The Bad Penny

Katie Flynn has lived for many years in the north-west. A compulsive writer, she started with short stories and articles and many of her early stories were broadcast on Radio Mersey. She decided to write her Liverpool series after hearing the reminiscences of family members about life in the city in the early years of the century. She also writes as Judith Saxton.

Praise for Katie Flynn

'If you pick up a Katie Flynn book it's going to be a wrench to put it down again'
Holyhead & Anglesey Mail

'She's a challenge to Josephine Cox'
Bookseller

'A heartwarming story of love and loss'
Woman's Weekly

'One of the best Liverpool writers'
Liverpool Echo

'[Katie Fl⋯ ⋯ Cookson had o⋯ ⋯ters to life'

Also by Katie Flynn

A Liverpool Lass
The Girl From Penny Lane
Liverpool Taffy
The Mersey Girls
Strawberry Fields
Rainbow's End
Rose of Tralee
No Silver Spoon
Polly's Angel
The Girl from Seaforth Sands
The Liverpool Rose
Poor Little Rich Girl
Down Daisy Street
A Kiss and a Promise
Two Penn'orth of Sky
A Long and Lonely Road
The Cuckoo Child
Darkest Before Dawn
Orphans of the Storm
Little Girl Lost
Beyond the Blue Hills
Forgotten Dreams
Sunshine and Shadows
Such Sweet Sorrow
A Mother's Hope
In Time For Christmas
Heading Home
A Mistletoe Kiss
The Lost Days of Summer
Christmas Wishes

The Bad Penny

KATIE FLYNN

arrow books

Reissued by Arrow Books in 2004

20

First published in the United Kingdom in 2002 by William Heinemann
First published in paperback in 2002 by Arrow Books

Arrow Books
The Random House Group Limited
20 Vauxhall Bridge Road, London SW1V 2SA

www.randomhouse.co.uk

Addresses for companies within The Random House Group Limited
can be found at:
www.randomhouse.co.uk/offices.htm

The Random House Group Limited Reg. No. 954009

A CIP catalogue record for this book
is available from the British Library

ISBN 9780099436539

The Random House Group Limited supports The Forest Stewardship
Council® (FSC®), the leading international forest-certification organisation.
Our books carrying the FSC label are printed on FSC®-certified paper.
FSC is the only forest-certification scheme supported by the leading
environmental organisations, including Greenpeace. Our
paper procurement policy can be found at
www.randomhouse.co.uk/environment

Typeset by SX Composing DTP, Rayleigh, Essex
Printed and bound in Great Britain by Clays Ltd, St Ives plc

This one is for Jo Prince, because she reads all my books – and tells me what she thinks of them. Thanks, Jo!

Acknowledgements

First and foremost, I should like to thank Sarah Miers, School Sister, based at the Grove Road Health Centre, Wrexham, for the loan of invaluable books on District Nursing and Midwifery in the Twenties and Thirties. As usual, any mistakes are my own but if I happen to have got it right, it is thanks to Sarah Miers. The library staff at Wrexham were their usual helpful selves, particularly John Thomas, who acquired for me photographs of nursing uniforms of the time, and Nia Rogerson, who came up with an extremely helpful – and little known – book of reminiscences on nursing in the Thirties.

Karen and Ric Hague, whose book search service is unrivalled, also did yeoman work in providing books which were unavailable and out of print in Britain; many thanks. And if I have left anyone out, you must blame the M.E., which makes remembering anything that happened before yesterday extremely difficult!

Chapter One
Liverpool 1932

Patty Peel trudged across the snow-covered courtyard to where her bicycle was kept in the ramshackle shed against the jigger wall. It was eleven o'clock and a wild January night, and as she wheeled her bicycle through the narrow opening into the jigger she reflected that the only thing you could be sure about with babies was that they would arrive at the moment most inconvenient to midwives. What was more, this birth should rightly have been attended by Nurse Stoddard, since it was in her area of the city. But Stoddard was in bed with influenza, so all her cases had been passed on to Patty.

The family she was about to visit were the Mullins, who lived in Stanton's Court off Cuerden Street. Patty had been woken a bare ten minutes earlier by a ragged boy, blue with cold and wearing the thinnest, shabbiest jacket she had ever seen, totally unsuitable for such weather. 'Me mam's havin' the baby,' he panted, holding on to the doorjamb as though it were the only thing keeping him on his feet. 'Can you come, Nurse? And can you hurry, 'cos me dad's in a wicked temper and me mam's awful poorly.'

Patty was not particularly fond of children, but her heart went out to the Mullins boy. He wore cracked and gaping boots through which his bare, bluish-grey skin could be seen and he looked as though he had not had a square meal for a month. Yet he had clearly

1

run all the way from Stanton's Court to Great Homer Street, despite the fearful weather.

'I'll be there right away,' she had said briskly. 'You'd best come in while I get dressed.' She had hesitated before the last remark since she had little faith in the honesty of young boys, but she told herself that no one would leave a dog out in such weather and held the door wider.

The boy, however, shook his head. 'I dussn't leave me mam for long,' he said breathlessly, already beginning to back down the steps. 'She'll feel better when she hears you're a-comin' and me dad's less likely to start a ruckus if he knows you're on your way. Besides,' he added as he turned away, 'you'll have a bike, I reckon, and I'm on foot. No point in wastin' time while you wait for me. Just you come along as fast as you can, missus.'

Shrugging, Patty had closed the door and returned to her bedroom where her clothing and equipment were laid out on a chair by the bed, ready for just such an emergency. She dressed quickly and as quietly as possible, anxious not to disturb the sleeper in the second bed, nor to rouse the two young nurses who shared the room next door. The house belonged to a retired midwife, who had been a great help to Patty in the early days of her career but now seemed to resent her lodgers' frequent night calls. The previous week, she had given Patty and her room-mate notice to leave.

'I'm too old to be woke up every night of me life by you bangin' in and out,' she had explained, half apologetically. 'Ordinary nurses are different; their hours is more – more like shop-workers. Oh, I ain't sayin' you and Higgins are noisy or thoughtless because you're good girls in your way, but I've had

2

forty years of disturbed nights and I reckon that's enough for anyone. Besides, me granddaughter's got a job in the post office on Sir Thomas Street and she's needin' a room. Blood's thicker'n water so I told her she could move in come next Monday.'

Patty had been neither particularly surprised nor dismayed. Mrs Bogget's house in Great Homer Street was a meeting place for both friends and family and their loud voices and constant quarrels frequently disturbed her daytime sleep, as did the heavy traffic which roared along the busy main road. Her roommate was planning to move back into the nurses' home, but Patty had seen some pleasant dwellings in quiet side streets, still in her area, which would suit her a good deal better than Mrs Bogget's crowded and noisy dwelling.

But right now, head bent against the whirling flakes, Patty had no time to think about moving house. The area through which she cycled was not strange to her, but very soon she would leave Cazneau Street, turn down Richmond Row and enter the maze of tiny streets she must negotiate to reach her destination. That would not be too bad, provided she could make out the street names through the fast falling snow, but once she reached Cuerden Street it would be a different matter. The courts were always ill lit, if lit at all, and though Nurse Stoddard had drawn a little map indicating the Mullins's house, Patty was not too sure that she would be able to find it, what with the dark and the snow falling so thick and fast.

Presently, she turned into the first court and immediately her worries left her. Only one house had a candle burning shakily in an upper window and as she dismounted from her bicycle and leaned it against the steps, a small figure detached itself from the shadows and a husky voice said: 'You've done well, Nurse. I runned all the way but I only just got back meself. Here, bring your bike into the hallway. You don't want it getting iced up.'

'Right you are,' Patty said briskly, heaving her bicycle up the three worn stone steps, slippery now with snow, and pushing it inside. There was barely room for it against the banisters since the hallway seemed to have become a depository for all manner of rubbish. Boxes, bundles of rags, empty bottles and a pram so old that its entire body was falling off it in strips were crammed into the narrow space and Patty looked rather desperately around her for some sign of a kitchen where she could boil water and sterilise her instruments. She turned to the small boy. Outside her door, she had thought him eight or nine, but now she saw that he was twelve or thirteen, though miserably small and undernourished. She said: 'Where's the kitchen? I'll need boiling water and some clean cloths. Has your mam any baby clothes ready? A cradle? Some pieces of clean blanket?'

The boy looked at her as though he had no idea what a kitchen was, but said readily: 'Me sister's boiling water on the oil stove in the back room. There's eleven of us and Fanny's nigh on fourteen, so she knows what you'll be wantin'. We lined a nice box wi' bits o'blanket . . . I dunno about clean rags, though. Oh, miss, won't you go up to our mam? She were hollerin' somethin' awful earlier, but now it's nobbut little gasps and groans; I's bleedin' scared, so I am.'

Patty looked at the small, sharp face and headed for the stairs. When she reached the landing she had no need to ask in which room her patient lay, for both doors were open. One was ringed with frightened, childish faces. The children were clad in cut-down

4

coats, thin shawls and rags. It was plain the Mullins dressed up rather than undressed when despatched to bed. The other room was empty save for a large brass bedstead, upon which a woman lay. Her face was as white as the snow which fell outside, her eyes dark-shadowed, and she had bitten her lip until blood ran down her chin. She was covered with a thin patchwork blanket and even as Patty entered the room she tried feebly to struggle into a sitting position, as the great mound of her stomach contracted beneath its thin covering.

Now Patty saw there was a man standing by the bed who looked up as she entered. 'Thank Gawd you've come, Nurse,' he said hoarsely. 'She's in a bad way, my old lady. What'll I do to help?'

Patty pulled back the thin blanket and cast a professional glance at the woman on the bed. 'It won't be long now,' she said briskly. 'Fetch me a jug of hot water and a basin so's I can clean the child up when it's born, and I'll have a kettle of boiling water to sterilise my instruments.'

The man shambled gladly out of the room and she heard his footsteps thundering down the stairs and his voice raised as he repeated her requirements to the occupants of the back room. Having got rid of the husband, Patty turned to her patient once more. 'Not long now, Mrs Mullins,' she said gently, as she began to examine her. By the look of it she would need her forceps since the baby's head was only just showing. 'But you may need a little help; I think we should send your lad for the doctor. The baby's a big one and you're already weak from pushing. Why didn't you call me earlier?'

Mrs Mullins turned huge, dark-blue eyes up towards the midwife and Patty realised, with a small shock of surprise, that the other woman must have been beautiful once. Not even her state of health could disguise the long, curling eyelashes, the small, straight nose and the clearly defined cheekbones, though the long, dank gold hair was dull and lifeless and her skin unhealthily pale, with sores at the corners of her mouth and nose. 'I always try to have the baby before the midwife comes; it's cheaper, and Gawd knows, after eleven kids, you'd think I'd have no difficulty. What's more, I sent the lad to Nurse Stoddard's place first, not knowin' she were ill,' she whispered in a thread of a voice. 'As for the doctor, my lad wouldn't know where to go. Dr Carruthers is sick with the 'flu – he's the nearest.' Another contraction shook her and she stopped speaking, her face contorted with pain. When the spasm was over, she flopped back on to the thin pillows. Sweat was pouring down her face. 'Oh Gawd, I've never had it so bad before,' she muttered. 'It started yesterday . . . oh, Nurse, I can't go on much longer.'

'You won't have to,' Patty said, but her heart failed her. She knew the patient was too weak to go on pushing; it would definitely have to be a forceps delivery and it would have to be done quickly.

She sighed with relief as the bedroom door opened and the husband came back into the room. He was breathing heavily and carried a kettle, still belching steam, in one hand and what looked like a pudding basin in the other. 'I'll fetch water for washing when the kid's born,' he said gruffly.

Patty opened her black bag and tipped her instruments into the kettle. It might not be ideal but it was the best she could do for now and experience told her that only immediate action would serve.

*

6

Patty was right in thinking that the delivery would require forceps; what she had not anticipated was that, having successfully delivered a baby girl, she should realise that there was another baby, this time a breech presentation. Desperately, she tried to remember who was standing in for Dr Carruthers, but in the event any help would have been useless. The second baby was born dead, a tiny, puny, blue-faced creature, and within seconds of its birth Mrs Mullins, too, had quietly and undramatically simply ceased to breathe.

Patty, worn out and deeply unhappy, made the bodies of mother and child as presentable as possible. She cleaned the dead woman up and brushed her hair back from her face, noticing how very young and peaceful she looked. She put the dead baby in the crook of its mother's arm, then lifted the living child out of the box in which it had been peacefully slumbering, wrapped it in a piece of blanket and went slowly down the stairs to face the family.

By now, it was almost six in the morning. Patty entered the back room and immediately Mr Mullins surged to his feet, though Fanny remained seated, her small face anxious. 'Is it over?' he said hoarsely. 'Is Gladys all right?'

Patty's heart sank even further. She had thought him an ignorant and probably violent man, but now she saw, from the look on his face, that he had loved his wife in his own way. She opened her mouth to speak but the words caught in her throat. With tears running down her cheeks, she shook her head silently, then said: 'No, Mr Mullins, I'm afraid not. Your wife gave birth to twins but she, and the smaller baby, died a short while ago.'

Mr Mullins gave a great, despairing shout and began to weep. Beside him, Fanny followed suit.

Patty, thinking to comfort him, said consolingly: 'But you've got a beautiful little girl here.'

Mr Mullins had slumped down at the table again and buried his face in his hands, but at her words he lifted his head and glared at her, his bloodshot eyes burning with anger even though tears spilled from them. 'Another bleedin' girl? And what do you think I'll do with another bleedin' girl?' he screamed. 'It were her comin' that took away my Gladys. I've seven kids still livin' at home and Gawd above knows how I'll manage them wi'out my wife. Jobs on the docks is like gold dust with this depression an' all. I'm tellin' you, Nurse, if you don't take that kid out o' here I'll do somethin' desperate – smash it to a pulp wi' me own hands, very like. Take it to an orphan asylum, tell 'em I can't look after it – and don't you go sayin' who I am or where I lives, because if the authorities come down on me I'll not stand for it. I'll abandon me kids and get work aboard a ship, so there'll be seven extra on the parish, I'm warning you.'

Patty stared helplessly at him, glad that she had insisted that the younger children go to bed earlier. At least she only had the father's grief and not that of his large family to deal with. The kids were dirty, unkempt and undernourished, yet she had the strange feeling that they were still a family unit and a strong one. She, Patty, had been brought up in an orphan asylum, never loved and constantly harassed by the overworked – and probably underpaid – staff of that institution. She had never known what it was to go hungry, perhaps for days at a time, or to have inadequate rags of clothing, no proper bed, and dirt, the constant enemy, all around, but with a flash of perception she realised that the Mullins children would understand and share their father's anguish. In all the families Patty knew, the older children took on the responsibility for the younger ones, but it was the mother alone who looked after a new baby. With their mother dead, and the little ones already in their charge, the Mullins girls would only see the new baby as an additional burden.

Patty sighed and tightened her hold on the child in her arms. 'Very well,' she said, trying to make her voice both practical and kindly. 'The baby is not strong, and will be better off in an orphanage if you feel so sure that you can't take care of her. You'd best send for a neighbour, Mr Mullins, to see to your wife's laying out and to help with the arrangements for the funeral. Do you have relatives living nearby who might be willing to give a hand?'

Mr Mullins did not reply and Patty turned away. Fanny jumped up from her place at the table and came over to her. She was a thin girl with poor skin and dull fair hair, but her eyes were bright and the hand she laid on Patty's arm was gentle. 'Me dad's in a turble way,' she murmured. 'But we do have relatives not far away – me Aunt Edie and me Uncle Jim – and I know they'll help us to sort things out.'

'I'm glad of that,' Patty said tiredly, making her way out of the room and along the passage to the front door with the baby still in the crook of her arm. She picked up her bicycle and tucked the blanket-wrapped infant into the breast of her uniform coat while Fanny went ahead of her to open the front door.

As Patty wheeled the bicycle carefully down the steps, the child followed her and, when Patty would have mounted, laid a detaining hand on her arm. 'Where'll you put her, miss? The baby, I mean? I'd – I'd like to see her again, know folks is being good to her. It's true what me dad said; without me mam she wouldn't get brung up proper. Likely she'd starve, poor little bugger. The rest of us is hungry most of the time, but we gerralong, one way or t'other. This 'un's too little to help herself and we's too busy wi' t'other kids to take on a baby.' She pulled gently on Patty's arm. 'Can I have a look at her, miss?'

'Course you can,' Patty said gruffly. 'I don't know where I'll take her yet, but I'll see she goes somewhere decent, where she'll be fed and – and looked after. I'll let you know where she is in a couple of days.' She rebuttoned her uniform coat tightly to the neck, then turned towards Fanny once more as she mounted the bicycle. 'I'll come and see you in a day or two and tell you what's happening then.'

'Thanks, miss . . . Nurse, I mean,' the girl said gratefully. 'And don't think too badly of me dad. He were mortal fond of our mam, even though there were times . . . but least said, soonest mended; there won't be no more of *that*, any road.'

Patty watched until the child had disappeared back into the house, then began to cycle slowly out of the court and into Cuerden Street. It was still dark, though it was no longer snowing, but a glance at the cloudy sky overhead convinced her that there was more snow to come. She should try to get back to her lodgings before it started but first, of course, she ought to make some arrangements for the baby inside her coat.

However, it occurred to Patty that no one was likely to query the child's whereabouts. When the doctor finally arrived at the Mullins home, he would undoubtedly assume that Mrs Mullins had given birth to a baby which had died with her. Mr Mullins was unlikely to admit that there had been a living child also, and with their father's threat to abandon them the children would most certainly keep the fact to themselves. So it did not really matter if Patty took the baby home for a few hours before handing it over to the authorities. Officially, the child did not exist, and would not do so until she was formally handed over.

Patty reached Richmond Row just as the snow began to fall again. The road was still white from the previous fall and consequently slippery, so Patty dismounted and began to push her bike towards home. With a bit of luck, she might get a few hours' sleep before the baby began to bawl.

It took her forty minutes to reach home and when she finally entered her room, it was to find that Nurse Higgins had already left. Thankfully, Patty removed her outer clothing, laying the baby on her bed whilst she took off her lace-up boots. She looked down at the child and was suddenly smitten by a feeling of great tenderness. The Mullins baby was so small, so fair, so vulnerable somehow. Patty thought of this tender little creature facing up to life in an institution and her heart smote her. Orphan asylums were full of children who had lost one or both parents but Patty herself had been a foundling, unwanted right from the moment of her birth. Even her name had been plucked out of the air by reason of the fact that a policeman called Patrick O'Donoghue had found her in Peel Street. It was as well, Patty had frequently thought sourly, that she had not been discovered in Dingle station by a woman called Dorothy. Dotty Dingle would have been more than any child could have borne.

Patty put her hands behind her and untied the strings of the long white linen apron – now sadly soiled

11

– which reached almost to her ankles. Then she peeled off her black lisle stockings and began to unbutton her plain print dress, shivering a little as she did so, for it was very cold in the room. She pulled on her nightdress, shaking out her short blonde curls, and slid between the sheets, promising herself a couple of hours at least. Then she reached out and pulled the blanket-wrapped baby under the covers with her. Rather to her surprise, it was gloriously warm, like a little hot water bottle, and looking into the small, fair face Patty suddenly realised that she could not abandon this child to the sort of childhood she herself had led. After all, it was a pretty baby and girls were always adopted more willingly than boys. Surely there was someone, in this great city, prepared to lavish love on her? Why, for two pins, I'd keep her myself, Patty found herself thinking. She would be company – and how rewarding it would be to know that she had saved a little girl from the fate she herself had suffered.

Presently, on the verge of sleep, Patty remembered that the child was not an orphan. She had a father living and a name she could call her own; she was, in fact, a Mullins. If I keep her, I think I'll call her Marcia, Patty told herself dreamily. Marcia's a pretty name, much prettier than Patty. But I don't like Marcia Mullins, and even Marcia Peel sounds a bit odd. No, I'll call her Merrell. There was a lovely kindergarten teacher at the orphanage – Miss Merrell – who looked after the babies. She was the only person who really seemed to like me and took my side. I was so sad when she left to get married; I felt I'd lost my only friend in the world. Besides, Merrell is a pretty name and it goes quite well with Peel. Not that I could keep her for always, of course; just until I find someone really nice who's willing to adopt her.

And with that thought, Patty fell asleep and dreamed a beautiful dream in which Miss Merrell came to the orphanage and took little Patty away to be her own girl. There was no husband involved and the two of them lived in a dear little house in the country, surrounded by woolly sheep, bright pink pigs and other animals, all of which bore a strong resemblance to the inhabitants of the Noah's Ark which Patty had greatly admired in a rich family's nursery.

Patty awoke when the door of her room burst open and Higgins came in. She was a stout, square girl, with thick black hair growing low on her brow and a tendency to spots. She spent all her spare money on food and Patty sometimes thought the only thing that mattered to her room-mate was to have her stomach comfortably full. Like Patty, she was a midwife, but she still worked at the hospital and seemed to have little interest in anything outside her own ward. Patty frequently marvelled that she had ever chosen to live out and had not been at all surprised when Higgins had put her name down to move back into the nurses' home.

Now, however, Higgins stared at her, wide-eyed. 'Wharrever are you doin' still in bed, Peel? Don't you have some revisits to do today?' Her voice grew sharp, almost triumphant, and Patty, who knew that a good many of the nursing staff resented both her ability to pass examinations and her choice of working a district rather than remaining attached to a ward, stiffened slightly. Higgins must have noticed, for her voice took on a more conciliatory tone. 'I know you're doin' Stoddard's area as well as your own, so I'd have thought you'd be pretty busy, but I suppose you know your own business best.'

Patty stifled a wave of panic and sat up. Higgins was absolutely right, she did have revisits! What was more, there was something niggling on the edge of her consciousness, something to do with a call-out in the middle of the night, something . . .

The baby! The Mullins baby, which the father had rejected. She had meant to take it to an orphanage . . . no, she had decided to have it adopted, meant to keep it herself until a suitable couple could be found who were willing to bring up the baby as their own. Against her side, the baby stirred and Patty fished it out of the covers, still wrapped in its piece of blanket, and tucked it comfortably into the crook of her arm. She stared defiantly into Higgins's astonished face. 'I've been busy, and I just fell into bed at about seven o'clock, meaning to have a couple of hours' sleep. What's the time now, Higgins?'

'It's four in the afternoon,' Higgins said accusingly. 'Oh, Peel, you're going to be in awful trouble. And where did that baby come from? It don't look too healthy to me.'

'The mother died,' Patty said, after the briefest of pauses, during which her mind worked frantically on how much she should tell Higgins. 'It'll have to go to a wet nurse until the orphanage will take it in. Be a few weeks, the matron said.'

'Well, so long as you don't mean to keep it in here,' Higgins said grudgingly. 'Why, you don't even like kids, Peel! Still, I suppose for one night, anything's bearable, even a brat in your own bed.' She turned away, clearly losing interest in the topic. 'It's a good job for you there's so much sickness around. You can say you were struck down by the 'flu if anyone asks what you've done all day.'

Patty had been hastily dressing whilst Higgins

talked and now she turned to face the other girl, fastening her cuffs as she did so. 'I suppose you wouldn't keep an eye on the baby for me whilst I do my revisits?' she asked, without much hope. She and Higgins tolerated one another but had never been friends. Patty had always told herself she did not need friends; it was better to be independent and self-reliant. She had noticed that girls with friends depended on one another for almost everything. They went around in pairs, chattered and gossiped when they should have been studying and rarely achieved the sorts of results the hospital demanded. Still, it would have been useful now to have had a friend who could take the baby over whilst she was out on her rounds.

'Look after that brat?' Higgins said incredulously. 'You've gorra be joking! And don't you think you can leave it here while you swans off, 'cos I won't stand for it and nor will old Ma Bogget.'

With a sigh, Patty picked the baby up, tucked it into the front of her coat and buttoned that garment securely up to the neck before heading for the stairs. There was no point in pleading with Higgins and anyway her pride would not have allowed it. Fortunately, now that she was thoroughly awake, she realised that the best thing she could do was take the baby with her. One of her revisits was to young Mrs Blake, who had given birth to her fourth child and lost it only hours later. The family were poor and the young woman would be glad of the money Patty would pay her to breastfeed the baby until it was old enough to be weaned. As she descended the stairs, crossed the hall and kitchen and let herself out into the snowy backyard, it also occurred to Patty that Mrs Blake might just as well take the child off her hands for several weeks, at least. She would be breast-feeding it every four hours or so, which made it impractical for Patty to keep taking the child back. Things would be very much easier if Mrs Blake would agree to the arrangement.

Patty wheeled her bike along the jigger, deciding as she did so to make Mrs Blake her first call. There was no point in carting the baby round to all her patients, having to explain the reason for the child's presence. Fortunately, Mrs Blake was in Patty's own district, so she turned right into Penrhyn Street, crossed the Scottie and headed for the courts which lined Wright Street.

Mrs Blake was doing the washing when Patty arrived at her door. Doing the washing and weeping with a sort of steady helplessness which went to Patty's heart. Her three children were sitting on the rag rug in front of the kitchen stove, playing with a pile of empty boxes and tins. The floor was very wet and one of the children was actually floating a box on a puddle. Steam rose gently from the floor. Glancing around, Patty tried to hide the dismay that she felt, greeting the family cheerfully, but shaking her head reprovingly at Mrs Blake's occupation. 'Mrs Blake, you know very well you ought not to be exerting yourself so soon after a birth,' she said. 'Your sister offered to give a hand whilst you recovered your strength and that meant doing the housework and the washing and seeing to the children. Do you want to make yourself ill?'

Mrs Blake had turned back to the sink after greeting her visitor but now she moved away from it and collapsed on to a creaky wooden chair. 'I hears what you say, Nurse,' she said tiredly, 'but Elsie works at the pickling factory so she can only help mornin's and evenin's, and the washing's got to be done else there's no money comin' in.'

Patty knew that Ada Blake's husband had recently been laid off from his job as a van driver at the jam factory. Mrs Blake had told her that this happened quite often in January and February. 'We has to allow for it by saving up the money from the good months, when he works overtime – July, August and September mainly – but it still comes hard in the winter,' she had explained. 'So I has to keep me little jobs goin', whether I'm in the fambly way or no.'

Patty had thought that Mr Blake, knowing how things stood, might have planned the production of small Blakes a little more carefully, for three-year-old Amy, two-year-old Horace and one-year-old Annie had all been born in the early months of the year. Mrs Blake, however, seemed to take it for granted that she would continue to work throughout her pregnancies and bore her husband no ill will for the exhaustion which followed each birth.

'I know you need the money – don't we all? – but you really shouldn't do hard physical labour,' Patty said, for what felt like the hundredth time. 'And if your husband has been laid off, why isn't he here? He could give a hand with wringing out the sheets and putting them through the mangle. He could even take care of the children for you whilst you worked.' She felt a drop of water on the back of her hand and glanced up at the ceiling to see a crudely made wooden rack laden with dripping sheets above her. 'Don't you have a mangle?'

Mrs Blake looked as if she were about to dissolve into tears once more. 'It's broke,' she whispered. 'That's what Alf's doin', tryin' to get some part for it.

The handle come off when he were shovin' a big sheet betwixt the rollers – he'd folded it wrong – and I'm a poor hand at wringing out, which is why everything's so wet.'

'Oh, I see,' Patty said, rather blankly. It was usually the man's fault when something went wrong, or at least that was Patty's opinion, but in this case she could scarcely blame Alf Blake for the disintegration of the mangle, since he had been doing his poor masculine best to assist his wife at the time. 'But look, Mrs Blake, it isn't going to help either your husband or the children if you become really ill. The doctor will have to send you to hospital and then where would they be?'

'I dunno,' Mrs Blake whispered, tears welling up in her eyes once more and trickling down her pale cheeks. 'I does me best, but it all gets too much for me, honest to God it does, Nurse. The kids is too young to help and me neighbours can't do me work for me, though they're mortal good over messages and keepin' an eye on the little 'uns. Dolly O'Hara is doin' me bakin' and Mabel next door has said she'll iron these sheets when I've gorrem dry. They's awful good but I still feel so . . . so . . .'

Patty knew all about the helpless misery and depression which follows losing a child, though privately she thought that most of the women would be a good deal better off with fewer kids and could not truly understand the agony of loss from which they suffered. But she did know that the feeling existed and could be alleviated in one way at least. Accordingly, she unbuttoned her coat and produced the baby, holding it out to Mrs Blake. 'There's easier ways to earn money when you've just lost a little one of your own,' she said gently. 'The mother of this little

18

'un died giving birth and I'm looking for someone to act as wet nurse until young Merrell here can be weaned. They'll pay sixpence a day, and of course, anything extra you need . . .'

Mrs Blake's whole face lit up and she held out her arms with a sort of desperate hunger which made Patty glad she had never been a mother. In Mrs Blake's place, she found herself thinking, I wouldn't have wanted anything to remind me of the baby I'd lost. But it's different for me – I wouldn't have wanted the baby I'd lost either. She handed the child, still wrapped in its scrap of blanket, to the other woman and watched as the infant snuggled against her. 'Does this mean you're willing to take the job on?' she asked, as Mrs Blake pulled up her stained jumper and put the baby to her breast. 'If so, I'll pay you a week in advance and perhaps you'll oblige me by not slaving at laundry work until you're a good deal stronger than you are now.'

'The job? Oh aye, you mean will I have her,' Mrs Blake said dreamily, gazing down at the baby's mossy head as though it was the most beautiful thing in the world. 'I reckon wi' three an' six a week to help out, I won't need to go launderin' other folks' sheets for a while yet.' She glanced, half shyly, into Patty's face. 'Thanks, Nurse, I'm real grateful, but wharrif the feller comes and takes the baby off me? Fellers can be real awkward. He might gerranother woman or decide to have a go at bottle feeding. Will you tell 'im where the little 'un's been placed?'

Patty gave a short laugh. 'He's got eleven kids already, seven of 'em still at home. He's a docker so he's lucky if he works two days out of the seven. He doesn't want the little 'un. She'll go into an orphan asylum once she's weaned, or that's his idea at any rate. For myself, I'd sooner see her adopted by a decent family who can afford to take care of a little girl. Some of the orphanages . . . well, I've heard there's precious little care handed out.'

'That's true,' Mrs Blake said eagerly. 'But she'll do grand wi' me, Nurse, honest to God she will. I'll treat her like me own and Alf will be that glad of the money, he'll agree to anything. Merrell, did you say her name was? That's a rare pretty name.'

'That's right, she's called Merrell,' Patty confirmed, getting to her feet. 'You had clean rags and bits of stuff for your own baby which will do this one, won't they? I remember your Alf made a wooden cradle when young Amy was born; do you still have it?'

'Aye. No one don't throw baby stuff away until they's a lot older than me,' Mrs Blake said absently. She smiled down at the baby in her arms, then up at Patty. 'You'll be poppin' in from time to time, I take it, Nurse? You'll be able to see for yourself I'm doin' right by her.'

Patty began to count out three and sixpence upon the wooden draining board, then added three round brown pennies to the sum. 'A penny each for the kids for some sweets and tell 'em not to spend it all in the same shop,' she said grandly. She had heard the expression from others handing out largesse but had never used it herself before. 'Yes, of course I'll be visiting regularly, Mrs Blake, but I know you'll take good care of the baby; that's why I chose to bring her here. You're a very good mother – Merrell's a lucky little girl.'

Patty continued with her visits, finally wending her way back to her lodgings at ten o'clock at night. She was not as tired as she might have been since her long sleep-in that day had considerably refreshed her, but as she entered the shared kitchen, got out her loaf and began to make herself some toast she was aware of some rather strange, conflicting emotions. She had experienced considerable relief upon leaving the Blakes' house; she felt she had shed her responsibility for the tiny baby without a stain on her conscience. Now she could take her time in finding just the right place for little Merrell. Yet simultaneously with this feeling came another. She was actually missing the warm little bundle tucked inside her coat and found herself far more interested than usual in the mothers and babies as she did her rounds. She began to compare the infants with little Merrell, always to their detriment, and she realised, with considerable surprise, that she thought 'her' baby was by far the prettiest.

To be sure, there was not a great deal of competition. Many of the babies she delivered were far from perfect. Often after a ninth or tenth child the mother would be weary and worn out at forty and the new baby was already destined to suffer from a thousand ailments – rickets, skin disorders and lung disease being just some of them.

But Gladys Mullins must have been at least forty and was clearly undernourished, Patty found herself thinking as she held a slice of bread nearer the fire. Her other children are skinny and ill looking, yet Merrell is pretty and looks healthy too. I admit she's small – she weighed less than five pounds at birth – but her skin's clear and in all the time I had her she never cried once. Most babies I deliver cry a good deal, poor little brats.

So absorbing were her thoughts that Patty only realised the round was done when a thin thread of blue smoke arose from it. Shaking her head at her own preoccupation, she got margarine out of the pantry and spread it on the toast, then devoured it hungrily. She had not eaten all day and Patty was fond of her food. Indeed, it was one of the reasons why she had elected to live outside the hospital, because hospital food was boring, badly cooked and seldom sufficient to satisfy the appetites of hungry and hard-working young girls.

Patty impaled another slice of bread on the toasting fork. She had worked her way through almost half the loaf before she felt even partly satisfied and had drunk a great deal of tea, mixed with the best part of a tin of condensed milk. The loaf was hers but the tea and the conny-onny were not and Patty knew that old Ma Bogget would be bound to guess who had taken them. But I think I'm entitled since I missed supper, Patty told herself rebelliously, replacing the remainder of the loaf in the bread bin and rinsing the teapot so that the tea leaves swirled down the sink. She checked that the kitchen was tidy, with no signs of her recent feast, closed the front of the stove and damped it down. The girls all had a key to the back door, for nurses doing shift work often come home at peculiar hours, but Patty checked that the door was locked before making her way up to her room.

Higgins was already in bed and judging from the bubbling snores emanating from her had been asleep for some time. Patty checked her fob watch; it was almost midnight and she was suddenly aware how tired she was. She undressed quickly as she always did, folding her garments neatly and checking that her bag was provided with everything she might need should she get an unexpected call-out. Only when she was satisfied that all was as it should be did she climb into bed and snuggle down. She expected to

22

fall asleep immediately but instead she was aware of a funny little sense of loss. Puzzling over it, she realised with true astonishment that she was missing the baby, missing the soft warmth of it of course, but also missing the delightful sense of responsibility of which she had been conscious when the child had snuggled into her arms.

I must be going mad, Patty told herself. If I needed companionship I could get a kitten or a puppy. They would be far less trouble than young Merrell and just as good a friend, I'm sure. Anyway, I'm not going to let myself wallow in sentimentality, because that's what it would be. I don't want to see the kid stuck in an orphan asylum, or farmed out to someone who doesn't care for her. But I don't want her hanging round my neck and dragging me down either. I'll get her adopted the way I planned and never think of her again; it'll be best for her and for me too.

On that thought she fell asleep and if she dreamed of puppies with babies' faces, and kittens whose nappies needed changing, they were only dreams.

Chapter Two

Patty stood on the balcony of the Ashfield Place landing houses, looking down on the quiet cul-de-sac below and feeling a thrill of proprietorial pride as she did so. She had agreed to rent No. 24, which was the last house on the top landing and was ideal, she decided. The road was quiet with no through traffic, and because landing houses had modern amenities they were much sought after, so she knew she had been very lucky to be offered this one. She also knew whom she had to thank for her good fortune. It had been her friend and mentor, Mrs Ruskin, who had given her the name of the landlord and told her that a property was about to become vacant in the landing house.

It had been January when Mrs Bogget had given Patty notice to leave, but it was actually March before she found the sort of accommodation she had been seeking. To be sure, she had had to leave Great Homer Street barely five days after Merrell's birth, and had moved into another lodging house where even more girls were crammed into the small space available. Higgins, of course, had returned to the hospital as she had planned, far happier to be amongst her own kind in the nurses' home even though it meant constant interference and criticism from more senior nurses, and even those doctors who deigned to notice her existence.

Patty had chosen midwifery as a career chiefly

because it gave her the independence she had craved for so long. Moving into the hospital as a probationer after her years in the orphan asylum had merely been changing one sort of slavery for another. Probationers were considered the very lowest form of life in the hospital hierarchy. They were condemned to doing all the really dirty and unpleasant jobs, to working the most unsociable hours, to eating whatever food was plonked before them and to being constantly bullied and harassed by anyone who had worked at the hospital longer than they.

Patty's brains and determination had quickly singled her out from the crowd, but that did not make her either popular or particularly well regarded. Her fellow nurses frequently referred to her as 'Peel, that nasty little swot' and Patty, who had grown used to abuse at the orphanage, had had to grow an even thicker skin as a consequence.

When she had qualified, she had known at once where her future must lie, for her happiest days in the hospital had, in fact, been spent out of it, when she was doing her 'midder' training. For six whole months she had 'lived out' with Mrs Ruskin, an experienced midwife, and had revelled in her first real taste of freedom. At the orphanage, she and the other girls, once they were old enough, had done most of the housework, which included preparing vegetables, washing up piles of dishes and scrubbing the vast flagstones on the kitchen floor. Cooking on such a large scale had been beyond them, however, so when Patty had moved in with Mrs Ruskin she had been unable to boil so much as an egg. Under her mentor's guidance this had soon changed, Mrs Ruskin informing her grimly that she had always believed in sharing work equally. She had taught

Patty to boil, bake and fry, to make bread, cakes and pastry, to cook a blind scouse when money was short and to whip up a light omelette when eggs were the only thing available.

Alongside this domesticity came an excellent grounding in midwifery itself. Mrs Ruskin, despite her title, was a single woman and had as little time for men as had Patty herself. 'They has their fun with some foolish young gal and leaves us to set all to rights nine months later,' she told Patty severely. 'Most of 'em drinks their wages away and expects their woman to gerrup from childbed and cook 'em a good meal. What's more, they think she ought to work outside of a house, no matter how many brats they wish on her. Oh aye, when you've been a midwife as long as I have, you won't think much to men, queen.'

Mrs Ruskin's area had been a very poor one, with mothers frequently unable to provide any sort of clothing for their babies, let alone equipment. Patty grew accustomed to bathing new infants in old toffee tins, to sterilising her instruments by baking them in the bread oven or dipping them briefly in a kettle of boiling water and to wrapping her new babies in any bit of rag available. Mrs Ruskin taught her to respect the women who had so little in the way of material possessions and from whom so much was expected. The midwife herself loved both the women and children in her charge but this was something Patty was unable to emulate. Instinctively she had sensed that involvement was dangerous for one who wanted independence and self-sufficiency, but even so she had begun to admire the women in her charge and had been genuinely fond of Mrs Ruskin. The midwife had retired officially some two years earlier, but Patty often visited her and usually found her busily making baby clothes out of odd scraps of material begged from neighbours or from the stallholders on Paddy's market, or knitting bootees and matinee jackets to keep some fortunate child warm.

As soon as Patty had told her about Merrell, Mrs Ruskin had begun to work on some nightgowns for the child. Patty had handed them over to Mrs Blake and felt a thrill of pride the first time she saw Merrell appropriately dressed. The baby was progressing satisfactorily, putting on weight, seldom crying and smiling at anyone whose face swam into focus before her blue eyes. Patty was far too busy looking for lodgings and keeping up with her job to spare the time to take Merrell round to see her friend, but she determined that as soon as the lighter evenings came she would do so. She reminded herself that she meant to have the baby adopted, that there was no point in introducing her to Mrs Ruskin, but somehow she had done nothing about finding prospective parents for the child. It was another task for the morrow.

She had gone round to visit Mrs Ruskin one evening and admitted to her friend that she had had no luck in her search for a small house or even a few rooms to let. 'The nice places are too expensive and the cheaper places aren't really what I want,' she explained. 'I need a bit of quiet, Mrs Ruskin, as you well know. When you're working mostly nights, you don't want to get yourself into an area where there's a lot of noise during the day. I remember all too well what it was like living on Great Homer Street; the traffic never stopped and what with vendors shouting their wares and passers-by simply shouting, I seldom managed to drop off. Not getting your sleep is really bad because when you start work again, your concentration goes.'

'And that's no good in our line of work,' Mrs Ruskin had said placidly. 'Tell you what, queen, have you ever thought of trying a landing house? I happen to know there's one coming vacant shortly in Ashfield Place, behind Ashfield Street, and it ain't likely to be popular with old folk because it's on the top landing, right at the far end. It'll be quiet, too, because no one will have to pass your door to reach their own, if you understand me. What's more, the rents are that little bit higher, which means them with a dozen kids aren't likely to be able to afford it. What do you say?'

Patty had been cautiously enthusiastic. She had visited the landing houses several times and had been much struck by the compact and modern homes. Since Ashfield Place was right in the middle of her area it would be extremely handy for work, and she knew that landlords regarded midwives as good tenants because of their regular salary and high standing with the locals. Although such a house would cost a little more, she told herself that she would manage somehow, and was delighted when she went to see the landlord to hear that, in order to have a nurse on his premises, he was willing to reduce her rent. 'Don't tell anyone else though, Nurse,' he had said, grinning at her, 'or they'll all be expecting a reduction. But it's worth a lower rent to me to have a real, professional nurse in our lane. Gives folk a sense of security, like.'

So now here she was, standing on the balcony outside her very own home and wondering when she would be able to move in. She would need a bed, a chair, a table and some curtains. A washing-up bowl would be useful but not essential; her little house had running water and, to her great surprise, electricity –

or electric light at any rate. There was a big living kitchen, and three other reasonably sized rooms which she could use as she wished. To Patty, still sharing one small room with three other girls, it seemed like a palace. She actually considered whether she should get someone to share it with her, which would reduce the rent even further, then decided against it. If money grew tight as the weeks passed, then she might consider sharing again, but for now, at least, she would enjoy her independence and revel in her solitude.

The clatter of feet as someone climbed the metal steps below her brought Patty's thoughts abruptly back to the present. She glanced down at her fob watch; if she was to see Merrell before returning to her lodgings for supper, she had better get a move on. She decided she would go to Paddy's market as soon as she was able, and buy a mattress and one of the old iron bedsteads which she had seen stashed up behind one of the stalls. Then she would be able to move in. If she furnished her house bit by bit, whenever she could afford an item, it would soon be a proper home.

She was halfway along the landing when a young woman came bounding up the last flight of stairs towards her. She had untidy brown hair and was dressed in a shabby grey flannel coat and a pair of black boots. She was pulling off a bright blue headscarf as she approached and grinned amiably at Patty, showing a set of excellent teeth. 'Mornin', queen,' she said cheerfully. 'Was you after me? I bin to the clinic on Brougham Terrace, only just got back. Or was it Mrs Knight or Mrs Clitheroe you was after?'

Patty gave the young woman her most professional up and down glance, the look that could reduce an angry and difficult patient to mumbling acquiescence. 'I haven't come to visit anyone,' she said severely. 'Good afternoon.'

She went to pass the girl, who put a detaining hand on her arm. 'I'm Mrs Clarke,' she said eagerly. 'You're a nurse, ain't you? Are you sure you're not coming to visit me?'

Patty, wearing her uniform, was used to being accosted as she went around the streets in her area and guessed immediately that this young woman was a new mother-to-be and was expecting a visit from someone like herself. That would account for her visit to Brougham Terrace and for the air of eagerness with which she had approached Patty. She allowed herself to be detained, therefore, merely sighing before saying briskly: 'I'm Nurse Peel and this is my district, but I don't believe I've been given your name yet. No doubt, however, I shall be seeing you quite soon.'

She tried to detach the young woman's hand from her sleeve but Mrs Clarke said impetuously: 'Aw, c'mon! I'll put the kettle on and make us both a cuppa, then you can tell me wharrever I need to know. Save yourself a journey, see?'

'Mrs Clarke, I've a great deal to do . . .' Patty was beginning, but the other woman tugged at her arm, smiling blindingly up into her face.

'It won't take five minutes to boil a kettle 'cos I keeps the fire lit all day in this cold weather,' she said coaxingly. 'Be a sport, Nurse!'

Patty hesitated, but only for a moment. She knew it would not be sensible to make an enemy of a patient, and a patient, moreover, who was living on the same landing as herself, but she could not miss her visit to Merrell. The child was eight weeks old and beginning to respond in a way which delighted Patty. Besides, if she let this woman persuade her once, you never knew where it might end. Accordingly, she pulled herself free from Mrs Clarke's clasp and set off down the stairs, saying over her shoulder: 'I have a great many patients to see, Mrs Clarke, and cannot favour one above another; I shall doubtless be seeing you shortly. Good afternoon.'

Making her way briskly along Ashfield Place, she thought, a trifle ruefully, that it was a pity she had not gone in for that cup of tea, but decided she had done the right thing. She had no wish for a neighbour who was always popping in for free advice or a cup of sugar, and she thought that Mrs Clarke was very likely to be the chatty sort who lay in wait for any passers-by who might want to share a bit of gossip. Patty had always held aloof from neighbours and had made no friends amongst her nursing colleagues (apart from Mrs Ruskin, of course) and this had suited her very well. To be sure, she had always lived in poor neighbourhoods where the other women had clearly considered her to be very different from themselves and had not attempted to draw her into their circle. She decided, as she left Ashfield Place behind her, that she must make it plain to her new neighbours that she preferred her own company to other people's. If it was necessary, that was. People generally found her attitude so off-putting that they did not attempt to get to know her.

Now, walking along Limekiln Lane, she reached Wright Street and was about to turn down it when, out of the corner of her eye, she saw that Mr Glenny's shop was empty and, on impulse, went inside. After two minutes she came out again, carrying a bag of broken biscuits, a screw of tea and a tin of condensed milk. She had grown quite fond of Mrs Blake and thought that a small present for the other woman would be rather nice. After all, she had drunk a good few cups of tea in the Blakes' kitchen, sitting with little Merrell tucked into the crook of her arm. This would show Mrs Blake that she was not ungrateful.

Patty clicked along the pavement and turned down the jigger which led to the back of the Blakes' small house, crossed the courtyard and, after the briefest of knocks on the back door, entered the kitchen. The children were playing with an empty cardboard box, Horace towing the youngest child, Annie, around the floor by a piece of rope tied around the box, whilst Amy pranced behind shouting: 'Make way for St George!' in shrill tones.

Mrs Blake was sitting in the chair nearest the fire, with the baby on her lap. She appeared to be endeavouring to spoon some sort of food into Merrell's mouth and Patty stopped short. 'Mrs Blake! Whatever are you doing?'

Mrs Blake had started violently as Patty entered the room, and now a bright tide of colour mottled her neck and dyed her face pink. 'Oh – oh, Nurse,' she faltered. 'I – I don't understand it, honest to God I don't, but me milk's dried up on me. It – it happened this mornin'. When I went to feed her, she sucked and sucked and then began to howl somethin' dreadful. I – I don't have no teats, though I've an empty sauce bottle what I could use . . . Oh, Nurse, I'm ever so sorry.'

Patty sat down on the nearest chair with a thump. She knew very well why Mrs Blake's milk had dried up and guessed that the other woman knew too and was ashamed. But reproaching her was useless; the damage had been done. Mrs Blake was pregnant once more and nothing Patty could do or say would make any difference.

32

'It's all right, Mrs Blake,' she said, as gently as she could. 'Naturally, having lost your last baby, you and Mr Blake are anxious to have another child.' She put the bag of broken biscuits down on the table and went over to the stove, pulling the kettle over the flame. 'I've brought you some tea and some conny-onny because, heaven knows, I've drunk enough cups here and I thought it was about time I gave something back. If you can keep an eye on the kettle and brew the tea when it boils, I'll just nip back to Mr Glenny at the corner shop and see if he's got some teats. He seems to sell everything, but I shan't be more than a few minutes even if I have to go a bit further before I find one.' She smiled reassuringly at Mrs Blake. 'Cheer up! I was coming to tell you that I've managed to rent one of the landing houses on Ashfield Place, so I should have been taking Merrell away with me in a few days in any case. It will be easier to find adoptive parents if they can come round to my place and see Merrell for themselves. After all, most babies being offered for adoption are weaned on to the bottle at Merrell's age, if not earlier. What are you feeding her from that bowl anyway?'

Mrs Blake, who had begun to cry, apparently moved to tears by the gentleness in Patty's voice, swallowed convulsively and said: 'It's watered down conny-onny, Nurse. She'll take to it like a duck to water once you bring back the teats, but she don't care for the teaspoon. I reckon it seems mortal hard and cold in her little mouth.'

'Well, don't try to feed her any more. Just give her a cuddle until I get back,' Patty said briskly, as she left the kitchen. She was amazed at her own tact and also at her sudden resolve to take Merrell away with her as soon as might be. She had grown quite attached to

Mrs Blake and trusted her completely whilst she was breastfeeding, but realised that the other woman probably neither knew nor cared about the importance of sterilisation so far as bottle feeding was concerned. Annie was a pretty child but she had sores round her mouth, and though Mrs Blake did her best all three children suffered from both fleas and head lice. So far, Merrell had remained free from such afflictions, but Patty realised that the child would stand a much better chance of remaining unaffected if she were removed from the Blakes' home.

Presently, returning with a supply of teats and two more tins of condensed milk, Patty made up a feed with boiling water, then stood the bottle in a bowl of water to cool. When the milk was the correct temperature, she took the baby from Mrs Blake and settled down in the chair her hostess had occupied. As she had hoped, Merrell's annoyance over the spoon and her hunger contributed to the ease with which she accepted the bottle and presently Patty laid the baby across her shoulder and rubbed the small back gently, astonished at the feeling of warmth and affection which accompanied even this simple action.

'You was right, Nurse,' Mrs Blake observed, dipping one of the broken biscuits into her cup of tea and quickly transferring it to her mouth. 'Merrell's took to the bottle as though she's been on it all her life. When will you be taking her away from us?'

'The day after tomorrow,' Patty said, making a lightning decision. She had no idea how she would manage, living at No. 24 with almost no furniture and a baby to take care of, but manage she would. 'If I come round, say at six o'clock in the evening, when I've done my visits for the day, would that suit you?'

'Oh aye, we'll have her ready for you,' Mrs Blake

agreed at once. 'Does you have somewhere for her to sleep and cloths for her little bum? I know she'll want them lovely gowns your pal made, but if you're goin' to get her a proper cradle I'll keep that one Alf made. All me other babbies have slept in it, so it'll do grand for the next.'

'I'll take two of the gowns and a shawl, but leave you everything else,' Patty said recklessly. 'She's going to be adopted, after all, and I wouldn't let her go to a home where they couldn't afford to clothe her properly.'

At that moment Merrell gave an enormous burp and Mrs Blake laughed and took her from Patty, laying her down in the wooden cradle which she kept on an old rag rug, close to the fire. 'It'll be grand if I have a little girl of me own as pretty as this one,' she observed, tucking a piece of blanket securely around the child. 'Now Alf wants a boy, 'cos he says we've two girls already, but I've a hankerin' to have another lass. Still an' all, that's one thing we can't choose,' she ended, straightening up.

Patty smiled and took her outdoor garments off the hooks on the back of the door. She buttoned the coat up tight to her throat, for although March was well advanced the evenings were still very cold. 'Goodbye, Mrs Blake,' she said cheerily, lifting the latch. 'I won't come round tomorrow because I'll be busy moving my stuff, but don't forget to boil the water before you mix it with the conny-onny and then to cool the bottle. Oh, and the teats and the bottle should be boiled in a pan of water for ten minutes or so before each feed. Can you remember that?'

'Why's that?' Mrs Blake said idly, helping herself to another biscuit. Patty realised that because of the new life burgeoning within her Mrs Blake would find it far easier to part with Merrell than she would otherwise have done. She would have her hands full with her three youngsters and was probably secretly quite relieved to have her fosterling taken off her hands.

'We boil bottles and teats to kill off infection; there are germs in food or milk which is left in the air for too long,' Patty said. 'Simply washing them thoroughly isn't really enough. Boiling water kills most things though, as you can imagine.' She smiled at Mrs Blake and was about to let herself out of the house when she thought of something else. 'By the way, can you give the baby a feed just before six when I come to pick her up. It would be a great help if you could.'

Next day, Patty began to regret that she had decided to take the baby so soon. There were complications enough without adding Merrell to the mix. She had managed to arrange for another midwife to cover her district for the day but had not reckoned with the difficulty of acquiring a handcart and someone to push it. In fact, in the end, she gave up on the hand-cart and hired a tough-looking street urchin with a wheelbarrow. He was a cheerful and willing lad, the eldest son of one of her patients, and trotted up and down the stairs with his arms full of Patty's posses-sions. After a couple of journeys, during which he carted her bedding, what little clothing she possessed and her midwifery equipment from Mrs Evans's lodging house to Ashfield Place, she decided that he was trustworthy and got him to accompany her to Paddy's market. Here, she purchased the bedstead and mattress, a rickety wooden chair and a battered tin kettle. She piled her new possessions on to the wheelbarrow and, remembering she would need to sterilise bottles – for a while at least – added an ancient saucepan to his load. Then she despatched the boy to Ashfield Place, telling him to wait for her there.

Having done her best to equip her new dwelling, Patty bought a large canvas shopping bag and began to look for food. Apart from her sojourn with Mrs Ruskin, when she had both cooked and done the marketing, she had never shopped. Mrs Evans provided breakfast and an evening meal for her lodgers, and on their days off they made do with a snack midday meal. Now, faced with the enormous choice available, Patty was completely overcome. However, she was a practical girl and decided to buy only the things she would need over the next couple of days. After all, there were dozens of little shops both on Latimer Street and in the rest of the area surrounding her new home. Anything she lacked, she could find locally. Accordingly, she bought a screw of tea, several tins of condensed milk, a small piece of salt from the block, a large loaf of bread and a few other essentials.

Armed with these necessities, she set out for Ashfield Place.

By ten o'clock that night, Patty was sitting in her own chair, in front of her own stove, feeling exhausted but happy. A midwife's work is both physically and mentally tiring, but rehousing oneself in new property, Patty discovered, was even more so.

For a start, the landing house, which had been previously occupied by an ancient lady and her feckless, idle son, was filthy. When Patty had been shown round it by the landlord, he had assured her that this would be remedied before she moved in, but because of her sudden decision to take possession

37

early he had been unable to keep his promise and the place was still extremely dirty. Patty had given the boy with the wheelbarrow another sixpence to stay and give her a hand and, together, the two of them had toiled until late in the evening, washing down walls, scrubbing floors and cleaning windows. Strong carbolic soap had helped but Patty, very conscious that she was to bring a young baby here next day, disinfected the place so thoroughly that her young helper, wrinkling his nose, stated: 'It pongs like a bleedin' hospital.' Patty thought this fair comment but merely told him that the smell would fade, though the good done by the disinfectant would remain.

To Patty's dismay, the previous tenants had taken the electric light bulbs, and because she had not noticed she had not replaced them. She had despatched her young helper to buy a couple and later on had also sent him to buy coal and kindling; since she had never been a householder before, it had not occurred to her that she would need to light the fire in the stove before she could boil the kettle.

When the boy had departed, richer by half a crown, she had cut herself a thick round of bread, spread it with margarine and settled down before the newly lit fire. The kettle, purring away over the flame, made her think that a cup of tea would go nicely with the bread and marge, so she made a pot, poured herself a cup, and then returned to her chair, looking round her little kingdom with great content.

Presently, however, sheer weariness told her that if she did not get herself to bed soon she would fall asleep where she sat, so she made her way into her bedroom, removed the enormous overall in which she had been swathed, undressed and climbed into bed. She fell asleep at once.

Patty awoke to the pale grey light of dawn and the shrilling of her alarm clock. She half sat up, looking blearily around her whilst she fumbled with the clock mechanism; it always annoyed her sleeping companions when someone's alarm awoke the whole room. Then she looked around her and was mystified for a moment to find herself in a large, bare space, without another soul in sight. There were no curtains across the windows, no linoleum on the floor and, strangest of all, no cramped and crowded beds full of other girls. But since the alarm had gone off, she swung her legs out of bed, and even as her feet touched the floorboards she remembered. She had left Mrs Evans's lodging house – and all other lodging houses – behind her and was now the proud owner, so long as she paid the rent, of No. 24 Ashfield Place.

But there was no time right now to revel in the new life which she felt sure was beginning for her; she must get up, dress, and make herself some breakfast. She had a busy day ahead of her, and since she was back on duty once more might have a disturbed night as well. She was about to start dressing when she remembered that she had banked up the fire in the kitchen; why should she not get dressed there? It was extremely cold in the bedroom and since she did not possess either a basin or a ewer, let alone a wash stand, she might as well both wash and dress in the warm kitchen.

Feeling deliciously guilty, Patty scooped up her uniform, shoved her bare feet into her lace-up shoes and made her way into the kitchen. As she had hoped, the fire was still in, though smouldering sullenly, and a couple of jabs with the poker soon had it roaring up once more. Patty emptied the contents of the kettle into the bowl in the sink. The water was tepid but comfortable, especially when she thought of the scamped and chilly washes she had taken under Mrs Evans's roof. It was a pity there were no curtains but Patty draped a thin towel across the window before stripping off and having a thorough wash. After that, having dressed at speed, she refilled the kettle from the tap in the low stone sink and put it over the fire. It would have been nice to start the day with something hot, a bowl of porridge for instance, but Patty's forethought had not extended to such luxuries, so it would have to be tea and bread and margarine once more, since she could not spare the time even to toast the bread. Today would be a busy one, as most of her days were. Babies arrive at their own convenience and no doubt, when Patty went round to her stand-in's home, she would find some new names had been added to her list. Furthermore, it was not only other people's babies who would be her concern, for at six o'clock this evening she was fetching Merrell from the Blakes' house and would have to make provision for her.

Having got ready for the day ahead, Patty damped down the fire, cast a comprehensive look around her kitchen and headed for the door. If she had time, she would try to buy some more groceries; she was already getting tired of bread and margarine. Outside her door, she unchained her bicycle from the balcony railings, pushed it along the landing and thumped it down the metal steps, not bothering to go quietly since there were lights in most of the windows she passed. To her annoyance, it was raining, but Nurse Watkin, who had stood in for her yesterday, only lived a couple of streets away and, no doubt, would ask her in whilst they discussed Patty's patients. And when I get home tonight, Patty told herself dreamily, mounting the bicycle, Merrell and I will have each other for company in our own little home. The thought cheered her throughout a long and busy day.

It was a beautiful June afternoon, with the sun shining from a clear sky. Patty was heading for home with baby Merrell fast asleep in her bicycle basket and her black bag strapped on to the carrier. As she turned the corner into Latimer Street, the baby's weight caused the bicycle to keel dangerously and Patty reminded herself that she really must find someone to look after Merrell whilst she was at work.

Despite the best of intentions, she had not got round to finding – or even searching for – adoptive parents for the little girl and knew now that she would not willingly part with her. At first it had been simple to take Merrell with her whenever she was called out in the night. If it was raining, she covered the bicycle basket with an old oilskin bought from a stallholder in Paddy's market. If it was fine, a good thick blanket sufficed. Fortunately, Merrell was a contented baby who rarely cried and Patty found it easy enough to unhook the bicycle basket and take it with her into whichever house she was visiting. If the mother-to-be had older children, then Patty left them in charge of Merrell; if not, she took the baby with her into the bedroom whilst she delivered the mother. If a doctor was present, she would leave the basket somewhere near at hand, and so far no doctor had ever queried Merrell's presence, taking it for granted that the patient was looking after the child for a relative. Patty always made sure that she cycled away, with the baby in the basket, after the doctor had left.

During daylight hours, when she did her revisits, Patty explained that the child was in her charge until she was old enough to go to a children's home, and though this occasioned some sharp looks and smothered smiles Patty simply concluded that folk thought she was being taken advantage of. However, it did not worry her. She had registered the child's birth, putting her down as Merrell Peel with unknown parents, and this had never been queried. So long as no one enquired too closely into Merrell's origins, or tried to take her away, Patty was satisfied.

But now, Patty realised as she cycled up Latimer Street, she would have to do something about the child. She had never looked for anyone to share No. 24, since she found she could manage the rent quite comfortably and really loved having her own little home. She had begun to furnish it and had been delighted, and astonished, by the way her new neighbours and several of her patients had reacted when she had admitted she was fitting it up as and when she could afford to do so.

'You've gorra job on your hands,' Mrs Clarke had said, seeing Patty hanging up a line of washing across her part of the balcony. 'I dare say your littl'un makes a deal of washin' and I know you nurses have to have clean uniforms ever so often.' She had looked critically at the overall which Patty was pegging to the line. 'You have to starch 'em an' all, don't you? I starches Bill's collars – he's a clerk at Exchange station – and that's a messy enough job, Gawd knows.'

Patty assured her neighbour that the hospital laundered her uniform but not the overall she wore around the house but Mrs Clarke, undeterred, had continued. 'Mrs Knight told me you wasn't much of a hand wi' your needle. She said you'd bought some real nice curtain stuff for your front room but you didn't have no sewing machine so you was goin' to make 'em by hand. I've gorra sewing machine and now I've left work . . .' she patted her protruding stomach proudly, 'I've got time on me hands, like.'

'Really?' Patty had said, a little coolly. 'But I'm afraid I wouldn't know how to use a sewing machine, Mrs Clarke.' She remembered chatting to her next door neighbour, Mrs Knight, earlier in the week, showing her the material, explaining that she would be making the curtains by hand, that she was a poor and reluctant needlewoman, and now she regretted it. She had meant to hold aloof from the neighbours, keep herself to herself, but Mrs Knight had been so friendly, so interested, that she had unbent a little. And now look what was happening! Mrs Clarke was as good as saying that she, Patty, needed to borrow – probably to hire – a sewing machine in order to get her curtains made before next Christmas!

But Mrs Clarke had clicked her tongue impatiently. 'Give me a couple of bob to cover cottons and me time, and I'll do 'em for you,' she explained. 'I don't suppose you know, but I worked in a clothing factory afore I wed and I'm doin' out-work for them now. It brings in a bit o' splosh, helps wi' household expenses.'

Patty had stood staring at her, unable to believe this marvellous offer. She looked searchingly at Mrs Clarke's freckly face to see whether she was taking a rise out of her. But even if she were . . . 'How much would you charge me to make all my curtains, tapes and everything?' she enquired baldly. 'I've got material for the front room, but I'd want it for the rest as well.'

'Better let me get it for you,' Mrs Clarke advised.

'I'm a dab hand at findin' just the right stuff up the market. As for making 'em, say I charge a bob a pair? Us have got to stick together, you know, and I dare say when me littl'un's born there's things you'll be able to do for me.'

Normally, Patty would have responded crossly that she needed to be paid for her services, but Mrs Clarke's offer had been so welcome – and so unexpected – that she found she had no wish to snub the other woman. Instead, she said: 'It's very good of you, Mrs Clarke. Do you want me to – to measure up my windows?'

'Nah, course not,' Mrs Clarke said scornfully. 'They'll be the same as mine . . . and the same as Nellie's and Lizzie's. I made their curtains an' all, so if you want to see what sort of a job I do . . .'

'I'm sure that won't be necessary,' Patty said hastily. 'Are you sure four bob is enough, though? It seems very little for so much work.'

'It'll be more than four bob with the tapes and the material,' Mrs Clarke reminded her. 'Give me half a bar and we'll settle on a proper amount when I know what it's goin' to cost.' She lowered her voice. 'Mrs Knight's right next door to you, so I dare say you've met her son, Derek? He's ever so nice, everyone likes him. They call him Darky . . . d'you know him?'

'I've seen him about,' Patty said guardedly. Considering he was her next-door neighbour it would have been strange indeed had she not noticed him. Derek Knight had thickly curling black hair, very dark eyes and the sort of olive complexion that Patty usually associated with someone of foreign birth. He was also well over six foot tall and well built, so Patty supposed that most girls would think him good-looking, handsome even. 'I've not spoken to him, mind, only seen him once or twice when we're both coming in around the same time. I don't believe we've ever exchanged so much as a "good morning", to tell you the truth.' She did not add, as she was tempted to do, that she had no interest in Darky Knight, no matter how handsome he might be, and what was more was equally uninterested in all young men. It might be the truth – well, it was – but it was not necessary to tell Mrs Clarke how she felt. In fact, if she thought about Darky Knight at all it was because he seemed somewhat sulky, and was definitely not at all friendly, never even smiling when they passed one another on the stairs.

Mrs Clarke chuckled. 'I dare say you think he's stand-offish, but you'll get to know him better in time,' she said tolerantly. 'The fact is, he's still not gorrover the death of his wife. She – and their newborn baby – both died and he's norrover it yet though it were . . . let me think . . . yes, all of three years ago. He stayed in their place for the first year, but then . . .' she lowered her voice to a whisper, 'then they say he tried to top hisself, so Mrs Knight insisted that he come back here to live.' She sighed gustily, clearly enjoying the drama of her revelations. 'I thought you'd best know, otherwise you might put your foot in it, like. Now, about them curtains; tell you what, decide what sort o' colours and patterns you'd like for the material, write it down on a scrap o' paper and shove it, wi' the money, under me door. Does that suit?'

Patty began to say it would suit very well when a voice hailed Mrs Clarke in stentorian tones from the balcony below and she set off hastily towards the stairs. 'I'll bring the material round as soon as I've gorrit,' she called back over her shoulder. 'I'm comin', Maisie.'

Patty had returned to her kitchen, knelt on the floor and prised up one of the short floorboards. Beneath it, in an old Glaxo tin, were her savings. Now that she had a home of her own, Patty often blessed the fact that she had always been a saver and not a spender. There had been nothing worth spending money on whilst she lived in the nurses' home and worked at the hospital, and though the nurses complained of poor wages and insufficient food Patty had always managed to put some money away each month and was glad of it now. She extracted a ten shilling note from her hoard, noticing ruefully that the amount in her tin was steadily shrinking, and pushed it into an envelope. Then she replaced the Glaxo tin and the floorboard and stood up, going over to the table where she seized a stub of pencil and wrote 'Curtain money from Nurse Peel' upon the envelope. Then she took it along the balcony and pushed it under her neighbour's door.

That night was a busy one. With Merrell snugged down in her bicycle basket, Patty set off at ten o'clock to check on a first-time mother who thought her pains had started; then, later, the doctor sent a message that she was to go at once to another case to assist him with a breech birth. By the time she eventually tumbled into her own bed, dawn was greying the sky and she knew she would not get much sleep before her day's work began. Even so, before she slept she considered what Mrs Clarke had told her about her neighbour's son. Young Mr Knight had lost his wife and baby three years ago, according to Mrs Clarke's memory of the affair. Patty could not remember any such happening and she had been on the district for three years, perhaps a little over. But then she remembered that the young Knights might have been

46

living on the opposite side of the city at the time and put the whole matter out of her head. It was, after all, none of her business. But it was very sad, and explained, she supposed, why Darky Knight always looked so grim.

Patty turned over and pushed her face into the cool pillow. Sleep, she commanded herself, or you'll be no use to anyone in the morning. And presently, worn out, she obeyed.

Darky Knight had been about to step out of the front door and on to the balcony when the voices gave him pause. He stopped short, clicking his fingers impatiently. It was the bleedin' women, gossiping out there; he'd hang on a moment until they finished talking and went their ways, then he would set off for the docks. The pubs down there were always open for when the dockers came off shift. Fortunately, his mother had gone to do her messages some time earlier, or she would have chided him for lurking indoors on a fine and sunny day. What was more, she would have guessed just why he was unwilling to go out whilst the women were jangling on the balcony.

'There's no sense in avoiding our neighbours, even if they do happen to be young women,' she would have said. 'For God's sweet sake, boy, it's nigh on three year since you lost your dear Alison; isn't it time you started to live again? That young Mrs Clarke's a grand girl so she is, and the new one, the nurse . . . well, she's pretty as a picture and anyone can see she's been let down by a feller or she wouldn't be bringin' up that babby by herself, so she ain't on the look-out for a man of her own, if that's what you're afraid of.'

He would say he was not afraid, merely indifferent,

47

and his mam would snort and say that it was time he pulled himself together, began to meet people again, to go to dances, to the cinema . . . time he began to take a girl about. Despite himself, Darky grinned. In his heart, he knew that Mam was probably right. Alison and the baby had died a long time ago. It was time he at least tried to put it behind him. And you couldn't deny that the girl next door – Nurse Peel, wasn't it? – was a real little cracker. That abundant, white-blonde hair, the brilliant blue of her eyes, the rose-petal complexion . . . he had been amazed when his mam had told him, in a hushed voice, that she was single, seemed indifferent to the feller who had fathered her child, and apparently had no man in her life.

No relatives, either, he thought musingly now. Nor friends, for that matter. She had been in the flat for three weeks and no one had called to see her save those who wanted her professional services. Odd, that. A pretty girl in a good job . . . but even thinking that way made him feel a traitor to Alison's memory. His dear little love with her soft, reddish-gold hair, skin like milk dusted with golden freckles, her round, hazel eyes, the lilt of her soft Scots accent, the bubble of laughter never far away . . . he felt the familiar contraction of his stomach. Gone. Gone. Because they had married and he'd taken no precautions, and she'd got in the family way . . . nine months of marriage and then . . .

Darky felt the stupid rage begin to build, the rage which sent him out on drinking binges which had twice almost lost him his job. He closed his eyes and pressed his fists against them until he could see brilliant sunbursts on the blackness behind his lids. Then he leaned his forehead against the cool glass of the window and made himself listen to the talk still going on outside. Anything, *anything*, to stop him remembering, blaming himself . . .

'. . . he's still not gorrover the death of his wife. She – and their newborn baby – both died . . .' There was a short pause whilst Darky gritted his teeth and clenched his fists . . . how *dare* they discuss him, the common little trollops, how dare they so much as mention Alison! . . . and then one of them whispered: 'They say he tried to top hisself . . .'

Darky felt his stomach begin to turn over and hastily abandoned the window to hang over the sink. He remembered the night his mother had come calling, had found him lying on the kitchen floor . . . the smell of the vomit was in his nostrils now . . . but no one knew! Not a soul had ever said a word to him; even in hospital there had been no talk such as he had just overheard, no scandal . . .

He retched, then straightened, cold rage bringing him back to his senses. It would be that bloody, self-righteous Nurse Peel, that's who would be passing rumours around amongst the neighbours! Well, it just went to prove that you couldn't judge by appearances. He had thought her downright beautiful, had liked the slim strength of her, the way she held herself. Not like a soldier on parade as so many of them did, but straight-backed nevertheless, and with an easy self-confidence, too. Dammit, he had *liked* the look of her. But no more. One of these days he would tackle her about the wicked rumours she was spreading but not now, not yet. He needed to be stronger before he so much as spoke to an unmarried young woman, even if, like Nurse Peel, she was no better than she should be. She must be shameless, bringing her bastard to a respectable neighbourhood, hoping no one would think the worse of her, chatting to his mam whenever they were out on the balcony at the same time . . . and slandering him, Derek Knight, in foolish, spiteful gossip with another resident of Ashfield Place! Oh, yes, he would tell her a thing or two one of these days so he would! He would give her a taste of her own medicine, talk about her, tell folk about her love-child. But in the meantime he would take absolutely no notice of her. He would pass her on the stairs or going along the balcony without a word, ignore her if she called on his mother, refuse to mention her in conversation.

True to her word, Mrs Clarke bought cheap material and made all Patty's curtains. Though there was still a little constraint between them – Patty was still very much the professional midwife – she began to appreciate Mrs Clarke's breezy personality and to enjoy her visits to the Clarke house.

Perhaps it was because of Mrs Clarke's friendliness that other neighbours had begun to treat Patty with less formality. They called out to her in the street, sent their children round to ask if she had any messages, offered help when she ran over a piece of glass and tore a great hole in her bicycle tyre, and generally behaved as though they wanted her friendship and were willing to offer her theirs.

'I don't understand it,' Patty had said recently, when she had visited Mrs Ruskin. 'I've done my best to keep them at a distance but it doesn't seem to work. And to tell you the truth, I rather like the friendliness. I remember what it was like in Great Homer Street, and at Mrs Evans's; no one liked me very much – not that I liked them either – so I never got any but grudging help, even when I needed it badly.'

Mrs Ruskin had chuckled. 'It's the baby, my love,'

she had said comfortably. 'They all think Merrell's your own child and that means you aren't a superior being but just like them. Having a baby – and no husband – makes you human and fallible. See?'

Patty, who did not see at all, had given a non-committal mutter but thinking it over she realised her friend must be right. Because of her education and qualifications, she had always held aloof from the community she served and she knew she had not behaved any differently in Ashfield Place, yet the neighbours had taken her to their hearts. Smiling a little ruefully she realised she had a lot to thank Merrell for.

Now, Patty dismounted her bicycle and began to heave it up the iron stairway. It had been simple enough when Merrell was tiny, but now her weight made carting it upstairs really difficult. As she struggled, a figure came clattering down towards her, a tall, dark figure. It was difficult to identify him against the light but as he drew level Patty recognised Darky Knight. By now she was used to him ignoring her and expected nothing else, so she was considerably surprised when he looked at the baby in the basket, gave a martyred sigh, and turned back, grabbing the front wheel of the bicycle as he did so. He began to pull the machine up the remaining stairs, though without a word said, and Patty, breathless from the effort she had already expended, held her tongue until they reached the top landing. Then she said: 'Thanks, Mr Knight.'

He turned away and Patty essayed a small smile, thinking crossly that he might at least acknowledge her thanks, if nothing else. But Darky Knight did not reply. With averted head, he went past her and hurried down the stairs, two at a time. Patty now knew that he was an electrician at Lever Brothers; knew also from his mother that it was a responsible and well-paid job. They do shift work at Port Sunlight so he's probably in a hurry, she told herself, but she could not help feeling a little aggrieved. Why was he so rude to her? It was impolite to ignore someone who had spoken to you. Mrs Knight had said, excusingly, that her son was shy and had become even more so after losing his wife, but Patty had heard him talking to Mrs Clarke and other neighbours in a normal fashion. To be sure, he did not gossip but he was always polite to everyone, except herself.

It is a nasty thing to feel oneself disliked for no obvious reason, as Patty knew well, but she comforted herself by remembering that she had no interest in any young man and really had no desire for a friendship with Darky Knight.

As she wheeled her machine along to her own section of balcony, Patty's thoughts reverted to her problem: who was going to look after Merrell now that she was becoming too big for the bicycle basket? She told herself sadly that she could not go on as she did at present, lugging the child around with her. It was fair neither to Merrell nor to Patty herself, for at five months Merrell was beginning to take a considerable interest in her surroundings, and in a few weeks more she would be sitting up by herself and wanting to crawl or to shuffle along on her bottom, the way Patty had seen other children do. Unstrapping the basket, Patty took her bag in her other hand, then had to set it down to unlock her front door. Once this was done, she carried Merrell across to the kitchen table and put the basket down on it, then began to set about the tasks which she performed on her arrival home each evening. First, she lifted Merrell, gurgling happily, from the basket and wedged her into a corner of the one easy chair she possessed. Then she emptied her instruments into the sink and washed them thoroughly before popping them in a biscuit tin and placing it in the bake oven for sterilisation, for the fire was kept alight in the stove day and night.

Patty had noticed a couple of weeks before how intently the baby now watched her every movement and as she prepared the child's bottle, and a simple meal for herself, she spent a good deal of time chatting to Merrell as though she understood every word. Right from the start, she had realised that the child needed constant loving attention as much as she needed feeding, cleaning and clothing and had done her best to provide it. The lack of such attention in her own childhood had, she guessed, contributed to the deep unhappiness from which she had suffered in the orphan asylum, so she had decided not to take Merrell to a child minder who probably looked after fifteen or twenty small children. Besides, such a person would look after Merrell during the day but would be unable to do so at night, and Patty was on night call every other week. At present, she took the slumbering Merrell with her but this would not be possible for much longer. The baby was outgrowing the bicycle basket and had begun to murmur a sleepy protest when she was bumped down the metal steps and across the cobbled street.

But there's no way she's going to end up with anyone but me, Patty told herself grimly, watching the child's ecstatic face as she sucked enthusiastically at the bottle. I wonder if Mrs Knight might like to give an eye to her? On second thoughts, Patty decided this was not a good idea. Mrs Knight was a delightful lady but her son never took the slightest notice of Merrell and might be unpleasant to the child simply because of his dislike of Patty. If his sad experience of marriage and babies had affected his mind, Patty did not want him anywhere near her little girl.

Besides, there were bound to be plenty of other people who liked children and would take on the care of Merrell when Patty was unable to see to her. 'And of course, I'll pay whoever takes you on, my little sugar plum,' Patty told Merrell, smiling down into the blue, blue eyes. 'Oh, I wish I knew what to do for the best! But one thing I do know: you aren't going to land up in an orphan asylum!'

Merrell having finished her bottle, Patty offered her some of the rice pudding she had made earlier. The baby ate it with enthusiasm, and when she had finished Patty replaced her in the chair and began on her own meal. But even as she ate, her thoughts continued to revolve uneasily. It was no good putting it off; she simply must find a solution for her baby-sitting problem before it became insurmountable.

Patty, eating bread and jam, thought of her own life in the orphanage, the strict discipline, the lack of love. Slowly, she let her mind drift back, remembering . . . remembering . . .

Chapter Three
November 1914

'Patty Peel! Wharrever's the matter now? I've never known a child like you for whining and complainin'. Keep up wi' the rest of the kids or I'll see to it you get a good slappin' and no supper when we get home!'

'It's me shoes, miss,' Patty said. 'Them's too small. I don't think they *are* mine, any road. I think they're Betty's.'

Patty, with her feet throbbing painfully, had fallen further and further behind. At the sound of Miss Briggs's voice, however, she hobbled along a little faster, wincing at the pain from her crushed toes, to catch up with her partner in the crocodile.

The children from the Durrant House Orphan Asylum, on The Elms, were being taken for their twice-weekly walk. They usually went to Sefton Park and watched other children feeding the ducks, admired the Palm House and the aviary and, in summer, were even allowed to play for a little on the grass. Today, however, though they had walked as far as the nearest gates, they had not entered the park. Laura Reilly, who happened to be Patty's partner, had been caught chewing gum and Miss Briggs had immediately boxed her ears and announced that, thanks to Laura, they would all be punished, for Laura had refused to say where the chewing gum had come from. 'And I trust you other girls will see that Laura never does such a thing again, since she has spoiled your walk,' the teacher said severely.

'However, we have to stay out for at least half an hour, so we'll take a turn around the neighbourhood instead.'

Miss Briggs had called the crocodile of small girls to a halt whilst Patty caught up, and as the child rejoined them she said sharply: 'Betty's shoes indeed! It's so typical of you, Patty Peel, to blame someone else for what is your own fault. Did you not check that the shoes were yours before you put them on? And why, may I ask, have you not apologised to me for your tardiness?'

There was a short pause whilst Patty considered which question Miss Briggs wanted answered first, but even as she opened her mouth to speak Miss Briggs grabbed her by the shoulder and slapped the side of her face sharply. Patty fell back a pace and put a hand to her hot cheek, but she could not help thinking that if Miss Briggs had known the full story of Laura's chewing gum she would have got a good deal more than a slap on the cheek. Patty had found the chewing gum stuck to the iron railings round the park and had shared it with Laura. There had still been a trace of minty flavour in the grey and gooey mass and she had been enjoying her share when Miss Briggs had shouted at Laura. Naturally, Patty had immediately swallowed her own piece and, had it not been for the pain in her feet, would have worried quite a lot over what the chewing gum was doing in her insides. Suppose it gave her appendicitis? There was a rude song the girls used to sing, about the travels of a peanut . . . *that* had given someone appendicitis. However, she could not appear to be unmoved by the slap or Miss Briggs would grow suspicious, so she said, breathlessly: 'Sorry, miss. I were last down to the cloakroom and there were only

one pair of shoes left, so I had to put them on, didn't
I?'

She did not expect sympathy or even understanding but felt the familiar sinking of the heart
when Miss Briggs snapped: 'Last as usual, you mean.
Can nothing teach you not to dream your life away,
girl? Everyone else enjoys their walks and hurries to
the cloakroom for outdoor clothing and shoes, but not
you. Oh no, Miss Patty Peel comes in her own good
time, when she thinks she will.'

There was a titter from the nearest group of girls, no
doubt hoping to curry favour with Miss Briggs,
though Laura gave her a sympathetic look out of her
large, rather tearful-looking grey eyes. Patty knew
most of the girls resented her because she was at least
a year younger than they. The previous term she had
been in Miss Nixon's class with girls of her own age,
but had rapidly become so bored by the childish work
that her fellow classmates were stumbling through
that she had begun to be naughty and disruptive.
Miss Nixon, her gentle, undemanding form teacher,
had taken her to one side and explained, almost
apologetically, that she had suggested Patty should
be moved from Class 3 to Class 4. 'I don't have the
time to set you special work, which means you are
often idle and often, I'm afraid, rather naughty,' she
had explained. 'In a higher class, with older children,
you will find the work more challenging and be less
likely to get into trouble. I shall miss you, Patty,
because you are easily my brightest pupil, but to hold
you back would be selfish and not in the interests of
the rest of my class. So when the new term begins in
September, you will go to Miss Briggs's class, where I
am sure you will speedily find your feet.'

Patty had liked Miss Nixon but had known nothing

about Miss Briggs and was appalled to find that her new teacher was both spiteful and vicious, much given to hitting her pupils and inventing punishments which often affected the whole class.

In a way, Miss Nixon had been right; removed from the company of children her own age, Patty had had to work hard to catch up. Having done so, however, she found herself even more unpopular than she had been with her own age group. The older girls might have tolerated her had she seemed to struggle or ask for their help, but that was not Patty's way. She had simply slogged at her books, reading whenever she had time to herself, and questioning the teachers until she had no need to enquire further, for she understood what the lessons were all about. And then she had soared to the top of the class once more and had reaped the reward of being called a goody-goody, a know-all, and even teacher's pet.

This last, as Patty knew to her cost, was very far from the truth but it hurt her, even so. There was something about Patty's flaxen hair, round blue eyes and rosy cheeks which seemed to mark her out as someone to be watched, and the teaching staff, with one accord, blamed her whenever things went wrong.

Sometimes they were right, Patty acknowledged to herself, trudging along in the wake of the crocodile as it headed along Belvidere Road. Usually, they continued past St Paul's Church and the Hamlet before turning right into The Elms, but today Miss Briggs led her crocodile down a different street before they reached the church. Patty, with her mind divided between the lump of chewing gum in her stomach and the pain of her crushed toes, did not wonder why Miss Briggs had chosen a different way home; she just hoped it was quicker. She might not have noticed the name of the street at all had Laura not given her a poke in the ribs. 'This 'un's your street, Patty,' Laura hissed hoarsely. 'I never knew you had a street all to yourself!' As she spoke, she pointed to a neat nameplate and Patty was astonished to see that the other girl was right; this was indeed Peel Street. It was even spelled the same.

Patty's mind immediately abandoned both toes and chewing gum and began to revolve the strange coincidence of bearing the same name as a street. 'I wonder if my relatives live here?' she muttered. 'No, they can't do, 'cos it's quite near the Durrant, so I dare say they'd pop in to see me from time to time. It's strange, though, isn't it? I suppose it might have been named for me dad if he'd done something special. Oh, Laura, I wish I could find out!'

'I 'spect it's just a co . . . co . . .' Laura said. 'I 'spect it don't mean nothing, really. People who are special don't put their kids into orphan asylums.'

Patty gave this some thought and then, as they turned into The Elms, nodded agreement. 'I s'pose you're right. I say, what's today? Is it bread and jam tea or is it bread and dripping?'

'Bread and dr—' Laura was beginning when Miss Briggs, at the head of the crocodile, turned to shoot them a suspicious glance.

'Was someone talking?' the teacher said sharply. 'Patty Peel, if you want any tea you'd best button your lip.'

The head of the crocodile turned into the entrance to Durrant House and, fortunately for Patty, Miss Briggs became too busy ordering them to the cloakroom and fussing about the way they hung up their coats, changed their shoes and put on their smocks to bother her further that afternoon.

Meals were taken in the long dining room just past the cloakrooms. The children lined up in the corridor and were then marched in to have their meal, class by class. There was not room for the whole school to eat at the same time, and as one of Miss Briggs's pupils Patty was now in the second wave to be fed. Since meals were small and skimpy affairs, however, it did not take long for the little ones to finish their food and go along to their playroom at the end of the building. And presently Patty, Laura and the rest of their class took their places on the long wooden benches, bowed their heads for grace and, when the word was given, began to eat the bread and golden syrup which was today's fare. And very thinly the syrup was spread too, so that it was no more than a few golden bubbles distributed across the surface of the waxy margarine.

As luck would have it, Patty was seated at the extreme end of one of the long tables, right next door to the prefect, who handed out the food, saw to it that no one took anyone else's portion and generally kept order. Today, the prefect in charge of Patty's table was Selina Roberts. She was a tall, slender girl with mouse-coloured hair and light blue eyes and was a general favourite with the younger children since she always had time to answer questions or to read storybooks to those still not able to read for themselves. Unfortunately, talking in the dining room was forbidden but Patty, with Peel Street still on her mind, decided to take a chance. When the duty teacher's back was turned, she asked Selina whether she could have a word with her in the common room later.

'Of course,' Selina whispered, also keeping her eyes on the teacher, who was reprimanding someone at another table for eating too quickly. 'Is it a private matter?'

Patty nodded bashfully and adjusted the neck of her smock; in her hurry she had tied the tapes rather too tightly. Selina suggested that it might be more prudent to go into one of the empty classrooms, since the sight of a senior girl chatting with a child of seven would give rise to the sort of curiosity which neither girl wished to arouse.

When the meal was over, the children filed out in table order and presently Patty found herself in one of the junior classrooms, perched on a desk with Selina smiling comfortably at her. 'Well?' the older girl said. 'What can I do for you, Patty Peel?'

Patty hesitated, but only for a moment. She had so many questions that she wanted answered! However, to begin at the beginning was always a good plan, so she took a deep breath and plunged into her story. 'Selina, I'm seven years old, but I never gets no visitors. I think me mam and dad are dead – at any rate, when I were in the baby class, Miss Merrell told me they were dead – but even so, wouldn't you think I'd have other relatives? But none of them ever comes to see me, nor sends me so much as a line, come Christmas. Then, on our walk this afternoon, Miss Briggs brought us home by a different way and we found ourselves walking down Peel Street. Now I thought, it bein' so near the Durrant an' all, and my name being Peel . . . well I thought it might *mean* something.'

'Yes, it does mean something, though not what you're thinking,' Selina said. 'Do you mean to say nobody has told you that you're a foundling? There's nothing wrong in that,' she added hastily as she saw the puzzlement on Patty's face, 'I'm a foundling myself. It simply means that your mam and dad weren't able to look after you, so – so they left you somewhere safe, where you were bound to be found by responsible people who would take good care of you.'

Patty digested this, then said doubtfully: 'But what difference does that make, Selina? I mean I'm still the child of Mr and Mrs Peel, aren't I? The same as you're the child of Mr and Mrs Roberts?'

'Well, no, it doesn't mean that,' Selina said gently. 'In fact, your beginnings are a lot more romantic than that, Patty dear. Your mother may have been very young and perhaps she did not want anyone to know that she had given birth to a baby, so she wrapped you in a nice, bright red blanket and left you snugly under a hedge on Peel Street. I'm positive she must have waited to make sure someone found you, and indeed you were found quite quickly, for though it was a rainy night your blanket was almost dry when a scuffer came along, walking his beat, and saw you. He brought you to the nearest orphan asylum, which of course was the Durrant, and left you in Matron's charge. But because they did not know your mother's name, or anything about her, they named you partly after the scuffer, whose name was Patrick, and partly after the street.'

'So I'm not Patty Peel at all then?' Patty said doubtfully. 'It's just a make-up? Is it the same for you, Selina? Is there a Robert Street somewhere in Liverpool, where you were found?'

Selina laughed. 'No, not a Robert Street. I was dumped on Lime Street station, but there was a note pinned to the shawl I was wrapped in. It said *This is Selina. Please take care of her*. And the porter who found me was called Roberts, so . . . well, that was the surname they chose for me, since I already had a first name.'

'I think that's nice, that your mam cared enough to name you,' Patty said wistfully. 'I wish mine had named me. And to be left under a hedge . . .'

Selina laughed. 'Patty Peel's a lovely name,' she said bracingly. 'Much nicer than Selina Roberts, if you ask me. I'm just so thankful that they didn't call me Selina Lime, after the station, you know. But why did you start wondering about your relatives, Patty dear?'

'I've wondered before,' Patty admitted. 'But I just thought me mam an' dad must have died, and me relatives must be living far away. Only when I saw Peel Street I thought – I thought . . . and I looked at the houses, real posh they are on that street, Selina, and I couldn't help wonderin' if I had cousins or – or aunts or somebody living there. Come to that, why did my mam choose Peel Street? I bet it were because she lived there . . . you never know. I could ask around.'

'Matron would be furious if you tried any such thing. Even if you managed to escape and get back in again without someone on the staff seeing you, you can be sure some interfering busybody would tell her,' Selina warned. 'Look, queen, I used to worry about my mam an' dad, just as you do, but I could see there weren't no future in it. What's important . . . well, what's important to me, at any rate . . . is getting out of this place and getting a proper job so's folk won't need to know I come from Durrant House. I'm not saying there's anything wrong with the place, because they do their best and we get a decent education if we're bright enough to make use of our lessons. But when I'm grown up I want a good job, a husband and kids of my own, and I'm telling you my mam and dad don't matter to me any more. After all, if I'd mattered to them they'd not have dumped me on Lime Street station, even if they did give me a name. And what's a name, after all? I used to think if my mam didn't care enough about me to hang on to me, bring me up, then she'd no *right* to go givin' me a silly name like Selina. I would have loved to be called Polly, or Jane, or even Mary, like everyone else,' she ended, her voice wistful.

'Well, I think Selina's a lovely name,' Patty said obstinately. 'But I'm glad we're both foundlings, not just me. Are there others, do you know? And how did you find out about me, anyroad?'

'Now that I'm old enough to be useful I help Miss Freeman, the secretary,' Selina explained. 'All our files are in the basement and sometimes, when it's raining and I'm bored, I go down there and ferret around. I noticed that my file wasn't in with all the others but was on a different shelf . . . yours was there too . . . and I read them to see why we were kept separately. As for other foundlings, there are several, but I shan't tell you who they are. Matron doesn't go blabbing information like that about in front of the whole orphanage because she knows some people would jeer at us if they knew. But you and me, we're too bright to have the wool pulled over our eyes. Even if I'd not told you, you'd have found out for yourself, in the end. So no harm done, eh?'

'No, no harm done,' Patty echoed, hearing the tone in Selina's voice which meant that the questions must come to an end. She slipped off the desk, then hesitated. 'Thanks ever so, Selina, for telling me. I wonder if all the other kids know, though? I mean, I never have a letter or anything like that and no one visits me. You'd think they'd have guessed – but I didn't, did I?'

'No. But in fact if you take a bit of notice of other

people in your class you'll find that there are several girls with one parent, or brothers and sisters, or aunts and uncles, who don't get letters or visits, either. Your mam and dad can't visit you because they don't know where you are, but there's no excuse for the others. And I'll tell you what, I've just had a really corking idea. When I leave, next year, I mean to go into nursing. I had my tonsils out when I was ten and ever since then I've known that I'd rather be a nurse, and help people to get well, than anything else. Oh, you don't start as a nurse, of course, but I don't mind working my way up. I'll go as a ward maid or a kitchen worker or something until I'm old enough to become a probationer, and then I'll work like fury and be State Registered as soon as I can. And . . . this is the corking idea . . . I'll write to you, send you the odd present. What do you say to that?'

'Oh, Selina!' Patty gasped, quite overcome. 'Would you really? That would be just wonderful! Only . . . wouldn't Matron and the teachers mind?'

'It's none of their business. The letters will be addressed to you, so you will be the only person to read them. Only mind you reply – I'll give you my address – because it will be interesting to hear how you're getting on.'

'Oh, Selina,' Patty said again. 'And you can tell me all about your hospital and what job you are doing. And when I'm grown up I'll be a nurse too, just like you.'

From the moment Selina had told Patty about her past, things, Patty thought, had begun to improve for her. The other girls in her class grew accustomed to her and Patty, with an intelligence beyond her years, decided that being top of the class was making her more enemies than friends. She did not intend to let herself slip very far but realised that being second or third, or even lower sometimes, would make life easier for her.

Laura, who had to struggle to gain pass marks in any subject, turned out to be a good friend. Though not clever, she had a lot of common sense and, once she realised that Patty often acted thoughtlessly, gave her a great deal of good advice. 'You're very pretty, with that lovely blonde hair and such blue eyes,' she said earnestly one day, as they lay on their tummies in the Corporation Playing Fields, watching the rounders match in progress. 'People *want* to like you, they even want to be your friend, but you put them off by knowing best and by not listening when they try to tell you something. I know you're clever, but that shouldn't stop you from being nice, as well, and at the moment even the teachers pick on you, don't they?'

'Some of them do,' Patty admitted grudgingly. She was enjoying this rare treat and felt lazy and contented for once, the sun was warm on her back through her thin cotton dress. Presently, she knew, the teacher would start to call in those girls not already on the playing field itself, and Patty, who was not fond of games, would be forced to exert herself. She thought it was a pity that Laura had chosen this moment to deliver her lecture. 'But I'm being quite careful in class now, you know. I don't always put my hand up when I know the answer to a question and the other girls are much nicer to me now. Why, even old Briggsy isn't as bad as she was; Teresa and me were talking in the dining room queue yesterday and she shook us both but didn't slap either of us. Wharrabout that, eh?'

Laura laughed. 'You are much better,' she acknowledged. 'And then there's Selina, of course. She's the
most popular prefect in the school and everyone
knows she's your pal. Oh, I do like Selina most
dreadfully! She's nice to everyone and she'll give you
a hand if you need it, and though she's really clever
she never lets on. I'm thick as porridge, but when I'm
talking to Selina I feel – I feel as if I'm just as clever as
her, somehow.'

'It is nice, being friendly with Selina,' Patty
admitted, smiling dreamily to herself. 'I don't see
much of her, mind, and next year she'll have left – and
won't I miss her! Did you know she were going to be
a nurse when she leaves the Durrant?'

'No, but I'm not surprised . . .' Laura was beginning, when Miss Dawson's stentorian voice broke
across the sentence.

'Any girl not already on the pitch, to me, if you
please! Come along, come along, you aren't here to
idle away the afternoon watching others do all the
work, you know! My goodness, I hadn't realised how
many of you hadn't had a game yet, but there's still an
hour before we have to go home, so that's plenty of
time to get you on the move. Patty Peel, Laura Reilly,
you can both pick a team. Laura, you start.'

For an hour, therefore, the girls played rounders,
and when Miss Dawson clapped her hands and told
everyone to get into pairs for the walk home they
were all conscious of a pleasant glow. These trips to
the Corporation Playing Fields came perhaps two or
three times a summer, and were much prized even by
those girls who did not enjoy games. To be sure it was
a long walk from Durrant House, but it was a change
from the everlasting circling of Prince's Park. What
was more, Miss Dawson was not a disciplinarian and

seemed oblivious of the fact that, on the way home, instead of proceeding in a neat crocodile, the girls sauntered along in small groups, chattering and laughing, sometimes falling behind and having to run to catch up. Perhaps it was because she was only a part-time teacher, but whatever the reason it made her lessons, if you could call them lessons, extremely popular.

After that one trip down Peel Street, Miss Briggs had reverted to their usual route, so Patty had not even had the doubtful pleasure of traversing the road in which she had been left. As Patty and Laura strolled along, it occurred to Patty that this was the ideal opportunity to take another look at Peel Street. Miss Dawson, with the third and fourth years in her charge, would not have noticed had ten of them gone missing, and because they did not walk in pairs the fact that Patty was not with the others would certainly go unnoticed. However, in all fairness, she must take Laura into her confidence; if blame was to be cast at anyone, it must not be at her friend.

Laura was the only person to whom Patty had confided the secret of her beginnings and Laura had been much impressed. She herself was from a broken home, for her mariner father had gone off with a girl half his age and Laura's mother, left to bring up seven children, all under ten, had put five of them into orphan asylums. She had long ceased to either visit or even write to her daughter, but Patty knew that Laura clung to the hope that she would be reunited with her parent one day.

When Patty told Laura that she meant to sneak off and take a closer look at Peel Street, she half expected her sensible friend to raise an objection, but Laura was all in favour of the idea. 'I'll come with you,' she said excitedly. 'If we get a move on, we can easily get well ahead of Miss Dawson, then we'll have time to take a good look at the street and still rejoin the other girls before Miss D. starts getting them into line again. You know how everyone dawdles on their way back to the Durrant.'

Acting upon these words, the two girls slipped away from the others and were very soon traversing the streets which would lead, eventually, to their destination. Neither girl was at all familiar with the area but Patty stopped, every time she saw a sharp-looking urchin, to ask for directions and very soon they found themselves in the area they knew, with Prince's Park on their right.

'What exactly are you going to do?' Laura panted, as they entered Peel Street. 'There are lots of houses along here and you might have been found outside any of them. D'you mean to go up to the front door and ask?'

Patty stopped short and stared, round-eyed, at her friend. Until this moment, it had not occurred to her that visiting Peel Street was not an end in itself. Then she squared her shoulders and grabbed Laura's arm, tugging her towards the houses on the right-hand side of the street, most of which had handsome hedges before their neat front gardens. 'Selina said I were under a hedge, so we can miss out the stone walls,' she said. 'Would you say my mam probably had hair my colour, Laura? Only if I was to go to the door and someone what looked like me answered it . . . well, it might be my own mam, don't you think?'

Laura giggled but looked extremely apprehensive. 'If your mam lived here once, I don't reckon she lives here now,' she said nervously. 'No one don't dump a baby in their own front yard, or no one I've ever heard of, anyhow. She may well have lived nearby, but the more I think of it, the more sure I am that it couldn't have been in Peel Street. It stands to reason, queen; she may even have come off the train at Dingle station and simply chosen a decent neighbourhood – and a nice thick hedge – so's you'd be picked up the sooner.'

Patty stared at her friend whilst a cold feeling of dismay rose up in her. Laura was so sensible! Nevertheless, Patty told herself grimly, she would not give up so easily. She had intended to go to the front doors but decided, instead, to go to the back; perhaps one of the servants might remember a baby being found, you never knew. Suddenly, it was important simply to find out under which hedge she had been left. If she could discover that much, perhaps on subsequent visits she would find out much more. Resolutely, she seized Laura's arm and dragged her to the nearest front gate bounded on either side by a thick laurel hedge. 'We'll start here,' she said fiercely, towing Laura around the side path and scarcely noticing the size and splendour of the house in her determination to reach the back premises. 'Surely someone will remember a policeman finding a baby under a hedge!'

Laura sighed, but accompanied her friend and presently Patty banged the knocker on a back door which was almost as imposing as the front one. The door was immediately snatched open and a girl's head, with a maid's white cap perched insecurely on her bush of hair, appeared in the gap. 'Yes?' she said baldly and then, realising that it was two little girls who stood on the step, added belligerently: 'Wharra *you* want, eh?' Over her shoulder, she remarked to someone the girls could not see, 'It's nobbut a couple o' kids, miz Thornton, from that there orphing place up the road. I thought they wasn't allowed out, 'cept in a line, like.'

'Nor they is, poor little buggers,' a voice in the background said cheerfully, ''cept, o' course, when they's left under an 'edge, like the kid what was abandoned here a few years back.'

The face at the door turned its back on Patty and Laura in order to say, incredulously: 'Under an 'edge? I never heered nothin' o' that before, miz Thornton! But these ain't babbies. They's probably . . .' Here she turned to survey the girls critically. 'They's prob'ly six or seven.'

'We aren't. Laura's eight and I'm getting on that way,' Patty said, some of her old belligerence flaring. 'I come to ask you about that baby, but you don't know nothin', you just said so. Please may we speak to Miss Thornton?'

At this, another face appeared in the doorway, a round, red face, enhanced by steel-rimmed spectacles perched on a rubicund nose and topped by thinning grey hair. The woman looked fat and jolly and smiled down at Patty and Laura, though the eyes behind the spectacles which scanned them from head to toe were shrewd. 'Couple o' runaways, eh?' she said genially. 'I been cook here nigh on ten years and in all that time I've never seen any of them orphings, 'cept wi' a teacher and walkin' in a line. Here, catch hold o' these,' and, as if by magic, two buns, fresh from the oven, were handed down to them.

Both girls mumbled their thanks and took the proffered treat and Patty said hopefully: 'So you were here when the baby was left? Please, Miss Thornton, was it your hedge, the one at the front?'

'I'm Mrs Thornton, not Miss,' that lady said

grandly. 'All cooks is missus, young woman, as you'll learn if you go into service like most of them orphings do. I misremember if it were our 'edge – wait a mo', now I come to think, it were the privet 'edge, two doors further along. Why's you so interested, queen? Don't say you're that babby?'

'Yes, I'm that baby,' Patty acknowledged, feeling singularly foolish. 'But if it wasn't your hedge, Mrs Thornton, how is it that you know all about the baby – me, I mean?'

Mrs Thornton chuckled richly. 'Well, for a start, the scuffer visited every house in the neighbourhood next day, tryin' to find your mam. And, of course, servants like to have a chat over the garden wall now and again, same as their mistresses do, so the news got around like lightning, I reckon. The scuffer asked us whether there were anybody in the house – maids, I mean, not menservants – who'd been acting kinda strange lately. Come to that, he wanted to know whether anyone had gone out that day and not returned until dark, but we couldn't help him. In the end, he told us it were probably some poor gel from the slums who had chosen a good neighbourhood to leave her babby in the hopes that a rich couple might adopt it, same as in storybooks.' She sighed gustily. 'Only real life ain't like that and you got left in that there orphing asylum. Oh well, I dare say it ain't so bad, eh? I dare say you's happy enough?'

Laura began to agree but Patty said, hopefully: 'The food's awful poor, Mrs Thornton. We don't get cakes like the one you give us, not even at Christmas. Mostly, it's bread and scrape and mugs of weak tea or milk and water. But we have scouse once a week and a piece of currant loaf on Sunday.'

Mrs Thornton tutted. 'Well, folk keep telling me

there's a war on and I know there's all sorts of shortages in the shops, though it don't bother us, pertickler,' she said. 'But bread and scrape and scouse once a week . . . what sort of a cook feeds growin' girls on stuff like that? I reckon she oughter be ashamed!'

'I don't suppose the cook knows that girls get as hungry as boys,' Laura said timidly. 'As for the war, I don't think it's made much difference to our meals. They've been the same for as long as I've been at the Durrant. But of course, some girls is luckier than others; they get grub sent in from relatives occasionally. Mebbe Cook thinks we're all like that.'

'Oh, go on! They know very well I don't have no relatives, nor parcels of goodies,' Patty said stoutly. 'And the teachers don't get fed what we get. Sometimes there's lovely smells come out of the staff dining room, and one of the older girls told me that when she's on table-clearing duties she and her friends lick the plates before they take them through to the kitchen, 'cos the food's so good.'

The cook tutted again and disappeared for a moment, to reappear with two more buns which she handed to the girls. 'There you are,' she said gruffly. 'And if you ever gerraway again, I don't mind if you come and give us a knock. Shortages or no shortages, there's always plenty of good food in *this* house, and seein' as you're the babby what were found just up the road I'm a-willing to hand out the odd treat now and then.'

'Thanks ever so, Mrs Thornton,' the girls chorused. 'And thanks for the buns,' Patty added. 'You must be the best cook in the world, and if we ever get away again, we will come and see you, honest to God we will.'

'Well?' Laura said, as they regained the road once

more. 'If the scuffer tried to find your mam, Patty, and didn't have no luck, what chance have you got? I reckon we oughter give up and go back afore we're missed. Unless you just look at the hedge as you go past it, of course.'

Patty agreed reluctantly that her friend was probably right, but when they drew level with the privet hedge a large boy erupted from the gate in hot pursuit of a football which whizzed past Patty's nose, rebounded off the wall opposite and cannoned into her, making a muddy mark on the front of her brown gingham dress which, she knew, would be difficult to explain away. The boy, however, simply snatched up the ball and would have run back into the garden with it had Patty not resolutely barred his way, saying as she did so: 'Oh, excuse me, but I wonder if you could tell me whether you live there, in the house with the privet hedge?'

He was a large, well-grown boy with a heavy, rather sullen face and mousy hair which needed cutting, but he said in an imperious voice: 'What business is it of yours where I live? As it happens, I do, but what are you doing here, you nasty orphan brat? You aren't allowed to come down Peel Street; your way home is by Ullet Road. This is a good area, this is, and my father told your matron, after that baby was found in our hedge, that he didn't want scores of scruffy kids marching up and down Peel Street. So go on, clear off!'

Laura took hold of Patty's arm and tried to pull her away but Patty stood firm, excited by the mere fact that the only two people she had so far addressed, not counting the maid, had known about the abandoned baby. 'I didn't know we weren't supposed to come down Peel Street,' she said. 'But I'm trying to find out as much as I can about that baby. It was me, you see. Matron named me Patty Peel after the street and – and I was sort of hoping that someone might know something about my – my mother. I know it was night time when I was left and it was raining, but surely someone must have seen something, wouldn't you say?'

The boy stared at her for a moment and then gave a bellow of raucous laughter. 'You want to know about your mother?' he said incredulously. 'Well, that's easily remedied; everyone hereabouts knows. She was a little slut working the docks who met up with half a dozen sailors a night and got paid in pennies for her services. If you were to meet her, she wouldn't be able to tell you who your father was – it could have been any one of a dozen that night, I dare say. Why, she probably had a little bastard every nine months and dumped the lot of them; that's the sort of woman she was.'

Laura tugged urgently at Patty's arm. 'Don't listen to him,' she whispered. 'He's just making it up so's we won't walk down Peel Street no more. He don't know anything really.'

Patty, however, her cheeks flaming, did not move. 'You're a hateful liar,' she said furiously. 'Why, when I were found here, you were no more'n a baby yourself. I bet you don't remember anything about it, not anything at all.'

'Why, you cheeky little bitch!' the boy said, now equally furious. He grabbed one of Patty's plaits and swung her round by it, and in two minutes there was a furious fight going on with both girls doing their best to escape from their brutal attacker. A well-aimed punch from Patty, however, put a stop to the fight, for she struck the boy full on the nose and as soon as he saw blood spurting he clapped both hands over his face and, screaming imprecations at the top of his voice, disappeared back into his garden.

The two girls promptly took to their heels and ran all the way home, but as soon as they entered the cloakroom and had a chance to see the state they were in they realised they were unlikely to escape notice. Both girls had suffered in the fracas. Patty was blood-streaked and muddy, her dress torn, one plait unravelled and both knees grazed where the boy had flung her down. That the blood was not her own was one comfort, but both she and Laura realised that they would have to think up a very good reason indeed for the state they were in.

Even as they stared speechlessly at each other, the door at the far end of the cloakroom opened and Miss Dawson began ushering in her charges. 'At least we aren't late,' Patty whispered, beginning to replait her hair, though since she had lost the ribbon she knew it would not stay plaited for long. 'But that doesn't mean we aren't going to get into awful trouble!'

As a result of what had happened in Peel Street, Patty and Laura were forbidden to leave the house for a whole month, and this in glorious summer weather, too. It had been obvious to both teachers and other pupils that something had happened to Patty and Laura, but before they could think up a convincing reason for the state they were in – not the truth, obviously – Matron sent for them. She told them that she had had a complaint; a Mrs Tennant, who lived in Peel Street, had complained that two Durrant House girls had jeered and called names at her little boy as he played with his football in the garden. She said that the girls had attacked him, punching his nose so that it had bled fiercely, and had then stolen his football and had run off with it.

Faced by this tissue of lies, the girls had done their best to explain what had really happened, but Matron had been so furious over the fact that they had abandoned Miss Dawson's crocodile to go off by themselves that she had not seemed to hear a word. 'Two girls bullying a little boy is despicable, but disobeying every rule and abandoning your teacher is almost worse,' she said impressively. 'You will have no tea today and on Sundays, when your companions have currant loaf, you will have dry bread and water to drink, instead of tea. I hope this will be a lesson to you.'

'Yes, Matron. I'm very sorry, Matron,' Laura said, sounding as if she meant it, but Patty thought that dry bread was not so very different from their usual fare and cold water very little less palatable than weak tea. Fortunately, she did not say as much but perhaps there was something in the way she compressed her lips which made Matron suspect that she was not as sorry as she might have been for, a couple of days later, Patty was called again to the study, this time without Laura.

For a long moment, Matron and Patty stared at one another, then Matron said in a neutral voice: 'Sit down, Patty, I want to speak to you. I must tell you that I went round to Peel Street this morning to apologise to Mrs Tennant for what happened to her son. As it happened, I met young Master Lionel Tennant in the hallway. Far from being the small boy I had imagined from his mother's complaint, I thought him twelve or fourteen and clearly quite capable of looking after himself. I asked Mrs Tennant whether she had other children, thinking that I might have been mistaken, but she assured me that Lionel was her only child.'

She paused, as if expecting Patty to say something, but Patty had learned, from her previous encounters with Matron, that trying to give adults an explanation which they are unwilling to hear does no one any good, so she remained silent, her eyes fixed on the older woman's face.

'Mrs Tennant informs me that you had been enquiring about a baby which had been abandoned in Peel Street some years ago and whom you believed to be yourself,' Matron continued. 'How did you come by this knowledge? It is not something that I usually tell my girls until they are twelve or sometimes older.'

Patty's mind raced furiously. She had no intention whatever of disclosing what Selina had told her, but she realised that simply saying nothing would get her into even more trouble. Still gazing at Matron, therefore, she said steadily: 'I guessed. You see, I'd heard the maids talking about how one of the children had been found under a hedge on Peel Street. My name's Peel, so I set myself to finding out whether the baby under the hedge could possibly have been me.' She tried a very small, hesitant smile. 'That was why Laura and I walked down Peel Street, to see if I could discover anything more. There was a kind lady at the first house we went to, who remembered the baby and gave us a bun. Then I asked the boy—'

'You asked Master Tennant, you mean,' Matron said, but her voice was no longer quite as cold as it had been. 'What did you ask him, Patty?'

'I asked him if a baby had been found under his hedge,' Patty said, glad to be back on the straight and narrow path of truth once more. 'I said I thought I might be that baby, and – and he said some very nasty things, Matron.'

'I can imagine,' Matron said drily. 'Have you ever heard the expression *curiosity killed the cat*, Patty?'

Patty, who had heard it many times and usually applied to herself, agreed that she had. 'Only if you don't ask questions, Matron, how are you ever going to find out anything?' she asked, rather plaintively. 'When I was first moved into Miss Briggs's class, I had to ask a thousand questions or I would never have caught up with the other girls.'

Matron smiled. 'If you hadn't asked so many questions about the baby in Peel Street, you would not have been condemned to spend a whole month in the house,' she observed. 'Because you were in the wrong place, at the wrong time, and doing what you should not have been doing, part of your punishment will stand, but you may tell Laura that both she and yourself may have normal meals once more. And in future, Patty, if you are tempted to make off again to satisfy that rampant curiosity of yours, the punishment will be more severe. Go to a member of staff with your questions or, if all else fails, come to me.' A bell rang out and Matron got to her feet and walked over to the door, beckoning Patty to precede her through it. 'There's the dinner bell – off with you!'

As soon as she was able, Patty told Selina what had happened and admitted that Matron, though strict, had been very much nicer to her than she had expected. 'She seemed to understand that I wanted to know about me mam,' she explained. 'And she didn't nag me to make me tell more about how I discovered I were the baby under the hedge; she might have, I suppose. She never even asked which of the maids I'd heard talking about it, which is as well! Why, if I'm really good for ages and ages I reckon I might ask her if I could go round to Mrs Thornton's place once in a while. She invited Laura and me to go back . . . and those buns were the best thing I've ever tasted, Selina! And because Matron listened to me, I wanted to please her. You like her too, don't you?'

Selina admitted that she thought Matron was 'all right'. 'It's not her fault that we never get enough to eat,' she told the younger girl. 'Or that our coats and shoes are too thin for winter wear, or even that we don't get much in the way of treats an' that. It's the Board of Governors. They're that mean and cold you'd think they'd never been kids theirselves, yet one of the big girls told me, a couple of years back, that their kids – the Board of Governors' kids, that is – are all spoiled rotten and get whatever they want. No, Matron does her best for us one way and another, and wi' so many children in the Durrant she has to be pretty strict and see to it that we don't break the rules. Lots o' the kids simply hate her, but I'm glad you saw through the coldness and crossness to the softer person underneath.' Selina looked sideways at her young friend, smiling. 'And I'm glad you never told her . . . about me finding out who are foundlings and who aren't,' she added. 'I'd hate for Matron to know; she'd think me real sneaky and I'd not like that. Mind you, though I understand why you went off to Peel Street, you'd best not do such a thing again. It's temptin' for you, with the street so close, but I hope you've learned your lesson.'

Patty smiled and sighed, but asked Selina what she would have done, in the same circumstances. Selina laughed. 'I'd probably have done as you did,' she admitted. 'Of course you did wrong to run away from

Miss Dawson the way you did, but you're being punished for that, and it's taught you something, Patty. Boys are not like girls. They're rough and spiteful and can be violent. In future, steer clear of boys. Not that I suppose you're likely to go prowling up and down Peel Street again. Why should you? You know all there is to know about what happened on that day, nearly eight years ago, so there's no point in further investigation.'

'But I only went to one house in Peel Street – and spoke to that beastly boy,' Patty said reflectively. 'Other people might know other things.' She sighed. 'I wish I could find that policeman, the one called Patrick, the one I'm named after. Mrs Thornton said he went to *all* the houses and spoke to everyone. He really might be able to tell me something about – about whoever left me under that hedge.'

'Yes, but according to what you told me, he got absolutely nowhere,' Selina reminded her. 'Please, Patty, don't go hunting for one scuffer called Patrick in a city where half the police force have Irish connections. If it's "meant", you'll find out anyway without having to get into hot water. And now I'm going to do some revision because the exams are less than two weeks away.'

For some time after her escapade, Patty was really good. She obeyed the rules, never strayed from the crocodile in which the girls were marched to and from the park, and concentrated on getting her schoolwork done as best she could, though she still made sure that she did not shine unduly above her fellows. Selina was a great comfort to her. The older girl understood Patty's longing for affection and, though she could not be seen to favour one girl above the others, she managed to see a good deal of Patty.

Best of all, Selina must have had a word with Matron, because shortly after the month indoors was over, Miss Briggs came to Patty as she sat outside on the paving stones in the back garden and told her that Matron had heard she had a friend living nearby who would be glad to see her occasionally. 'I don't think it can be a relative, since you are . . .' Miss Briggs began, then abruptly changed tack, a flush mantling her cheeks, '. . . since you have never mentioned relatives before. Anyway, Selina has offered to take you round to see this . . . this person. Being Senior Prefect, she is someone who can be trusted, so if you've simply made up a story to get away from Durrant House from time to time, you may be sure Selina will not hesitate to tell me.'

For a moment, Patty was completely baffled and probably looked it. She started to say that she did not understand, that she had made no such claim, and abruptly remembered her interview with Matron. She was almost sure she had told the older woman about Mrs Thornton's kindness; that must be it then. So instead of the denial that was on her lips, she said demurely: 'Oh, that will be Mrs Thornton. She's – she's just a friend. Did Matron say when we were to go, Miss Briggs?'

Miss Briggs heaved an exaggerated sigh and cast her eyes up to heaven. 'Why do you think I came out here to talk to you, Patty? Matron says you may go today and Selina is waiting for you in the front hall.'

Both Patty and Selina secretly wondered whether Mrs Thornton would be as glad to see them as Patty had implied, but they soon realised their fears were groundless. Mrs Thornton ushered them into her kitchen with real enthusiasm, sat them down at the big, well-scrubbed table and, after she had made everyone a cup of tea and handed round a tin of home-made biscuits, settled herself opposite them and began to talk. She wanted to know all about Durrant House and the staff there and about their meals, which fascinated her because she could not see the need for such a regimen. 'Porridge for breakfast every day of your lives, and nothing else?' she said incredulously. 'And nowt but pea soup for your dinner, two or three times a week? And baked beans in gravy? It's enough to turn the strongest stomach.'

'It's the bread and marge every day for our tea which is most boring,' Patty said. 'There used to be jam sometimes, or golden syrup, but now Cook says there's a war on, so it's just plain bread and marge. And we used to have weak tea at breakfast and dinner and watery milk at teatime, but now it's watery milk or cold water all the time, because of the war as well.' She gave a contented sigh, looking around the warm kitchen and holding a large piece of shortbread in one hand. 'I wish you were our cook, Mrs Thornton! If you were, I'm sure we'd still have jam sometimes, because Letty – she's one of the big girls who works in the kitchen – says Cook takes all sorts home in her bag of an evening.'

'Well I never did,' Mrs Thornton gasped, looking truly shocked. 'Still an' all, the pair of you must come and see me a couple of times a week – say Tuesday and Friday – and I'll have some food ready to line your little stummicks. How about that, eh?'

'It would be lovely, if it were allowed,' Selina said regretfully. 'But we aren't allowed out more than once a fortnight, you know. Most of the girls go to relatives on a weekend, but that's relatives. I don't think friends are quite the same.'

Mrs Thornton suggested that she might become an honorary aunt but Selina explained that, since she too was a foundling, it was unlikely that they would be believed. The cook tightened her lips at this, but said mysteriously that she would have a word with someone in authority and see what she could do.

Mrs Thornton really must have intervened, for the girls were given permission to visit the house in Peel Street every Friday afternoon. She must have had a deal of influence in some quarter, too, for jam appeared in the Durrant House dining room once more, and twice a week the cold water was replaced by a mug of tea. It might only be sweetened with saccharin but it was still a good deal more sustaining than cold water.

Because Selina had asked her to, Patty did her best to forget about her origins, but one Friday afternoon, when she and Selina entered Mrs Thornton's kitchen, they were surprised to find a large policeman sitting at the table and drinking a cup of tea. He grinned at the two girls. Mrs Thornton, who was stirring a large pot over the fire, pushed back wisps of hair from her forehead and greeted them cheerfully. 'This here's Sergeant O'Flaherty,' she said. 'He walks this beat now and then and usually pops in for a word wi' meself and it occurred to me that he might know the young constable what found you under the hedge, Patty dear. So when he came by earlier I axed him to call round now, so's you could hear what he's got to say.'

Sergeant O'Flaherty cleared his throat. 'It were young Paddy O'Hara what found the baby under the hedge, but he went back to Ireland five years ago. His uncle died, d'you see, and left him a nice little business. Paddy had married a Liverpool girl and

84

they'd a couple o' young 'uns, so I dare say it were a sensible move. He were a good policeman, though, and did his very best to trace the baby's mam, because he thought she must have abandoned the baby only minutes before he found it. It were August and a mild night but it had begun to rain as Paddy turned into Peel Street. Yet the blanket weren't even damp, so he scouted around a bit, trying to find whoever had left the baby there.'

'Did he see *anyone*?' Patty asked eagerly. Her heart was thumping so hard that she felt sure it could be heard all over the kitchen. 'Did he think the girl had gone into one of the houses on Peel Street? Or might she have run up to Dingle station to catch a train? Only if she come from there, why didn't she leave me on the platform?' She turned to her friend. 'Selina here was found on Lime Street station. As it was raining, you might have thought my mam would have left me at the Dingle if she were going that way herself.'

Sergeant O'Flaherty shrugged. 'Who can tell, queen? When a gal's in trouble, she don't always think clearly. But I tend to favour your theory – that she'd not come far. I reckon what happened was this: she meant to take the baby to the orphanage and leave it on the doorstep, knowing that it would be looked after there.' He grinned ruefully as Patty began to shake her head. 'No, no, the Durrant ain't nearly as bad as some orphan asylums. Your matron's a good woman and you girls always look neat and tidy, which is more than can be said for some, believe me. But let me finish me story. Your mam were headin' for Durrant House when all of a sudden, who did she see comin' towards her but Constable O'Hara. She knew what she were goin' to do were wrong and she

85

guessed that if she walked past him he'd notice the baby in her arms, might even stop to ask her what she was doin' out on such a night. She dared not risk being questioned, so she whisked round and hurried off in the opposite direction, pushing the baby – that's you, miss – into a nice, thick hedge to shelter it from the rain which was already beginning to fall. She guessed that the policeman would see you – perhaps she even hung around, hid behind a gatepost or some such, to make sure that you were found.' He cocked an eyebrow at Patty. 'Well, queen? Does that sound possible to you?'

'Yes, it does,' Patty breathed, her eyes shining like stars. 'I don't feel so bad about me mam leaving me now, Sergeant. I still wish I could find her, though. It 'ud be grand to have a mam of me own.'

On their way back to Durrant House, Selina gave Patty's hand a comforting squeeze. 'Are you happier now, Patty?' she asked gently. 'Sergeant O'Flaherty told you all he could. And will you promise me that you won't go searchin' for any more information – or not until you're a good deal older, at any rate? Only I'm leaving the Durrant in October to start work at one of the hospitals and it will only worry me if I keep imagining you running away and getting into trouble for it.'

'I promise I won't go chasing off until I'm older,' Patty said obediently. 'Oh, Selina, I shall miss you so much! But you'll come back and see me, won't you? Matron says that when you leave I can take another girl round to Peel Street on a Friday afternoon . . . you might meet us there. I'll take Laura, of course, though she isn't a foundling. When she's ten, her mam says she'll have her home from time to time, on a weekend, and if she's allowed she'll take me with her.'

'That sounds grand, queen, but don't set too much store by it,' Selina advised. 'I'm sure Laura's mam means well but it isn't only Laura she's put in an orphan asylum, you know. There's three brothers in the Father Berry Home and a little sister in the nursery. But as soon as I've got a room of me own, you can come there. Why, once I'm earning, we could go to the cinema, the theatre . . . we could have all sorts of fun. And you know, Patty, I would never let you down.'

'Oh, Selina, thank you,' Patty gasped. 'Things are looking up for me, aren't they? I'm really glad I found out about Peel Street or none of this would ever have happened. You know, I'm going to be a nurse like you when I'm grown up, but if I weren't, I think I'd be a cook like Mrs Thornton. She makes the best food in the world, doesn't she?'

Agreeing, Selina led the way into Durrant House just in time to join the queue for tea, but for once neither girl was eager for her slice of bread and margarine; Mrs Thornton's generosity had seen to that.

Chapter Four
July 1932

For all Patty's intentions, she had not yet asked any of her neighbours for help with the baby. Mrs Clarke would have her hands full with her own little one once it was born, and though Patty had grown quite fond of the other woman she could see that one baby would be enough for Mrs Clarke to deal with at present. Close observation had convinced her that Mrs Knight and Mrs Clitheroe would not do at all. Mrs Clitheroe had two small children and very little patience. When one passed her doorway, it was often to hear her shouting at her small son and daughter and Patty was determined that Merrell should know nothing but love in these crucial first months of her life. But the doctors were beginning to look askance at her small companion, and Nurse Stoddard and Nurse Watkin obviously thought that she should give the child up for adoption. If there was trouble over Merrell, Patty knew that her colleagues would not support her but would, in effect, throw her to the wolves.

'Hey, Nurse Peel! Mrs Owens on the second landing wants to sell her pram. It's old and battered but it's got four good wheels and the hood and apron ain't too worn. Are you lookin' for such a thing for young Merrell there? She offered it to me but I'm superstitious; there ain't no way I'll buy a pram till after me baby's born. Want to come down now and take a look at it?'

Patty swung round. It was Mrs Clarke, wearing a big beam and a smock dress so distended that she looked like a rubber ball.

'A pram!' Patty said. Could this be the answer to her problem? If she had a pram, she could leave the baby outside the houses where her patients were confined – or she could do so at this time of year, at any rate. In winter it would be different. And come to think of it, she told herself ruefully, it would scarcely do to leave the child outside at night, either. Still, it would be nice to have a pram. Merrell was getting jolly heavy, and the more she thought about it, the more an idea began to grow in her mind.

'Well? Have you got a moment?'

Patty smiled gratefully at her neighbour and bent to pick Merrell off the old piece of blanket on which she was lying. 'Yes, I'm really interested in a pram,' she said. 'Thank you very much for thinking of me, Mrs Clarke. How much is she asking, do you know?'

'Well, she's *askin'* ten bob,' Mrs Clarke said as the two of them clattered down the stairs. 'But I don't s'pose she expects to get that much. For someone wi' a grosh o' kids, mind, it 'ud be worth every penny, but then folk wi' a grosh of kids don't have ten bob, so I dare say she'd settle for seven and six.'

They reached the end of the stairs and turned on to the lower landing. Mrs Clarke made straight for No. 14. It was a warm day and the front door was open, but she knocked on it anyway before shouting cheerfully: 'Hey up, Mrs Owens! I brung a pal to see the pram.'

Mrs Owens appeared so quickly that Patty thought she must have been expecting a customer when she heard their tread on the iron stairs. She was a small, round woman, with big, light grey eyes and a tiny, tight little mouth. She stared at her visitor with great interest and Patty guessed she had been told about the nurse who lived on the upper landing and was intrigued to find her on her own doorstep.

'Good morning, Mrs Owens; Mrs Clarke told me you had a pram for sale,' Patty began, but Mrs Owens clearly did not think it polite to start talking business before one was even introduced.

'Good morning, Nurse. Ain't it a fine day?' she said, her eyes darting all over Patty from head to toe and taking in the baby in the crook of her arm. 'That's a fine little lass you've got there. I dare say you've been told I were widdered last year but I'm still mortal fond of babbies.' She held out her hands invitingly. 'Can I have a hold?'

Patty, smiling, handed Merrell over. A month ago she would not have done so, but as she got to know her neighbours better she began to realise that most of them were both reliable and trustworthy. They might have very little money, but what they had they used to the best advantage, and the women who lived in Ashfield Place seemed to be better off – and perhaps more enterprising – than those who inhabited the cramped, old-fashioned and unhygienic courts.

Mrs Owens took the baby and looked down into the small, fair face, her own expression softening. 'Ain't you a little beauty, then?' she crooned. 'Wharra little princess. How old would she be, Nurse?'

'She's almost six months, and she's got two teeth already,' Patty said proudly. 'She's getting a good deal heavier, too, and beginning to try to sit herself up.' She leaned forward and brushed a lock of fair hair from the baby's forehead. 'You're getting on just fine, aren't you, Merrell?'

'Merrell! That's an unusual name,' Mrs Owens

remarked. 'I dunno as I've ever heard it before.' She looked quickly up into Patty's face and then downwards once more into Merrell's. 'Who do you reckon she favours, Nurse? Is it her dad?'

'No, I don't think so,' Patty said, surprised. 'But of course, I only met her dad once and that was quite a long time ago. I suppose I ought to have gone back and visited him again but somehow I've never got round to it. Anyway, I doubt he'll be much interested in Merrell now. He's got half a dozen other kids, you see.'

Mrs Owen looked startled and shot Mrs Clarke a quick glance under her eyelids before remarking sagely: 'Well, if that ain't fellers all over! Still, I reckon the little 'un's a good deal better off with you than with him.' Abruptly, she became businesslike. 'Now about this pram, Nurse. It's in excellent condition 'cos I've never used it for carrying wood or coal or anything of that nature an' I've always kept it clean an' nice. Me daughter Beryl had it for her two little 'uns but she's like her mam, real house-proud, so it's not one whit the worse. I expect Mrs Clarke told you I were hopin' for ten bob but I could knock off a shillin' for an outright sale.'

Handing Merrell back to Patty, she began to demonstrate the pram's various functions. The handbrake still worked; it was, as Mrs Owens had claimed, immaculately clean; and though the apron was sadly worn, it still looked waterproof.

'I'll take it,' Patty decided. 'I'll have to go back for the money, Mrs Owens, since I was hanging out my washing when Mrs Clarke told me about the pram but I won't be a tick.'

'Leave the little lass wi' me,' Mrs Owens said eagerly. 'Just whiles you run upstairs, I mean. My

Beryl's children are seven and ten, so it's a treat for me to hold a little babby.'

'She isn't very little,' Patty said ruefully. 'That's why I shall be so glad to have the pram. Carrying her on my hip is all very well but when I've got my midwife's bag, with all my medical equipment in it, poor Merrell is almost more that I can manage.'

'Ah well, you'll have the pram in future,' Mrs Owens said comfortably, as Patty and Mrs Clarke hurried along the landing and up the stairs. As they gained the upper floor, Patty could hear Mrs Owens beginning to sing a lullaby and smiled to herself. Who would not love Merrell, she thought as she returned to her own flat and picked up her purse. I wonder why she was interested in who she looks like, though?

And presently, humping the pram up the stairs with Merrell inside it, she put the question to Mrs Clarke. 'Why do you think Mrs Owens asked if Merrell looked like her father? I mean, small babies just look like other small babies, don't they? And from what I can remember, which isn't a lot after six months, Merrell looks more like her mother, I think.'

Mrs Clarke giggled. 'More like yourself, you mean. I think she's ever so like you, both of you bein' fair an' all, and I'm sure Mrs Owens thinks the same. She's not a bad old body, but she's curious as any cat. What she wanted to know was why you ain't livin' wi' Merrell's father. Of course, we're all interested,' she added honestly. 'Most folk is too polite to ask and anyway, fellers bein' what they are, most of us reckon you've been let down.'

Patty was so surprised that she almost let go of the pram handle. So Mrs Ruskin had been right. The women in Ashfield Place had all assumed that

Merrell was her own child, probably a love child since no man had appeared at No. 24, and this was the reason why they had accepted her so completely. For a moment, she wondered whether to disabuse Mrs Clarke, tell her the true story, but then she hesitated. Believing her to be one of themselves, the women had given her the sort of uncomplicated friendship she had never received in her adult life. If she told them she had adopted the child – and adopted her unofficially, at that – she had no doubt that their attitude would change. Without even meaning to do so, they would distance themselves from her once more. She would go back to being the professional, the midwife with a regular salary coming in, someone to be respected but never loved, never fully accepted. Was that what she truly wanted?

Once, Patty would have unhesitatingly told the truth and withdrawn into her shell again, but that was the old Patty; the new Patty was so different that, looking back, she might have been two separate people. The Patty of now did not want to revert to the Patty of yesterday. She was proud of Merrell and discovered she was quite happy for people to assume that the relationship between them was that of mother and daughter. Mr Mullins was very probably not as black as he was painted, but she could not bear to think of his reclaiming the child. If everyone assumed that the baby was hers, then Merrell would *be* hers.

The silence, it seemed, had lasted rather long for Mrs Clarke. She tugged timidly at Patty's sleeve. 'Merrell's father is your business an' no one else's,' she said. 'If you don't want to talk about him then you don't have to. Why, Etty Darville – she lives on the ground floor – she's had three children from three different dads and she's married to another feller now and no one thinks the worse of her for it. Not very much worse, anyway.'

Patty giggled. 'I must meet Mrs Darville sometime,' she said cheerfully. 'But I'm not like that, you know, Mrs Clarke. I got Merrell by – by accident, you might say, and I'm certainly not interested in getting myself a husband. I – I don't like men very much, to tell you the truth.'

'You shouldn't judge 'em all by one who's let you down,' Mrs Clarke said reprovingly. 'There's good fellers an' bad and you just have to look out for a good 'un. But there, I dare say you know that.'

They had reached Patty's door by now so they said their goodbyes; Patty thanked Mrs Clarke sincerely for telling her about the pram and then pushed it into No. 24, closing the door behind them. The pram made the room seem small but Patty guessed that she would soon get used to it. She went and fetched a pillow from her bedroom and propped Merrell up against it so that the child could watch her as she made their tea. 'Aren't you a lucky girl to have a special place all of your own?' she said as she moved around the room. She picked up Merrell's flannel rabbit and the rattle she had bought from a vendor on the Scotland Road, and popped them into the pram with the child. 'Just you sit there and play with your bunny and presently you shall have some lovely bread and milk.'

Much later that evening, when Merrell had been bedded down for the night, Patty sat by the fire and began to plot. The moment Mrs Clarke had suggested that she should buy the pram, a picture had popped into her head. As she did her messages, she often saw large and shabby prams with babies and small children perched within being pushed along the pavement by older children. Most of these children were shabby, dirty and neglected-looking and some of them were undoubtedly taking care of younger brothers and sisters while their parents worked.

Why should I not take advantage of a system which obviously works very well, Patty asked herself. It would mean virtually adopting another child because of my night work, but it need not cost me very much and it would be a good grounding for some little girl in the ways of keeping house. The more she thought about the idea, the more it appealed to her. Other people did it, as she knew very well. There had been girls at the Durrant whose older sisters had been 'loaned' to aunts, uncles or even friends who needed help with their own children. It was quite common for a man, left a widower, to 'borrow' a niece to assist him in running his family until such time as he might remarry or until a child of his own was old enough to help. Now that Patty was considering the idea for herself, she realised that the obvious thing to do would be to return to Stanton's Court and speak to Mr Mullins about the possibility of hiring one of his daughters to help her to bring up little Merrell.

Even thinking about it, however, sent a cold shudder through Patty's slim frame. So far as she knew, Mr Mullins had never revealed that his wife had had twins and that one of them had lived. Patty had told him that the child was small and weak so he might honestly believe that the second twin had died too. If she went boldly to his house and told him that this was not the case he could turn nasty. He could even try to blackmail her, or take the baby back, or threaten them both. The possibilities were endless. Yet though she shrank from it, Patty was sure that she should go to the Mullins with her request. It was their right, and because she had taken Merrell it was also Patty's duty to appeal first to the family.

However, the week was a busy one and it was not until several days later that Patty was able to take her day off. In the interim, she had delivered five new babies, which naturally increased her workload during the day, so when her day off came round she was faced with a great many household tasks and thought, wistfully, how nice it would have been to have someone to help her. Nevertheless, she washed and polished with a will, baked four large loaves of bread and made a batch of currant scones. Then, telling herself that she could draw back at any moment, she popped Merrell into her pram, slung a string of beads across the front of it and set off towards Stanton's Court.

It was another warm and sunny day. A light breeze lifted the hair which fell across Patty's forehead and tousled the baby's fair curls. Whilst she was in her own area, Patty was constantly greeted as she walked; mothers, children and tradesmen all had a kind word for Nurse Peel and wanted to admire her baby. Once she crossed the invisible dividing line between Stoddard's district and her own, however, she noticed the change at once. Folk nodded respectfully as they recognised her uniform, but glanced incuriously at the baby in the pram, never stopping to chat. Patty began, without realising it, to walk more slowly. The school holidays had begun and the pavements were crowded, and when she reached the Scottie and began to pass the courts she saw that they were gay with children skipping rope, bowling hoops and playing ball. Frequently, of course, the hoop was just a circle of metal from a barrel, the ball a bundle of tightly lashed rags, and even the skippers used a piece of orange box rope which they had begged from a greengrocer, but that did not lessen the youngsters' enjoyment of the games they played. Ragged and ill fed they might be, but such children, Patty considered, were a good deal happier than those in the orphan asylums. The regimented and strictly controlled life of such orphans compared very unfavourably with the freedom and natural gaiety of the street children.

By the time Patty reached Cuerden Street, she was so worried about her reception by the Mullins family that she seriously considered changing her mind, pretending that she had just been taking a walk and returning to Ashfield Place. Indeed, she might have done so, had she not been accosted by an elfin-faced child in a filthy pink dress, who caught hold of the handle of the pram, pulling it to a halt.

'Oh, Nurse, it's you, ain't it? You're the one who come to our house when our mam died. I reckernise you! I'm Maggie Mullins – do you remember me?'

'Yes, of course I do, Maggie,' Patty lied valiantly. The only Mullins girl she could clearly remember was Fanny, the eldest. The rest had been a sea of unidentified faces. 'How are you, love? And how is your father?'

'I'm awright, but – but things have changed, miss. Me dad's brung in a woman to help wi' things. He told us to call her Auntie Ethel. We doesn't like her at all, miss – Nurse, I mean – but Dad reckons we'll all settle down together, given time.'

'I'm sure your dad's right and Auntie Ethel will help him to keep the family together,' Patty said pacifically. 'It's hard for a man left a widower, you know, Maggie. When your mam was alive I expect she did just about everything in the house, didn't she? Cooked, cleaned, sorted the little ones, baked the bread . . .'

'I don't remember,' Maggie said, rather defensively. 'I don't think she cooked much 'cept for stews 'n' that. But so far, Auntie Ethel don't even do that much. It's bread and scrape mostly wi' Guinness for her and me dad to wash it down. As for keeping the family together . . .' her voice quavered on a sob, '. . . she's already sent the two youngest to the Father Berry Home 'cos she says she can't be doin' wi' so many kids. And now she told Dad I were useless, just another mouth to feed and why didn't he send me to her Aunt Flo, who's past eighty and mad as a bat. Only if they do send me, I'll run away home, see if I don't!' she finished defiantly.

Patty stared helplessly down into the child's small, tear-stained face. Maggie looked no more than ten, but she seemed a sensible child. 'I'm so sorry things aren't working out for you, queen,' Patty said gently. 'But perhaps I might be able to help. I've come to see your father, to ask him whether he would consider allowing one of his daughters to live with me and the baby here. You see, at present, I have to take her with me whenever I'm called out, but she's getting too big for such a life. I remembered that your sister seemed to take full charge of the younger ones whilst your mother was – was ill, so I thought perhaps your dad might . . .'

Maggie had been concentrating all her attention on Patty but now she swung round and stared hard at the baby. Merrell, seeing herself so intently regarded, beamed and held out her hands towards the little girl and Maggie turned towards Patty once more. 'Is that – is that *our* baby,' she enquired incredulously. 'I 'member Fanny saying that there were two and that our dad told you to take the livin' one away 'cos he couldn't be doin' with it. But Fanny reckoned the poor little bugger had been purrin one of them orphan asylums, and we wouldn't never see it no more. Oh, miss – Nurse, I mean – is this really our baby? Only . . . only she looks ever so like our Laurie did when he were a nipper.'

Patty decided to take the plunge. 'Yes, Merrell is your little sister,' she admitted. 'But because your dad said she was to go to an orphan asylum, I've never told anyone else that she's really a Mullins. Everyone believes she's my own little girl and because I couldn't bear to see her put into an institution – couldn't bear to lose her, come to that – I've let people go on believing she's Merrell Peel. I'm Nurse Peel, you see.'

'Oh, Nurse, ain't she the prettiest thing?' Maggie breathed, reaching out a filthy little hand and timidly touching the baby's cheek. She straightened up, giving a gusty sigh as she did so. 'But it ain't no manner o' use askin' our dad to let Fanny go, 'cos Auntie Ethel treats Fanny like a perishin' slave and makes her do most of the work. Fanny keeps saying she'll be off one of these days to get herself a proper job where she's paid money for skivvyin' an' I do think she'll go because she were furious when the little 'uns went. As for Biddy – she's thirteen – they won't let her go either 'cos they'll want her to take Fanny's place when she leaves school.' The child turned beseeching eyes up to Patty's. 'I suppose I wouldn't be no good?' she asked wistfully. 'I'm eleven, and though I'm small, I'm ever so strong. What's more, the woman hates me; she'd be happy to see me go off and live somewhere else.'

'I think you would do very well,' Patty said gravely. 'But I must have your father's permission before you can come and live with me. Is he at home at present?'

'Aye, he'll be there,' Maggie said. 'When me mam were alive, I were real fond of me dad. He tried ever so hard to get work and when he were in the money he gave most of it to Mam, just keepin' back a bob or two so's he could have a drink of an evening. But now he's like a different person. Fanny says that Ethel leads him round by the nose and it don't seem as if he's got time for his own kids. Auntie Ethel's gorra girl of her own, Sadie, she's five. Our dad moons over Sadie as if she were the bleedin' Queen of England, and never suggested purrin her into an orphanage when Auntie Ethel took our little ones away.'

The two of them had been talking in Cuerden Street but now Patty began to push the pram towards Stanton's Court. At the entrance, however, she paused for a moment and addressed her small companion. 'Maggie, what I'm about to suggest may seem strange to you, but I truly think it is for the best. If you will look after Merrell while I'm gone, I'll speak to your father – and Auntie Ethel – by myself. I shan't mention Merrell or say that I have a baby which needs looking after; I'll let him assume that I simply need help because I'm working full time. I shall offer to pay him a small sum once a month and I'll tell him that you will bring the money when you visit him, so that he can see you are being well looked after and adequately fed. I don't mean him to visit me at my home. Do you think he will object to that?'

'Oh, miss!' Maggie gasped. 'Do you *really* want me? I'll be ever so good, honest to God I will. I'll run your messages, sweep your floors . . . oh, I'll do wharrever you tell me and of course I'll take the greatest care of Merrell and I won't never tell no one she's me sister. As for our dad objectin', I can't see it. He wants to please Auntie Ethel more'n anything else and a bit of money comin' in reg'lar will be a great help. The only thing is, I dare say he'll want it weekly. It ain't that he won't trust you – everyone knows nurses is real responsible and trustable – but he'll reckon four weeks is too long between payments.'

'Well, it's up to you,' Patty decided. 'If you don't mind walking all the way from my place to Stanton's Court once a week, instead of once a month, that's fine by me. But you won't be able to bring the baby so you'll have to come when I'm at home to look after her.'

Maggie began to agree enthusiastically that she would be quite willing to come back once a week when something occurred to her. 'Wharrabout school, miss?' she said doubtfully. 'We often misses school, us Mullins, but it don't do to draw attention to yourself and if folks see me on the streets, runnin' your messages in school time, then I reckon we'll both be in trouble.'

Patty smiled. The more she knew of Maggie, the more she liked her. Her last remark proved that Maggie was both thoughtful and conscientious. 'Of course you must continue your education,' she assured her young friend. 'I've very good neighbours and I'm sure one or other of them will give an eye to Merrell when I'm working during term time. A great deal of my work is done at night, however, and I often don't get home until eight or nine in the evening when I have a lot of revisiting to do. Now can you think of anything else which needs talking over?'

There was a thoughtful pause, then Maggie shook

her head. 'No, I think that's all,' she said. You go in now, miss, in case Dad decides to go down the pub for a quick 'un. I'll take good care of – of Merrell. Is it all right if I push her up and down the street? Only I don't want folk from the court wonderin' what I'm at.'

'Yes, that'll be fine; you are a sensible child, Maggie,' Patty said gratefully. 'I think you should come back with me right away, don't you? If your father agrees, then you can collect your things, say your goodbyes and join me as soon as you can. I'll walk very slowly along Scotland Road, stopping to look in the shops and perhaps do some marketing, and you can catch me up when you are able.'

'Right, miss,' Maggie said gaily. She seemed to have given up the struggle to remember Patty's title. 'Oh, aren't I just glad I met you?'

Patty laughed, straightened her shoulders, and set off for the Mullins home.

Later that afternoon, Patty pushed the pram, with Maggie hanging on to the handle, across Ashfield Place. There had been no difficulty in getting Mr Mullins to agree to letting his daughter move in with Patty. Indeed, when the sum of half a crown a week was mentioned, he had positively glowed.

'You bein' a nurse makes it all respectable, like,' he had said, while his new lady friend lurked in the background, feeding shop biscuits to a fat, fair-haired five-year-old. 'If our Maggie comes back each week, the way you say she will, I don't see no objection, no objection at all. As for schoolin', she's a bright kid – reads and writes like a clerk already – so we won't argify about that.'

'But she will continue to go to school, Mr Mullins,' Patty had reminded him. 'Apart from anything else, I would soon have the Schools' Inspector down on me for letting her sag off. You need have no fear on that score.'

'Well, isn't that just grand?' Mr Mullins had beamed. 'I can see you an' me will gerralong just fine, Nurse.' He had turned to the woman, beckoning her forward. 'This is me lady friend what's helpin' me wi' the kids an' that,' he had said vaguely. 'We's gerrin' married when I find a decent job, ain't that so, Eth?'

Ethel had agreed that it was and presently Patty handed over five shillings, explaining that she was paying an extra half-crown on this occasion, so that Mr Mullins would be able to buy something nice for his other children. 'But in future it will be half a crown a week, as we've agreed, also paid in advance when Maggie comes to see you,' she had said firmly. 'Thank you, Mr Mullins, Mrs er . . .'

'I'm Miss Halliwell,' Ethel said quickly. 'And thanks to you, miss.'

'Is this where you live, Nurse Peel?' Maggie asked in an awed voice, breaking into Patty's thoughts as they turned and began to heave the pram up the metal steps. 'Ain't it posh, though? I've never been in a landing house, but there's a girl at school whose aunt lives in one and they've got runnin' water in the house – runnin' out of a tap I mean, with a sink an' everythin'.'

'Well, these houses have running water and a sink and electric lighting in the rooms,' Patty said. 'I'm afraid you can't have your own bedroom since I'll want you to share with Merrell. She'll be in your charge when I'm out at night, so I just hope you're a light sleeper! I'll make you up a bed with the cushions off the couch and buy you a proper one as soon as I'm able.'

Maggie nodded confidently, trotting along the landing beside her and staring curiously into the windows as they passed. 'I'm sure I'll wake the minute she does, 'cos I never slept through when Laurie and Gus were crying,' she said. She giggled suddenly. 'What did our dad say when you told him I'd be coming back to fetch me clothes?'

'I don't remember him saying anything,' Patty said, surprised. 'Why?'

'Because I ain't got any,' Maggie said briefly. 'He give me an' old skirt of Ethel's – she were that mad, she swore at him – and the blouse what Fanny bought, and that was it.' She grinned up at Patty. 'When Fanny sees her new blouse is gone, I reckon it'll be the final straw. She'll take off like a rocket and Auntie Ethel will have to find someone else to do the chores.'

Patty laughed, but at this point they reached the front door of No. 24 and very soon Maggie was being shown round. Patty enjoyed the child's wide-eyed approval of everything she saw and decided that she, Maggie and Merrell would all settle down very nicely once they had grown used to each other's ways.

Maggie was much impressed by the fact that Merrell had a bath every Friday night but not nearly so impressed when Patty told her that in future she, Maggie, would have a weekly bath too, and a strip-down wash daily. 'But there ain't no need,' Maggie wailed. 'I ain't dirty – or not very dirty, in any event. I brush me hair before I goes to school and washes me hands and face. Won't that do?'

'No it won't,' Patty assured her. 'I'm a nurse, Maggie, and it's very important that my home and the people I live with are clean. I visit women who have just had babies, and of course the little babies themselves, and such people are at a low ebb and easily infected. Dirt breeds germs, you know, and if you were to handle food with really filthy hands, then the food could become infected. So I'm afraid it's a daily wash and a weekly bath so long as you're living with me. Is that clear?'

Maggie was inclined to be a bit sulky and muttered that she was not a nurse and was therefore unlikely to pass on any germs which might hang around her, but when she found that Patty heated water for bathing, and did not expect her to climb into a cold tub, she was somewhat reconciled. When the bath was ready and Patty ruthlessly plunged her into it, she gasped and whimpered, and when the strong carbolic soap was rubbed into her mop of fair hair and the suds ran down into her eyes she screamed and threshed as though she were being torn in two. But when the bath was over and she was wrapped in a towel and settled before the fire, with a bowl of steaming bread and milk in her lap, she grew cheerful once more, telling Patty that for such a bowl of food she would have endured being in the water twice as long.

'I'm glad to hear it,' Patty said, mopping the spilt water off the floor and heaving the tin bath over to the sink, to throw away its contents. 'Because, Maggie, my dear, you've brought some little visitors with you which only a great deal of washing will banish. Fleas, fortunately, drown very quickly, but head lice are a different matter. Presently, I shall have to do your hair with a steel comb and lotion. It isn't very pleasant – it's very strong-smelling indeed – but if we keep at it, it will do the trick.'

'D'you mean to say you can stop me head itchin'?' Maggie said incredulously. 'I hates the feelin' that things is creepin' round on me scalp and I hates bed bugs an' all; they bite like tigers, don't they, miss? – I mean Nurse. When me mam were alive, she spent ages tryin' to get rid of 'em but Dad is too busy an' that Ethel don't seem to mind 'em.'

Patty had noticed the larger bites amongst the fleabites on the child's body, and guessed that they had been caused by bed bugs. She knew the unending battle which most of the women living in the courts waged against the disgusting creatures, but had always managed to keep clear of them herself. The accepted method of suddenly leaping out of bed in the middle of the night and nabbing the creatures on a bar of softened soap was not one she had tried personally, but her informants had assured her it was the only way to make a capture since the bugs are nocturnal and shun even a glimmer of light. 'It is extremely difficult to get rid of bed bugs once they're dug into a house,' Patty admitted. 'I'm told they live deep in the mattress and even burrow beneath wallpaper or a layer of whitewash, but we are very fortunate here. The building is relatively new and everyone has a thorough spring clean each March or April and whitewashes the walls regularly. I'm afraid, Maggie, that I'm going to burn the clothes you were wearing, so it's a good job your father gave you the skirt and blouse, because you'll need them tomorrow. For tonight, you can wear one of my nightgowns. It will be miles too big, but at least it's clean. And since there are no bed bugs here, that's one thing you won't have to worry about. Now if you've finished your bread and milk, I'll start on your hair.'

Maggie raised no demur and very soon Patty was pulling the fine toothcomb through the child's fair locks and anointing her scalp with the strong-smelling lotion. Although the task was a distasteful one, Patty worked with a will. She knew how easy it was for one child to infect another with head lice and had no desire to see poor little Merrell's fine fair hair crawling with insect life.

As she laboured, Patty thought that this was one task she had never envisaged. It was odd, because her work took her into some of the worst slums in the area and she constantly saw signs of fleas, lice and bed bugs on the bodies of the women she nursed, and on their tiny new babies too, after only a few days. But since it was not part of her job to attack such things, she merely gave advice and hoped that the mothers would follow it. Now, however, the problem was hers as well as theirs and she realised for the first time that had she lived in less salubrious surroundings, the battle would have been a constant one.

'Phew. Wharra pong!' Maggie said sleepily, as Patty finished her work and began to tidy away the lotion and the comb. 'Me hair's awful wet, miss – I mean Nurse – and the stuff stings me scalp somethin' cruel.' She smiled up at Patty with watering eyes. 'Guess you needn't worry I'll miss Merrell tonight! I reckon I shan't sleep a wink for the stinging.'

Patty took the kettle off the fire and poured hot water into a bowl, then added some cold. Then she got out the carbolic soap and approached her small companion once more. 'I quite agree, you wouldn't sleep a wink with that stuff on your hair; it would probably burn straight through the pillow,' she said cheerfully. 'Come to the sink and put your head over the bowl and we'll soon get rid of that smelly lotion and any horrid little bodies which are still around, for I'm sure they'll be well and truly dead by now. Then I'll dry your hair on a clean towel, pop you into a nightdress, and I'm sure you'll sleep like a top. Merrell's very good and only wakes in the night if she has a pain or if she's cutting a tooth. She has her first feed at half past six, but I shall deal with that, since I have to get up early to start my revisits. Unless I'm called out in the night, but if I am, I'll stick a note on your bedroom door, telling you where I've gone and how to feed Merrell and so on. And you'd better call me Patty,' she added, 'since we're going to be living together for some time, I hope.'

'It don't sound very respectful,' Maggie said, bending her head over the basin of water. 'Wharrabout Miss Patty? I keeps tryin' to remember to call you Nurse . . . I suppose miss won't do?'

'No it won't,' Patty said decidedly. 'Would you rather call me Auntie? I could put up with that, I suppose.'

'Auntie Patty,' she spluttered, her tone considerably muffled and difficult to hear against the slosh of water as Patty emptied the jug over her. 'Lors, Auntie Patty, you bleedin' near drowned me that time!'

'Sorry; I was a bit enthusiastic,' Patty said. She raised Maggie to a standing position once more and enveloped her head in a small towel, then began to rub hard. Presently, she slid the nightgown over Maggie's head and smiled at her. 'There! Now you're as sweet and clean as Merrell herself and very soon you'll be as fast asleep as well. Is there anything you want before you go off to bed, Maggie? You know there's a lavatory at the end of the landing, don't you? And there's a chamber pot under your bed because you won't want to go traipsing along the landing in the middle of the night.'

'Reckon I'd best slip along to the lavvy afore I goes

to bed, then,' Maggie said, heading for the door. Patty stepped in front of her.

'This is a respectable area, young lady,' she said severely. 'Folk don't go marching around in their nightgowns, bold as brass. You'd best slip my old jacket round your shoulders, for decency's sake.'

'Right you are,' Maggie said with unimpaired cheerfulness, though Patty could tell by the look she shot her that the younger girl thought she was as mad as a hatter. 'I shan't be long.'

When Patty awoke next morning, she wondered for a moment where she was, for usually Merrell's cooing and bubbling roused her. Today, there was only quiet and the early sunrise coming in through the gap in the curtains. Sitting up in bed, Patty abruptly remembered how her life had changed. Merrell was in the small bedroom next door, with Maggie to look after her, so if Patty wished she could cuddle down again and have an extra half-hour in bed. She sighed luxuriously and leaned back on her pillow. But old habits die hard. She had an alarm clock which would wake her in good time if she were to set it, but she realised that she was ready to get up, so swung her feet out of bed and padded out of the bedroom and into the kitchen. She had a good wash in cold water at the sink, dressed in the clothes she had laid out ready the night before, then set about preparing for the day ahead. Her sterilised instruments and all the things she would need for her revisits she popped into her black bag. She got the loaf from the cupboard, together with a pot of jam and a slab of margarine, and made herself two thick sandwiches. She had a full day ahead and was unlikely to be able to return to Ashfield Place for a midday meal, so the sandwiches were stowed in her black bag as well. After that, she stirred up the fire, made herself a round of toast and, when the kettle boiled, brewed a pot of tea. Then, satisfied with her preparations, she poured a second mug of tea and carried it into the smaller of the two bedrooms, where all was peace and quiet. Merrell still slumbered in the old wicker bicycle basket, which she was rapidly outgrowing, and Maggie slept too on her makeshift bed. Patty stood the mug of tea down beside the girl, and went across the room and drew back the curtains. This room faced the back of the building and was always dim, even at midday.

The sound of the curtains being drawn back must have wakened Maggie for she sat up, yawned and then, as her eyes fell on the tea, gasped. 'Oh, miss – I mean Auntie Patty – I must have been real wore out, 'cos I don't remember a bleedin' thing after I lay down. Is that – is that mug of tea for me? I do hope you didn't have to come in to Merrell in the night, only I were that tired . . .'

'It's all right, all three of us were very tired indeed, so none of us woke,' Patty said reassuringly. 'I've stirred up the fire and made Merrell's bottles up for the day. If you bring the baby through into the kitchen to feed her, I'll show you where I keep things. Drink your tea before it goes cold.'

Maggie reached for the mug and began to sip, her eyes looking huge over the rim. 'Thanks ever so,' she said, between mouthfuls. 'I'll make the feeds up meself once I knows how. Is it just milk she has or can she take a bite or two? By the time our Gus was as big as your Merrell, he were eatin' spuds, rice pud . . . most everything we ate, in fact.'

'Yes, Merrell does have tiny amounts of soft food if it's well mashed up,' Patty said. 'Finished the tea?

Then come through into the kitchen – you can dress yourself later – and we'll sort out your tasks for the day.'

By the time October arrived, Patty, Maggie and Merrell were quite a little family unit. Maggie proved every bit as competent and sensible as Patty had hoped, and when she returned to school Mrs Clarke, who was by now the proud mother of a bouncing baby boy, was glad enough to earn a couple of bob by taking care of Merrell from nine until four on schooldays. Patty, as her midwife, had delivered her child and the two women had grown fond of each other. Mrs Clarke had been easy-going, possibly even a little feckless, but with the birth of her baby all that changed. She and her young husband were as proud as peacocks of their offspring and determined that he should have the best life possible. Mrs Clarke, therefore, questioned Patty closely as to how she should bring up young Christopher and took all Patty's advice to heart, including the methods of hygiene which Patty herself practised and Mrs Clarke, in the days before Christopher, would have thought unnecessarily fussy.

Because of this, Patty had no fears in leaving Merrell with her friend. Patty knew that Merrell's nappies would be changed whenever necessary, that the dirty ones would be steeped in a bucket of cold water and that the wet ones would be run under the tap before Mrs Clarke put them in the bag Patty provided to carry them home in.

Mrs Clarke had offered several times to wash the nappies when she did Christopher's, but this Patty would not allow. She liked to do as much as she possibly could for Merrell herself and quite enjoyed seeing a line of nappies blowing in the breeze, on her own section of landing.

Maggie visited her family in Stanton's Court weekly. Patty had no objection to the visits and knew that Maggie was careful never to let it be known that she was looking after her own sister. In the nature of things, it was inevitable that a member of the Mullins family, or even a neighbour or friend, would eventually see Maggie pushing a pram with a baby inside it. In order to explain this away, Maggie had told her family that she baby-minded for anyone in the neighbourhood willing to pay her a few pence, and since this was common practice in the courts no one ever questioned her.

What was more, when Mrs Clarke was busy, there were now two babies tucked up snugly in the big old pram, and quite often Maggie obliged any neighbour who wanted a baby minding or a small toddler kept happy for an hour or so. She never took money from Mrs Clarke, but as soon as Patty realised that Maggie was quite happy to take on other children she told the girl that if she was offered money for baby-minding, then she could accept it. 'I don't see why you shouldn't have a bit of pocket money to spend on sweets, or hair ribbons, or whatever,' she said vaguely. 'After all, you earn the money by being a great help to me, but your dad gets all of it, doesn't he? I don't suppose he ever gives you the odd penny or so?'

Maggie didn't answer directly. Instead, she said: 'There's a lorra children in our house. Poor Biddy works harder than I do, I can tell you, especially now that Ethel woman's took herself off. Our dad is desperate to get Fanny back, but she's holdin' out, says she'll only come home if Laurie and Gus can come too.'

When Maggie went home to Stanton's Court it became a regular habit for Patty to have a hot bath and the lice lotion standing by against her return. The girl never complained, but Patty knew that she was beginning to feel ashamed of the state of her father's house. She even felt a little guilty because she was not at home and this was something which Patty knew she would have to tackle, for by now she valued Maggie highly. The girl was sweet-tempered, generous and genuinely fond of children. She was a quick learner, seldom having to be told twice how to do a task, and was becoming proficient at cooking, cleaning and most of the household tasks which Patty had once had to cope with unaided. Patty could not imagine how she would manage without Maggie but the truth was, she had never realised before quite what a menace household parasites could be. It was financially impossible for her to burn poor Maggie's clothing every time she came back from Stanton's Court, but she could, and did, soak the girl's clothes in the bath water overnight and this generally seemed to suffice. She wished she could get the Mullins to tackle the problem at their end, but was beginning to accept the sheer impossibility of such a task.

In the end, Patty decided to have a talk with Maggie. 'You mustn't feel guilty because you bring back the odd flea or a few nits when you go to visit your father,' she said gently. 'It isn't their fault that they are plagued with such things and I don't mean to blame them for it. The courts were built over a hundred years ago. They have no running water and no indoor sanitation either. Most of the houses share one tap and one lavatory, and no matter how hard people try bed bugs, fleas, lice and black beetles are far too firmly entrenched to be easily killed off. But as you know, queen, a nurse has to be especially careful that she doesn't carry germs – or insect life – into the homes she visits. You have seen me coming back some evenings and hanging all my clothing on the line outside whilst I get in the bath and give myself a good scrubbing. That's when I can tell I've picked up fleas myself and must be rid of them before they take up residence in number twenty-four. So please, Maggie, don't feel your family are letting us down, because they aren't. Only – only you wouldn't want to see Merrell covered in bites, would you? And I know how glad you are not to be plagued by such things yourself.'

She and Maggie had been sitting companionably on either side of the hearth; Maggie engaged in making a ball for the baby out of spare scraps of wool and two milk bottle tops and Patty sewing diligently away at a new overall for herself. 'Oh, Auntie Patty, I know everything you've said is true, really, but I can't help thinking if I never went home we wouldn't have the problem,' Maggie said distressfully. 'But I do know you're right. Just about everyone in the court, even Miss Edith Turnbull, who's ever so smart and a piano teacher as well, gets sick and tired of trying to get rid of bed bugs and that. And if you're afraid I might go back home to help me dad and the younger ones, I never ever will. It's probably awful selfish but I don't reckon I'd make any real difference to them and I *do* make a difference here, don't I?'

Patty felt her heart lift with relief and knew that a broad smile spread right across her face. 'You do make a difference, love,' she said fervently. 'You're the best thing that ever happened to me, you and Merrell, and I hope you'll stay with us . . . oh, until you marry some nice feller and want a home of your own.'

'Well I will then,' Maggie said decidedly. 'We's a real little family, ain't we, Auntie Patty? And if it made things easier, I'd tell me dad I've gorra stop me weekly visits but would come every other week instead. Only I'm bound to say, if I did that, I think he'd come callin', or send Biddy round to fetch the money. And that wouldn't suit us, would it?'

'No it wouldn't,' Patty agreed immediately. 'But I never told your father my address, and he never asks. Have you mentioned it?'

'Not me,' Maggie said, stifling a giggle. 'But you know what lads are, Auntie. They gets all over the city, poking their noses in where they ain't wanted. I seen little Jacky, what lives next door, in Stanton's Court, playin' wi' Reuben Pilling what lives on the bottom floor here, the other day. He saw me an' all, said hello and watched me heavin' the pram up the first few stairs, so I reckon everyone'll know where we lives by now.'

Patty sighed. She had hoped to keep her address a secret, but had guessed it would be impossible. Children, even more than adults, roamed the city streets, inquisitive as cats, and the Mullins children would be no exception. And to do Mr Mullins credit, Maggie had been living in Ashfield Place for three months now, and he had never come calling. Maggie reported that he was extremely grateful for the weekly payments, and even though he was now working he had not suggested that Maggie might return to her own home. Things could be a lot worse, Patty told herself and turned to Maggie. 'Now, how about a drink of cocoa before we go to bed?'

'I'll make it,' Maggie said eagerly, laying down her own work. She went over to the cupboard and got out the tin of cocoa, spooned some into two mugs, then turned back to Patty. 'Someone said the other day that – that you were in an orphan asylum when you was a little girl. Is it true, Auntie Patty? And is that why you wouldn't put Merrell in one?'

For a moment, Patty was startled; who had been discussing her past so freely? Then she remembered an incautious remark she had made to Mrs Clarke about orphan asylums in general and Durrant House in particular and thought, ruefully, that her friend must have put two and two together. 'That's right. I was brought up in an orphanage,' she said briefly. 'It isn't something I'd wish on anyone, Maggie. No one was cruel to me; we were fed and clothed, though never generously. I was often hungry. But there was no love, no feeling of belonging, no family affection. I didn't want that for Merrell.'

Maggie said no more, and went off to bed apparently satisfied. But when Patty went to her own room, her mind flew back across the years to the Durrant and to her life there. She climbed between the sheets and burrowed into the pillow, remembering, remembering . . . .

116

Chapter Five
May 1917

Outside the windows of Durrant House a light and drizzling rain was falling. Patty, sitting next to Laura, nudged her friend in the ribs with an impatient elbow. 'Look at that,' she hissed, nodding towards one of the long windows. 'It's raining *again*, and I bet Miss Arnold won't let us go to the park.' She sighed impatiently. 'And if anyone else says it's because *there's a war on*, I'm sure I shall scream!'

It was a Saturday morning so the day, though by no means free, was less rigidly disciplined than weekdays. Patty had been hoping that they might be taken to the park where they were now allowed, occasionally, to play sedate games of ball, or even such things as Grandmother's Footsteps or Relievio. Matron had softened with the years and had agreed with some of the older girls that if they were willing to supervise such games, they helped to keep the younger children healthy and happy.

'Well, I don't see why you should expect to go to the park. Today's the day the new matron takes over,' Laura pointed out. 'Everything will change; it's bound to. New brooms sweep clean, they say, and they call this matron the prison wardress, don't they? I'm going to write a letter to my mam to remind her again that I'm supposed to go home from time to time, now I'm eleven. If things get strict again, like they was when we were younger, I'll scream even louder than—'

'Laura! You are quite old enough to know the rules and to obey them! If I see you talking again, you will get a detention.'

Laura and Patty immediately bent over the thin gruel which was all they had for breakfast, though Patty flashed an indignant look at the prefect who had spoken. Her name was Maria Wickes and she was disliked by almost everyone at the Durrant. How different from Selina, Patty thought sorrowfully, who had been universally popular. And of course, Laura was probably right. This Miss O'Dowd was bound to try to make herself felt as soon as she took command. Life was never easy for the inhabitants of Durrant House, but Patty was sure that a new matron would see to it that the girls had even less freedom than before. As she neared retirement, the present matron had slackened the reins a good deal, and a good many of the rules had not been so strictly enforced. Naturally, other teachers had followed her example, so that, despite the shortages caused by the war, life at Durrant House was actually easier.

With the prefect's eye upon them, Patty and Laura dared not talk again, but spooned in the thin gruel, drank their milk and water mixture and, as soon as the word was given, left the dining room. They made their way to their common room, glancing hopefully out of the windows as they entered, but rain was still falling steadily, which probably meant that they would not be allowed to go outside until the weather improved. However, there were no classes to be attended, and the girls were free to chat among themselves as they got out the knitting that had become a part of their attempt to help with the war effort. The teachers and the Board of Governors supplied them with old woollen garments, which they unpicked, washed and rolled into balls. At present the girls in Patty's class were knitting squares, which were then crocheted together by some of the older girls, to make a whole blanket.

'I wonder if Selina will have a few hours off today,' Patty said wistfully as she and Laura carried their knitting over to the window seat. 'If she has, perhaps she'll call for me and take me out somewhere. Even a walk round the park or up and down Ullet Road would be a treat after being cooped up in the Durrant all week.'

'Yes, I know what you mean,' Laura said, rather dolefully. Ever since Selina had left, she and Patty had visited Mrs Thornton in Peel Street on Friday afternoons, sometimes meeting Selina there and always being treated by the cook with warmth and generosity. Mrs Thornton saw to it that they enjoyed a good tea at least one day a week. Her employer, a Miss Jessica Larkin, was a well-known philanthropist, giving both time and money to a number of good causes. She very rarely visited the kitchen regions, but had done so on one occasion when Patty and Laura had been enjoying hot buttered scones and cups of tea at the kitchen table. Mrs Thornton had unblushingly introduced the girls as 'me nieces, what's in the Durrant House orphan asylum up the road and comes to visit me from time to time', and Miss Larkin had greeted the girls in a friendly but absent manner, assuring them that they were welcome to visit her house whenever they were free to do so.

'Your aunt is an excellent cook and a good, kind woman,' she said in her high, fluting voice. 'I know these orphan asylums do their best, but what with the war and shortness of money the children have a restricted diet and very few treats, which does not lead to strong bones and general good health.' She smiled kindly, if myopically, down at the two girls. 'So you must visit your aunt whenever you can and have a good tea,' she instructed them. 'Then you will grow up to be strong and healthy, able to hold your own in the world.'

So far as Mrs Thornton, Patty and Laura were concerned, this made the girls' visits official, and whenever they were able to do so the girls made their way to the kitchen of the big house on Peel Street and were always welcomed there. However, for the past two Fridays they had been unable to see Mrs Thornton. Miss Larkin, immensely relieved now that America had entered the war, had given two garden parties in aid of the troops, and because of all the preparation – and cooking – that this had entailed Mrs Thornton had regretfully advised them to steer clear for a couple of weeks.

'After dear old George's proclamation concerning food shortages and cutting down on bread consumption, you'd expect Madam to think twice about holding a cream tea in aid of the troops, but not she! "If we aren't to be allowed to eat bread, then you must make a great many scones, Cook," she told me – as if she didn't realise that scones are made with flour and it's flour the country's short of! But there you are, we shall just have to contrive.' Mrs Thornton had looked at the girls worriedly. 'I feel that mean, askin' you to miss your weekly visit twice, but I'll be that busy . . . but the following week, just you come round as usual and I'll make sure you get a good tea, shortages or no shortages.'

The girls had heard the king's proclamation read out in church and had thought, with real dismay, that this would mean even less food set out for them in the dining room. Bread and margarine was served to them for tea almost every day and dinners, never lavish, had been reduced to a thin vegetable stew two or three times a week, with baked beans in gravy or a bowl of virulent green pea soup the only alternatives. But it was no use grumbling; when the girls did so, they were informed, frostily, by the hated Miss Briggs, that the king and queen and the rest of the royal family had been restricting their intake of bread since February and had also cut down on potatoes.

'But I bet the king and the rest of the royal family get lots of things to eat that we could never dream of,' Laura had muttered rebelliously in her friend's ear. 'It's all very well to cut bread and potatoes down when you've got alternatives, but we haven't. I'm sure there are no children in the whole of England as skinny – and as hungry – as we are. I'm sure that if they really cut the bread and potatoes they give us by a quarter, we'd bleedin' well starve.'

Patty had agreed wholeheartedly with her friend's conclusion but it appeared that even the Board of Governors – and Cook, of course – realised that the girls could not survive on anything less than they were getting already, so though the slices of bread at teatime were possibly a little thinner cut, everyone was still given a complete round together with their mug of milk and water. Jam had disappeared two years earlier and tea was just a memory. 'Well, tea is brought in from abroad, and the German U-boats sink a great many of our ships, so they say,' Selina had said. 'I suppose tea is a luxury really, which we must learn to do without. But the other things the ships bring – flour, sugar, and such – are essential to keep body and soul together.' She had smiled teasingly down at Patty. 'I know the food at Durrant House is terrible and never nearly enough, but I promise you, queen, that nurses don't fare much better. We're often so hungry that we hang around the kitchen waiting for the patients to finish their food and if they leave so much as half a round of bread and butter, or a piece of potato, someone will gobble it down at once.'

'But you do have some money so you can buy yourselves extras,' Patty had pointed out, her mouth watering at the thought. 'I remember you telling me that all your spare money went on food when you first started training as a probationer.'

Selina had chuckled. 'I shouldn't grumble,' she said with a smile lighting her beautiful grey eyes. 'The patients are ever so good, particularly the soldiers. Their relatives bring in fruit and sweets and little cakes and the soldiers hand a good few such presents on to the nursing staff. But you've got Mrs Thornton, haven't you, queen? I know she treats you right well.' She had paused for a moment, and then had said thoughtfully: 'When I've passed my exams, Mrs Thornton has promised to teach me how to cook. I'm looking forward to it quite as much as I'm looking forward to being a fully fledged nurse.'

So now Patty and Laura sat in their common room, knitting half-heartedly and hoping that the rain would soon stop. Patty's tummy was rumbling aggressively, as though the mere thought of food had made it realise how empty it was, and when she spoke she actually raised her voice to drown out its mutterings. 'I wish your mam would ask us home, Laura,' she said wistfully. 'Of course it's grand going to visit Selina but I don't think they really approve of her having someone who is not quite ten in the nurses' home. When it's raining, we sneak up the stairs to her room and toast bread in front of her gas fire. But we aren't supposed to so if the weather's fine we wander round the shops or just go for walks.'

'Selina's working today, isn't she?' Laura asked, diligently knitting away. 'I wonder whether the new matron will let Selina take you out, though, Patty. It's not as though she were a relative, after all.'

'I shall say she's me cousin,' Patty said loftily.

Laura snorted. 'If you think old Briggsy wouldn't tell her it were a lie, you've got a higher opinion of the woman than I have,' she said roundly. 'Still an' all, I suppose it's worth a try. And anyway, the staff like us to go out of a weekend because there's more food for the others to share around.'

'That's true,' Patty said thoughtfully. 'I tell you what, though, Laura, if your mam does invite us to go round to her place even once, then whenever Selina's free we can pretend we're going to see your mam. The staff are far too busy to check up on things like that and you know Selina is happy for you to come out with us from time to time.'

Laura put down her knitting and stared admiringly at her friend. 'I always knew you were the brightest of us,' she remarked. 'Why, if you and Selina went off together and then met me at an agreed place, I could have an afternoon to meself, wandering round the shops and mebbe visiting some of me relatives. I still remembers where they live, more or less, and though they haven't taken any notice of me since I've been in the Durrant, I reckon it's just out of sight, out of mind. I've often thought if I turned up on their doorstep they'd welcome me in, especially me Aunt Annie. She's got a dozen kids and her old feller's in an' out of work like a jack-in-the-box, but they're all real good-natured. Me mam used to say Aunt Annie 'ud share her last crust with a blind beggar, so I'm sure she'd ask me in so we could have a good jangle over a cuppa.' She beamed at Patty. 'Oh aye, that's a grand thought of yours, so it is.'

'Ye-es, only first of all, we've got to persuade your mam to ask us round to her place,' Patty reminded her friend. 'They'll check up the first time, you know they will. From what other girls have said, your mam will have to come round here in person and agree times, dates and so on. Tell you what, Laura, let's write to her this very afternoon. Or . . . I wonder if I could persuade Selina to take me round to your mam's place? I could ask her meself, explain what a lot it means to us.'

'We'll try both,' Laura said. 'I'll fetch paper and a pencil.'

She was on her feet and heading for the door when it opened abruptly. Miss Briggs stood there, and beside her, already dressed in the familiar uniform, was a woman who must be the new matron. Patty stared. The woman was massive. She must be six foot tall and was as broad as a policeman with enormous shoulders and a great, jutting bust. The uniform looked as though it were already straining at the seams and the little white frilled cap perched on her bob of thick dark hair made her head look even larger. Her face, when Patty's eyes fell upon it, was not prepossessing. Her eyes were small and set amidst rolls of fat, her red cheeks looked as hard as apples and her mouth was just a thin, determined line above her rolling chins. No wonder the older girls had christened her the prison wardress, Patty thought. Their old matron had been gaunt and spare but her expression had not been unpleasant and Patty could not remember her ever glaring at the assembled orphans in such a ferocious manner.

Patty was just wondering whether she ought to get up when Miss Briggs stepped forward and spoke in ringing tones. 'Girls! All stand to welcome our new matron, Miss O'Dowd. She would like to say a few words.'

Miss Briggs stepped back as the girls rose obediently to their feet and Miss O'Dowd stepped forward. Patty thought she probably smiled at them – at least the rolls of fat rearranged themselves – and then she spoke. For such an enormous woman she had an extraordinarily thin, high voice but Patty, stealing a glance around, saw that no one smiled. 'Good morning, children.' She paused and the girls chorused obediently: 'Good morning, Matron.' There was another pause before Miss O'Dowd spoke again. 'As you know, I came to Durrant House a couple of weeks ago to meet the staff and the senior girls, and from today I take up my position here. I am sure I don't need to tell you that I have a great admiration for the work done by Miss Capper, your previous matron. However, she was nearing retirement and became, I believe, rather – lax in her attitude to some of the rules.' She paused again to sweep the assembled girls with a cold and fishy eye. 'You will soon find that I am not the type of person to relax any rules unless, of course, I think it would be for the good of Durrant House. I may make changes but I must emphasise that I shall expect instant obedience from all of you. Punishments have not been particularly severe in the past but I am a great believer in showing my displeasure in a way which will not be easily forgotten. Spare the rod and spoil the child is my motto; there is a cane in the corner cupboard of my study and I shall not hesitate to use it upon wrongdoers. Bear this in mind, obey the rules and do nothing without first asking permission, and I am sure we shall get along very comfortably. And now I will leave you to continue with your war work – I take it you are all employed in doing something towards the war effort?'

'The girls are making blankets for hospitals in France and some are writing their weekly letters home,' Miss Briggs said. 'If it had not been raining, they would have gone to the park for an hour or so of leisure.'

Miss O'Dowd sniffed and turned towards Miss Briggs: 'Satan always finds mischief for idle hands to do,' she quoted sourly. 'Leisure time should be spent in improving both the mind and the body, but we'll discuss that later. She turned back towards the children. 'That will be all, girls; you may recommence your tasks.'

For a moment there was complete silence as the door closed behind the two women, then a low buzz of conversation broke out. Patty could see that everyone had been shocked both by Miss O'Dowd's appearance and by her words. In the past, the staff – and Miss Capper – had been strict, sometimes unfair, but they had never approached their work with the steely determination which had gleamed from Miss O'Dowd's eyes. If she tries to stop me from seeing Selina and visiting Mrs Thornton, then I'll make sure she regrets it, Patty told herself, but knew the threat was a hollow one. A child was always powerless against adults and could only rebel in her heart and mind unless she wanted to court disaster.

Laura jerked at Patty's arm. 'Wharra terror,' she exclaimed in awed tones. 'One hard slap from her and you'd be dead, I reckon. As for her cane – well, I don't like the sound of that at all. I reckon we ought to write that letter straight away, no messing.'

Patty agreed and the two of them spent the next half-hour explaining to Mrs Reilly that it was now truly important that Laura be allowed to visit her home sometimes at weekends. When the letter was finished, Patty scribbled a hasty note to Selina and the two girls went along the corridor to the secretary's room, where stamps and envelopes were available. The children were allowed one stamp and one envelope per week, though few of them availed themselves of the privilege.

When the girls entered the room, Miss Briggs was sitting behind the desk, poring over a large ledger. She looked up as the girls entered, raising her thin brows in enquiry. 'Yes?'

'Please, Miss Briggs, may we have a stamp each and an envelope?' Laura said politely. She was usually the spokeswoman when Miss Briggs was the teacher being addressed since Miss Briggs's hostility towards Patty was renowned. 'I've written a letter to my mother and Patty has written to a friend.'

Both girls expected the teacher to pull out the long middle drawer of the desk and to extract stamps and envelopes, albeit grudgingly, but instead Miss Briggs simply held out her hand. 'Give the letters to me,' she said crisply. 'If they pass muster, I will see that they are posted.'

Both girls stared at her, round-eyed. 'But – but it's a letter to – to my mam,' Laura gasped. No one never reads our letters, Miss Briggs!'

Miss Briggs smiled unpleasantly. 'No? But that was in Miss Capper's time. Miss O'Dowd has already stipulated that all letters must be read by a member of staff. If anything of which Miss O'Dowd does not approve has been said, then the letter will have to be rewritten without the offending sentence or paragraph.'

Laura looked hunted and Patty knew she had told her mother about Miss O'Dowd and implored Mrs Reilly to help her escape from the new regime occasionally. Patty knew at once that if Miss Briggs set eyes on the words, there would be terrible trouble. And as for herself . . . well, the letter she had written to Selina had included a full description of the ogress now in control.

Miss Briggs clicked her fingers impatiently. 'Come along, come along,' she said briskly. 'Why are you hesitating? I've explained that this is one of Miss O'Dowd's new rules. Is that not sufficient for you?'

Patty took a deep breath, scrumpled her own letter into a ball and took Laura's from her unresisting fingers. Fortunately, there was a small fire burning in the study grate and before Miss Briggs had more than opened her mouth, both letters were in the flames and burning brightly. 'We changed our minds, Miss Briggs; we don't want stamps and envelopes after all,' Patty said in her most sweet and reasonable tone. 'We're very sorry to have bothered you.'

Miss Briggs did not pretend to misunderstand them. She smiled coldly and let her eyes return to the ledger once more. 'I expect you will want to rewrite your letters yourselves,' she said sarcastically. 'No doubt you will go back to your common room and inform the other children how things stand. All incoming mail will, in future, be opened and read by a member of staff. Your friends and relatives will doubtless wish to know things have changed.'

'Yes, Miss Briggs, thank you, Miss Briggs,' the girls

chorused, but once outside the door they stared at one another with very real dismay. 'Thank the Lord you gorrem in the fire before old Briggsy snatched 'em out of me hand and read every word,' Laura said, pale to the lips. 'Oh, Patty, Durrant House has never been a bed o' roses, exactly, but it's going to be *awful* from now on.'

And Patty, returning to the common room to write a very different letter to Selina, could only agree.

By September, the girls were growing used to the new broom. Miss O'Dowd, known as 'old dowdy' to the girls, ruled with a rod of iron and had a strange idea that orphans should not be given privileges since such treats softened them and did not prepare them for the hardships they would meet when they went into the outside world. Discontent and muttering became usual, even amongst the meekest residents of Durrant House. In fact, the only good thing about the new matron's iron rule was that it drew the girls together as nothing else could and made the rest of the staff into allies rather than enemies.

It clearly never occurred to Miss O'Dowd that every time she punished the girls by handing out wholesale detentions, one of the teachers had to give up her own free time to monitor that detention. The walks in the park and the gentle games they played there were as much a relief for the staff who supervised them as for the girls themselves. And when Miss O'Dowd began to cut their meagre food supply even further, the resident nurse told the matron bluntly that she was not saving money but simply moving it from the kitchen to the sanatorium. 'What I'm trying to say, Matron, is that with even less food to line their stomachs, the children are twice as likely to come down wit' one of a dozen ailments which decent food could help to prevent,' Nurse Mitford said bluntly. 'It's bad enough, to be sure, when a measles or mumps epidemic sweeps through Durrant House wit' out having children weakened by poor nutrition so that they come out in eruptions of boils or suffer from continual hacking coughs.'

Since Nurse had tackled Miss O'Dowd in the sanatorium, an exact account of the conversation had spread like wildfire from the patients to the rest of Durrant House and there was much admiration for Nurse Mitford's daring in standing up to her superior. At the time, a sick child had reported, Matron had huffed and puffed and said she was as aware as Nurse Mitford of the importance of feeding the children a nourishing meal at least once a day. 'I wouldn't dream of depriving them of anything but luxuries,' she had said stiffly. 'But I see no need to pander to their appetite for sweet things by providing a piece of currant loaf at Sunday teatime. And meat heats the blood; less meat won't harm them.'

Nurse Mitford had snorted inelegantly. She was a great favourite with the children, a round, apple-cheeked little woman with a strong Irish brogue, who worked unceasingly on behalf of her charges and managed to make sure that the food in the sanatorium was a good deal better than that served in the dining room. Now, she fixed Miss O'Dowd with an accusing eye. 'I'm not after saying that a slice of currant bread will make or break the health of a child. I'm after pointing out that the kitchen staff have noticed there's no meat any more in the twice-weekly stew and that the gravy is just gravy browning. What's more, growing children need milk and what they're getting these days is so diluted with water that you can see the bottom of the mug through it. Don't tell me there's a war on, Matron, because no one's more aware of it than I, but sure and don't I know the girls should have their share of what food is available and at present they don't.'

To the girls' delight, Nurse Mitford's words had had their effect. The twice-weekly stew had been a great treat and the girls had mourned its replacement by a sort of thin vegetable soup. Upon its return to the table once more, they all rejoiced. When a second course was introduced, usually consisting of bread pudding or stewed fruit and custard, they felt themselves privileged indeed, even though puddings were still only served two or three times a week, and thanked Nurse Mitford in their secret hearts for every delicious spoonful.

Patty's friendship with Selina continued, and to Patty's amazement this was due to Miss Briggs. Miss O'Dowd had issued a command that all relatives who might want to take the girls home over the weekend, or during the school holidays, must come to Durrant House so that she might make sure they were suitable. When Patty put in her own request that she might be allowed to visit Selina when the older girl had time off, she had described Selina as her cousin, her dead mother's sister's child. Miss Briggs, who had been in the room taking notes for Miss O'Dowd since the secretary was busy elsewhere, had opened her mouth . . . and closed it again. Whether she had been thinking that it would be nice to be rid of Patty from time to time it was impossible to say, but Patty was grateful to her, nevertheless, and, instead of deliberately annoying the teacher whenever it was possible, began to try to see the older woman's good points. At one time she would have said that Miss

Briggs had no good points and was both surprised and pleased to discover that she was wrong. Miss Briggs had a sharp tongue and a nasty way with her, but she could be understanding and even amusing on occasion.

On this particular day, Patty and Selina had planned a trip across the water. Selina knew a village with a small general store in the back room of which the proprietress served customers with an excellent and very reasonably priced tea. She had been there before with nursing colleagues and was eager for her young friend, too, to enjoy the treat. She called for Patty early in the morning, looking very respectable in her navy-blue skirt and coat with a small hat perched on her light brown hair. Patty, of course, was in Durrant House uniform and carried her Burberry over her arm, for it was a warm and sunny day, though Patty noticed, as they made their way down to the Pier Head, that there was a coolness in the breeze which lifted the hair from her face.

Once aboard the ferry, Patty began to relax. She always felt that whilst they were in walking distance of Durrant House, someone might be sent to bring her back and she might lose her treat. It was always possible that an incautious remark could reveal to the matron that Patty was a foundling and could not, therefore, possibly possess a cousin, but so far this had not happened. And as the ferry docked in Woodside, Patty took Selina's hand and beamed up at her. 'It's so grand to see you, Selina, that I wouldn't mind if we just spent all day sitting on the quayside and chatting.'

Selina smiled back and squeezed her hand. 'It's the same for me, queen,' she said. 'I love telling you all the little things that happen on the wards and how

I'm getting on with the work. Of course, us probationers talk amongst ourselves all the time, but it's nice to tell someone else what is going on – someone who isn't working in the hospital herself, I mean. And believe it or not, I really love hearing about the Durrant and what goes on there.' She chuckled. 'Things at the hospital don't seem nearly so hard when I think of what you poor kids are going through.'

'Oh, it's not all bad,' Patty said cheerfully as they made their way to the nearest bus stop. They meant to take a bus ride to within three or four miles of the village which was their destination, for despite the fact that she was on her feet all week, often running from ward to ward, Selina liked to spend a good deal of her spare time walking in the fresh air. She often told Patty that walking and the countryside were the two things she enjoyed the most, and Patty knew, with a sinking of the heart, that once she was qualified Selina would try for a post in a rural community, rather than in one of the big and busy hospitals in the city. Selina had assured her that they would keep in touch, but Patty knew it could not possibly be the same. Patty had years ahead of her before she would be able to join a hospital herself, and then there would be more years of training. At the end of that time, if she passed all her exams and did well, she might be able to apply for a post at Selina's hospital, but secretly she doubted she would ever do so. And anyway, she reminded herself, as the two of them scrambled their way up the stairs of the bus towards the upper deck, Selina's got ever so pretty since she left Durrant House and started curling her hair and using a bit of make-up. She'll go and get married and have kids of her own and she won't need me at all.

But the day was too lovely to waste it in regretting something which might never happen. 'Are you still on Women's Surgical?' Patty asked as soon as they had settled themselves comfortably. 'Or are you back with the soldiers again? Who is your sister? I hope you've moved on from Sister Richards, because she was such a horror.'

'No, it's Sister Eagles now, and I'm general dogsbody on one of the medical wards,' Selina said cheerfully. 'It's a nice ward and the nurses and patients are friendly and optimistic. We've had a lot of cases of trench foot and some of the dear fellows do get better and regain almost full use of their limbs, though others are not so lucky. It's interesting nursing them because they need a great deal of attention and dressings need to be changed constantly, of course, which is one task that the fully fledged nurses are only too eager to hand over to us probationers.'

For some while, Selina kept Patty amused with tales of life on the ward and in the nurses' home, but when they got off the bus it was Patty's turn to describe in detail what was going on at Durrant House. 'And you'll never guess what's happening in Peel Street,' Patty told her friend. 'Mrs Thornton's moving on! She and the gardener at number twelve are getting married and moving out to Crosby, where they are taking up the posts of housekeeper and general handyman to an old lady. Apparently, she asked Miss Larkin to find her a reliable married couple. Miss Larkin knew that Mrs Thornton and Mr Hedges were planning to get married, so she suggested they should apply and of course they got the job.'

'Golly!' Selina said, round-eyed. 'But won't Miss

Larkin miss her cook most dreadfully? And what will you and I do with no house in Peel Street to visit on a Friday afternoon?'

'Oh, Mrs Thornton says she'll have a word with the new cook when she's appointed,' Patty said, trying to sound optimistic. 'Anyway, I'm luckier than most orphans because I've got you, Selina.'

Patty thought she had spoken no more than the truth and enjoyed a wonderful day with her friend, but when she returned to Durrant House she was immediately hauled into Matron's study. Completely unsuspecting and still flushed with pleasure from her day in the open air, she hurried into the office and looked questioningly at Miss O'Dowd. 'Yes, Matron? Nellie Beasley said you wanted to see me.'

'Indeed I do,' Miss O'Dowd said ominously. 'Earlier today, I had cause to ask for some files to be brought up from the basement; yours was amongst them and I have now discovered that you are a liar and a cheat. I don't know where you go to when you pretend to be with your cousin, but I do know that you have no cousin. You are a foundling, abandoned by your parents, who were, no doubt, people lacking moral fibre of any sort. Your connection with the house in Peel Street is not that of niece to the cook. I understand from your file that you were abandoned in Peel Street which is, of course, why your name is Peel. You will not rejoin the rest of your class but will be put back a year, and you will not be allowed out any more with this girl Selina. Nor will you again visit the house in Peel Street.'

Patty stared in astonished disbelief at the woman before her. 'You can't possibly put me down a year, Matron,' she said at last. 'It would mean doing the work twice, and anyway I'm nearly always top of the class I'm in. I've done nothing wrong, apart from saying Selina was my cousin instead of my dear friend. It's not my fault I'm a foundling and – and Mrs Thornton has been wonderful to me. Please punish me in some other way, if you must, but not by taking my friend away from me or putting me in a lower class.'

'Don't question my decisions,' Matron said icily. She reached behind her and picked up the cane and whilst Patty was still standing, staring at her, she came around the desk, moving incredibly fast for such a large woman, and caught Patty two stinging blows across the cheek. 'I hope that will teach you a lesson,' she said breathlessly. 'You are a wilful and deceitful child and must be taught the error of your ways. I shall tell—'

But Patty had fled the room, a hand to her stinging cheek, and half an hour later she had also fled Durrant House and was crouched beneath a bench in Prince's Park, sobbing and terrified, but determined never to return to a person who could behave as Miss O'Dowd had done.

Patty got very little sleep that night. Fortunately, the weather was still warm, and before running away she had had the foresight to take out her winter coat and to put on the stout lace-up boots which the girls all wore in wintertime. Had she been able, she would have stolen some food since there was no way she could provide herself with so much as a penny piece, but she had had no opportunity. Tea was the last meal of the day the children were given and it had been long over before Patty had returned from her day out. After escaping from Miss O'Dowd's study, she had gone straight up to her dormitory and in feverish haste had arranged a bolster in her bed, to look as though she were curled up beneath the covers. It was the time of day the children spent in their common rooms and the teachers and the rest of the staff had some small degree of freedom, so no one was lurking in the corridors. Patty slid out of the side door and simply ran as fast as she could, not heeding in which direction she went. She had actually returned to Prince's Park when darkness fell because it seemed considerably safer than the streets, but even in her anguish and misery she knew that it would not be a good place once the park keepers arrived the following morning. As soon as it grew light, therefore, she made her way out of the park and headed towards the docks. She had no idea where she would go or what she would do, but was simply eager to put as much distance as possible between Durrant House and herself. Naturally enough, she thought wistfully of both Mrs Thornton and Selina, but realised she could not take either of them into her confidence. They would not approve of the way she had been treated, but even so they would not be able to harbour a runaway orphan. They would have to hand her over to Miss O'Dowd and, even though she understood, she knew it would harm the relationship she had built up with the only friends, outside the orphanage, that she had in the world. If she meant to run away – and stay away – she must do so unaided. As she walked along the quiet pavement, wondering where to go, she remembered with nostalgic pleasure the previous day spent in Selina's company, and this gave her an idea. The ferry had been crowded; she thought it was quite possible that a child alone might get aboard the ship unnoticed and ticketless, and reach the further side without being caught or questioned. Then – ah, then – the rich countryside would stretch out before her, with all its infinite possibilities. Immensely cheered by the thought, she set off for the Pier Head.

Despite the fact that it was term time, Patty was pleased to see that there were a fair number of children amongst the many adults crossing and recrossing the quayside. This meant that she would not be picked out immediately as a truant, though she wished, desperately, that she had managed to find some means of disguising the brown gingham dress, which was all Durrant House provided in the summertime. In fact, however, the dress was to be her salvation for presently, as she made her way towards the landing stage, someone laid a hand on her arm. Patty jumped quite six inches and prepared to run, believing for one awful moment that a member of staff – perhaps even Matron herself – had spotted her. Before she could do more than jump, however, she turned her head and saw a skinny boy, four or five inches taller than herself, whose toffee-coloured hair fell in a straight fringe across his forehead. He had light brown eyes and a confident air though he was dressed in ragged trousers and a grey flannel shirt several sizes too big for him. 'Sorry I scared you,' he said, 'but ain't that an orphanage uniform youse wearing? And judgin' from the way you jumped, you've lit out from the place, like what I have. I doesn't want to get catched and sent back and I reckon they'll be huntin' for one kid, norra couple. Pity about that there dress, but when it's gorra bit dirtier no one won't think twice. You catchin' the ferry? Gorrany money? I's headin' for Ireland, but it may take a while to get there. Where's you goin'?'

Getting over her initial fright, Patty stared at him

curiously. He was extremely dirty and barefoot and probably about her own age, but he had a sort of cheerful independence, which made him appear older. 'Yes, I was at Durrant House,' she admitted, sinking her voice. 'We've got a new matron and she hates me.' She turned her face so that the cheek with two red weals across it was towards him and touched the wound with careful fingers. 'She hit me with a cane so I ran away. I say, is that *your* uniform? Only it – it doesn't look much like one.'

'I snitched the shirt off of a washing line, the day afore yesterday,' the boy said cheerfully. 'The trousers is mine, but I ragged them up a bit, and I sold me shoes and socks to someone in Paddy's market yesterday afternoon. I got a bob for 'em, 'cos the shoes was almost new,' he added proudly.

'I never thought of that,' Patty said admiringly. 'I guess I'd look better without boots, wouldn't I? More like other kids, I mean. Do you reckon you could sell mine for me?'

The boy looked down at Patty's feet. The winter boots had been new last autumn and still looked hardly worn. 'Yeah, I reckon I could,' he said, rather doubtfully, 'but wharrabout walkin', queen? You don't look to me as though you're used to goin' barefoot. It's different for me; until last summer, I were barefoot all the time and even in the orphanage, I took me shoes off whenever I could. Hated the feel of 'em, see? They cramped me toes up somethin' cruel.'

'I reckon I'd rather be barefoot than in these boots,' Patty said, having thought the matter over. 'Besides, I'm getting awful hungry, so any money we get for the boots we could spend on food.'

'Right,' the boy said with alacrity. 'We'll walk inland, then, see what we can find.'

Patty fell into step beside him, wondering why she did so. Her only previous encounter with a boy had been with young Lionel Tennant in Peel Street and that had not exactly filled her with loving kindness towards the male species. In fact, she had both feared and disliked boys ever since, so why was this one different? Patty shot a sideways glance at him, then decided that it was not looks which counted. He was a runaway, as she was, and seemed much more worldly-wise than herself. For all her much vaunted intelligence, she had not thought of selling her boots, nor had she realised how conspicuous they made her in a part of the city where almost every child she met was barefoot. In the circumstances, she decided, she would do well to forget her prejudices against boys and accept both his companionship and any help he might offer.

'We'll come back here later, I reckon,' the boy said presently, as they passed Prince's Dock and turned up Leeds Street. 'There's canny houses down by the docks where you can get a real good meal for less than a tanner. What's more, we mustn't forget we're goin' to need money if we mean to cross the water. Come to that, we'll need food wherever we are. There's a limit to what grub we can pinch, particularly at this time of year, when there's very little in the way of fruit and veg left in folks' gardens. Can you sing?'

They were passing Exchange station at the time and Patty stopped, staring at her companion, wide-eyed. 'Sing?' she echoed. 'Well, I dunno. I suppose everyone can sing, can't they? But what made you ask?'

The boy jerked his head towards the station entrance and Patty saw a skinny little man in a bright

140

red shirt and royal blue trousers, with a shiny peaked cap on his head. He was playing on a thin black pipe and every now and then a passer-by would toss him a coin which he caught, with amazing dexterity, in his right hand.

Patty looked doubtfully up at her companion. 'Do you mean we could make money, as he's doing? Only I don't think anyone would pay to hear me sing, and I can't play a pipe – well, I don't have one!'

'No, but I have,' the boy assured her. He rooted round in his pocket and produced a penny whistle. 'Before they took me into St Peter's Orphan Home for Boys, I often played the whistle so's me mam could dance to it – and sing, of course. It weren't so good in country places, 'cos there ain't much money about, though folk often gave us fruit and veg an' that. But in big cities we did awright. I reckon you an' me could keep body and soul together and it's better than beggin'. Scuffers don't like you beggin' but they'll turn a blind eye to a bit o' street music. Can you dance?' he asked, as they turned left into Vauxhall Road.

Patty looked longingly at the shopfronts they passed, her mouth watering over the display of cakes and loaves in the window of Richard Taylor's. 'No, I can't dance, nor walk a tightrope, nor juggle, nor do any other sort of circus acts,' she said firmly. 'Were you and your mammy circus folk?'

The boy grinned but shook his head. 'No, though that were a good guess. Some people call us gypsies but we're really fair folk – or at least we were when me dad were alive. It were a grand life, never stayin' in one place for long, always movin' on, bringin' fun and entertainment wherever we set up. Me mam ran a hoopla stall and me dad did a knife-throwin' act, as well as servicing the traction engines and doin' all sorts of engineering work. But after he died, Mam had a struggle to manage and Texas Ted, the Riding Master – that's the boss of the fair we were with – tried to get fresh with her. When she wouldn't go along with what he wanted, he kicked us out and took our caravan for his fancy woman. Mam said it wouldn't matter, we'd do OK by ourselves, but we needed a big city, so we came to Liverpool. It were grand for a bit, except we went into digs. They was awful poor – the food were dreadful, and the bed bugs nigh on the size of cats. Then two winters ago, Mam went down with pneumonia and died ten days later.' He grabbed her arm and the pair of them crossed the busy road and dived down Burlington Street. 'Hey, I never even asked your name. I'm Toby Rudd.'

'I'm Patty Peel,' Patty said readily. 'I come from the Durrant House Orphan Asylum for Girls, on The Elms, up by Prince's Park. It's a hateful place, or it is now, with Miss O'Dowd in charge. It weren't so bad with the old matron, but this one's wicked as they come and the size of a mountain. Have you tried playing your pipe for money, Toby? Did it work?'

'Yes, and I got fivepence three-farthings, only it got took off me by a bigger feller,' Toby admitted ruefully. 'I put a battered old tin down beside me to take the money and this great bullyin' brute of a boy just snatched it up, money an' all, and made off afore I could take the whistle from me lips. But if there were two of us, the one who was singin' could put the money in a pocket – or up her knicker leg for that matter – because she'd have both hands free, see?'

'Yes, I do see. I got beat up by a big boy once, when I were only seven,' Patty told him. They paused to look, hungrily, at a corner shop from which enticing smells of various foods drifted out to their nostrils.

'This here's Scotland Road; do you want to take your boots off or will you keep them on your feet till we gets to Paddy's market?'

'I'll keep them on my feet,' Patty said decidedly. There were a great many people crowding the pavements and even walking in the road and most of them, she thought apprehensively, looked quite capable of snatching her boots, which represented her dinner, and making off with them. Whilst they were on her feet – and tightly laced up – she told herself she would give anyone trying to nick them a good kick in the face, and that would put a stop to any thoughts of theft.

'Toby, why did you light out?' Patty asked curiously, as they made their way along the crowded pavement. 'I told you why I went.'

'Oh, I means to meet up wi' another fair as soon as I'm able,' Toby said airily. 'There's fairs and fair folk plying their trade all over the country, you know. Why, for all Texas Ted thinks he's so wonderful, he ain't nothin' special. There's bigger and better what 'ud take me on like a shot once they knew I were lookin' for work, like. Me dad taught me how to service the steam engines and to drive them and there's no sideshow I couldn't man, I reckon. Wharrabout yourself, queen? I mean, I knows you left 'cos the old witch hit you, but where's you headin'? Have you got a mam or a dad, or aunts and that?'

Much though Patty liked Toby Rudd, she decided that vagueness was her best course. 'I dunno; I dunno exactly where I'm heading,' she said absently, as though she had a million places to choose from. 'I've got relatives all right, but this time I thought I'd try to

143

cross the water. There's lovely country over there –
my friend Selina took me for a day out yesterday – and
I reckoned I could sleep in haystacks and live off the
land, like they do in storybooks. What about you?'

'Well, I wouldn't say you'd do awful well at this
time o' year,' Toby was beginning when he broke off
abruptly. 'Here's the market, just about the best place
to shop in the whole of the 'Pool,' he said authori-
tatively. 'Come on, gal, and don't argue when I starts
to bargain over them nice boots o' yourn. Awright?'

'The more money we get the bigger the dinner I'm
going to eat,' Patty said joyfully. 'I say, aren't I glad
you and me met up! But how come you know about
places like this, and that – that canny whatever it was
you told me about just now?'

'Mam and me were on the streets, buskin', for the
best part of a year before she died,' Toby explained,
leading her between the many fascinating stalls with
which the market was crowded. 'You gets to know a
place awful well when you're doin' that.'

'Buskin'? What's that when it's at home?' Patty
asked curiously, following close on his heels and
actually taking hold of the end of his shirt, for it
would, she felt, have been all too easy to lose him in
the crush of bargain-hunters who surrounded them.
'Something to do wi' the fair, is it?'

'Not really. It's what you might call street
entertainment, I suppose,' Toby said. 'Buskers are the
fellers – or women, or kids – who move up an' down
theatre or cinema queues, playin' or tellin' stories or
singin' songs for a few coppers. Now here's the stall
where I selled me shoes. Take 'em off and hang 'em
round your neck by their laces . . . and do *try* not to
look like a perishin' orphan who needs some money.'

Patty would have enquired indignantly just how

she was supposed to do this, but taking off her boots without being knocked over by passers-by proved to be a task which required all her attention, and by the time she had the laces around her neck Toby was pulling her towards the stall he had selected, breaking into a positive hymn of praise to the excellence of the boots the moment he caught the stallholder's eye.

The stallholder was a wispy little woman with fair hair going grey, rather protruding pale blue eyes and quick, bird-like movements. Her stall was piled with second-hand clothing and there was a large section given over to footwear. It did not need the significant jerk of his head to draw Patty's attention to his shoes. They were the only pair on the stall which did not look as though they had been owned – and worn – by half a dozen people before being sold to the little stallholder. Though the stallholder gave them both a bright smile, Patty was sure she would be sharp as an eagle where bargaining was concerned and feared for her new friend's self-esteem, but she need not have worried. Toby gave as good as he got whilst laughing and joking with the woman, and even when she pointed out that the boots were winter ones and would be 'eatin' their bleedin' heads off for the next four or five weeks 'cos no one won't buy winter boots at this time o' year,' Toby was not dismayed.

'Oh aye, so you'll feed 'em wi' boot blacking twice a week, will you? You can't fool me, missus, them boots will go up in price a couple o' pence or even a tanner, so by the time folks is buying for the winter they'll have gained a couple o' bob and probably cost you all of three-farthings in blacking.'

This made the woman laugh and after one more, rather half-hearted attempt to get Toby to reduce his asking price, she sighed deeply, stood the boots at the back of the stall and passed a handful of small change across the counter.

The two children turned away and were soon back on the Scotland Road once more. Here, Toby would have given the cash to Patty but she shook her head. 'I've got no pocket and me knicker elastic's a bit weak; you take care of the money,' she hissed. 'What about my white socks, though, Toby? Shouldn't I take them off as well? They're my Sunday ones, because I'd been for a day out just before I ran away.'

Toby's eyes brightened. 'Take 'em off,' he said at once. 'Another copper or two won't come amiss. Or shall we give 'em to her? I wouldn't mind doin' that, 'cos next time we wants to sell something, it'll be easier.'

'Yes, you give them to her if you want,' Patty said grandly. She had liked the stallholder and quite saw the good sense of a small free gift. 'But what else can we sell, Toby? I won't sell my dress, and I used my coat like a blanket to sleep under last night, so I'd rather not sell that.'

Toby looked critically at the thin brown coat which Patty had tied round her waist, knotting the sleeves in front of her. 'Well, we won't sell it yet,' he said. 'You may need that if it gets any colder.'

Patty felt a smile spreading over her face. It was clear that Toby did not envisage being recaptured too quickly and she was beginning to suspect that what Toby wanted, he usually got. In this case, he wanted his freedom, as did she, so with a bit of luck they really might get away, even stay away.

The two children made their way back into Paddy's market and Toby handed the stallholder the white socks. 'Because next time we wants to sell something, you'll mebbe remember we give you the socks, and make us a good price,' he said, grinning at the woman. 'We'll be seein' you, missus.'

Once outside in the sunshine again, they headed for the nearest canny house and were soon settled in a steamy, smoky little room, filled with chattering, laughing workmen, all intent upon catching the waitress's eye. The tables were made out of old orange boxes, the plates were enamel and the cutlery was tin, but the food, when it eventually came, was excellent. Patty thought it immensely superior to orphanage food, compared it favourably with Mrs Thornton's lovely cooking, and was soon scraping her plate clean with a piece of bread and drinking the last of a mug of strong, sweet tea.

'That were prime, weren't it?' Toby said, as they left the establishment. 'Is we goin' to cross the water or ain't we? If you're set on it, we'll try to get aboard the ferry today, but for meself, I think we need a bit more money. Will they be lookin' out for you yet?'

'I dunno,' Patty said truthfully. 'This is the first time I've run away and I can't remember anyone else ever doing so. What difference does it make?'

'Why, 'cos they'll watch the ferries, o'course, and they'll put the word out to the scuffers to keep an eye on anywhere that a kid might use to kip down in,' Toby said, rather scornfully. 'They'll guess we'll make for the countryside or mebbe even for Ireland, which is where I want to go. Me mam and dad both came from Ireland, years ago, and I've a grosh of relatives there, not all of 'em fair folk. So if it's all the same to you, I'd rather stay in the city and get some pelf so's we can pay our way for a while.'

'And how do you mean to get this money?' Patty asked, rather suspiciously. 'Not by nicking stuff?'

'I telled you. We'll busk to the folk waitin' to get into the theatre or cinema or we'll hang about the stations or the tram stops, and I'll play my whistle and you can sing,' Toby said. 'But if you want something to wear what's a bit less obvious than that dress, then I reckon we'll have to do a bit o' robbin'. Or we could buy somethin' plain and cheap off of that woman what took your boots,' he added thoughtfully. 'What do you say? Shall we get us some money first and then think about catchin' a ferry?'

By this time, Patty already had a good deal of faith in Toby's judgement. If he thought they should stay in the city and earn some money, then she was sure he was right. She said as much, and that evening, when he insisted that they walk out to the suburbs to find themselves somewhere to sleep, she went willingly, though by the time they reached the destination he had in mind she was extremely tired.

'Here we are,' Toby said cheerfully. They had stopped outside a fence of chestnut palings, beyond which were a great many garden plots. Each one had some sort of edifice – a shed or shelter of some kind – erected upon it. The gate into the area was padlocked but Toby and Patty climbed it with ease, dropping down on the other side. It was growing dark by now, but Toby led the way, unerringly, to the shack he had in mind. He ignored the door, which was also padlocked, but went round the back where he carefully removed one of the planks of which it was constructed, squeezing his way into the dark interior and beckoning Patty to follow. 'I've been here several times and no one ever comes near nor by after dark. What's more, there's a pile of sacks in the corner which make a nice soft bed, and if you don't mind a bit of dirt there's usually a bag of potatoes or beetroot or carrots what the feller's taken from the clamps but not took home yet.'

He rooted around and presently he and Patty were curled up amongst the sacks, crunching carrots. 'I could do with a drink of water,' Patty said sleepily, 'but I don't s'pose there's a tap around, is there?' The grit from the carrots had lodged, rather uncomfortably, in her teeth and for the first time she actually missed one aspect of the orphanage: the small pink toothbrush and the round tin of tooth powder which stood on the washstand in her room.

But Toby, it seemed, was equal to most things. 'Yes, there's a tap, so's the fellers what owns the allotments can water their plants,' he said sleepily. 'I usually wash the carrots and spuds under it and have a drink before I settle down, but tonight I was so tired I forgot. Want to come wi' me? Only I've got nothing to bring water back in.'

Patty was about to say that she would go with him when sleep fell upon her as abruptly as a blind descending and she knew no more.

For three glorious days the two children enjoyed their newfound freedom. They did exactly as Toby had planned, playing and singing to the queues of people waiting for admittance to theatres and cinemas in the evenings and doing quite well, especially when Toby began to turn somersaults and cartwheels in between sessions on the penny whistle. He tried to teach Patty to walk on her hands but she was not very good at it, saying it made her feel sick to stay upside down for very long. However, her small, sweet singing voice brought in a good many pennies, though Toby told her that folk paid because she had such pretty yellow

hair and such an appealing look rather than because
they liked her voice.

'You've gorra learn some more sad songs like
"Danny Boy" and "Keep the Home Fires Burning",'
Toby told her earnestly. 'There were tears dripping
off the nose of that fat old woman, what said her son
was in France, when you sang, "Danny Boy". In fact,
most o' the queue were cryin'. It's odd, ain't it, that
they puts more money in the tin when you makes 'em
cry than when I makes 'em laugh.'

Patty thought it was odd too but agreed they
should take advantage of adults' strangenesses and
the two runaways continued to enjoy their free life
and the warm and sunny weather.

Despite Patty's fears, they had not, so far, been
reduced to stealing since their nights were spent in
the allotment shed and the money they made from
busking provided them with one good, cooked meal
a day, as well as a variety of snacks – wet nellies,
cinnamon sticks and an occasional ounce of toffee or
Everton Mints. Although they found the cinema and
theatre queues lucrative places beside which to sing
and play, they had to be careful just where they plied
their new trade. An attempt to do so on Lime Street
station had led to an ugly encounter between themselves and a couple of down-at-heel ex-servicemen
who entertained travellers by playing on an
accordion and a mouth organ. They did not mean to
let a couple of kids invade their pitch. Both men had
been injured in the war – one lacked an arm, the other
a leg and an eye – but this did not stop them from
giving Toby and Patty a good hiding. Limping away
from the station with ringing heads and tingling ears,
the children decided that they had been unwise to try
to horn in on what was obviously a very profitable

business. They never stayed long in one spot, anxious to avoid the attention of the scuffers. 'For once they notice us, they'll remember there's a couple of kids gone missin' from orphanages,' Toby said gloomily. 'But never mind, eh? We's done awright from the flatties, and I guess we'll just give the stations a wide berth in future.'

'Flatties?' Patty said enquiringly. She was growing used to the strange expressions Toby came out with but this was a new one. 'Or did you say fatties?'

'No, you were right first time. Flatties is what fair folk call the customers,' Toby explained. 'I dunno why, except that when you're on a brightly lit roundabout, or one of them stalls, faces just look like flat white discs – you can't tell one from t'other.'

That night, when they returned to the shed to sleep, Toby produced a cocoa tin with a triumphant flourish. 'Something to carry water in,' he told her. 'We can have a proper supper tonight 'cos I bought two of them Cornish pasties from George Kelly's on Heyworth Street while you was queuing for a drink by the water tap. They was goin' cheap 'cos Kelly's never sell two-day goods.'

Patty thought this was grand and the two of them had a proper little midnight supper. They even lit a candle, though it was only a stub of a thing which someone had thrown out with the rest of their rubbish, and by its light they drank cocoa-flavoured water and ate their Cornish pasties, not bothering with the carrots tonight since Toby said they would save them for breakfast.

After such a feast, both children slept soundly – overslept, in fact, since a ray of sunshine falling on her face was the first intimation to Patty that day had arrived. She jumped out of her bed of sacks, shook her fellow conspirator by the shoulder and told him in a hissing whisper that they'd best make themselves scarce. 'We're late; there's folks abroad already,' she hissed huskily. 'Best get away before we're caught.'

They managed to sneak out of the shed without being seen and climbed rapidly over the gate, Patty scratching her leg rather nastily on some barbed wire. Then they made for the docks and the canny house which, they knew by now, would sell them a sausage sandwich for a couple of pence. Because they were late, they did not go first to a tap to clean themselves up, but raked their fingers through their hair and brushed off the dirt and crumbs as best they could before presenting themselves at the counter.

'Toby, I think we'd best go somewhere different tomorrow,' Patty said thoughtfully, as they strolled along, watching people hurrying past them. 'The woman who served us in the canny house gave me a very funny look, I thought. You said we don't want folks noticing us but I reckon it's a bit late. She has – noticed us, I mean.'

Toby pulled her to a halt and looked at her critically. 'You do look a bit of a mess,' he observed. 'I hadn't noticed before, but you've got bits of straw in your hair and there's a sort of line round your neck where you've washed so far and no further. Mind, there's plenty o' kids who look a deal worse than you do. Most of 'em rove the docks beggin' for pennies or offering to cart shopping or goods of some description for anything they can get. As for the cane marks on your cheek, they're beginning to fade. No, I reckon we're safe enough if we just disappear each time we see a scuffer. What'll we do today?'

'I don't know,' Patty said, rather helplessly. 'I don't know anything about the city, except what you've told me.' She looked wistfully across at the waters of the Mersey, gleaming gold under the autumn sun. 'Do you remember telling me about New Brighton? I suppose we couldn't . . . ?'

'No, we couldn't,' Toby said bluntly. 'It's too soon; I told you they'd be watchin' the ferries and they will. Give it another two days, and we might get away with it, especially if we could get some dark handkerchief to hide your hair. Tell you what, though, there's always the canal.'

Patty had heard of canals in her geography lessons, had even seen pictures of them, and was intrigued to learn that there was a canal in Liverpool. 'Could we go there?' she asked eagerly. 'I remember one of the teachers saying ordinary folks, folks like us, live on the canal in barges painted all over with pictures. I'd love to see them.'

'Yes, we can go there, and what's more there's all sorts you can do by the canal,' Toby told her. 'If we goes up by Tate & Lyle's – that's the sugar factory – we can go for a swim. There's outlets from the factory which lead directly into the canal and the water the factory has used is warm as toast. All the kids in these parts who can't afford to go in the swimming pool muck about in the Scaldy, as they call it. Can you swim?'

'I expect so,' Patty said. She assumed that if one could walk and run, one could probably also swim, but when she told Toby this he assured her she was mistaken.

'It's quite different; you use your arms and legs like a frog does, not a bit like walking or running,' he explained. 'Dogs are the only ones who swim like they run – there's a swimming stroke called a doggy paddle – but even that's got to be learned. Tell you what, you can dangle your legs in the water and watch me and when you think you can do it, you can have a go. How about it, eh?'

The two children had a wonderful time by the canal and this was fortunate, since it proved to be their last day of freedom. In their haste to leave the shed on the allotment that morning, they had left a good many clues behind them: the end of the stub of candle, a great many crumbs from the Cornish pasties, and the cocoa tin half full of water. When they returned to the shed that evening, all unsuspecting, they had barely taken the planks out at the back and crawled inside when they were frozen in a beam of torchlight and a deep voice said triumphantly: 'Gotcher! Willy, guard the back! So that's the way you got in, you young ruffians!' It was the shed owner, who, as he told them, had realised as soon as he saw the candle and the cocoa tin that someone had been sleeping rough in his shed. Further investigation had revealed that someone had also been eating his carrots and, incensed by the thought that the hard work he had put in was being harvested by another, he had told the local bobby of his suspicions.

Constable Willy Robson had immediately put two and two together and, as it happened, made four. All the police were on the look-out for two kids missing from two different orphanages; if he apprehended them, it would be a feather in his cap, or rather his helmet. So he and the allotment owner had lain in wait and as soon as the constable clapped eyes on Patty's startlingly white-gold hair he had known that he had been right. These were the missing orphans and he would doubtless be lavishly praised by his senior officers for his perspicacity in capturing them.

Constable Robson asked the allotment owner if he

wished to press charges – the vegetables had been stolen after all – but the man said he would not do so. 'They'll be in enough trouble wi'out me complainin' over a few missin' veg,' he said gruffly. 'As for sleepin' on the sacks, there were no harm in that. And I'd rather the mice ate up the crumbs they left than gnawed their way through me new season's carrots.'

Patty and Toby, both held in the firm grasp of the law, looked at him with real gratitude. He was a short, bald man whose pale blue eyes behind ancient, steel-rimmed spectacles were as innocent as a baby's, and when he smiled Patty saw that his gums were also like a baby's, since he did not have a tooth in his head. Constable Robson seemed rather disappointed that he would not 'press charges' and tried a couple of times to impress him with the enormity of what the children had done, but fortunately it made no difference. 'I'm not even sure as they did eat any of me carrots,' the man said obstinately, when Constable Robson said it was his civil duty to prosecute. 'Gerralong with you, Willy, weren't you never a kid yourself? Didn't you never go scrumpin' apples in other folks' orchards?'

Strangely enough, this brought a reminiscent gleam to the constable's eye. 'Boxing the fox, we called it in Dublin,' he said dreamily. 'Oh aye, everyone did it in them days. So you reckon nickin' the odd carrot is no worse'n boxing the fox, do you? Well, I dare say you're right and it's certain sure they'll be in deep trouble enough when I gets 'em back to the places they've run away from.' He jerked their wrists, though not unkindly. 'Come on, young 'uns, it's the police station for you and a nice cell until we've informed Durrant House and St Peter's that we've got their runaways. A'course, you'll be on bread an' water till you're fetched, 'cos that's all we ever serves in police stations.'

Everyone laughed except Patty, who thought it was the truth. But presently they were taken to the police station where they were given large mugs of lovely hot tea and a thick round of bread and dripping each. Whilst Constable Robson went to make his report, they had their one chance, as it turned out, of a private word and used it to good advantage.

'We'll gerrout again,' Toby whispered hoarsely, 'because it's been grand, hasn't it? We might have made it to Ireland – or at least to the Wirral – if we'd not overslept last night and left clues for the old feller to find. You gals take your walks in Prince's Park, don't you? Same as we do, only I reckon we go different days and different times.'

Patty nodded. 'Yes, we do,' she said eagerly. 'But we never see other kids from orphan asylums, or not that I've noticed. Why, what are you planning, Toby?'

'There's a stone wall, partly tumbling down,' Toby said rapidly. 'It's gorra loose stone shaped like a dog's head what's well within my reach, so you'll be able to reach it too. If I gerraway again, I'll shove a note behind the stone, telling you where I'll be and at what time, then you can make a break for it as well. But if you goes first, you leave a note for me – OK?'

'It sounds all right, but we only go to the park once a week, or sometimes twice,' Patty said worriedly. 'And when the weather's bad, we don't go there at all because it makes a mess of our boots and we get mud splashes on the skirts of our coats. You could leave me a message and I might not see it for a couple of weeks.'

Toby sighed deeply. 'It's the best I can think of,' he said. 'Tell you what, if me note's still there after a day or so, I'll come round to Durrant House, and get a message to you somehow. Hey up, someone's comin'. Norranother word.'

He was right, someone was indeed coming. Miss Briggs and a spare, cold-eyed man in a grey flannel suit entered the room together and, almost as though they were twin souls, began berating their charges simultaneously. Patty and Toby bowed their heads beneath the storm and only spoke to say how sorry they were and how deeply they repented their naughtiness, for this had been agreed between them whilst they drank their tea and ate their bread and dripping. And presently, their mentors took them back to their orphan asylums, Miss Briggs saying sourly, as she pushed Patty ahead of her into Durrant House, 'Not that I worried over you, Patty Peel! I knew you'd turn up again, like a bad penny.'

For Patty a weary vista of detentions and circumscribed meals stretched ahead. She had expected to be hauled up before Matron, but on this occasion, at least, she was spared that fate. Laura told her, as they lay in their beds that night, that Miss O'Dowd had been called back to her previous position to take over for a short period since her replacement there had become ill. But Patty neither knew nor cared if this were true. All she knew was that, had Miss O'Dowd been present, her punishment would have been a good deal more severe. Miss Briggs might not like her – did not like her – but because of the new matron's behaviour to the staff Miss Briggs was taking a positive pleasure in ignoring what she imagined were Miss O'Dowd's wishes, and treating the runaway with a certain amount of leniency.

Patty realised she would not be allowed to see Selina until her running away had been forgotten, however, and accordingly, over the next few weeks, she concentrated all her efforts upon being a model pupil and a meek and obedient child. By the time Miss O'Dowd returned to her post Patty's absence was truly a thing of the past and, since the matron did not allude to it, Patty hoped that she either had not heard about the runaway or had simply let it slip her mind.

Patty was too wise, now, in the ways of adults to expect to be allowed any treats or outings for some time to come, and though she looked behind the stone in the wall whenever she had the opportunity she guessed that Toby, too, would be closely watched for a while, at least. By the same token, of course, her trips out with Selina and her Friday afternoons at the house in Peel Street became a thing of the past, and Patty did not refer to them. She would bide her time, wait until Matron had a day off or departed on some mysterious errand, and then she would ask permission to see her dear friend again.

The days became weeks, Christmas came and went, and Patty was still being an exemplary pupil. A few days before Christmas, Laura's mother had come up trumps at last and invited her daughter – and her daughter's friend – to visit her whenever they were allowed. Both girls seized the opportunity joyfully for now Patty could resume her visits to Selina with no one the wiser since the staff – and presumably Matron – thought that she was at Mrs Reilly's tiny house off the Scotland Road. Gradually, as spring became summer and summer faded into autumn once more, Patty almost gave up hope that she would ever see or hear from Toby again. But she did not forget him. Over and over, when she lay in her narrow bed with the other girls snoring and snuffling around her, she relived those exciting three days of freedom, and longed to find a note behind the stone in the wall. Sometimes she thought she saw him as the crocodile of girls from Durrant House wended its way through the streets or the park. Sometimes, when she and Laura set off for a day with Mrs Reilly, she would imagine that the boy ahead of her was Toby, but when she hurried and caught him up it was always a stranger.

No one but Laura knew anything about her friendship with Toby, because she had always pretended she had spent the three days alone. Miss Briggs, it appeared, had merely been told that both orphans had been recaptured, not that they had been recaptured together, so that was all right. Patty had even been cautious about telling Selina, because her friend had warned her about the unreliability and general mischievousness of boys and might scold her for trusting one of them, but when a year had gone by without a word from Toby she decided to take her friend into her confidence, and was glad she had done so.

'You were lucky because Matron was away and Miss Briggs didn't tell on you, but I don't suppose your pal Toby had the same luck,' Selina had said wisely, when Patty told her the whole story. 'But when you ran off, queen, you were running from injustice. This young feller, this Toby Rudd, hadn't been whacked across the face with a cane or wrongly accused, had he? He was just trying to get away, back to his own folk. He'll do it again just as soon as he can I don't doubt, but that doesn't mean you should. From what you've told me you're in good standing at Durrant House right now, and you're eleven years old so you've not got all that long to go before you're a trusted senior, with a deal more freedom. Just keep your nose clean and work hard and you'll gerrout of the orphan asylum legal-like, without having half the scuffers in Liverpool on your trail. Isn't that a good deal better than running off again, getting caught, and being in a heap o' trouble?'

Half reluctantly, Patty agreed that it was, but she still kept looking behind the loose stone in the wall, half hoping that, one day, there would be a message from Toby.

But as time passed, she began to think that Toby must have gone. He was clearly the sort of boy who would not meekly sit down and wait until he could legally leave the orphanage and besides, unlike herself, he had a destination – a destiny, almost – in mind. There might have been a note, taken by some other child, or there might not have been, but she began insensibly to believe that Toby was either dead – horrid thought – or gone from the city. And though she continued to look in the wall whenever she was able to do so, there was never a note, never a word.

Patty still dreamed but she ceased, in her heart, to hope.

Chapter Six
Spring 1933

'Well, Mrs Brierley, your pulse and temperature are both normal,' Patty said, having scrutinised the thermometer which she had just removed from her patient's mouth, 'and little Miss Brierley seems to be doing well. Have you any worries? If so, you can tell me about them whilst I check your stomach.' Patty placed her hand flatly on the woman's still swollen abdomen and pressed down gently but firmly, to check that all was well with the uterus. 'Any pain or discomfort, Mrs Brierley? I've already dealt with the baby's umbilicus and everything there is fine.'

'Yes, Nurse. I'm gettin' sort o' crampy pains,' said the young woman lying in the rumpled bed. 'They aren't there all the time but they comes now and again. I s'pose you could say they was a bit like early labour pains, though not – not quite as bad. I – I hopes as they ain't nothin' serious?'

'Oh, no, don't worry, it's just a sign that everything's going back into its proper place,' Patty assured her patient. She drew the blanket up over the other woman's stomach and smiled down at her. 'Where's your mam, queen? She told me yesterday, after Baby was born, that she'd be staying with you for a week or so, but there was no sign of her when I came through the kitchen.'

'She came round early and got breakfast for all of us – that's herself, me and me old man – and now she's gone home to see to me dad and the house before

161

doin' the messages, but she'll be back in time for dinner,' Mrs Brierley explained. 'She's that delighted with my little Flossie that she could scarcely tear herself away.' She looked shyly up at Patty. 'I think she loves this one all the more 'cos I lost the first,' she finished.

'Very understandable,' Patty said briskly, beginning to put her instruments back into her little black bag. 'I expect your breasts are feeling a little swollen and sore? You know that this is merely the milk coming in; has Baby been fed today?'

'Oh aye, and she sucked like a right 'un,' Mrs Brierley said. 'Me mam's goin' to deal with the dirty nappies and gowns and so on, but when can I gerrup, Nurse? I know I'm lucky being an only child so Mam's only got me to worry about, but I'd like to be able to help out a bit.'

'Give it a week if you can,' Patty said, thinking ruefully of the many mothers on her district who had no choice but to get up, sometimes within hours of the birth. 'No need to stay in bed all that time, mind; you can sit in a chair by the fire, make a cup of tea, potter about gently. But no heavy work and no leaving the house. And when I say you can do these things, you shouldn't be up for more than an hour or two a day.' She reached the door and turned to smile at her patient. 'See you tomorrow, Mrs Brierley.'

The visit to Mrs Brierley was typical of many Patty paid that day. She saw one patient who had given birth to her fifteenth child; a puny, large-headed little creature whose constant wailings were already causing the family much annoyance. She visited a mother of twins, who met her at the door with her five-day-old babies tucked into her shawl, since she intended to do her messages before the other kids came back from school. Remonstrating with her would have been useless, but Patty persuaded her to return to the kitchen so that she could take her pulse and temperature and check her physical well-being, after she had first examined the twins.

'It's a mortally cold day, despite the sunshine,' Patty said gently, as she changed the dressings on the babies' umbilical cords. 'Why don't you ask a neighbour to do your messages, Mrs Smith? It really isn't good for you to go out into this wind, carrying two great babies so soon after the birth. Come to that, it isn't very good for the babies either!'

Mrs Smith was a big, ginger-haired woman, with a squint and most of her teeth missing. She was clearly astonished at Patty's words but agreed, rather doubtfully, that perhaps the wind was a bit keen. When Patty offered to go next door, she was quite willing to accept help.

Patty left the house after half an hour, wondering how Mrs Smith's large brood managed to survive. She knew it was largely ignorance and not deliberate neglect and could not help wondering what sort of a man Mr Smith was. Despite attending three of Mrs Smith's lyings-in, she had never yet met the master of the house. However, it was none of her business and, as usual, she had other patients to visit, so she bicycled briskly along the narrow, dirt-splattered roadway towards her next case.

As soon as she reached the house, she knew that there was trouble here which she could not deal with alone. The new mother, a woman in her late forties, lay groaning and tossing amidst filthy sheets in the tiny bedroom. When Patty took her pulse, her heart sank, for it was racing at an incredible speed and her temperature was 104 degrees. She seemed to know

Patty but ordered her, quite sharply, to take the baby out of the room since the child's wails had given her a terrible headache. 'What's more, you only brung out one of the babies; there's another in there, I'm sure of it,' she wheezed hoarsely. 'Me stummick is swole up like a bleedin' balloon and it hurts me somethin' cruel. You've gorra do somethin', Nurse.'

Patty looked round the room. There was no sound from the baby fast asleep in its makeshift bed but she realised that her patient was delirious and almost certainly suffering from puerperal fever. Patty went to the head of the stairs and called down to the eldest child present, a girl of fifteen or sixteen. She told her to boil water and to send someone for the doctor and then began, grimly, to do what she could for her patient.

Much later, knowing that the woman was in good hands, Patty left the house. Dr Carruthers was held in high esteem by all the midwives and, though he had looked worried when he first entered the bedroom, a few quick-fire questions and an examination had been enough to reassure him that this was not the deadly strain of the disease.

'There's no septicaemia present since there has been no vomiting, and the abdominal wall, though distended, is by no means rigid,' he told Patty. 'Infection is obviously present, so you had best go home and disinfect your clothing and do all that is necessary. I'll get a replacement to finish your visits and someone else to see to things here. Thank you for calling me in good time, Nurse.'

When she got home later that afternoon, she had done no more than bath and change her clothing before a knock came on the door. Patty crossed the room and flung it open. Mrs Clarke stood there, looking anxious. 'Oh, it *is* you, Patty! I thought it were when you passed me window. Have you a moment? Can I have a word?'

'Yes, of course,' Patty said, ushering the other woman into her warm kitchen. 'Where are the children?'

'They're asleep in the pram. It's just outside your door,' Mrs Clarke explained. 'I won't risk bringin' them in, because I were just off to do me messages when I saw you pass, so they're well wrapped up, the little darlin's.'

'That's all right then; I'll pull the kettle over the flame,' Patty said, suiting the action to her words. 'I could just do with a cuppa. I wonder if Maggie has left me any scones?'

Maggie proved to have left several scones, so Patty buttered two of them, made two cups of tea and then glanced enquiringly across at her visitor. 'Well, has something gone wrong? I know Merrell can't be ill or unhappy because you'd have told me straight off.'

'No-o-o, but it ain't exactly good news, or not in one way, it ain't,' Mrs Clarke admitted. 'D'you remember when we first met, I told you I'd been workin' in a clothing factory? Well, they've offered me me old job back on an increased salary and me old feller says I should take it. Naturally, I can't look after Merrell or Christopher when I'm workin' so me and Ronnie talked it over and the upshot was I went along to Mrs Knight's flat and – and axed her if she'd be willin' to have Christopher whenever I were workin'. I told her I was sure Maggie would have both kids durin' the school holidays and – and I think Mrs Knight got hold of the wrong end of the stick. Anyroad, she said she'd be delighted to have both Christopher and

Merrell – she even said she'd give Maggie a meal, when she were off school – so – so I said I'd have to talk to you first and here I am.' She had been looking down at the floor but now she shot an anxious glance at Patty through her lashes. 'I hope I done right. I know you're friendly wi' Mrs Knight, her being next door to you, an' you know she loves kids. She's ever so good wi' babies and often says how she envies other women her age who've got grandchildren round them all day. So what d'you say, Nurse?'

Patty opened her mouth to reply and immediately remembered how thin were the walls of the flats. She hoped, desperately, that neither Mrs Knight nor Darky were home at this moment. She said uneasily: 'Oh, I do like her. She's ever so nice and she's really fond of Merrell as well. She made her the pink flowered Vyella dress which I keep for best and she knitted the pink cardy which she wears over it. I do agree she'd be a marvellous person to look after the babies, only – only what about Darky?' Patty had lowered her voice still further on the last few words but Mrs Clarke, it seemed, had no such inhibitions.

'Oh, men don't count when it comes to lookin' after babies,' she said. 'He won't have nothin' to do with either Christopher or Merrell. Mostly he'll be out at work – he's an electrician out at Levers, you know – but even if he happens to be workin' some weird shift, he won't take no notice of 'em. I told Mrs Knight we'd pay her five bob a week between us, but to tell you the truth I think she'd ha' done it for love, she's that fond o' kids. So what d'you think?'

Patty felt as a Christian must feel in the arena when the lions come roaring in. It was all very well for Mrs Clarke but Patty happened to know that Darky greeted her with casual friendliness when they met.

She had even seen him bend over the pram and make some remark about the way Christopher was growing, though he always ignored Merrell and had continued to look through Patty rather than at her whenever they met. 'Well . . . is she in now?' Patty hissed. 'More to the point, is young Mr Knight in? I don't suppose you've noticed, but he doesn't like me at all – won't even give me the time of day when we meet. I can't think he'd welcome his mam having Merrell because it would mean either Maggie or myself being back and forth quite a bit.'

'Are you sure Darky don't speak to you?' Mrs Clarke said, her tone incredulous. 'I know they say he's quiet and has been ever since his wife died, but he's never rude – or not to anyone I know, at any rate. He often asks after the kids when he meets me wheeling the pram and usually comments on how they're growin'. He chucks Merrell under the chin and tells her she'll break hearts one of these days, just like anyone else might do.'

'Oh!' Patty said, considerably surprised. 'Well, perhaps he doesn't hold any grudge against Merrell then, but he definitely doesn't like me. Honest to God, Mrs Clarke, he won't meet my eye if he can help it. But if he has no choice, he'll glare at me as though I were his worst enemy, and so far as I know I've never offended him in any way.'

After a few moments' frowning thought, Mrs Clarke's brow cleared. 'There may be a reason for the way he treats you,' she said thoughtfully. 'His wife died giving birth to a dead baby. Mrs Knight says the baby were comin' awkward, upside down and round about. Breech I think they calls it. Darky weren't there o' course, but his mam were and she wanted the midwife to call the doctor as soon as she realised how tired young Mrs Knight were gettin'. Apparently the midwife – she were an elderly woman called Mrs Thripp – refused to get the doctor, saying she'd managed many a breech birth without help from anyone. She and the doctor on call that night were sworn enemies and she were determined to manage alone.

'In the end, Mrs Knight defied her and sent someone for the doctor but by the time he arrived it were too late; mother and child were too far gone to save either and the doctor made no bones about tellin' Darky that if the midwife had called him sooner, it might have been possible to save them. I've heered Darky's pals say that he hates all nurses, especially midwives, so probably he don't see you as a person but just as a member of the profession. Does that explain it, d'you think?'

'I suppose it might,' Patty said thoughtfully. 'Well, he can like me or dislike me, I'm indifferent to how he feels, but I dare not risk his interfering with Merrell in any way. I'll have a chat with Mrs Knight, I think, before making up my mind.'

'Yes, you'd best do that,' Mrs Clarke agreed, getting to her feet. 'But fancy you not havin' a bit of a weakness for Darky! All the girls is crazy about him, and he's got a real good job and a nice regular salary as well. I didn't know him before he married, but I believe all the girls were wild for him then, including his wife, o' course.' She sighed deeply. 'Oh, his wife were lovely. She was from Edinburgh and had beautiful red-gold hair, ever such white skin and the softest, prettiest Scotch accent you can imagine. He were heartbroken when she died – who wouldn't be – but everyone thought he'd marry again because until he got wed he were a real one for the girls. He goes to dances now, and to the flicks, and when Levers take parties of workers to the coast for a day, he goes along wi' the rest. The girls at Levers say he's always polite and friendly enough but never singles any one person out for special attention. It's an awful shame 'cos he's so good-looking. He reminds me of Rudolph Valentino only o' course Darky's hair is curly, not all slicked back. Anyway, if he don't speak to you I reckon it's just because you're a nurse.'

'Oh, that makes it much easier to bear,' Patty said with a sarcasm which passed Mrs Clarke completely by, for she nodded vigorously.

'Yes, it does, because you know it ain't personal,' she said. 'Why's you home at this time of day, anyroad? You're earlier than usual; does that mean you want Merrell back now?'

'Better not,' Patty said. 'All my instruments have to be sterilised and things like dressings burned 'cos I've been nursing a contagious case. As soon as I'm able, though, I shall go round and talk to Mrs Knight. Then I'll come round to you, so if you'll hang on to Merrell till then I shall be very grateful.'

As soon as Mrs Clarke had left Patty finished her work and then set out for the house next door. Mrs Knight welcomed her in and, as Mrs Clarke had done, asked her what she was doing at home in the middle of the afternoon. Patty looked round cautiously as she explained what had happened, but there was no sign of Darky. She knew he worked shifts at Levers but guessed he was doing days at present, so accepted Mrs Knight's offer of tea and shortbread and a seat by her glowing stove. There was no need to tell Mrs Knight why she was there. Her neighbour beamed at her and said expansively: 'Ada Clarke explained she were goin' back to work and that you'd both like me to keep an eye on the little 'uns durin' term time,' she said. 'I were downright honoured to think that you'd trust me with little Merrell, but I can promise you she'll have every care while she's under this roof, same as Christopher will, of course. It were a terrible blow to me when young Alison died and lost her baby, because I've always longed for grandchildren. But there you are, there's sadness in every life and my poor lad has had to suffer more than most.'

'Yes, I've heard that young Mrs Knight died tragically,' Patty said gently. 'I'm so sorry, Mrs Knight. But are you quite sure that your son won't mind you taking Merrell in? It might bring the sad times back, make him realise what he's missed. I wouldn't want that to happen. And what about when he's on a night shift and needs quiet during the day so he can sleep?'

'Oh, don't you worry yourself about that, queen,' Mrs Knight said comfortably. 'When Darky's doing a night relay – they call 'em relays and not shifts at Levers – I'll take the babies out walking in their pram if I think they're goin' to disturb him. He has cousins living out Bootle way and two of the girls have kids of their own, all under school age. Darky fairly dotes on 'em, seems to find it easier talkin' to kids than grown-ups, to own the truth. I just wish he'd meet some nice young woman and settle down with her, but he says it's too soon. "Four years is a long time," I tell him but he says he can't forget and what's more he don't want to. The Father told me that time is a great healer, and though Darky may never forget his little wife, one day he will be able to remember her without pain. When that happens, he'll be ready to take up his life again.'

Patty made sympathetic noises and presently she

and Mrs Knight got down to business and talked through the arrangements which must be made as soon as Mrs Clarke returned to her factory bench. Mrs Knight repeated her offer to give Maggie and the two little ones a midday meal during the school holidays but Patty, unwilling to commit her little friend until they had talked it over, said vaguely that the question would not arise for a while.

'Maggie and I will have a good old jangle this evening and sort out times and so on,' Patty assured the older woman. 'I can't tell you how grateful I am for your kindness, Mrs Knight. I really don't trust a child minder to do the right thing by Merrell; I shall be far happier knowing that she's in your charge.'

'Aren't I just lookin' forward to the summer now!' Mrs Knight said, accompanying Patty on to the landing. 'I don't mind telling you, Nurse, that it's been a pretty lonely life for me, wi' Darky working. And he's a changed feller since Alison's death. We used to have a hand of cards before the fire in winter, or he'd bring pals in for a few drinks and some sandwiches. I'm mortal fond o' whist drives and I used to belong to the Townswomen's Guild but I give that all up after Darky came back to live in Ashfield Place.' For the first time she looked a little confused. 'It – it seemed kind o' mean to go out and about on me own affairs when my poor boy was stuck in, wi' nowt but memories.'

'Well, perhaps looking after the children will be good for both of you,' Patty said. 'After all, you'll be wanting to take them out in the afternoons, especially when summer comes, and I don't see why you shouldn't start going to whist drives again because I believe your son goes out most evenings.'

'Well, maybe I will,' Mrs Knight said. She sounded

very much more cheerful. 'To tell the truth, Nurse, I've let things slide a bit, but wi' the little 'uns to keep me busy during the day I reckon I'll be more cheerful altogether. Tell you what, how about you an' me takin' ourselves off on a bit of a spree – wi' the kids, of course, an' Maggie – one weekend. We could go to Rhyl by charabanc when summer comes; it 'ud be good for all of us.'

Chuckling to herself, Patty opened the door, and said it sounded like a good idea. Although she had been uncertain at first, she felt now that Mrs Clarke's suggestion had been a good one from which they would probably all benefit. Satisfied that she was doing the right thing, Patty returned to her own home, poked the fire into a blaze and began to prepare their tea.

'You've done *what*?' Darky's voice rose and his mother put a finger to her lips and jerked her head significantly at the party wall between their flat and that of Nurse Peel. 'Mam, you're impossible! You can't want that . . . that little tart in and out of here whenever she pleases, just because—'

'Derek! I oughter make you wash your perishin' mouth out wi' carbolic soap! Just who d'you think you're callin' a tart? Merrell? Or young Maggie? Come to that, you can't possibly mean Nurse Peel herself – a nicer, more sensible young woman never breathed! Why, she's bringin' her little one up beautifully, never stints what she spends on her, no doubt constantly goes without herself . . . and she's the same wi' young Maggie, what's no kin o' hers! I were talkin' to Maggie only the other day and she told me that Nurse Peel pays Mr Mullins half a crown every week so's she can keep Maggie livin' wi' her and the littl'un. There's not many what would do that; many a family teks on a cousin or a niece to help wi' their kids but they're more likely to ask for money than to hand it over. And what's more, if anyone hears what you've been sayin' there'll be no question of me taking care of Nurse Peel's little girl or the little Clarke boy and I really want to have them. They'll be company like, so I'll thank you to keep a civil tongue in your head when you're talking about our neighbour. Indeed, I'm ashamed that any son o' mine should think such things, lerralone say 'em.'

Darky tightened his lips, though he felt the hot colour rise to his cheeks. The trouble was, he had never told his mam what he thought of Nurse Peel, never admitted that he had listened to her spreading gossip about himself. Perhaps he should have done so. As it was, his dislike must seem illogical. He took a deep breath and tried to speak out boldly. 'The truth is, Mam, I overheard her tellin' Mrs Clarke that I'd tried to top meself after Alison died. I've done me best to forget that awful time and, as I've told you – and I told the police – it were an accident. I were just so desperate for a night's sleep that I took too many aspirin tablets. I don't deny I were terribly unhappy but I'm not a fool. If I'd really meant to kill meself, I'd have done it properly, not made such a poor job of it.'

He tried to make the last remark sound light and amusing but his mother did not smile. 'Look, son,' she said. 'You spend too much time dwelling on what's past and gone. If Nurse Peel told Mrs Clarke anything she don't know already, I'll be rare surprised. After all, no one can cover up police inquiries and you being lugged off to hospital in view of all your neighbours. Nurse Peel didn't even live here when you was brought back to my place, so if you ask me it's likelier that young Ada were explaining to the nurse why you lived here wi' your mam and don't go out wi' girls much. And if you want to stop that sort of gossip, there's an easy way to do it: go out more; start acting like other young fellers instead of stalking around lookin' miserable.'

It had not occurred to Darky until his mother had said so but now, thinking it over, he realised that it was quite possibly Ada Clarke who had done most of the gossiping. Even so, he still did not like the thought of Nurse Peel's having the run of his home, and decided that if he did not stop it now he would be in no position to do so later.

'Well, son? I can read you like a book! You know I'm right, don't you. It were Ada tellin' Nurse Peel and not the other way round.'

'Yes, I reckon you're right at that,' Darky said grudgingly. 'But she's a bleedin' midwife and it were one of them what caused Alison's death, you know it were. What's more, I told you before, Mam, she's no better'n she should be. She comes here wi' her love-child, bold as brass, tellin' decent women like Ada Clarke and Lizzie Clitheroe how to run their lives . . .'

'Nonsense,' Mrs Knight said briskly. 'I know it were a long time ago but it's no secret that your dad and me wed because you were on the way! The trouble was we'd had a long engagement, and an understandin' even longer than that . . . but you wouldn't call me a tart, would you, son?'

Darky grinned, admitting defeat, he knew, and suddenly not minding all that much. 'Not twice I wouldn't, Mam,' he said. 'So all right, I shouldn't have called her a tart, but with you, Dad were always in the background, eager to get wed an' make an honest woman of you. I've never seen a feller near number twenty-four. Why, the girl ain't even courtin' from what folks say.'

Mrs Knight sniffed. *'From what folks say,'* she mimicked. 'So who's gossipin' now, eh, lad?'

Darky laughed outright and turned to give his mother a hug. You had to admire her spirit and quickness of mind; it would be a clever feller who could put one over on his mam. 'OK, OK, I give in,' he said, still smiling. 'If you want to look after half the neighbourhood then it's up to you, and I'm sure Nurse Peel will pay you regular and behave as she ought and I'll try to be polite if I possibly can.'

'A decent feller's polite to all women,' his mother said reprovingly. She went over to their pantry and began to get out the ingredients for tea. 'As for dislikin' someone because of their job – well, I've never heard of anything so foolish! Your father were run over by a brewer's dray delivering ale to the pub on the corner but it hasn't stopped you from enjoying a pint, nor I don't steer clear of the Jug and Bottle in case I might see the driver who killed your dad. Live and let live, I say, and I don't go blamin' folk for what they had no hand in. It's time, chuck, that you did likewise.'

'I'll do me best, Mam,' Darky said. He knew his mother was right really. It was high time he stopped dwelling on what had happened and could never be put right and started building his life again. He had contemplated getting a place of his own over the water, perhaps in Port Sunlight itself, but the recollection of how cold and lonely his little terraced house had seemed after Alison's death put him off such a move. Unless he remarried, he told himself, he would prefer to stay at Ashfield Place, despite the long journey to work.

'Oh, damn!' Mrs Knight said suddenly, putting an oval plate and a loaf of bread down on the table. 'I'm right out of margarine, son. Pop down to the corner shop, like the good feller you are, and get me half a pound of Stork. It won't take you a minute.'

'OK, Mam. I'm glad you're supporting Levers by buying our products,' Darky said, grinning. He left the flat and hurried along the balcony to clatter down the stairs two at a time, and was almost at the bottom when he saw young Maggie coming up.

The child grinned. 'Hello, Mr Knight,' she said politely. 'Off to work, are you?'

'No, I'm gettin' the messages for me mam,' Darky said. He decided to start as his mam meant him to go on and fished in his pocket for some loose change. 'Tell you what, queen, want to earn yourself a penny? Me mam wants half a pound of Stork margarine. Would you like to get it and deliver it to our place?'

'Sure I would,' Maggie said gratefully, taking the handful of cash. 'But where's I to go?'

'The corner shop will be fine, duck,' he said and returned to his home, feeling a positive glow of rectitude. He told his mother that Maggie had gone for the margarine and Mrs Knight nodded approvingly. 'She's a grand little lass,' she observed. 'When the school holidays come, I'm arrangin' to give her a midday dinner, along o' the two babies. I'll enjoy it, you know, having youngsters about me.' She smiled a trifle wistfully up at her tall son. 'I'm glad we're pullin' together over me givin' an eye to the kids,' she said gently. 'It ain't the money – you've always been generous – it's just that I miss having young things about me. To tell you the truth, I can't wait for Monday mornin' when Ada Clarke starts work at the factory!'

It was a bright August day. When Patty arrived home, she found Maggie and Mrs Knight facing one another across the kitchen table whilst the two children played happily on a large blanket surrounded by cushions. Merrell was walking now and Christopher beginning to toddle, though he had frequent falls, hence the blanket. For a moment, she stood in the doorway surveying the scene and reflecting how very lucky she was. Everything had worked out well, with Mrs Knight clearly enjoying the children's company and the children loving her dearly. Merrell, who was already talking quite a lot, called her 'Nanna', and Christopher was already trying to follow suit. As for Maggie, she had taken to Mrs Knight's ways like a duck to water and was eager to learn anything the older woman could teach her. Even though it was the summer holidays and Maggie was now officially in charge of the two children, she spent most of her day with Mrs Knight. They shopped together, and went to the park to feed the ducks, or to the playground for the swings and slides. They ate together at dinner time, and Mrs Knight appreciated Maggie's help. She very sensibly worked out the finances of such meals, but since she only charged for ingredients Patty often felt guilty and so had begun to suggest that dinner should be prepared alternately in Nos. 23 and 24.

Maggie, looking up, smiled at Patty in the doorway. 'We had our dinner here today,' she said cheerfully, 'and Mrs Knight has been teaching me to make lemon barley water.' She turned to her companion. 'We've made gallons, haven't we? Enough for both our families with a bit over for Mrs Clarke, because Mrs Knight says lemon barley water is good for babies when the weather's as hot as this. D'you like it, Patty?'

Patty had longed ceased to be 'Auntie' as far as Maggie was concerned. She was beginning to say that she was very fond of lemon barley water and could do with a glass of it right now when Merrell, who had been piling garishly coloured wooden bricks into a tower, spotted her. She jumped to her feet, knocking the tower all over the place, and rushed across the room, squeaking: 'Mummy! Mummy! Mummy back!' and hugging Patty so tightly around the knees that she nearly pulled her over.

Laughing and staggering a little, Patty picked the child up, hugged her and plonked a kiss on her shining fair curls before remarking: 'Yes, all right, queen, you're right, I'm home!' She turned to Mrs Knight. 'I'm being honoured by the hospital, Mrs K. They're sending me a trainee midwife to live here for six months and learn our ways. I'll have to buy another bed, of course, but I shall be reimbursed. Her name's Ellen Purbright; she's from Formby, and once she's installed it will make the work a good deal easier. She's a bright girl, just like her name, full of fun and not at all in awe of the senior staff the way I was when I worked on the wards. Why, as soon as she heard she was to stay with me, she suggested that we might like to get to know one another on a more informal basis before her actual training starts. I was a bit doubtful at first, but I've agreed and we're starting tonight. No one at the hospital knows that there are three of us in this house and quite honestly I want it to stay that way, so I need Nurse Purbright to be on my side, if you know what I mean. I didn't want to refuse to take her, that *would* make folk suspicious, so it seemed a good idea that we should meet socially a few times. Then I can explain . . .'

'I'm very glad you're going to have a companion of your own age, and I do think you ought to go out and about wi' your own kind,' Mrs Knight said at once. 'All work and no play make Jack a dull boy, and you work every hour God sends, as I well know, what wi' the job and your little fambly here. As for not wanting the people at the hospital to know about Merrell, I can understand that, though I'm not sure that deceiving folk ever pays, in the end. Still, you go out and enjoy yourself wi' your pal. I'll keep an eye on all at number twenty-four.'

'Thanks ever so much,' Patty said gratefully. 'Actually it won't be just meself and Nurse Purbright, we'll be with three or four other nurses from the Stanley Hospital, so it will be quite a social event for me. Of course I'll put Merrell to bed before I leave and Maggie will put herself to bed when she feels tired. But I'd feel happier, Mrs K., if you know where I am and can give Maggie a hand if anything goes wrong while I'm away. She can knock on the wall the same as she does when I'm on nights.'

'She's never knocked on the wall yet, but I know what you mean,' Mrs Knight admitted. 'I don't usually go to bed afore midnight, and I dare say you'll be back home by then, though I'm a light sleeper and a knock on the wall at two in the morning would wake me up, you may be sure. Where's you goin', queen? Somewhere nice, I hope.'

'We're going to the Daulby Hall,' Patty said rather gloomily. She had no desire to prance around a dance floor with a young man's arms about her but had felt she could hardly say so when the other girls were being so friendly and trying to include her in an outing for the first time. 'I don't know if it's really my kind of thing, but the others seem to think I'll get along all right.'

'Of course you will,' Mrs Knight nodded, getting to her feet and beginning to lay the table for their supper. 'Why, Nurse, you're pretty as a picture, though you don't seem to realise it! All that lovely, wavy blonde hair is enough to set you apart, to say nothing of the trimmest figure!'

Patty had decided to grow her hair and now wore it in a neat bun on the nape of her neck during working hours, thinking that it looked more professional than the bob she had favoured when she first came to Ashfield Place.

'You ought to have a grosh of admirers . . . come to that, you oughter be married to some good-lookin' feller who would spoil you a bit, make a fuss of you!' Mrs Knight went on.

'It's nice of you to say so,' Patty said, taking off her uniform coat, hat and apron and donning the calico overall which she usually wore around the house. 'But I'm really not at all interested in being married or courted or anything like that. I want a proper career, that's what I want, and enough independence to have a little house of my own in the country one day, with a nice piece of garden to grow cabbages in and mebbe some fruit. Then I'd need a run for some hens, perhaps a pig . . . and a dog called Rover and a cat, too. That's what I'm aiming for, Mrs K.'

Her neighbour looked astonished. 'And no man? Wharrabout a feller who can be a dad to young Merrell here? Don't you think your life would be easier wi' two of you earnin', and a feller to dig the garden and plant them cabbages? No pretty young woman can manage without a feller, queen.'

'Well, I can,' Patty assured her. 'I don't need a feller here, so why should I need one in the country?'

'The country's lonelier than the city,' Mrs Knight said. 'Still an' all, if that's what you want, queen . . . oh, I forgot to ask. What are you wearin' to this here dance?'

There was a moment of astonished silence, then Patty said: 'Why, a clean print uniform frock, of course. What else should I wear?'

'I guess your pals will be in dance dresses,' Mrs Knight said mildly. 'You know the sort o' thing – taffeta, or artificial silk, wi' a full skirt and mebbe a flower pinned to one shoulder. Oh, queen, you must know wharr I mean.'

'Yes, I think I do know, only I've never had any need of that sort of dress,' Patty said, after some thought. 'Won't a uniform dress do, then?'

'No it won't,' Mrs Knight said at once. 'Tell you what, though, you can always borrow something. Young Ada Clarke used to be a great one to dance afore she wed. She'll likely have at least one dress what'll fit you, and she doesn't have a mean bone in her body, young Ada. She'll see you right. Best go along there at once and explain.'

So Patty went, cap in hand she felt, to Mrs Clarke and presently returned with what she said, in an awed voice, was the most beautiful garment she had ever seen. It was cut low across the breast, with a full swirling skirt which reached almost to her ankles, and the colour was a sort of misty grey-blue which did wonderful things for Patty's fair complexion and blue eyes.

'That'll do you a treat,' Mrs Knight said with satisfaction. 'Well, I trust you'll come round some time tomorrer, tell me how things went. And I'll keep an eye out for the kids, like I promised.'

'Thanks, Mrs K., you're a real friend,' Patty said gratefully. 'Mrs Clarke asked if I had any dance shoes, but I thought my navy sandals would do. They're ever so comfy . . . and anyway, since I don't know how to dance I dare say it won't make much difference what I wear on my feet.'

Mrs Knight glanced a trifle doubtfully at Patty's sturdy, flat-heeled sandals, but agreed that comfort was the thing. 'No one won't stare at your feet, norrin that dress,' she assured her young friend. 'Now I'm off back to get Darky's tea, but you have yourself a good time, chuck!'

Patty prepared Maggie's tea, fed Merrell and popped her into bed, and then began the preparations for her own evening. To her surprise, she rather enjoyed it. A strip-down wash, a quick dusting of baby powder – she had no other – then clean underwear and over that the borrowed dress. She brushed her hair hard, then slid from the pocket of her uniform dress the lipstick Mrs Clarke had insisted on lending her and applied it before the small, spotted mirror. It gave her face a sort of focus, she supposed doubtfully. Then she went to the long mirror in which she always checked her appearance before setting out for a day's work. Seeing her reflection, she almost gasped. She looked – oh, different! Pretty, carefree, like a society belle off for an evening's fun.

Maggie, looking up from the French knitting which was all the rage at school right now, whistled beneath her breath. 'You look stunning, Patty,' she said admiringly. 'Ain't Mrs Clarke clever, though? She must have made that dress, because she told me once that she makes all her own clothes.'

'She's kind as well as clever,' Patty said, slipping her coat over her shoulders and checking that her purse was in her pocket. 'If I had a dress like this I don't know that I'd want to lend it to anyone else, it's so beautiful. Now be good, Mags. I'll be in before midnight, I expect.'

'Bet you ain't never been out so late before – apart from work,' Maggie said. 'Have a grand time, Patty. I'm going to ask Mrs Clarke if she'll teach me to make a dress like that.'

Patty laughed and headed for the door. 'You'll probably finish it in time for your wedding,' she said jokingly. 'Don't forget, queen, if you need any help just knock on the wall. And don't stay up too late. I'll see you in the morning.'

Patty had agreed to meet her colleagues outside the dance hall and was glad to see that she was not the only person waiting about. There were several small groups of girls and some young men as well and she stood by a pretty, dark-haired girl in a black taffeta skirt and white blouse, hoping that it would not be long before the others turned up.

Presently, the other nurses began to congregate and included Patty easily in their conversation, asking her about working on the district as though they were really interested. Nurse Purbright was last to arrive and came panting up at a run, then linked her arm with Patty's in the friendliest way. 'We'll stick together, us two,' she said rather breathlessly. 'We can dance together to start with, before the lads have got our measure, I mean. The other girls say you don't go dancing much.'

'Well, never,' Patty admitted, suddenly wanting to confide in this easy-going, attractive young woman. 'I've been so busy . . . and then I've got responsibilities which you don't know about yet. I – I live with a – a baby called Merrell – she's past eighteen months and toddling – and a young girl, Maggie, who helps me in the house and looks after Merrell when I'm busy.'

Her new friend looked at her with considerable awe. 'And someone said you were a dull stick! You're really a dark horse,' she gasped. 'My Gawd, they don't know you at all, do they? I'm real fond of kids and they like me, so it'll be grand sharing a house with you and your baby; we'll all have a great time together, I'm sure, just like you and I are going to have this evening. I know you don't go out much, the others told me . . . unless they're wrong about that as well?'

'I'm too busy to go out much,' Patty said ruefully. 'But with you sharing the house with me, I hope things will be easier.'

'I'm sure if we all pull together we'll have time to enjoy ourselves as well,' Nurse Purbright assured her. 'And we're certainly going to enjoy ourselves tonight, just wait and see.'

And entering the dance hall, taking in the brilliant lights, the equally brilliant dresses, and the air almost of carnival which seemed to make the lights shimmer even more brightly, Patty was sure that her new friend was right. It reminded her of the only other real, grown-up party she had ever attended, which had been the night the war ended, and that had been – oh, an unforgettable night. It had remained in her memory as clear and bright and beautiful as it had been at the time. Smiling at the recollection, Patty left her coat with the cloakroom attendant and walked, with Ellen's arm still linked in hers, towards the gleaming dance floor.

Chapter Seven
November 1918

The 'flu epidemic which had been sweeping Britain reached Durrant House in early November. At first, only four or five of the younger girls appeared to have been affected, but once it had taken hold it spread with astonishing rapidity so that staff as well as children began to take to their beds.

Matron was one of the first adults to go down with it and was so ill that she was admitted to hospital, for the staff were either too poorly themselves or too busy nursing the children to be able to cope. Patty and Laura, on the other hand, had had heavy colds at the end of October and this appeared to have given them some sort of immunity. Along with a dozen or so other girls, they remained unaffected, and it was these orphans who suddenly found themselves, for the first time in their lives, free of the rules and restrictions which had shaped their days until now.

Rumours that an armistice had been signed and would take effect on 15 November reached Durrant House. Patty and Laura were helping Cook by peeling potatoes and were surprised to find several members of the staff crowding into the kitchen. 'You two – Patty and Laura – the war is officially over and we are to take down the black-out blinds,' Miss Briggs said, and Patty saw that there were tears of joy in the teacher's eyes. 'There won't be any more of those terrible Zeppelin raids,' she told them. 'And though they say rationing of food won't stop at once, things should be easier. Ships will start bringing in oranges and bananas, as well as sugar from the West Indies and other things. She considered for a moment, then added: 'You'd best not go into the sick bay because we can't afford to have the entire school ill with 'flu, but take the rest of the blinds down as soon as you can.'

'What shall we do with them, Miss Briggs?' Laura asked as they set out to begin their task. It was a cold, grey day and Patty hoped the teacher would tell them to make a bonfire in the small square of garden. It would have been grand to do something really cheerful because despite the ending of the war the crisis over the 'flu epidemic had had a depressing effect on everyone. However, it was not to be.

'Pile them up in the downstairs cloakroom,' Miss Briggs said. 'They're mostly paper with wooden slats, but before we destroy them I shall have to see what Miss O'Dowd thinks. As you will realise, with so many children and staff ill there will be no one available to teach you so you must make yourselves useful in any way you can and try to be good. When you've taken down the black-out blinds you had best report back to Cook. No doubt there are some small tasks which need doing – both the kitchen maids have gone home to help with the illness in their own families – and of course in a place this size there is a great deal of brushing and dusting to occupy anyone not otherwise engaged. Now, off with you; I'm going back to the sick bay to see if the nurses who have been brought in to help need anything.'

Despite the fact that they were set to work on some task or other by every adult who clapped eyes on them Patty and Laura really enjoyed the day. There was a feeling of suppressed excitement amongst those who were well enough to realise the significance of what had happened on the Continent earlier in the week, and even the sickly ones began to sit up and take notice when they were told that today, Friday 15 November, was officially Victory Day.

When the girls were sent out on messages for Cook they were smiled upon by total strangers, one old lady even handing them a threepenny piece each for sweets. The greengrocer offered them, without being asked, a fine piece of rope to skip with, and when they were passing the pub on the corner a man shifting barrels gave Patty a rough hoop and told her not to bowl it along the roadway but to use the pavement. 'It's safer, because if I know anything, queen, it's goin' to get rowdier and rowdier as the day wears on. Why, there's to be fireworks tonight, and a huge bonfire ... right out in the street an' all.'

'Isn't everyone nice today?' Laura said as, heavily laden, they made their way back to Durrant House. They had thoroughly enjoyed their shopping trip and had felt truly grown up, paying for goods with real money and stowing them in the capacious baskets with which they had been provided. 'Is it just because the war's over, do you suppose? D'you think anyone would notice if we went back to me mam's when we've handed over the messages? Only if we stay in the Durrant we'll be working as hard as they can make us, Victory Day or no Victory Day.'

Patty thought it over, but decided that it would not be allowed – or not by Miss Briggs, at any rate. To be sure, she was much nicer now that there were fewer pupils to boss about and fewer teachers and staff to support her, but even so . . . no, she would not let them go that day. Regretfully, she told her friend that if they were going to see anything of the Victory celebrations it would have to be clandestinely, because otherwise old Briggsy would see that they worked until they dropped.

'But I don't mean to let anyone stop me going out this evening,' Patty said grimly, as they chopped cabbage at the kitchen sink. 'We've worked like slaves ever since the 'flu started; I think we ought to have some fun now and then.'

'We don't work as hard as the older girls,' Laura pointed out. Once a child was thirteen she was expected to do a good deal of the housework and to perform such tasks as preparing vegetables for Cook. It helped to keep the place decent without having to pay extra staff and Matron said it was good training for later life, when probably ninety per cent of the girls would become domestic servants of one sort or another. 'And they don't just work hard because everyone's ill with 'flu, either, they do it all the time.'

'Oh, it's excellent training for later life,' Patty said in the sort of booming, self-righteous voice Miss O'Dowd used when addressing the children. 'Horrible old hag! I bet she hasn't used a floor-mop for years and years, if she ever did. So I'm off out this evening . . . what'll you do? Honestly, I think we're safe enough. Everyone who's fit will go out, and the rest won't notice what's happening.'

'I'll come wi' you when you light out,' Laura said with decision. 'Only think, to have to tell folk when we's grown up and married, wi' kids of our own, that we stayed in on Victory Night and never saw so much as one firework, or half a bonfire!'

'We'll pretend we're going up to bed, tired out, and then as soon as it's quiet we'll make our way into the city centre, because that's where all the fun will be,' Patty planned busily. 'I might meet me pal Toby . . . if he's still in St Peter's, that is. But anyway, we'll have a good time!'

The rest of the day passed quickly and supper was served earlier than usual since there were so few well enough to eat it. Meals were being taken in the staff room, so the children ate rather better than usual since Cook could scarcely serve two or three different menus, but as soon as they had cleared the long table and washed up they were told to make their way to bed.

'It may get a little noisy later, so try to get to sleep early,' Miss Briggs told them as she shepherded them towards the stairs. She was now the senior member of staff and was clearly taking her position as Matron's deputy seriously. 'I'll not wake you too early tomorrow morning; the bell will go off at eight-thirty instead of seven o'clock, because I shall probably not get to bed myself until late.'

'And why do you suppose that is?' Patty said sarcastically as the two of them sat on their beds waiting until they considered it safe to leave the building. 'Because she's nursing sick patients or peeling spuds for tomorrow? Not her! She and the others will all be off on the razzle, don't tell me any different!'

And presently, when they dressed in their warmest things and crept down the stairs, the house did seem uncommonly quiet. No light came from under any door, and when they rather timidly approached the front door it was to find it both unbolted and unlocked.

'There you are!' Patty said triumphantly as they slipped out. 'The only reason for not locking up is because you want to get back in later. I thought the staff would take the opportunity and nip off out, same as we are. Come on, queen, let's find us a tram to take us up to St George's Plateau. That's where all the fun will be, you mark my words!'

They reached the Plateau and were soon joining in the dancing and singing, watching the fireworks whiz skywards, gazing enviously at the queues of eager people around the hot chestnut sellers, grabbing for balloons which someone was blowing up and then releasing into the windy darkness. At first the two girls clung to one another, but then they were swept into a dance, one they had never seen or heard of before, but it was easy; someone shouted at them, 'Just watch me and do what I do!'

The tune was catchy, the words the same: 'Who were you with last night, out in the pale moonlight?' Legs kicked, arms windmilled wildly, people pressed closer to the man with the mouth organ who had started the singing. His tiny instrument still managed to produce enough noise for the crowd to follow. 'It wasn't your sister, it wasn't your ma, ah, ah, how naughty you are!'

Patty was singing as loudly as anyone else, kicking as madly. She held a balloon in one hand and her hair had come loose from its neat plaits and flew around her shoulders as she tossed her head to the rhythm. Presently the dance surged in a different direction, and as she got further from the source of the music she realised that she had not seen Laura for several minutes, perhaps as long as half an hour! Hastily she tried to move back, to look around, but it was impossible. The crowd was good-humoured, but though she wriggled her way back towards where she could last remember seeing Laura, she was unlucky. Her friend had been swallowed up, as she had.

Patty felt a momentary stirring of fear. It was dangerous to be out alone in a huge crowd; people could get trampled underfoot, seriously hurt, killed even. And she and Laura had vowed to stay together. But it was no one's fault. All she could do, now, was to make her way back to Durrant House and hope that Laura would do the same.

But knowing what one should do and doing it are sometimes two different things. Patty made her way back towards Lime Street station and then began to head in the direction from which she thought they had come. The only trouble was, she did not perfectly remember the way back – they had been on a tram, after all – nor could she recognise landmarks with the pavements, roadways and every little square and gap in the houses black with people. All the shops round here were closed, that went without saying, but the pubs were open. Every now and then, men and women stumbled and swayed their way out from the brilliantly lit doorways and some of the folk outside, eagerly waiting for just such an opportunity, stumbled and swayed their way inside. And presently, Patty found her arms taken by two plump and pretty young women, one of whom shouted in her ear: 'Most o' the pubs has run out of ale, chuck, but who cares? I could get drunk as a lord on water this evening! Me boyfriend were fightin' out there on the Continong, but he'll be comin' home to me and we'll get wed . . . oh aye, I could get drunk on water tonight!'

Patty tried to say she was happy for her new friend, but then someone staggered out of a pub with a full glass in his hand and gave it to the young woman who had just spoken. She drank, then held the glass beneath Patty's nose and Patty realised that she was extremely thirsty and took a good long draught. It was bitter, not very nice at all, but it quenched her thirst and she was in the middle of thanking her new friend when the movement of the crowd wrenched them apart once more. Patty was actually lifted off her feet and carried along, to be deposited, presently, in what she took to be some sort of public garden since there were bare-branched trees overhead and earth beneath her feet.

She glanced a little wildly about her; why had the crowd come here? She could see no sellers of hot chestnuts, no balloons floating in the air. Then she realised that, ahead of her, someone had stretched a rope between two trees . . . and a figure, lithe and brightly dressed, was dancing, actually dancing, upon the tightly stretched rope!

It was an act! There were tumblers doing somersaults, the tightrope dancer, a man setting light to a huge taper and then apparently swallowing the flame he had produced . . . it was, in fact, some sort of fair or circus!

Patty pressed forward. Suppose, just suppose, that Toby had joined up with these people, was here, within a few feet of her! There were several children of about her own age in the gaping audience and presently she saw a thin boy just ahead of her. She stared; was he wearing the uniform of the St Peter's boys? It looked remarkably like it, and he looked very like Toby Rudd. Patty felt the heat rise in her cheeks and excitement made her bold. She must get to Toby, if it really was Toby, and right at this moment she was sure it was he! Pushing as hard as she could, slipping through every little gap, sometimes hacking at ankles and elbowing stout stomachs, she squiggled through the crowd until she was near enough to grab the boy's arm.

'Toby? Is it really you? Oh, I've searched and searched . . . I found the brick easily, but . . .'

The boy turned round. It was not Toby. Patty's disappointment was so painful that for a moment she was literally unable to speak. She felt as though someone had struck her a hard blow in the stomach, rendering her breathless as well as voiceless. But she could not just stand here; the boy would think her a complete idiot! She let go of his arm and tried, through the waves of disappointment still engulfing her, to smile.

'Oh! I'm sorry . . . I thought . . . I thought you were a pal of mine, someone I've not seen for – oh, for months and months. You looked just like him – from the back that is – and you're wearing the sort of thing he wears. But I see now I was mistaken . . .'

'Did you say his name were Toby?' the boy grinned. 'Only there's a Punch an' Judy man what's goin' to do an act presently and his little dawg's called Toby. I knew it were a dog's name, but I never thought it could be a feller's an' all.'

'A dog's name!' Patty felt the hot blood of fury rise in her cheeks. What an ignorant, rude boy he was, to say such a thing. She longed to give him a hard slap and tell him that Toby was a grand fellow, both bigger and handsomer than himself, but, just as she was about to do so, someone called her name. Patty swung round, completely forgetting the boy; had Laura caught up with her at last?

But it was not Laura. The face she had begun to believe she would never see again grinned at her, not a foot from her shoulder. It was Toby. He was wearing a rough brown jacket and ragged trousers, and despite the coldness of the day he was barefoot, but it was Toby all right, looking delighted to find her. 'Toby!' Patty squeaked. 'Oh, I've kept my eye on the loose brick but there's never been a message so I'd quite given up. What's been happening to you?'

'Three days after you and me were on the loose, I got away again,' Toby told her, speaking rapidly. 'I never had a chance to leave you a message 'cos this time I cleared off wi' an' old pal o' mine. He were one of them fellers with a barrel organ and a little monkey – I knew him from me old life – and he were lookin' for a young feller to take the hat round when his act were over. So he and me joined up . . .'

'I though wi' a name like Toby you was a-goin' to say the feller had lost his monkey and wanted you to take its place,' a voice said, rather jeeringly. 'I just told that gal there weren't no fellers called Toby, only little dawgs, but I see I were mistaken.'

It was the boy Patty had addressed first. Patty hoped that Toby would punch him on the nose, but Toby just gave him a disparaging glance and continued with his story. 'I told the old feller – his name were Mac – that it weren't safe for me to stay in Liverpool, so we made our way to Manchester, earning money as we went. He were an Irishman though, desperate keen to get back to the old country as he called it, and we were makin' our way back to Liverpool to catch the boat for Dun Laoghaire when he were took ill. He died in a little village and Parson buried him there. He were real kind to me – I didn't tell him I'd escaped from an orphan asylum, mind you – and put me in touch with Flanagan's Fair . . .' He jerked his head towards the group of performers Patty had been watching. 'That's them, or some of 'em, rather. We decided to split up 'cos the boss reckons we make more money that way. I'm takin' the hat round, or was, but when we's on a proper gaff I do all sorts. I looks after the hoop-la stall, barks for the fat lady and the thinnest man in the world, sells herbal medicine, cooks sausages to sell to the flatties . . .'

'There! I said Toby was a name for a dog and norra feller and I were right,' the other boy said triumphantly. 'Fellers don't bark, but dogs does. And what are flatties when they're at home?'

Once more, Patty hoped that Toby would thump the other boy, but instead he said quite patiently: 'It's fair talk. A barker stands outside a tent where a show's being given and tells folk what they're goin' to miss if they don't pay up their money and go inside.' He grinned at the boy. 'And you're a flattie; so's young Patty here. It's show people's name for the rest of you.'

The boy opened his mouth and Patty shot him a menacing look. She was sure he meant to make some unpleasant remark about Patty the flattie, but her intention to punch him on the nose herself if he did so must have shown in her eyes for he only said: 'Well, now you've cleared that up, what say we go an' gerrus a paper o' chips? I'm in the money, I am.'

'It'll take us hours to fight our way through the crowds,' Toby pointed out. 'Tell you what, let's link arms, the three of us, with Patty in the middle, and we'll see what else there is to see. A feller wi' a hot pie just went past; I wouldn't mind a hot pie.'

The rest of the evening was magic so far as Patty was concerned. She and Toby managed to lose the other boy and had a delightful wander through the streets, now oohing and aahing over fireworks, now biting into a deliciously charred potato from the heart of the huge bonfire, now drinking fizzy red cherryade out of a bottle stoppered with a glass marble. They danced the two-step and then the turkey trot; they sang many of the songs which the soldiers had sung in the trenches and watched, uncomprehendingly, as both men and women wept at the sound of the familiar tunes. To them, this was a victory celebration, and having known nothing of the war – and in Patty's case, at least, nothing of the pain of loss – they thought that every face should be smiling and every man and woman rejoicing with them.

When, at last, the stars began to fade and the sky to pale in the east, Toby accompanied Patty back to The Elms. He told her how sorry he was that he could not take her back to the fair with him, but explained that it would only lead to trouble for his friends, the Flanagans. 'Because you're a girl and only eleven,' he told her, 'the scuffers would be after you, and wi' that light yellow hair you ain't exactly easy to miss, are you? I'm fourteen so I'm all right now.'

'But I want to go with you,' Patty said tearfully, clinging to his jacket sleeve. 'I've never wanted anything so much in my whole life. I could be really useful. I'd work ever so hard . . . I'm good at housework and I can cook . . . oh, Toby, do take me back with you.'

'It's no use, Patty. There ain't much that girls can do in a fair unless they've been raised to it, like. Besides, didn't you tell me last time we met you was goin' to be a nurse when you growed up? A fair is no place for a nurse!'

Patty acknowledged the truth of this last remark but wished that she had never told Toby about her ambition. Nursing sounded awfully tame when compared with the life Toby was leading, but in her heart she knew the latter was not for her. Selina had fired her enthusiasm for looking after people, making the ill well again, and besides, she liked order and neatness and guessed that life on the gaff, with its constant moves, would be chaotic. Nevertheless, she hated the thought of losing touch with Toby, and said as much.

'Well, now that the war's over, Mr Flanagan, my boss, is talkin' of goin' over to France this winter to find new sideshows. He says a showman's life is good over there, particularly on the south coast, where there's still plenty of money in folks' pockets,' Toby told her. 'We'll be back in England some day, but I can't say when. Mr F.'s got big ideas – he's a rare one for takin' on new acts – and he's heard of a feller somewhere in France who's selling a galloper – that's a roundabout to you, Patty. He reckons it'll go cheap and he's dead keen to buy one because with a big attraction like that he could be Riding Master of his own fair in no time, which is what Mr F. and his wife have always wanted. They used to have three sons but Bob and Samuel were killed in the war, so that only leaves young Teddy. I'm sorry about Bob and Sam, of course I am, but Mr F.'s treated me real good since they went an' I know he needs me. Once he's got the galloper, I'm the only one who knows how to drive it and service it, which will make me really valuable. We'll work our way across the country, endin' up meetin' this feller what owns the galloper. But knowin' Mr F., we'll pick up half a dozen other acts or curiosities along the way. So next time I sees you, you'll probably be in a nurse's uniform, tendin' the sick.'

'Can't we make some arrangement?' Patty asked wistfully, as he turned to leave her. 'Couldn't you come back – oh, say in a year's time – so's we could see each other and catch up? We could meet on Lime Street station, under the clock, say one year from today.'

'I might be still in France . . .' Toby was beginning but some of the disappointment she felt must have shown in Patty's face for he suddenly grinned at her and tweaked a lock of her hair. 'All right, but a year's too soon. Why not in five years?' he said. 'By then we'll have a good bit of news to tell one another because we'll both be working. Of course, it's hard for me to say where I'll be in a year. The war's disrupted things, you see, so we'll be having to make new arrangements, I guess. But in five years things should have settled down a bit and I should be able to make plans. Right, on the fifteenth of November, 1923, at twelve noon, we'll meet under the clock on Lime Street station. And if I just can't be there . . . well, how about the following year? Same time, same place, but 1924. That way, if I'm out o' the country or up in the north of Scotland or somewhere in 1923, we can still get in touch. If I'm not there, you'll know I'm still abroad or unable to get to Liverpool. OK?'

'If I'm not there, you'll know I'm dead,' Patty said mournfully. 'But wouldn't it be safer if I say I'll be on Lime Street station at noon on the fifteenth of November every year? Oh, I don't mean before the five years,' she added hastily, seeing a slight frown appear upon his brow. 'I mean after 1924. I know fairs move around and I know you might not be able to come to Liverpool, but I don't mind spending a few minutes in Lime Street station once a year. Honest I don't. Would that be all right?'

'Well, all right,' Toby said. He looked hunted. 'I'll do me best to be there in five years' time, honest to God I will. But now I'm off or they'll think I've been blowed sky high by a rocket or ate by a Welsh dragon. Take care o' yourself, queen.'

'Goodbye, Toby, and good luck!' Patty responded.

She stood watching until he had disappeared then turned, with a sigh, towards Durrant House. And the next five years. It seemed a terribly long time before she and Toby would meet again.

By a great piece of luck, as Patty turned into the drive of Durrant House, she saw a small figure approaching her from the direction of Peel Street. It was Laura. The two girls re-entered the house together and, despite the fact that it was five o'clock in the morning, stayed awake for a further thirty minutes, exchanging experiences.

Next morning, they somehow managed to get out of bed when the bell sounded but were so pale and listless that Miss Briggs, fearing more 'flu victims, sent them back to bed for the rest of the day. They were happy to obey her, but by four o'clock conscience got them up and dressed, and downstairs once more. They were glad they were able to give a hand since more girls – and another member of staff – had gone down with the 'flu and conditions were chaotic.

'You'd best go and help Cook; she's making a nice stew for those able to eat it and a big tureen of semolina pudding for those who can't stomach ordinary food,' Miss Briggs said, putting a hand to her head and looking distracted. 'There was a message for you, Patty, but I can't recall what it was. Oh, I think a friend of yours has got the 'flu. Anyway, get on with your tasks and perhaps tomorrow, if things are easier here, it might be possible for you to visit her. Selina, that's who it was!'

'Oh, poor Selina,' Patty muttered as she and Laura made their way to the kitchen. 'I know nurses get the 'flu just like ordinary people, but I hope they get better treatment as well. I will try and see her tomorrow, if Briggsy agrees.'

But for the next two days, both girls were so busy that they scarcely had time to think. November 15 had been a Friday, but though the girls usually had a little more freedom at the weekend, on this occasion they were forced to remain in Durrant House. On the Saturday morning, two of the older 'flu victims, Miss Dodds and one of the kitchen staff, died, which meant that Miss Briggs had her hands full, though another member of staff, Miss Collins, did her best to take the older teacher's place. Then, on Sunday, two of the orphans died and another two went down with the 'flu and were admitted to hospital since Miss Briggs felt that they could no longer cope alone. On Monday, however, Patty was sent out to do the messages with the faithful Laura by her side, and as soon as they were well clear of The Elms Patty told Laura that she meant to visit Selina's hospital before she did anything else. 'Because there might be some little thing we could get her whilst we're visiting the shops,' she told Laura. 'Selina's been a good friend to me and she must have wanted me to know she was ill or she wouldn't have sent the message. Come to think of it, it's odd that she sent a message at all, knowing how difficult it is for us to get out of the Durrant.' She clutched her friend's arm. 'Oh, Laura, suppose she's very sick, suppose she – she were to die? Let's hurry!'

They reached the nurses' home and made their way towards Selina's room but were stopped by a flustered-looking nurse whom Patty recognised as one of Selina's friends. 'If you've come to see Selina, you won't find her here,' she said. She looked at Patty with an odd expression on her face. 'But – are you sure you ought to see her, queen? She's very, very ill, but surely they told you that?'

'No one told me anything,' Patty said, her heart beginning to jump about in her chest in a very frightening way. 'Miss Briggs said there was a message for me but so much has happened. Several people have died of the 'flu and others have gone sick . . . if Selina isn't in her room, where is she?' She clutched the older girl's sleeve. 'She – she isn't going to die, is she, Nurse?'

'She's very ill,' the older girl repeated. 'Look, I know you're a good friend of hers so I'll take you along to the ward and, if Sister agrees, you can see her. I went in yesterday morning, so perhaps she'll be better by now, more – more herself.'

By now Patty was desperate to see her friend for herself. She, Laura and the nurse hurried across to the main hospital and began to thread their way through various corridors. The double doors at the end of the children's ward were open and Patty glanced in. This was the ward Selina liked the most and talked about with great enthusiasm. As her eyes passed across the rows of cots and small beds, something stirred in the back of Patty's mind, but then she was hurrying on once more, too concerned about Selina to follow up a vague feeling that she had seen something of importance.

On the ward, Sister came hurrying out to meet them as soon as they went through the double doors. The nurse explained who Patty was and Sister looked at her for a long moment, her expression a mixture of doubt and sorrow. 'I don't think it will hurt her to see you for a moment, dear,' she said at last. 'She was asking for Patty – that's you, isn't it? – when she was first brought in. But not your friend, she can wait in the corridor. Nurse Mitcham, you take the child down to Nurse Roberts's bed, but she must not stay for long, and if Nurse Roberts shows any signs of distress you'd best bring her away at once.'

'Yes, Sister,' Nurse Mitcham said. She took Patty's arm and led her along the ward, saying in a low tone: 'She's at the far end, queen, on the left-hand side. There's screens round the bed to try to keep the noise to a minimum, but most of the women in here are too sick themselves to chatter much.'

They reached the screens and slipped inside them, and then Patty clutched her companion's arm and gasped with shock. Selina was lying almost flat on the bed, with various tubes and bottles attached to her person. But what horrified Patty most of all was the state of her. Her body seemed to be a mass of bandages and her face was black and blue; her nose looked broken and two of her front teeth were missing. Her eyelids were puffed and blackened, though she seemed to be asleep, and her breathing was laboured.

Patty turned to her companion. 'I – I thought she had the 'flu,' she muttered. 'But this isn't like any 'flu I've ever seen. Oh, Nurse, what on earth's happened to her?'

'It were on Victory Night,' the nurse began, but at the sound of their voices the figure on the bed moved slightly and gave a deep, tearing cough. Patty flew to the bedside and took one of Selina's hands gently in both her own. She could see the gleam of Selina's eyes beneath the puffy lids and noticed blood seeping from the corner of her mouth. Terrified, but determined not to show it, she spoke gently. 'It's me, Patty. Don't try and talk, Selina, because it must hurt even to speak. I came to ask if there was anything you wanted but I'm sure Sister will tell me what you need. I'm going to stay with you for a little, Sister said I might, so just you go off to sleep again, if you can.'

There was a short pause and then Selina spoke, her voice no more than a harsh whisper. 'Victory Night,' she said. 'I was minding my own business . . . coming back to the hospital . . . down near the docks . . . sailors . . . attacked me . . .'

'Oh, Selina, how dreadful to hurt you so,' Patty cried, gently stroking her friend's bruised and battered fingers. 'But don't try to talk, you mustn't talk, it will only tire you.'

'Must tell you . . . warn you . . .' Selina mumbled. 'I'm not pretty, never have been, but you're pretty. Men . . . wicked . . . wild animals . . .'

'Yes, yes, I can see what they've done to you,' Patty said distressfully. Tears formed in her eyes and began to trickle slowly down her cheeks. 'They must have been mad, as well as wicked, to attack you. Oh I wish I could do something to help you!'

'You can. Be very, very careful. Don't trust any men,' Selina said. She spoke clearly now, almost forcefully, and the hand in Patty's stirred a little. There was a weak pressure from her fingers, the bruised and battered mouth seemed to try to smile and then Selina said, with a sort of desperate satisfaction: 'I fought them. I fought like a tiger, Patty, but it weren't no good. Be careful, little Patty.'

'I will, I will,' Patty promised her, her own voice choked with tears. 'But you'll get better, Selina, you'll be better soon, then we can get the scuffers to search for the men who did this.'

Selina sighed. 'Thirsty,' she said vaguely. 'So thirsty.'

Nurse Mitcham picked up a glass of barley water which was standing on the bedside locker and began to prop the patient up on her arm to offer her the glass. Selina's head came forward as though to drink but suddenly Nurse Mitcham turned her head slightly and said in an authoritative voice: 'Go back to your friend, queen. I'll – I'll just make Selina comfortable and then I'll follow you.'

Patty made her way out of the ward and back into the corridor, so shocked and shaken by what she had seen that she could scarcely think straight. She told Laura a little of what had happened whilst they waited for the nurse to join them, but when she emerged from the ward she went straight past the girls and into Sister's small office. After about five minutes the two of them emerged, the nurse to go off on some errand of her own whilst Sister came towards Patty and Laura. 'My dear, I'm afraid your friend has died,' she said gently. 'It's a merciful release since she had dreadful internal injuries and could not have survived as anything but a helpless invalid. I'm so sorry to be the bearer of such sad tidings, but I thought you would rather hear now than later.'

That night, Patty could not sleep. She lay in her bed and thought about Selina. A kinder, more generous girl had never lived, she told herself, so why should she die such a horrible – and protracted – death? She had been attacked last Friday but had not died until today, Monday. It seemed a cruel thing that she should have suffered for so long when, according to Sister, she had been far too badly injured to live. Why had the doctors not given Selina something which would have ensured her sleep until the end came? For Patty thought she would never forget that harsh breathing, the moan Selina had given only a few minutes before her death.

When they had got back to Durrant House, she had told Miss Briggs what had happened in the fewest words she could find and then asked permission to go to her dormitory. Miss Briggs had looked at her and what she saw in Patty's face must have affected her for she had actually taken Patty's hand and given it an encouraging squeeze before saying that she thought that a bad idea. 'Your grief is understandable and must be given full rein, but it does not do to shut oneself away from the world and wallow in misery,' she had said, and though her voice had been brisk, there was more kindness behind the words than Patty had ever heard from her lips before. 'Helping Cook to prepare and serve the evening meal will take your mind off what has happened, at least for a little. I don't mean to be hard on you, Patty, for I know how fond you were of your friend, but I promise you that the less you dwell on what has happened, the better it will be for you in the long run. You want to be able to remember Selina with affection and pleasure, not as a sort of nightmare which haunts you. Believe me, I know what I'm talking about. My fiancé was killed at Gallipoli in 1915. I – I let myself dwell on what had happened to him and how he had died and now, when I try to see his face in my mind's eye . . . but anyway, my dear, I don't want you to go down that path.'

Lying in the dark and staring towards the lighter square of the window, Patty told herself that one should never judge people until one knew their full history. If she had known that Miss Briggs had lost her fiancé and was haunted by bitter memories, it would have been far easier to understand her and to make allowances for the bad temper and spite which the teacher had frequently displayed. She's been much nicer lately, too, Patty told herself. I suppose it's because she has taken her own advice and has stopped thinking about her fiancé whilst running the orphanage and nursing the sick. Why, this evening, I almost liked her – I *did* like her! And in future, I'll try to be cooperative and do as she says without grumbling or making a fuss. And I'll remember Selina as she was on our day out, when the sun shone and the sky was blue and we ate our picnic on the banks of the stream and talked about what we would do when we were both truly grown up.

In the opposite bed, Laura stirred and mumbled something beneath her breath and Patty, hunching the covers up to her ears, reminded herself that she really must get to sleep or she would be no use to anyone in the morning. And useful I must be, if I'm to follow Selina's example and become a nurse, she told herself. It would be hard to cast from her mind the dreadful picture of Selina as she had seen her last, but she realised that it must be done. Selina's advice, however, must not be forgotten. Selina had said that men were animals, that not one but several of them had attacked her. Patty still wanted to find out who had caused her friend's death, still wanted revenge, but she knew in her heart that such men were probably visiting sailors and would never be punished for what they had done. But I know now that underneath, all men are beasts, Patty told herself as she felt the first waves of sleep approaching. I'll never trust a man, never, never, never . . . and Patty slept at last.

It was not until the day after Selina's funeral that Patty remembered glancing into the children's ward on her way to visit her friend. Several times she had been vaguely aware that something had happened which was important to her, but because of her misery over Selina's death she had been unable to concentrate, to think what it was she had seen. But quite suddenly, as she and Laura hurried along Dingle Lane on their way to the shops, a mental picture of the children's ward popped into her mind and she knew at once what had caught her eye. So stunning was it that she stopped in her tracks, a hand flying to her mouth, and Laura, staring at her, said worriedly: 'What's up, queen? What have we forgot? Oh drat, don't say you didn't pick up the purse!'

'No, it isn't that,' Patty exclaimed. Before her eyes, the picture of the children's ward still danced. Ten or twelve cots and an equal number of small beds – and each of the cots bore a scarlet blanket! It had never occurred to Patty before, but now it struck her it was possible that her mother had had some connection with the hospital – why, she might even have worked there. Red blankets were not something one often saw, and if her mother had been a nurse, then she would have had access to such things. What was more, it would explain Patty's own deeply rooted conviction that she should join the nursing profession as soon as it was possible for her to do so. She knew Selina's own attitude had been partly responsible, but that was just coincidence. Surely her mother must have been a nurse?

'Patty?' Laura's voice was impatient. 'What on earth's gorrin to you, queen? You're standing there like a perishin' statue! *Have* you forgot the purse?'

'No, I've got the purse all right,' Patty said. 'And it isn't what I've forgotten so much as what I've remembered.' And, as briefly as she could, she told

Laura what she had seen in the children's ward and the significance of the red blankets.

'But if your mam were a nurse, surely the other nurses would have noticed if she were expecting a baby, wouldn't they?' Laura asked, as they continued towards the shops. 'You can tell when a woman's having a baby; remember Mrs Flagg?'

Mrs Flagg was Laura's mother's neighbour. She had eleven children and seemed, to the girls, to be constantly pregnant.

'I know what you mean,' Patty admitted. 'But girls can be really sly when they're expecting babies; Selina told me about one of the nurses who got herself into trouble. She had pains and they thought it was her appendix, so they shovelled her into a bed and the next thing they knew, pop! She'd had a dear little baby. Selina was cross because they kicked her out – the nurse who had the baby, I mean – but she went home to her mam and left the baby with her and then joined up to a different hospital and no one the wiser. So I dare say, if my mam had had her baby somewhere less public, she could have got away with it.'

Both girls slowed as they turned into Minshull's butcher's shop. Cook had told them to try the Park Road shops before going further afield since she wanted bones to make stock, and large marrow bones were a commodity which could probably be purchased locally more easily than in the city. She also wanted a large slab cake which could be softened with custard to make an acceptable pudding for the invalids. Since Mrs Clarice Parry, who owned the confectioner's shop next door to the butcher's, reduced her prices when such slab cakes began to go a bit stale, there was little point in the girls going elsewhere.

There was a queue in the butcher's and the girls joined the end of it, hoping that Mr Hughes would still have some bones left by the time they reached the counter. 'I dare say you're right about your mam being a nurse and getting a blanket from the hospital,' Laura remarked quietly as the line of women edged forward. 'Tell you what, Patty, you want to get to know some of the older nurses on the children's ward. I've always thought your mam must have had very blonde hair, like yours, because I don't reckon your mam or dad could have been dark-haired, do you? Then, when you know them – the older nurses I mean – you can ask them if they knew a girl wi' hair your colour about a dozen years ago. You never know, they might remember and be able to tell you something useful.'

'It's a grand idea, but I won't be able to do it until I'm a nurse myself,' Patty pointed out. 'Nurses are always so busy – haven't you noticed, Laura? Selina was always breathless when she came off the ward and though they aren't allowed to run in the hospital corridors – unless someone haemorrhages, that is – they all seem to develop a sort of gliding walk which is nearly as fast as running. But when I start my training I'll do as you suggest, I reckon.'

Later that day, as she peeled a mound of potatoes for Cook, Patty thought regretfully that it was a pity she did not have some good reason for going into hospital and talking to the nurses. I'm a child still, though I feel very old since Selina's death, she reminded herself. If I were to catch this 'flu I might end up on the children's ward and be able to ask all the questions I want. But of course, I might die and I don't want to do that, not before I've had any sort of a life of my own. The trouble is, in half a dozen years, when I can go in as a probationer, most of the older nurses will either have forgotten what happened so long ago, or will have left. I wonder . . .

A week later, Patty was on the children's ward as a patient. It had not been nearly as hard as she had supposed to gain admittance to the hospital. First she had complained of stomach ache, and then, after Miss Briggs had dosed her with syrup of figs, she had really had stomach ache. After that, she had gone quietly into the sick bay and abstracted a large bottle of the hated purgative, dosing herself with it each night until she was so weak and so ill that she had felt it safe to convincingly collapse almost on the doorstep of the hospital. She was picked up by two porters – her skin had crept with horror as they took hold of her, for she could not forget that it was men, possibly just like these, who had attacked Selina – and carried into the hospital, ending up, as she had hoped, on the children's ward. What she had not bargained for was that they would leap to a totally wrong conclusion, so that she woke up, two days after her admission, to find herself without an appendix and in a good deal more pain than she had experienced after her generous doses of purgative.

Laura, who had been in on the secret, had been shocked to hear that her friend had actually had an operation, but when she came visiting had been overcome by giggles, much to Patty's annoyance. 'Just you stop laughing, you nasty girl,' Patty had commanded. 'And don't you go having your appendix out because it hurts something horrid. I almost wish I'd never started the whole business. Whose idea was it, anyway?'

'It was my idea that you got into the hospital by

fakin' it,' Laura admitted. 'But it was your own silly idea to go guzzling all that syrup of figs. You poor thing! But Miss O'Dowd's back, large as life and twice as nasty, so you'll not be regretting you aren't at the Durrant.'

'No, and I'm to go to a convalescent home for three weeks, when I'm well enough to be moved,' Patty said, trying to hitch herself up in bed and sinking back on her pillows with a groan. 'It's a place in the country. The nurses say it's lovely, so that's a sort of special treat for losing my appendix. Or that's how I look at it, at any rate.'

'What did the surgeon say when he found your appendix was right as rain?' Laura asked curiously. 'Good thing he didn't decide to whip out something else while he were about it – good thing he didn't fancy liver for his lunch!'

'Shut up, you horrible girl!' Patty said. 'I told you, laughing hurts. As for what the surgeon thought, I've not got the faintest idea. They don't tell you *anything* in here; they won't even tell me how long I'll be on this ward before I go off to be convalesced.'

The ward was a busy one but Patty was the oldest inhabitant at the moment, most of the beds and cots being filled with very much younger children. So Laura did not scruple to lean forward, having checked that there were no nurses around, and ask Patty how her search for her mother was going on.

'Better than I thought,' Patty said, lowering her voice. 'It was a piece of luck that Nurse Cummings was sent to the ward the night after my operation. I was dreadfully uncomfortable and so thirsty, and the day nurses wouldn't give me a drink in case I was sick. Then Nurse Cummings came along because one of the other nurses had contracted the 'flu and she was ever so kind. At about two in the morning, she made herself a cup of tea in the little kitchen place over there and asked if I'd like a cup. My tongue was hanging out like an Abraham's carpet, so of course I said I'd love one and she came and sat on my bed while I drank it. We chatted a bit and although I felt pretty horrible I suddenly realised that she might know something. I said I believed my mother had worked in the hospital eleven or twelve years ago, and asked Nurse Cummings if she remembered a girl with very pale hair like mine.'

'Didn't she ask you what her name was?' Laura asked. 'That would have been my first question.'

'Well it wasn't hers,' Patty said aggrievedly. 'Do *listen*, Laura, and stop chattering. I guess she thought her name was Peel, the same as mine, because after some thought she said she *did* remember someone, though she couldn't be sure of when, exactly, the girl worked on the ward. She said she was ever so pretty and had the makings of a really good nurse, but then she thinks she may have got ill or taken a job away, because when Nurse Cummings was next seconded to the children's ward the fair-haired girl had gone.'

'And you think that the fair-haired girl might have been your mother?' Laura said, her voice rising to a squeak. 'Oh, if that isn't the most romantic thing . . . did she say whether the girl had a feller? Come to that, did she give her a name? It would help you a good deal if you knew the name, queen.'

But here Patty had to shake her head regretfully. 'No, and I couldn't very well ask, could I? But I'll find out, don't you fret. I've not gone to all the trouble of sticking meself in hospital and losing me appendix just to give up when I've scarcely started. Oh aye, I'll find out whatever there is to find out, you may be sure of that!'

Patty was on the children's ward for a full week, but she made no further discoveries. Indeed, when she saw the night nurses coming on to the ward, standing in a neat line, heads cocked, expressions intelligent, she looked hopefully for Nurse Cummings, but did not see her. And though she looked every night, the middle-aged nurse did not return to the ward whilst Patty was there and no one else evinced the slightest interest in a fair-haired girl who might have nursed on the ward a dozen or so years before.

'I were scarcely out of leading reins twelve years ago,' the youngest probationer told Patty. 'What was her name, chuck, this blonde you're so interested in? Why not ask Sister? Or Matron, come to that – they're both old as the bleedin' hills.'

Patty hastily disclaimed any particular interest and changed the subject. She told herself she did not want any trouble and decided that despite her efforts she would learn no more from the staff of the children's ward. But she did make casual enquiries about the red blankets and was told, proudly, that they had been a gift from a rich benefactor to 'cheer up' the children's cots.

'It were a Mr and Mrs O'Grady, what brought their little kid over from Dublin for special treatment,' one of the nurses told Patty. 'The kid were cured – it were all of twenty years ago, mind – and he bought the blankets and left a sum o' money so's they could be replaced when they got worn. Kind of him, weren't it?'

'Very kind,' Patty said solemnly, thinking that this, at least, was no more than the truth. As a tiny baby she herself had been wrapped in a warm red blanket – and speedily found because it was so noticeable, according to Selina. And when at last she left the hospital and was taken, in a big, old-fashioned wagon, to the convalescent home just outside the city limits, she felt that she had not done too badly. She had discovered that a fair-haired girl had worked on the children's ward around the time of her birth and might well have been in a position to have prigged one of the red blankets. And best of all, she had conquered the sick fear of the hospital which had attacked her the first time she had entered the premises after Selina's death. Now, the hospital was once more the place in which she wanted to work when she grew up, especially since she was now almost certain that her mother had once been, if not a nurse, at least a worker in that same hospital.

Laura visited her in the convalescent home and so did Miss Briggs. The older woman came with a bag of broken biscuits for Patty and sat rather stiffly in the big, sunny visitors' room, telling Patty all about her fellow orphans, how the teachers were managing and what Miss O'Dowd thought of the way they had coped during the crisis.

'Because we've lost so many staff, the matron is having to be a little more flexible,' she told Patty. 'To own the truth, my dear, I don't think she'll stay at Durrant House for very much longer.' She glanced sideways at the younger girl. 'She isn't cut out to take care of little children and I think some members of the Board of Governors actually realise it. I don't think for one moment that they will appoint a member of the existing staff since we are not qualified nurses, but I'm sure they will choose someone not quite so – so unbending this time.'

And so it proved. The new matron was younger, a plump woman in her forties, with frizzy brown hair forever escaping from her cap and a good deal more sympathy with her staff and charges than Miss O'Dowd had ever shown.

So the next few years passed pleasantly for Patty and Laura. They had both decided on a nursing career, and worked grimly towards that end. Together, they studied hard and often popped in to the hospital to chat with the nurses and listen to their grumbles about life there, and how the senior staff treated them little better than slaves. But the two girls were not to be discouraged. They wanted to nurse the sick and were determined to do so.

Chapter Eight
August 1933

Patty, Ellen and their companions made their way to a cluster of chairs which they reserved by putting their handbags on the seats. Patty looked a little doubtful. She would have had no fear of anyone's stealing her usual handbag since it was an elderly and battered object which she had owned – and treated harshly – for many years. But Mrs Clarke had insisted on lending her an evening bag made of blue-grey velvet, and though it contained little beside a few pennies and a handkerchief, Patty thought it a very desirable object. Ellen, however, assured her that it would be safe as houses left on the chair seat. 'Everyone bagses their seat with a handbag and there'd be a rare outcry if folk at dances couldn't trust one another,' she said airily. 'Besides, there's nearly always someone left out when the dancing starts and they'll give an eye to the handbags while we're on the floor.'

One of the other nurses gave an admiring whistle. 'I say, Peel, wherever did you get that dress?' she demanded. 'I've never seen you here before and I thought you didn't go to dances, but that dress is just the most gorgeous thing I've ever seen. Did you buy it specially?'

Patty shook her head ruefully. 'It isn't really mine at all. I borrowed it from a friend,' she explained. 'You were quite right; I don't go to dances but my friend is a dressmaker and makes most of her own clothes, so she lent me this.'

The other girl reached forward and ran a hand along the soft silk of Patty's full skirt. 'Wish I had a friend who could sew like that,' she said wistfully. 'Well, Ellen said we was to come early so we could teach you the steps of the most popular dances, so we'd better get on and do it.' The music struck up what Ellen told Patty was a waltz, and very soon she began to thoroughly enjoy herself. She had never realised that dancing was so easy – or perhaps it was because Ellen and the other girls were good teachers. At any rate, by the time the hall began to fill up – with young men as well as young women – Patty felt herself quite capable of dancing the waltz and quick-step, though some of the more modern dances, such as the charleston and the black bottom, had yet to be conquered. When a couple danced an exhibition tango, Patty was really impressed, though she had no desire to follow their example. 'I'm surprised the poor woman's backbone is still intact,' she said to Ellen as they watched the couple, both thin as sticks, circling the floor. 'If you find that girl lying in a bed on Women's Surgical tomorrow morning, then she'll only have herself to blame.'

When Mrs Knight had told her son that she was giving an eye to the kids next door since Patty had gone to the Daulby Hall with a group of nurses, he had shrugged his indifference and turned away, but inwardly he was interested. He had never known Patty to go out anywhere except in the course of her work as a midwife and had often wondered at this. Most girls went to the cinema, the theatre or a dance hall at least a couple of times a month before they were married, but Patty had never once asked his mother to keep an eye on the kids except when she was working. 'Your tea's on the table,' Mrs Knight said presently. 'It's boiled bacon and mash, one of your favourites.'

'Thanks, Mam,' Darky said, taking his seat at the table. He did not want his mother to think he was interested in Patty – it would give her quite the wrong idea – but he did want to know just why their sober and reclusive neighbour had suddenly decided to go dancing. With his mouthful of potato, he said thickly: 'What's special about tonight, Mam? That Peel never goes anywhere, not to my knowledge. Don't say she's trapped some poor fellow at last!'

Mrs Knight sat herself down opposite her son and picked up her knife and fork, then paused. 'The feller what gets young Patty Peel will do awright,' she said severely. 'But she ain't gone with a feller, she's gone with a group of nurses. Not that you're interested,' she added sarcastically.

'No, I'm not interested,' Darky said instantly. 'Only it seems kind o' strange. Pass the salt, Mam.'

Mrs Knight shoved the tin of Cerebos across the table and snorted. 'If you think a pretty young gal going to a dance is strange, then it's you ought to ha' his head examined. And where's "please" gone, may I ask? I've brought you up to know better than to miss out the magic word, young feller.'

Darky laughed at this and relaxed perceptibly. When he had been a small boy, the mere mention of 'the magic word' had brought a 'please' or 'thank you' to his lips and now he grinned at his mother and asked her how she had spent her day. Very soon, Patty and the dance had been forgotten – he hoped – and by the time Mrs Knight had served treacle pudding and custard, harmony had been restored.

At about nine o'clock, Darky took his jacket from

the hook on the door and told his mother he was going down to the pub. 'And mebbe I'll go down to the Pier Head after that to get a breath of fresh air, because it's been such a stiflingly hot day,' he told her. 'So don't sit up for me.'

'As if I ever did,' Mrs Knight said, laughing. 'I wouldn't mind a breath of fresh air meself, but of course I've gorra keep me eye on next door. Still, I reckon I'll take a chair on to the landing for a while; I can hear Maggie just as well from there if she shouts me.'

'Right,' Darky said, swinging open the door. 'See you at breakfast then, Mam.'

Mrs Knight watched her son striding off down Ashfield Place and smiled grimly to herself. He couldn't fool her! She knew her son had been interested in young Patty Peel from the first moment he had set eyes on her and she considered it a very good thing. Darky had taken no notice of any woman, save herself, since his young wife had died, so even though he made no secret of the fact that he disliked Patty, his mother thought it a good deal healthier than the sort of indifference with which he had regarded other young women.

She remembered her son as he had been before his marriage: going off to dances, taking girls to the cinema or the theatre, going down to the pub with a crowd of his pals. There had been outings of every description, many of them organised by Levers, and Darky had missed none. He had been popular with everyone, fellers and girls alike, and had seldom spent an evening at home.

All this had changed, of course, after his marriage. Alison was not a gregarious girl but meek and compliant, far too anxious, Mrs Knight considered, to please her new husband. Darky had joined a group doing amateur theatricals, helping the electrician to light the stage and making scenery, but Alison had chosen to stay at home and await Darky's return.

With Alison's death, however, all such activities had ceased and now Darky seldom went anywhere, save to work and to the pub, where he rarely drank more than a pint and consequently returned home, after no more than an hour, as sober as he had left. Mrs Knight had no desire to see her son drunk, but she would have enjoyed seeing him more relaxed, easy once more with his fellow men. Old friends had come round to the house when he had first moved back to Ashfield Place but most of them were married by now and even those who were still single failed to persuade Darky to join them. He was always polite; he was grateful for their efforts, but preferred, he said, to remain at home.

But unless I'm much mistaken, me laddo will end up at the Daulby Hall this evening, Mrs Knight told herself, as she dragged her chair on to the landing and sank gratefully into it, fanning her face with the copy of the *Echo* which Darky had brought home, for even out here it was breathlessly hot. I don't suppose he'll ask her to dance – or anyone else for that matter – but at least he'll be in a ballroom amongst young people his own age. And maybe, who knows, he might meet someone who takes his fancy. Or he might even realise he's misjudged young Patty and begin to act a bit more friendly. A little breeze lifted the hair off Mrs Knight's hot forehead and she wondered how Patty was enjoying her first dance. She had looked downright beautiful in Mrs Clarke's lovely dress. Surely, when Darky saw her all dressed up, with that wonderful hair tumbling in loose waves across her shoulders, he would be impressed. Mrs Knight heaved a sigh. She knew her son too well to think he would change his opinion just because of a pretty dress, but she could not help hoping. Now that she was looking after the children for Patty and Ada, it would make life very much simpler if Darky was not antagonistic towards Patty. Darky got on well with Ada Clarke and seemed carelessly fond both of little Christopher and of Merrell. This attitude contrasted so strongly with the way he treated Patty that it made his mother uneasy.

By now, it was growing dark, and Mrs Knight decided she might as well go back indoors and begin to get ready for bed. She would open her bedroom window as wide as it would go and lie on top of the covers, hoping that the heat would dissipate as night drew on. The heat wave had lasted most of the month but surely it would pass soon? This was England, after all, though it might as well have been tropical Africa, she thought as she re-entered the stuffy house.

Presently, in her cool cotton nightdress, she lay down upon her bed, intending to listen for the return of Patty and her son, but the day had been a long and tiring one, and soon she slept.

Darky entered the ballroom in company with a group of young men who had arrived at the same time as he and took up a position in a dark corner of the large room. He spotted Patty almost at once, recognising the gleam of her blonde hair immediately, and was surprised at how different she looked. He had never seen her wearing anything but uniform, with her hair coiled into a bun on the nape of her neck, but now she was in a smoke-blue dress and her hair, pale as moonlight, fell in loose waves well past her shoulders.

The girls she was with were not known to him, but he thought them a pleasant enough crowd. He had no intention of approaching them – in fact he had no idea what his intentions were – but when a chair became vacant near him he sat down, deciding that, since he had paid for admittance, he might as well at least take a look at the talent on offer.

He was still watching the girls when the orchestra struck up a waltz and the young men began to move across the dance floor to where the girls were sitting. A fair young man in a shiny blue suit looked as though he were heading for the nurses and Darky stiffened, but when he reached them the fair-haired one paired off with a little redhead and Darky relaxed once more. It was not that he cared whether Patty danced or not, he told himself virtuously, but he did not like to think of some innocent young man getting involved with her before he knew of her circumstances. Why those circumstances should prevent her from dancing, Darky could not have said. His whole attitude towards Patty was confused and irrational, but his disapproval was so strong that it coloured everything. Even his mother's championship of the girl annoyed him. He wanted nothing to do with Patty, was not interested in her, did not care what she did, or with whom . . . yet he seldom took his eyes off her.

Presently, his fears were realised. A tall, dark-haired young man approached the group, singling Patty out. He bent towards her, clearly asking her to dance, and led her on to the floor. Propelled by he knew not what instinct, Darky promptly jumped to his feet, crossed the floor and found himself standing in front of a very young girl in a very bright pink dress. She had thin, frizzy hair and her eyes, when she glanced up at him, stared fixedly at each other, but Darky had already blurted out: 'May I have the pleasure of this dance, miss?' before he realised that the last thing he wanted to do was take to the floor with a partner so young and so extremely plain.

However, the deed was done. The young girl got to her feet and proved to be almost as tall as he, which was an advantage since, what with her height and breadth, she almost hid Darky from view. She was clearly delighted to be asked to dance and said breathily, as soon as they were on the floor, 'Thanks ever so much, mister! I been sittin' there wi'out anyone so much as glancin' at me for half an hour an' it's bleedin' borin' when everyone else is havin' a good time. Me name's Annie Halligan; what's yours?'

Darky quashed a craven desire to tell her he was Charlie Chaplin. How his pals would jeer if they could see him now! But he was not a cruel person and knew that the girl could not be more than fifteen, if that, so he said, 'I'm Derek Knight. How do you do, Miss Halligan?'

'I'm doin' fine *now*,' the girl said. Darky felt that this was a very inaccurate remark since Miss Halligan had trodden on his toes twice and was clutching his hand so tightly that he was sure sweat was pouring off their palms on to the floor. 'I say, mister, ain't it hot? My old feller – that's me dad – was in India before he married me mam and he says it's as hot here as it were there. You ever bin in the army, mister?'

Oh, God; plain, sweaty, and now chatty as well, Darky thought mournfully, guiding his large partner round in a circle so that they might follow Patty and the dark young man at a safe distance. However, as

Miss Halligan got over her awkwardness, she began to relax a little and proved to be quite a good dancer. Darky did not go in for the twiddly bits but he and Alison had attended dancing classes for a year before they married, so he was reasonably competent and managed to keep Patty in sight without making his partner suspicious.

Having taken Miss Halligan back to her seat when the waltz ended, Darky had not intended to dance again, but Miss Halligan's small crossed eyes were pleading when he thanked her for the dance. 'You'll axe me again, won't you, chuck?' she said baldly, before he could escape. 'It's been grand, having someone to dance with. I were beginning to wish I'd not come because me cousin, her what brought me, went off wi' some of her pals to sit at t'other end of the room, and when I tried to folley her she told me to clear orf and not meddle wi' me betters. She di'n't want to bring me at all,' she added dolefully, 'but I'm stayin' wi' me auntie and she made her. Auntie's gone orf to visit another sister and di'n't want me along,' she finished.

Telling himself that he was unlikely to find another young woman behind whom he could hide whilst he watched, with increasing annoyance, Patty's growing friendship with her partner, Darky agreed that he and Miss Halligan would have another dance 'later' and made his way back to his secluded corner. I won't wait much longer, he told himself. There's no alcohol here and I could do with a drink after hoisting Miss Halligan around the floor. Yes, I'll quit this place soon.

When the orchestra struck up again, several of the men who had been standing idly on the opposite side of the dance floor converged on the girls. Patty knew all her companions' names by now. There was Ellen of course, slim and energetic with curly brown hair and laughing eyes; then there was Murchison, the one who had admired her dress; Beckett, a lively redhead; Matthews, a tall buxom girl with glasses and freckles and easily the best dancer; and Pringle, a plump and giggly girl with a strident voice and acne. She was astonished at how easily they had got to know one another, for in all the years she had worked at the hospital before going on to the district she had never made a real friend. She supposed, now, that it had been her own fault. She had been so keen to do well in her chosen profession that she had resolutely refused to socialise with her fellow nurses. This had made them think her a 'dull stick' and had led to Patty's never really getting to know any of them.

Of course, on the district, fraternisation was doubly difficult. Because of the volume of work, free time was precious and used for such tasks as shopping, cleaning one's home and, in Patty's case at least, visiting the only person in the area she knew well: Mrs Ruskin. She met other midwives when they were called to the hospital for meetings but that was strictly work, and though Patty knew that many of the girls often went off after such meetings for a cup of tea and a bun, she had never accepted invitations to join them.

I've missed an awful lot, Patty concluded, as the girls in her group began to be taken on to the floor by various young men. I've been really foolish but I'll know better in future. Why, Ellen has not even moved in with me yet and already she's made a difference to my life.

As she pondered, Patty's eyes had rested, without

225

really seeing him, on the figure of a tall young man who was approaching their group. She guessed that he was coming across to ask one of the girls for a dance and was astonished when he stopped in front of her. 'May I have the pleasure of this dance, miss?' he said. He had dark hair, slicked back from a broad forehead, and spoke with a local accent. When he caught her eye, he smiled rather shyly.

'I – I'm not a very good d-dancer,' Patty stammered. 'I'm a beginner really. Are you sure . . . ?'

Next to her, Matthews giggled. 'If you'd like to change your mind, chuck, I'll give you a turn round the floor,' she said, addressing the young man. 'Though Patty's doin' all right for a beginner.'

The young man blushed fiery red but continued to stare down at Patty, looking so miserable that she took pity on him and got to her feet. 'Don't say I didn't warn you,' she muttered, as he led her on to the floor. 'My pal's a really good dancer, an expert you could say. But I'll do my best.'

'Well, I'm norra great dancer meself, not like them fillum stars . . . John Gilbert and them . . . but if we both do our best, mebbe we'll get by,' the young man said as he took her, somewhat gingerly, in his arms. 'I hope I won't tread on your toes,' he added, looking down at Patty's feet in their sturdy sandals.

For the first time since he had asked her to dance, Patty smiled. 'I'm likelier to tread on yours, and if I do, you'll know it,' she told him. 'And who's John Gilbert when he's at home?'

Her partner was holding her a little away from him so she was able to look up into his face, and she saw his astonishment. 'He's a fillum star and he dances real good,' he said. 'Don't you go to the cinema, miss? Or are you a nurse, like the others? I've not seen you

226

with them before but we all know the nurses; lovely girls, every one of them. Why, you'd think with all the running round they do that they wouldn't have no energy left for dancin', but they quick-steps and waltzes wi' the best of 'em.'

'Yes, I'm a nurse,' Patty said, rather guardedly. For some reason she felt reluctant to tell a perfect stranger that she was a midwife. She decided to tell a part of the truth, however, and added: 'But I'm on the district, so I don't have much time to myself and I don't mix a lot with the other nurses, as a rule. What do you do?'

The young man told her that he was a clerk in an insurance office and added that his name was Albert Kennedy. He said this with such a question in his tone that Patty realised she must respond in kind. 'I'm Patty Peel,' she said rather gruffly. 'Do you live round here, Mr Kennedy?'

Mr Kennedy replied that he was only a tram ride away, and by the time the dance ended Patty felt a good deal more self-confident. Mr Kennedy might not be the greatest dancer in the world, but once he had got over his initial shyness he had been a pleasant and unexacting partner. Despite her fears, Patty had managed to follow him without either treading on him or being trodden on and she felt a little surge of satisfaction as he led her back to her seat, thanked her formally and said that he would ask her for another dance when they had both had a cool drink, for the heat of the day still lingered.

For the rest of the evening, Patty danced with everyone who asked her to do so. She was soon able to tell those who could dance with flair from those who simply plodded round the floor, and enjoyed dancing with the former a good deal more than with the latter. She also noticed that the really good-looking men often had not bothered to learn to dance properly whereas the plainer ones seemed to enjoy dancing for its own sake. She mentioned this to Ellen and her friend laughed and said: 'You're an observant one, you are! Now you mention it, you're quite right. Handsome fellers don't bother much with the twiddly bits because they know they can get a girl so long as they can do the basic steps, but the plain ones take pains. I'd sooner dance wi' a feller who knew what he was doin' than one who trampled all over me feet, even if he looked like Gary Cooper.'

During the interval, the girls went to the bar and bought soft drinks which they carried out of the dance hall, first having the back of their hands stamped so that the management would know they had paid their entrance fee and let them back in. It was cooler out here, the stars bright in the dark sky, and the girls perched on a handy wall and chatted amongst themselves. Patty was surprised and amused at how quickly the talk became nursing talk. They discussed various sisters, the wards they ran and the patients on them, and Patty realised that this must be how the young men had discovered the girls' occupations, since she imagined that no one would volunteer the information. She had often heard it said, when she was doing her training, that for some reason men considered nurses to be 'fast'. She supposed it must be because nurses saw their patients in pyjamas or nightdresses – or even in nothing at all – and were thus presumed to be willing to do a little more than give their escorts a goodnight kiss. She herself had not told anyone she was a nurse, apart from Mr Kennedy, who had guessed at her occupation after a glance at her companions.

As the evening drew to a close, Patty thought that all her new friends had behaved in an exemplary fashion. They had danced with a great many young men but had not encouraged any of their partners to return to join their group. Other girls in the dance hall had not acted so sensibly. There had been shrieks of laughter and a good deal of horseplay, and Patty had also noticed that some of the young men had used a dance as an excuse to fondle their partners. If the girls did not object, some went further, though not on the premises. This had happened outside, during the interval, and Patty had been shocked by it and truly grateful that the girls she was with had kept themselves to themselves.

'Last waltz,' Ellen said cheerfully as the orchestra struck up once more and the lights dimmed. 'Whoever you dance the last waltz with may expect to walk you home, but just tell him you're with us – unless you like him a lot. If that's the case you can go off with him, but between ourselves I wouldn't advise it. Meself and the rest of the girls have been coming to dances here for months and we know who's decent and respectable and who isn't. You'll be safest to stick wi' the rest of us until you've got a bit more experience under your belt.'

Patty agreed that this seemed sensible and accepted Mr Kennedy's offer of the last waltz, sure that he would behave himself, and so it proved. He held her a little closer and hummed the tune to which they danced as they glided round the floor. When the music ended, he thanked her with all his customary politeness and said he hoped to see her again next week, to which Patty made a non-committal reply. Then he hurried away from the dance floor, no doubt eager to catch his last tram, and Patty joined the queue for coats. Outside the hall once more, the girls waited by the door until the group was complete and then set off in the direction of the nurses' home at the Royal Infirmary on Pembroke Place. Ellen was still living with the others in the nurses' quarters, and when they reached the home Patty suddenly realised that there would be no one to accompany her to Ashfield Place. However, she spent so much time on the streets at night, in her capacity as a midwife, that she was not at all nervous. She said goodbye cheerfully to her new friends, assuring them that she did not mind the walk home and turning down Ellen's suggestion that she and one of the other girls should accompany her.

'Good lord, Ellen, when you're on the district you go in and out of some dreadful areas, late at night or in the early hours, and never think twice about it,' she said robustly. 'I know you and I will be together most of the time whilst you're doing your midder training, but once it's finished and you take up a post on the district – if you do – then you'll soon grow accustomed.'

'Well, if you're sure . . .' Ellen said doubtfully. 'Good night then, queen, see you tomorrer. All right if I come round in the evening? I'll bring some of me stuff so when I come to stay I won't have to make two journeys.'

Patty agreed to this, adding the rider that if she was out, she would tell Maggie to expect a visitor, and the two girls parted, Ellen to hurry into the nurses' home and Patty to begin to wend her way through the dark streets.

She had just passed Holy Trinity Church on St Anne Street when she heard a commotion ahead of her. She peered in the general direction of the noise but could see nothing and, deciding it must be a late night party which had spilled on to the street, continued on her way. She was passing the dark mouth of a narrow jigger by the Drill Hall when half a dozen young men in seamen's rig burst out of it. Several clutched beer bottles and all were swaying and probably drunk and Patty crossed the road, aware for the first time of the deterrent of a nursing uniform and a bicycle. Had she been mounted on her trusty steed, she would have either whizzed past them or taken another route, but she could scarcely do this on foot. She would just have to hope that the young men would not notice her.

Because it was such a warm night, she was carrying her navy coat over one arm, and was still wondering whether it would be wiser to stop and put it on or simply to hurry past the convivial group with her face turned away from them when she was spotted. 'Shurrup, fellers, there's a l-lady presen',' one of the men shouted. 'A l-l-lovely l-lady, beautiful as a fairy, begod!' He came towards her, a beaming smile almost bisecting his large red face, the hand not holding a beer bottle held out towards her. 'Wharra lovely lady! She's goin' to be Harry's little friend, ain't you, queen?'

Before Patty could think of a sufficiently crushing reply, another man came lurching towards her. He had a draggly little beard and was bald as a billiard ball but he, too, was beaming broadly. 'L'il darlin', acushla, querida,' he crooned, in a broad Irish accent. 'She's *my* li'l girl an' I'll fight anyone who says different, so I will.'

The other men, jeering and shouting, were making their way up the road and ignoring what was happening behind them. The first man, clearly taking offence at the second man's attitude, grabbed Patty by her left arm, and before she had even begun to take evasive action Baldy had seized her right elbow. 'Less o' that,' the red-faced one commanded. 'Get your filthy paws off me lickle piece of stuff.'

For answer, Baldy swung a wild fist in the general direction of Red Face, missing him completely and having to hang on to Patty in order to remain upright. Red Face laughed jeeringly and put his arm round Patty's waist, trapping her right arm between their bodies and holding her so tightly that she could have cried with the pain of it.

'Let me go, you vile creature,' she gasped. She tried to kick Red Face, endeavouring to wrench her arm free from Baldy's grip, but neither manoeuvre was successful and just as she was considering a scream – for she was beginning to feel like the wishbone between two Christmas revellers – Red Face swung a fist the size of a ham and hit Baldy squarely in the mouth. The smaller man crashed down on to the pavement, his head hitting the kerb with a sickening thud. Patty, all her nursing instincts aroused, went to go to his assistance but was prevented by her captor, who twisted her to face him, saying gloatingly: 'Tha's his goose cooked, me lickle princess. Now you an' I can have a lovely time wi'out no stupid Irish git putting his oar in.' He chuckled evilly. 'Or anything else for that matter.'

'Let me go, you fool; can't you see he may be badly hurt?' Patty said desperately. 'I'm a nurse; if he's concussed or if you've knocked his teeth down his throat . . .'

'A nurse, is it?' Red Face said. If anything, he tightened his hold. 'Well, an' isn't me luck in tonight? Just you come along o' me and leave that lickle bastard to find his own woman.'

He began to drag Patty towards the mouth of the jigger from which he had emerged, but Patty struggled as fiercely as she could. 'I tell you, he's hurt,' she shouted. 'Didn't you hear his head whack against the kerb? And there's blood running from the corner of his mouth!'

Red Face gave a contemptuous snort. 'The poor bugger's drunk so he'd ha' fell floppy like,' he said thickly. 'An' that ain't blood tricklin' out o' his mouth, it's Guinness. How much do you charge, princess?'

Patty was about to say that she was not a prostitute so did not charge, but then realised that this could well be a mistake of colossal proportions. In his drunken state, Red Face would no doubt assume she had fallen for his charms and was in effect free. So she said, furiously: 'I am not that sort of woman, but if you continue mauling me I shall charge a hundred pounds a minute.'

Slightly to her surprise, this remark actually seemed to give him pause. He let go of her with one hand to fumble in his pocket, then announced, in a wheedling tone, that she would have to mek do with five bob, 'cos that were all he had left after a night out on the ale. 'But if you give me a good time, I'll do the same for you,' he added persuasively. 'A hundred pounds a minute . . . you must be very, very good!'

By now, they were well into the jigger and pretty well out of sight of the main street, and Patty realised that she would have to act quickly if she was to escape from this most dangerous and disagreeable situation. Red Face was manoeuvring her into the corner between a wall and a gate, and once he had got her pinned there she guessed she would be at a disadvantage. She hoped that her kicks and punches would be sufficient to stop him taking the ultimate action, but was beginning to doubt it. She had every intention of screaming as loudly as she could, although she realised that such an action in such a neighbourhood might bring not help but just the opposite. Indeed, as Red Face pinned her against the wall with all his weight and began to fumble with her clothing, she saw, past his shoulder, a figure lurching towards them up the alley and saw that horrible little Baldy was neither dead nor badly injured, but was returning to the fray.

Patty began to scream but a huge hand promptly covered her face and Red Face's leg caught her behind the knees and tumbled her to the ground with him on top of her. Almost choking, she bit wildly at the palm of the man's hand and began to heave and squirm, suddenly remembering that she was wearing Mrs Clarke's beautiful dress; if it got torn or ruined, it would cost her a month's wages to buy Mrs Clarke something similar.

But the dress was replaceable and her life was not. She had read stories in the *Echo* of girls who had been raped and murdered by drunken seamen and she could never forget what happened to Selina. Her friend had fought but it had availed her nothing. Suddenly, it was no longer something that happened to someone else; it might well happen to her, Patty Peel, who had responsibilities and had scarcely begun to live yet. Patty wrenched her arm free and punched wildly and rather ineffectually at her attacker. Then she grabbed him by the hair and began to tug as hard as she possibly could. Out of the corner of her eye, she saw that Baldy had arrived and was staring down at them and shifting from foot to foot like an excited child who wants to join in a game but is not sure precisely how to do so.

'Help me!' Patty shouted, but her voice came out as a tiny whisper. 'Please, please help me!' But Baldy continued to stand by, watching, whilst Red Face began to fumble with Patty's clothing once more.

Despite his resolve, Darky had stayed in the ballroom to the bitter end. He had danced several more times with Miss Halligan, closely observing Patty's gyrations with her various partners and disapproving. Why could men not see what sort of a girl she was? But he supposed there were a great many men who were on the lookout for a girl like Patty; a girl with lax morals and a fall of glorious golden hair. The last thought surprised and annoyed him since he had not meant to think of how pretty she looked this evening, with her cheeks flushed, her eyes sparkling and her mouth curved into a small, happy smile. Looks didn't matter, he reminded himself severely; character mattered, and not only was Patty an unmarried mother, she was a member of the hated profession, the profession which had caused the death of his wife.

Nevertheless, when the group of nurses left the dance hall, he followed them at a discreet distance. He reasoned there was safety in numbers so thought that the girls would get home unmolested, but decided to follow them anyway. His mother, he told himself virtuously, was fond of Patty, and if Mrs Knight found out he had been at the dance and had not seen Patty safely home, she would blame him if anything went wrong.

Darky had no intention of letting it be known that he was keeping an eye on the girls, however. He kept well back, sauntering along with his hands in his pockets. When they reached the nurses' home, he was surprised when the whole group of girls disappeared inside it, leaving Patty to continue alone. Then he remembered that the girl was out almost every night in the course of duty and scolded himself for being such a fool as to worry that she might run into trouble. She must be well used to warding off unwanted attentions; if they were unwanted, of course. But common sense told him that she could not do her work as a midwife and double as a woman of the streets, so he continued to follow her.

When the group of seamen lurched on to the pavement in front of her, he was a good way behind, having relaxed his vigilance. He saw Patty grabbed by two seamen, saw the scuffle between the men and, in the dim light from the street lamps, thought that the girl had pulled herself free. She must have hurried on and would be well clear of trouble by now. Then there was a mutter, some drunken shouts, and a large man threw a wicked-looking punch at a smaller, balding fellow. It connected with a thump and the man fell to the ground, and suddenly Darky could see Patty clearly again. The tall fellow had his arm round her and she seemed to be looking down at the smaller man lying at her feet. Darky quickened his pace; the small man was hurt. For a moment Darky concentrated on the injured seaman, and when he looked up again Patty and the large man had simply disappeared. He began to run. Had they gone into a house nearby, or had they simply continued to walk down Cazneau Street and were now out of sight? It was possible they had gone into a doorway with amorous intentions and Darky had no wish to make himself ridiculous by interfering where he was not wanted.

He slowed his pace once more and saw the small

man suddenly shamble to his feet and stand, swaying uneasily for a moment, before disappearing down a jigger which Darky had not previously noticed. Then he heard the scream.

Patty almost gave herself up for lost when a third figure loomed up behind Baldy, but she continued to struggle as hard as she could. It was impossible to shout since Red Face still had a vast hand across her mouth, and in any case his weight had squashed all the air out of her lungs and she could only wheeze and give tiny muffled squeaks.

It was difficult to see exactly what happened but Patty suddenly had the impression that Baldy actually sailed through the air, landing for the second time that evening with a jarring thump. Then the third man grabbed Red Face and hauled him to his feet before delivering a punch which rattled Red Face's teeth. 'Whazzat? Why, I'll kill you, you interferin' . . .'

The third man hit him again and this time Red Face sank to his knees, remaining for a moment in a praying position before slowly toppling over side-ways on to the cobbles.

Patty managed to get tremblingly to her feet, then tottered over to the wall and leaned against it, feeling quite unable to remain upright without assistance. She glanced apprehensively at the third man and said, in a small, shaking voice: 'Oh, thank you, sir. I thought they were going to kill me, but I'll be all right now.' She indicated the two men sprawling on the cobbles. 'I don't think they'll trouble me again, thanks to you.'

The third man came across to her but did not attempt to touch her. 'Can you get back to Ashfield

Place, Miss Peel?' he asked. 'I'm going home meself so I can lend you an arm if you need it.'

Patty gasped and peered at her rescuer in the faint starlight, for the jigger was not illuminated by street lamps. 'Mr Knight?' she said in a small voice. 'It *is* Mr Knight, isn't it? Oh, I'm so grateful. I hate to think what would have happened if you hadn't come along. I don't know why those men picked on me because I took no notice of them . . . if you wouldn't mind walking slowly, I'd be most grateful for your escort, because I feel all shivery and strange.'

'Yes, it's me,' Darky admitted. 'Those fellers were both drunk as lords. They'd likely have picked on any woman who walked alone, thinking that she were no better than she ought to be. In future, if you'll take my advice, you won't never walk the streets at this hour without someone you can trust beside you. Where'd you been, anyhow? Not workin', not in that dress.'

Patty gasped, remembering the dress, and glanced down at it as they crossed on to the Scotland Road. To her relief, it did not look torn, but it was impossible to see if it had suffered much from the dirt of the street. She thought, hopefully, that a good wash might well bring it back to its original state. She turned to Darky. 'I – I borrowed the dress from Mrs Clarke and went dancing with some of the nurses from the hospital,' she said, her voice still very shaky. 'Two of the girls offered to walk me back to Ashfield Place but it seemed so silly – I mean, I'm out most nights, in all sorts of weathers, and nothing like this has ever happened to me before, thank God.'

'No, but you're usually on a bicycle and in uniform,' Darky pointed out, his tone rather righteous. 'You should have had more sense, Miss . . .'

But Patty's heaving stomach and battered frame

was taking its revenge. She turned away from her rescuer, fell to her knees on the pavement, and was violently sick into the gutter.

The rest of the walk home was accomplished more or less in silence. Darky tried to match his usual pace to her slow one, but he kept giving impatient sighs and Patty soon began to resent what she felt was an implication that she could have walked faster had she chosen to do so. Accordingly, she went even more slowly, and when she tried to explain exactly what had happened he merely grunted in reply. Once more, Patty felt that Darky Knight was not interested either in her recent plight or in the cause of it, and since she was aching in every limb she started to feel angry as well as vulnerable and miserable. She was truly grateful to him for rescuing her but felt sure that he would not have done so had he realised it was she who had been attacked. If she had been a total stranger, she had no doubt that he would not merely have offered his arm, but insisted that she take it; might even have put an arm round her waist to assist her faltering footsteps instead of sighing deeply whenever she slowed. In short, Patty's gratitude was soon liberally laced with righteous indignation. She had not encouraged those hateful men to believe that she would welcome their advances and she felt, suddenly, that Darky was accompanying her back to Ashfield Place rather as a prison warder accompanies a difficult and rebellious prisoner. So she said nothing more until she reached her own front door, when she turned to him. 'I don't know why you're being so extremely unfriendly, Mr Knight,' she said, her tone brittle with suppressed anger. 'You're acting as though I somehow got into that dreadful scrape on purpose, and I can assure you I did not. I was

239

attacked, for no reason, by drunken seamen and it might have gone badly for me had you not turned up. I'm very grateful for your interference and shall be more careful in future. Good night!'

She had been looking steadily up into Darky's face as she spoke and saw his mouth tighten and a frown line appear between his brows. He opened his mouth as though to speak, then shut it again, and Patty turned the key in her front door and shot inside. Once there, she flopped down in a chair and began to cry, making sure that she did so silently, in case Darky still hovered out on the landing. Within seconds, however, she heard the Knights' front door shut and realised that Darky had not even responded to her farewell. She had felt cold and shaky as she entered the familiar kitchen but now the warmth of righteous anger burned up in her, drying her tears and stiffening her backbone. Darky Knight was rude, unkind and altogether hateful and the next time they met he would not need to ignore her because she meant to ignore him.

Darky, in his bed in the room next door, lay awake for some considerable time. He was furious with himself because he had been so ungracious; had, in fact, not so much as given Patty a hand to scramble off her knees after she had been sick. He had stood back, watching as she vomited helplessly into the gutter. Half of him had wanted to rush forward and pull back the long gold hair, to put a sustaining hand on her forehead and then to help her tenderly to her feet. Unfortunately, the other half had been saying, 'Serves her right for encouraging the fellers, giving the wrong impression. Why, she danced with everyone who asked her and then came breezing down the road with her hair loose and her shoulders bare – what did she expect? She looked like a tart touting for business and got treated like one. And then she had the nerve to tell me I was unfriendly. What else did she expect? I didn't want to give her the impression that I was a customer! Why, if I'd acted friendly, she might have thought I was expecting favours in return for rescuing her! You can't be too careful with that type of girl.'

Darky heaved the covers over his shoulders, but it was a long time before he fell asleep.

Chapter Nine

Patty woke late next day because she had slept straight through the alarm, and as a result had to scramble through her ablutions. As she dressed herself in a clean, starched uniform, she could hear Maggie and Merrell chattering away in the kitchen and was glad that the children did not know of her ordeal the previous night. Merrell was far too young to understand but Patty had a shrewd suspicion that Maggie would understand all too well and determined to spare the child a story which could only upset her.

Examining herself in the piece of mirror propped up on her chest of drawers, she decided that very little of her ordeal showed in her face. To be sure, there was a bruise on the side of her jaw and her upper arms and calves were black and blue, but her black lisle stockings disguised her legs adequately and the cuffs and sleeves of her dress performed the same function for her arms. Satisfied on that score, Patty brushed out her hair. She was conscious, as never before, that soft and shining hair attracted men of the wrong kind and was determined never to wear it loose again. Then, making her way towards the kitchen, she chided herself for such thoughts. How ridiculous she was being! The men had been drunk and had been eager for a woman – any woman – with whom they could have their way! If it had not been her, it would have been someone else, regardless of length and colour of hair, bareness of shoulders or elegance of dress. She remembered Selina and sick horror arrowed through her. Men were beasts, no better than animals; if she kept that in mind and steered clear of them in future, she would be as safe as anyone could be.

Entering the kitchen, she smiled gratefully at Maggie, who was pouring tea from the big brown pot into two enamel mugs. Swathed in one of Patty's big calico aprons, the child looked a real little woman and it struck Patty that even Maggie, who was only twelve, was not safe from the attentions of such men as Baldy and Red Face if she happened to be in the wrong place at the wrong time. Oh, God, Patty thought fearfully, I must warn Maggie, make sure she's safe. She's a pretty kid now she's properly fed and looked after . . . what can I do to keep us all safe?

'Mornin', Patty,' Maggie said cheerfully, pushing one of the mugs of tea towards her. 'Did you have a good time at the dance? I've put Mrs Clarke's dress in to soak – what happened? Did you have a fall? It were pretty dirty. I'll make you some toast because you won't have time for anything else, will you?'

Patty took the cup of tea gratefully and subsided into a chair. Now, she told herself, was the time to warn Maggie about men without frightening the child or making it too obvious. She said carefully: 'Yes, I did have a fall. A feller – a feller got a bit too friendly like and I had to make off in a hurry. It – it was after the dance, when I was coming home. I fell on the cobbles and knocked my head and that made me kind of giddy.'

'Oh, poor Patty,' Maggie said sympathetically. She had speared a piece of bread with the toasting fork and was holding it out to the stove. 'I know it's awful hot in here – and just as hot outside – but it's my day to go round to Stanton's Court wi' me dad's money, so I shan't be stuck in the stuffy house. I'll damp the fire right down when I leaves.' She took the piece of toast off the fork and handed it to Patty. 'You have the first one, queen, because you're in a hurry and Merrell and I ain't,' she said cheerfully. 'Mrs Knight is taking Merrell and Christopher to see her sister Ruby what lives out at Bootle, and then they're goin' on to Seaforth Sands so's the kids can build sandcastles and that. I'm joinin' them when I've paid me dad, so we're all havin' a real nice day.'

She put out a tentative finger and touched Patty's jaw. 'That looks like a thumb print,' she said curiously. 'And there's four more paler ones under your chin – did someone grab you, Patty?'

Patty decided that she would have to admit to some of what had happened the previous night or Maggie might draw her own conclusions – and they might be the wrong ones. Slowly, she said: 'Yes, a feller did catch hold of me. But I got away, so that was all right. The thing is, Maggie, I was out late at night, in a flimsy dress, with my hair down, and I think – I think men sometimes don't quite understand, when they're drunk, that girls don't fancy . . . um . . . well, kissing total strangers and that. So, in future, if I'm out at night after a dance, or a trip to the theatre, I'll make sure I don't walk home alone.'

'Oh aye, a feller with the drink on him isn't what you might call reliable,' Maggie agreed. 'You were lucky to gerraway with a bruise or two, Patty. But when Nurse Purbright comes to live here there'll be two of you most of the time, won't there?'

Patty agreed that this was so and began to make herself a carry-out. She would be hard pressed to get round all her revisits, late as she was, and would have no chance to get home for a snack at dinnertime. When she was almost ready, she took Merrell out of her high chair, gave her a kiss and told her to be good for Nanna Knight. Then she sat the little girl down in the playpen which Mrs Knight had given her, and reached up to the peg for her navy gaberdine.

It was not there, and all in a moment Patty remembered that she had had it over one arm when she had been stopped by Red Face and Baldy. She gave a gasp and clapped a hand to her mouth. The gaberdine was expensive and a part of her uniform; it would take her months to save up for a replacement.

'What's the matter, Patty?' Maggie said. 'Don't say you left your gaberdine at that dance hall place you went to!'

'No, I didn't leave it there,' Patty said hollowly. 'It was such a hot night that I didn't put it on, though. I had it slung over my arm. Oh my God, I must have dropped it when that feller . . . Damn, damn, damn! And I was determined not to talk to Darky unless he spoke to me first, but now I'll simply have to. He might have noticed where I dropped it . . . he might even remember where I was when he . . . oh, damn, damn, damn!'

Maggie stared doubtfully at her across the kitchen table. 'He'll be at work,' she observed. 'Never mind, Patty. It's a really hot day and no one's likely to tell on you for not wearin' your coat. They'll think you've got it rolled up in your bicycle basket. As for Mr Knight, if you don't want to ask him about the coat – and I understand why you don't want to – then I'll ask Mrs Knight if she can find out what happened to it.'

'No, don't trouble Mrs Knight,' Patty said quickly.

245

'I'm going that way myself, so I'll set off now and see if I can find it. If I can't, I'll call in at the nearest police station. Perhaps some honest person will find it and turn it in to the scuffers. I really don't want any more trouble.'

After Patty had hurried out, Maggie picked Merrell off the floor, sat her on the draining board and began to get her ready for their trip out. She worked automatically, chattering to the baby and occasionally singing a nursery rhyme, but her mind was in a whirl. Reading between the lines, it looked as though Patty had indeed been roughly handled when walking home from the dance, and Maggie concluded that the attacker had been Darky Knight. Why else should Patty think that Darky might know the whereabouts of her gaberdine? Maggie was well aware that Darky did not seem to like Patty, but she was equally aware that when a man was drunk his feelings were not to be relied upon. She imagined that he must have approached Patty with a view to doing whatever it was that grown-up people did, and been rejected. In those circumstances, most of the men Maggie knew, including her own father, would have turned nasty, or if not nasty at least indignant. Maggie liked Darky but thought him quite capable of grabbing Patty round the face if she annoyed him enough. He was big and strong, a good six inches taller than Patty and a great deal heavier, so naturally a rejection, which would make him feel small, might lead to reprisals.

Maggie finished dressing the baby and sat her in the big, old-fashioned perambulator. She damped the fire down and closed the front of the stove, then pushed the pram round to Mrs Knight's house. Her neighbour opened the door, revealing that Christopher had

246

already arrived and was sitting in an ancient high chair eating bread and jam. Maggie wondered whether to enquire as to Darky's whereabouts, but decided against it. She knew Patty was no tale-clat and would not dream of telling his mother how Darky had mistreated her, so she had best keep her own mouth shut. However, there could be no harm in mentioning the coat, which might have been dropped almost anywhere, she supposed. So as soon as the normal greetings were over she told Mrs Knight that Patty had lost her gaberdine on her way home from the dance the previous evening. 'So if anyone tells you they found a nurse's coat – it had a name tag an' all, with Nurse Peel written on it – perhaps you could tell us,' she said hopefully, going over to the sink and fetching a damp cloth to wipe the jam from Christopher's little face. 'I dare say it's gone for good – it were a real nice, expensive coat – but I thought I ought to make a push to gerrit back for her. She's goin' to the scuffers herself, so you never know . . .'

Mrs Knight clucked sympathetically. 'I'll keep me eyes open,' she said. 'And I'll ask Darky whether he knows anything about it; he were out last night an' awful late comin' home as well.' She chuckled. 'And he were in a nasty temper, muttering to hisself and shuttin' the door a lot more noisily than usual. It ain't like me laddo to have a drop too much, especially as I suspicioned he'd gone to the dance at the Daulby Hall, but something had put him out of sorts, that I *do* know.' She crossed the kitchen and began to wash up the breakfast things.

Maggie seized a cloth and began to dry for her. 'Thanks, Mrs Knight. I do hope Patty's coat turns up. Mebbe, with everyone keepin' an eye open, she'll gerrit back.'

'If it don't turn up soon, I'll tek meself along to Paddy's market and see if there's a navy gaberdine on one of the stalls,' Mrs Knight remarked. 'If a kid finds it – or someone dishonest – they'll cut out the name tag and sell it to one of the stallholders, like as not. No one who ain't a nurse is likely to want to wear it; the uniform's too well known for that.'

Maggie thought this a good idea and said so, but Mrs Knight's remarks had strengthened her suspicion that Darky had been in some way involved in Patty's experience. The two of them had never been friends and now, Maggie thought dismally, it was even less likely that they could bury the hatchet, whatever that hatchet might be. By the time she reached Stanton's Court, however, she was beginning to look forward to the day. After all, she reasoned, a bit of a spat between a man and a woman was no rare thing and often merely indicated that they were interested in one another; perhaps this would be the case with Patty and Mr Knight. It had certainly been so with her own mother and father. They had rarely quarrelled and were, she knew, deeply fond of one another, but that had not prevented unpleasantness when her father was in the money and able to take more drink than usual. Maggie was truly fond of her father but had long accepted that too much drink made him violent. Yet the violence passed as the effects of the drink ebbed away and he was always heartily sorry after he had hit out and hurt someone. Mr Knight, Maggie was sure, would be just the same. Perhaps he would apologise to Patty and things could get back to normal. Maggie, hurrying up the stairs to the ramshackle rooms in which she had been born and bred, hoped fervently that this would be so.

*

Patty had a hectic day trying to catch up and was extremely glad that Ellen would be joining her the following week. Despite her hurry, though, she went into the police station and enquired about her coat, unfortunately without success. It had not been handed in and the desk sergeant, displaying a jaundiced view of humanity, advised her to leave it a couple of days and then to try the stalls on Great Homer Street and Paddy's market. 'If it were a decent dark gaberdine, whoever found it will likely sell it on rather than keep it,' he said. 'You've looked where you thought you dropped it?'

Patty, who had visited St Anne Street earlier in the day, without success, nodded and assured the sergeant that she had retraced her route but had seen no sign of her precious coat. 'I'll take your advice, though, and try the second-hand clothes stalls, just as soon as I can spare the time,' she said. 'Thank you very much, Sergeant.'

When she finished work that evening, it was late and she was extremely tired, but when she reached home it was to find that the children had not yet returned. She had bought the makings of a salad from Stanley Rawsthorne's on Scotland Road and now she set about hard-boiling some eggs to go with it. She and Maggie would eat the salad but little Merrell would be happy with what she called a 'dippy egg' and some bread and margarine cut into 'soldier boy fingers'. Since this could not be prepared in advance, Patty was listening for the sound of Maggie dragging the pram up the stairs when a knock sounded on the outer door. Pushing back wisps of damp hair from her face, for the heat was building up in the kitchen, Patty went to the door, thinking that Maggie and Mrs Knight must have carried the pram, as they sometimes did when Merrell was asleep. However, when she opened the door, it was not Mrs Knight or Maggie who stood outside on the landing, but Darky Knight. For a moment, she looked up into his face, thoroughly startled, wondering what on earth he was doing there. But then he thrust something towards her and Patty's gaze dropped to his hands. He was holding her gaberdine!

'What on earth . . . *where* on earth . . .?' Patty stammered, holding out her hands for her coat. 'I thought I was never going to see it again! But – but you walked home when I did. How . . .? Oh, but I'm extremely grateful; buying a new one would have cost me a month's wages.'

'When I got home it were too hot to sleep,' Darky said gruffly. 'I got out of bed to get meself a drink of water and while I was fetching a mug I suddenly remembered you'd been carrying something over your arm when I first saw you – something you weren't carrying when we left that alley. Well, it were awful hot and I fancied a walk so I just – just sort of strolled down to St Anne Street, keeping me eyes peeled. It were up that jigger, kicked into a corner of the wall. I thought you'd likely need it so I picked it up and brought it back.'

He did not meet her eyes as he spoke but stared over her left shoulder as though there were someone more interesting behind her. Patty, taking her property, began to try to thank him but he cut her short.

'It's all right,' he said gruffly, angrily almost, Patty felt. 'Only next time you go out of an evening, you'd best choose your company a bit more carefully. Next time there might be no one about to—'

Patty felt her cheeks go hot and cut across his

words without compunction. 'Just *what* do you mean by that?' she asked furiously. 'I didn't choose to be so much as spoken to, let alone hauled off up that jigger! I was making my way home as quietly as I could – why I even crossed the road when I saw those men come bursting on to the pavement – and the next thing I knew, one of them had grabbed me! And what do you mean, *when I first saw you*? You're not trying to tell me you stood by and watched whilst I was – I was molested?'

She was staring furiously into Darky's face and saw the flush creep up from his neck; saw, too, that he was beginning to look angry. She would have liked to retreat, but held her ground. 'Well? Just what *were* you doing in St Anne Street last evening, Mr Knight?'

'I don't see that it's any of your business, Nurse Peel,' Darky said coldly. 'I'd – I'd been round to a friend's place and I didn't recognise you, as it happens. I saw a feller put his arm round your waist and thought no more of it . . . well, I could see you were willing . . .'

It was too much. 'I was *not* willing and you may go to the devil, Mr Knight,' Patty said. She saw him beginning to open his mouth and slammed the door in his face, turning the key in the lock as she did so. Then she rushed across the kitchen, threw herself into one of the fireside chairs and indulged in a hearty fit of weeping.

It was a good thing, she reflected later, that Mrs Knight had kept the children rather longer than usual. By the time Maggie and Merrell returned, Patty was in command of herself once more. She had brushed her gaberdine coat and it was hanging on the back door; Mrs Clarke's beautiful dress hung beside it, washed, dried and ironed. Supper was on the table and Patty herself was calmly pouring milk into Merrell's little mug and cutting her bread and margarine into fingers. Maggie's first remark, as she hung her own thin jacket on the back of the door, was: 'You've got your coat back! Oh, Patty, I'm ever so glad! And we've had just about the best day ever. Mrs Knight let us take off our clothes, except for our knickers, and we bathed in the sea! We dug in the sand and made sand pies and lovely castles and Merrell and me collected shells to decorate the castles with. Then Mrs Knight's sister, Mrs Widnes, gave us a lovely tea with home-made scones and jam, and a plateful of little pink shrimps. It were lovely, honest it was.'

'I'm glad you had a good day and yes, I got my coat back,' Patty said guardedly. 'There's salad for supper with hard-boiled eggs, and a dippy egg for Merrell. I'm just going to put it on now.' She suited action to her words and presently the three of them took their places and began to eat.

'Where did you find the coat?' Maggie asked, reaching for her mug of tea. 'Was it at the police station after all?'

'No. Mr – Mr Knight found it lying in the road. He brought it round on his way home from work,' Patty said briefly. She began to spoon the white of the egg into Merrell's eager mouth. 'This young lady may have had a good tea, but she's still very hungry, I see.'

She half expected Maggie to continue to question her over the recovery of her coat but Maggie shot a shrewd glance at her, opened her mouth to speak, and then closed it again. And then the business of the evening, which was to get everyone first fed and then washed and changed and into bed, took over, and the affair of the coat was forgotten, or so Patty hoped.

Merrell was not talking very much yet though she was beginning to make a big effort to be understood, and as Patty washed and changed her she chattered constantly about her lovely day, though most of what she said might have been in a foreign language for all the sense Patty could make of it. She said as much to Maggie as the two of them made their hot drinks later and prepared to go to bed, but Maggie said, wisely, that children did things at their own pace. 'My little brother Freddie scarce said a word until he was three,' she told Patty. 'And Harold was chattering like a magpie when he were no more than eighteen months. But now Freddie's top of his class and Harold's just run of the mill. So it don't do to worry yourself over Merrell not saying a lot, 'cos it don't mean a thing.'

Much heartened by this matter of fact approach, Patty went to bed and eventually to sleep, though all the cutting remarks which she could have said – should have said – to Darky Knight kept her awake for a good hour.

'Now! If you've got your balance, if you're quite sure, then I'll give you a shove and you can see if you can stay on the bike for a few yards without coming face to face with the cobbles,' Patty said breathlessly, trying to hold the bicycle upright whilst Ellen sat on the seat, clutching the handlebars and wobbling wildly from side to side. 'All right? Say "go" when you're ready.'

Patty was teaching Ellen to ride a bicycle. For the first week, Ellen had hurried after her on foot, but this was frustrating for Patty and exhausting for Ellen so, on Sunday, the two of them had gone round to Nurse Gundry's neat little house to ask her if she might consider hiring her bicycle to them for a few weeks.

Nurse Gundry had been on the district for all her working life, and had retired three years ago. However, she still used her bicycle, pedalling furiously along the most crowded thoroughfares and padlocking the machine whilst she went shopping, bargaining fiercely for any goods which had taken her fancy. Patty knew that the older woman was considered eccentric but, nevertheless, she liked her. Whenever illness struck and the district found itself suddenly shorn of nurses, the authorities knew they could always rely on Gundry to step into the breach. She had been a little doubtful about asking the older woman for the loan of her bicycle, but to her pleasure Nurse Gundry had not hesitated. 'You're welcome to have a borrow of it weekdays, 'cos at this time of year I reckon walking is a nice change from bicycling,' she had said. 'But come the weekend I like to cycle into the country, wi' me little tent strapped to me back and me grub in the carrier. So can you have it back here by, say, eight o'clock of a Friday evening? As for payin' me, I wouldn't take money from a nurse, not if I were ever so. And as soon as Purbright here decides to stay wi' the district, we'll all go down to Paddy's market and I'll choose a good sturdy machine for her to buy. How's that?'

Patty and Ellen had been delighted, but Patty had not reckoned on the extreme difficulty of teaching a grown woman to ride a bicycle. Ellen had never ridden one in her life and was frankly scared at the idea of having to brave the traffic. Patty pooh-poohed this, assuring her friend that she would soon grow accustomed, but that had been before she had actually seen Ellen and bicycle together. Ellen had no natural sense of balance and though, so far, they had only practised in Ashfield Place, Patty was beginning to dread their first foray into proper streets. Maggie, who had never ridden a bicycle until she had come to Ashfield Place, had told Ellen that she had mastered the art in two days, but Maggie was not afraid of falling whereas Ellen was terrified of it, and frequently fell off because she forgot to pedal and kept screaming and closing her eyes in anticipation of disaster.

Today, however, Ellen was determined to learn and was concentrating on what she did and refusing to panic. As a result, she actually managed to ride the full length of Ashfield Place, though turning at the bottom was beyond her as yet. In fact, as soon as she put on the brakes, she fell off, saving the bicycle from a tumble with some difficulty and then turning to beam at Patty. 'Not bad, eh?' she said breathlessly. 'I'm goin' to get it right this evening if it kills me! You wait and see, Peel. When you set off for work on Monday, I'll be cycling alongside you.'

'Not if you can't turn corners, you won't,' Patty said. 'Still, you're getting on pretty well. And you must learn to stop properly; pull on the brakes slowly and then lean sideways, so that one foot goes on to the ground. Are you ready to have another go?'

By the end of the evening, when it was growing dusk, Patty wheeled Nurse Gundry's bicycle up the steps and padlocked it to the balcony rail. Then she and Ellen went into the house to join Maggie. Merrell was in bed but Maggie had just brewed the tea and was pouring it into three mugs. She looked up and smiled as the girls came in. 'How did it go?' she enquired. 'There weren't nearly as many screams and bumps as usual!'

'No, because tonight I had an audience,' Ellen said

mysteriously. 'There were this feller . . . he were keepin' well back so it were difficult to see his face at first, but later he came downstairs and crossed the Place and went off somewhere. My, but he's good-lookin'! The best-lookin' feller I've seen since I left the hospital. He must live somewhere on our landing, but I don't reckon I've seen him before.' She sighed deeply. 'He's lovely when he smiles. He's got the whitest teeth and he's ever so tanned. But you wouldn't have seen him, Patty, because you were watching me and you had your back to him. I reckon he must be a neighbour, though, unless he were just visiting.'

'I imagine you probably saw Mr Knight,' Patty said indifferently. 'But don't waste your time making sheep's eyes at him, Ellen. He doesn't like nurses.'

Ellen giggled. 'I thought all men liked nurses,' she objected. 'They've got some weird idea that we're more – more cooperative than girls in other professions. Anyway, you can't dislike someone 'cos of the work they do, surely?'

'Mr Knight can,' Patty said, sitting down thankfully and beginning to sip her tea. 'It seems unreasonable – well, it *is* unreasonable – but he blames midwives for his wife's death.'

'Oh, he's married, is he?' Ellen said, then took in the full meaning of Patty's words. She brightened. 'D'you mean he's a widow?'

It was Patty's turn to giggle. 'A widow is a woman, you fool,' she said. 'But yes, he's a widower, if that's what you mean. I don't think he's interested in girls, though. His wife died four years ago and his mam told Mrs Clarke – she lives further along our balcony – that he's not taken a girl out since.'

'You'd better keep your voice down, Ellen, 'cos he

lives next door,' Maggie advised, speaking for the first time. 'He often goes out of an evening, but Mrs Knight's always there and the wall between the flats ain't all that thick.' She eyed Ellen curiously. 'Don't you have a boyfriend, Ellen?'

'I have hundreds of men eager to spend their money on me,' Ellen said airily, then leaned across the table and chucked Maggie under the chin. 'You are daft, young Maggie! I'm a nurse; doesn't that mean anything to you? Nurses are lucky if they get one evening off a week and then we're often too tired to go out and have a gay old time. Why, Patty here only came to the dance hall once and that took some arranging. Still, if I had a handsome feller like Mr Knight living next door to me, I'd make him change his mind about nurses, see if I wouldn't.'

'You do live next door to Mr Knight,' Maggie observed, 'and you'll go on living next to him until you decide you want to go back to the hospital, I suppose.'

'I'm not sure that I do want to go back to the hospital,' Ellen said thoughtfully. 'I know I've only been on the district a short while but I really like it, honest to God I do. And although we work ever so hard, at least you are your own boss,' she added, addressing Patty. 'If you decide to do all your revisits in the morning and have an hour off in the afternoon for your messages, provided you keep up with the work that's fine. The authorities don't care how you arrange your day as long as the job gets done.' This time she turned to Maggie. 'It's so different on the ward, you wouldn't believe. Even when there's nothing to do, which isn't often, a senior staff nurse, or Sister, will tell you to count blankets or draw sheets or they'll decide the walls need washing down or the floor could do with an extra polish. Then there's the ward kitchen and the sluice and the patients' lavatories – oh aye, Sister would invent a job rather than think of you being idle for ten minutes. No, give me the district any time.'

'That's good to hear,' Patty said. 'I was talking to Mrs Ruskin a couple of weeks ago – telling her that you were coming to stay with me, Ellen – and she said she'd had dozens of nurses doing their midder training with her and only four of them had actually stayed on the district. She said lots of nurses, though they grumble like anything, prefer the regulated regime of the wards to the more informal approach on the district. So I shall count myself really lucky if you decide to join us.'

Despite Patty's fears, by the following Monday Ellen insisted that she could ride well enough to accompany Patty on Nurse Gundry's bike, so the two of them set off. As they made their way to their first call, Patty warned Ellen that they were about to visit a very unhygienic house. 'You'll soon get to know which patients can't cope and which can,' Patty said. 'Mrs O'Connor has eight children and a husband who drinks more than he should. Consequently, money is scarce and Mrs O'Connor has to work away from the house. That means she's often too tired to do much more than feed the kids and drag herself to bed, so bugs have a fairly easy time of it.'

'Oh, I know all about bugs,' Ellen said cheerfully. 'When we delivered that baby last Thursday night and there were all those little red things hopping around in the orange box Mrs Allen was using for a cot, I nearly died, but you just shook the blanket over the fire – and there were lots of little crackling sounds and neither of us said a word. Afterwards, you told me they were fleas. So that was me baptism of fire.'

Patty laughed. 'Oh, it's almost impossible to get rid of fleas, especially when the weather's so warm,' she said. 'But until the baby came Mrs Allen scrubbed and scoured the whole house three or four times a week. I wouldn't hesitate to accept a cup of tea and a biscuit from her. Mrs O'Connor isn't like that, though! I doubt if she's ever had a bath in her life; her hands are always grimy and her nails are black. It doesn't do to say so, of course, but all the children have nits and the youngest two simply squat on the floor when they want to go to the lavatory; you have to watch where you step!' Patty laughed again at Ellen's stricken face. 'So if Mrs O'Connor offers you a cup of tea, say you've only just had one. It doesn't do to hurt folks' feelings, and sometimes, when a patient is very pressing, you have to accept a mug of tea and either drink it or pour it away when she isn't looking. These people are desperately poor but they have their pride – it's about all some of them do have – and we're always careful not to injure that pride.'

'I won't forget,' Ellen said fervently. 'How old is Mrs O'Connor's baby? Will we visit her often?'

'Little Tommy was born eight days ago. I did all the revisits whilst you were doing other things, because I didn't want to put you off,' Patty said frankly. 'But now you can ride the bike we'll be working much more closely, and I'm afraid I shan't be able to spare you the less pleasant visits.' She turned her bicycle into a noisome side street and then into a jigger which led off it. 'These houses are back to backs, so there's only one door. It leads straight into the kitchen from a tiny yard so get ready to tread carefully, ignore bugs and fleas and refuse all offers of refreshment!'

Patty and Ellen had a long and tiring day but, Patty thought, a satisfying one. They went in and out of their patients' homes, doing the jobs which needed doing, offering sympathy and advice and solving small problems. They also delivered a baby which was not due for another week. The mother was a skinny, frightened girl of fifteen or sixteen – no one mentioned the father – and Patty allowed Ellen to bath the tiny scrap in a biscuit tin and then sent her out to a neighbour's house to beg or borrow some pieces of blanket in which to wrap the child and some rags to act as nappies. The girl was still living at home, surrounded by younger brothers and sisters, with a hatchet-faced mother who kept grumbling that she had enough to do with her own brood and clearly resented the added burden of an unwanted grandchild.

'I mentioned adoption the first time I visited but the old woman nearly blew my head off, though you wouldn't think it to hear her today,' Patty said as they cycled off to their next visit. 'The girl's a poor little creature with no mind of her own. If you ask me, that baby doesn't stand much chance. Still, there isn't much we can do about it. Women like that girl's mother resent anything they see as interference, even if it's for their own good. But maybe it'll all work out. If the old woman is still resentful and unhelpful tomorrow, I'll suggest adoption again.'

'You've got to be really brave on the district,' Ellen observed as they pedalled along. 'In hospital, it's the doctor or the matron – or even Sister – who suggests that a child might be offered for adoption. And in hospital the patients are – are sort of cowed. I s'pose all the clean sheets and rustling uniforms and bossy women terrify them.

It makes them a lot easier to deal with, though.'

'Yes, I'm sure you're right,' Patty agreed. 'Take the next turning on the left, Ellen. You've been here before – it's Mrs Merrick. Do you remember her? She'll make us a nice cup of tea, and I must say I'm gasping for a cup.'

'That last woman offered us a cup of tea,' Ellen reminded her. 'What excuse did you make? You couldn't very well say we'd just had one because we were in her house almost four hours!'

'I said it was very kind of her to offer but we dared not stop or we'd be late for our next four or five visits,' Patty said demurely. 'Actually, Hatchet Face is probably a good deal cleaner than some, but I still couldn't fancy anything she made. She probably spits in the tea of anyone who doesn't take her fancy and I expect she still remembers I suggested adoption, so I'm probably in line for some mark of disfavour.'

By the time all their visits had been completed, it was nearly six o'clock and the rush hour was well under way. Patty wondered whether to tell Ellen to push the bicycle but the thought of delaying still further their return home to the meal which awaited them was not welcome. Instead, she simply advised Ellen to take great care. 'Buses and trams come awful near and other cyclists whiz past and cars cover you in dust,' she said. 'You're still a beginner on the bike, so just go slow, follow me and don't let the traffic fluster you, then you'll be all right.'

Ellen agreed to do as she was bidden and the two of them set off into the increasingly heavy going-home traffic.

'Darky! Darky Knight! Where do you think you're off to in such a hurry?'

Darky, pushing his way off the ferry, turned to see who was addressing him, then groaned inwardly. It was one of the girls from Levers, a machine operator in the flakes department. She was a bold, brassy piece who made no secret of the fact that she wanted to get to know him better. Darky disliked her, and was frequently embarrassed by the bawdy remarks which were always made in a voice just loud enough to be heard, but could be denied if she were challenged. In Levers, of course, he was 'Mr Knight' to all the staff. Even brassy Bet would not have dared to address him as Darky during working hours, but obviously she considered that once free of the factory environment she could call him anything she liked. Darky's feet met terra firma and he considered pretending that he had not heard, but even as he did so he remembered that he had turned back, that their eyes had met. Sighing, he slowed his pace, and presently Bet caught him up and grabbed his sleeve.

'Phew! I thought you were never goin' to hear me shout,' she said, pulling him to a stop and standing far too close for comfort, so far as Darky was concerned. 'I wanted to tell you there's a gang of us hirin' a charabanc for a trip down Rhyl while the hot weather lasts. It'll cost four bob a head and that includes us dinners. Want to come along?'

'No thanks. I'm busy at weekends,' Darky said promptly. He had no wish to get involved with factory outings planned and masterminded by brassy Bet, though it would never do to say so. Bet was a forceful character, and though the other girls did not like her they respected her ability to tackle the bosses and to make life unpleasant for anyone who stood up to her.

'Who said owt about weekends?' Bet said immediately. Darky noticed, with satisfaction, that she was having to trot to keep pace with his longer strides. 'You never even asked me what day it were planned for.'

'Well, surprise me,' Darky said cordially. 'Tell me you've arranged a trip for mid-week, you being so clever an' all.'

Bet sniffed. 'It's next Sat'day,' she said sulkily. 'We're startin' out at six in the morning – there'll be five pick-up points, two of them in the 'Pool – and we reckon we'll be home by midnight.' She pulled him to a halt once again, then stepped in front of him so that he had to look at her as she spoke. 'Be a sport, Darky. It 'ud make my day if you said you'd come along – and I'd see you enjoyed yourself. I'd make sure, personally, that you had a damn good time.'

As she spoke, she ducked her head and looked up at him through her lashes. It was a frankly inviting look and one which caused Darky's spine to tingle in a most unpleasant fashion. Had the look been cast at him by someone he found attractive, it might have been a different story, but Bet repelled him. She was a tall, green-eyed bottle blonde and she was known to be easy, despite the fact that she had married a sailor a couple of years ago. Her husband was on the transatlantic liners and consequently away for fairly long stretches of time, and it was known to most of the workers that Bet liked company during her periods of enforced grass widowhood. But the girl was looking up at him, her lips parting, her mouth beginning to curve into a smile. She must have thought that his silence meant he was seriously considering her offer, Darky thought crossly. Best put an end to it now.

'Sorry, I've plans for this Saturday,' he said briefly. 'But there'll be plenty of other takers, no doubt. Good day to you.'

Bet, however, was not to be put off so easily. 'Whadda you mean?' she asked indignantly. 'I don't give up so easy, chuck. I live only a couple o' streets away from you, so we'll bleedin' well walk home together and you can bleedin' well listen while I bleedin' well try to change your mind.'

Despite himself, Darky felt a grin spread across his face. You had to admit it, Bet was a trier. She was unsnubbable too; most girls would have flounced off after his first refusal, but Bet was plainly made of sterner stuff. In fact, he thought as she fell into step beside him, you would be forgiven for thinking she had read encouragement in his firm refusal, for she actually had the nerve to tuck a hand into his arm, saying as she did so: 'Off we go then! Now, about this trip to Rhyl . . .'

Darky considered being really unpleasant, so that she was left in no doubt of his feelings, but then he remembered that he would have to face her in the factory next day. She was quite capable of lying in her teeth and pretending that he had "tried it on" when she had approached him about the trip to Rhyl. Or she might say he was so stuck up that he would not go on a factory outing with other workers. She could tell any lies she liked, and though she would probably not be believed, it would do little to improve the atmosphere at Levers. Darky's boss was always emphasising that the staff should be friends and not just colleagues. If word got back to him that Darky had been churlish and arrogant, then it would not improve his chances of promotion. Sighing, Darky continued to walk at a pace which suited Bet and to invent in his head a cast-iron reason for remaining in Liverpool next Saturday.

*

Patty and Ellen managed quite well despite the heavy traffic, until they reached Vauxhall Road. It was so crowded with vehicles and people, to say nothing of trams, that Patty turned her head to advise Ellen to dismount, but her friend was twenty yards behind her and concentrating grimly, Patty thought, on simply staying on the bicycle. She had no attention to spare for anything else so Patty, who had dismounted, set off once more, threading her way through pedestrians and stationary vehicles along the busy street. She slowed her pace, however, and when Ellen was a mere five yards behind turned to remind her friend that they would presently take a right turn into Silvester Street. 'You'd best dismount, Ellen,' she bawled as loudly as she could. 'It's safer to push the bikes across when there's so much traffic about.'

She saw her friend nod and pull out to pass a stationary cart. But she did not slow down as she came up to Patty, instead continuing to cycle straight on, with a desperate look on her face. Initially baffled, Patty suddenly realised, with horror, what had happened. Ellen's wheels were stuck in the tramline and Ellen did not realise it. Patty saw her wrench wildly at the handlebars, heard her despairing wail of 'Patteeeeee' as she sailed past. Then a tram came charging along and Patty's horror turned to sick disbelief. If the driver did not realise . . . if he hit Ellen . . .

Patty cast her own bicycle down into the gutter and sprang forward and, as she did so, saw a tall young man with a brassy blonde hanging on his arm stop for one moment and then leap into the road.

It was Darky Knight!

Bet was still hanging on to Darky's arm in the most infuriating way when they stopped on the edge of the kerb in Vauxhall Road, meaning to cross and go down Silvester Street. Their ways would part here, Darky hoped, but he was not too sure that Bet really was heading home. He knew, of course, that she did not live in Ashfield Place, for everyone knew everyone else in the landing houses, but he supposed, despairingly, that she might live in one of the courts off Latimer Street or even on Westmoreland Place or Bendledi Street. If so, then she really was heading home and not simply accompanying him in order to find out where he lived. He decided that whichever proved to be the case, he would have to summon all his courage and tell Bet – only he would call her Miss Grainger – that he did not believe in fraternising with fellow workers outside the factory. Then he would walk away smartly, and surely even brassy Bet would not choose to follow him in such circumstances.

They were waiting on the edge of the kerb when he saw Patty and the new girl who had taken up residence next door cycling towards him. Patty drew her machine to a halt and looked over her shoulder at her companion, but to Patty's obvious surprise the other girl cycled straight past. Darky was wondering why she had done such a thing, for the way home led down Silvester Street, when realisation came to him. He had seen Ellen learning to ride the bicycle so knew her to be a beginner and guessed at once that her wheels were stuck in the tramline. Even as the thought crossed his mind, he heard the tram thundering down on them and saw Ellen wobble dreadfully as she tried to glance behind her.

He pushed Bet away from him and leaped forward, seeing out of the corner of his eye that Patty had thrown her bicycle down and was running towards her friend. Darky got there first. In a couple of strides, he grabbed Ellen round the waist and heaved her off the bicycle. Then, with the warning jangle of the tram's bell sounding in his ears, he dragged the bicycle out of the tramline and got all safely to the pavement, just as the tram thundered past.

'Who do you think you're pushing, you ignorant . . .' Bet was beginning, but then she must have realised what had happened and, by a miracle, fell silent. People were pressing around them, congratulating Darky on his quickness, telling Ellen what a lucky escape she had had, offering gratuitous advice on keeping out of the way of tramlines in the future.

Patty, panting up breathlessly, took the bicycle from Darky's hands and propped it carefully against the kerb. 'Thank you very much, Mr Knight,' she said in a small, tight voice. 'I did my best to reach her but I was too far behind.' She turned to Ellen. 'It was all my fault, queen. I never warned you about the tramlines, but I've got so used to avoiding them myself that I suppose I just didn't think. Are you all right? No bruises or bumps? Can you wheel your own bicycle or do you want me to take the pair of them?'

'I think I'm all right,' Ellen said. Darky saw that she was crying and imagined it was relief after her narrow escape from, if not death, at least serious injury. She turned her face towards Darky, her tear-filled eyes shining with admiration and gratitude. 'I don't know how to thank you, Mr Knight! You saved my life – and you saved my bicycle too. I were almost as worried about the bike as about myself because I borrowed the bike from Mrs Gundry and she'd never forgive me if it came to harm.'

Darky muttered that it was all right and turned to

leave the two girls, then remembered Bet. She was still standing where he had left her but with a very much softer expression on her face, and as soon as she saw that the two girls had left him she came hurrying to his side, saying: 'Well, and who's a bleedin' little hero then? You saved that gal from a horrible accident, there's no doubt o' that; I never seen anyone move so fast in me life, nor act so brave. Wait till I tell the gals at work what you done.'

'I just happened to be nearer than anyone else,' Darky said gruffly. 'Don't you go blabbin' at work, Miss Grainger, or you'll be in my bad books.' A brilliant thought occurred to him. 'It 'ud only embarrass my young lady.'

Darky felt he could almost see Bet pricking up her ears. 'Young lady?' she said suspiciously. 'What young lady? They say, in Levers, you haven't had no young lady since . . . not for years,' she amended.

Darky laughed. 'Why do you think I dived into the road and risked me own life to get young Ellen out of trouble?' he asked. 'I've not known her all that long, as she's only just moved into our neighbourhood, but I suppose you could say we've got an – an understanding.'

There was a short pause whilst Bet digested this, then her eyes narrowed suspiciously. 'Are you tryin' to tell me that girl's your young lady?' she asked incredulously. 'Well if so, you've a bleedin' funny way of showin' it! Why, you let the two of them go off wi'out so much as a word. If she'd bin your young lady, you'd ha' give her a kiss and an 'ug, an' don't try to tell me different!'

'Ah, but you don't understand,' Darky said. He felt astonished at his own quickness of wit and ingenuity. 'Ellen's a nurse – a trainee midwife actually – and the

268

girl with her, the blonde, is her boss. She's ever so strict and spiteful to girls who have fellers – you know how spinsters can be. Why, if she knew I were courtin' Ellen, she'd make sure to get Ellen dismissed for some imaginary fault or other. What's more, she hates me and would do me any harm she could.'

Bet looked at him with round eyes. 'Aye, I know what you mean. There's some of the supervisors at work what has a down on particular girls and sets out to make them so miserable that they'll leave,' she agreed. 'Well, good luck, Mr Knight, wi' your romance. And now I'd best be off. Me mam'll have tea on the table and I'm off dancin' later so I must gerra move on.' They crossed the road together but Bet turned back along Vauxhall Road, confirming Darky's suspicion that she did not live in the vicinity of Ashfield Place. She took half a dozen quick steps along the pavement, then turned back. 'Why don't you bring your young lady on the charabanc trip to Rhyl?' she enquired. 'They're pickin' up at the junction of the Scottie and Silvester Street so you wouldn't have far to walk, and you won't find no other nurses on the trip, 'cos it's all Levers, as I said.'

'I dunno,' Darky muttered, feeling trapped. If he did not go, then Bet's suspicions would become aroused and she might try to follow him home again. But he did not know Ellen well enough to ask her out for the day and, in any case, was not sure that he wanted to do so. She was a pretty thing with her bouncy brown hair, clear skin and long, greenish-hazel eyes but, when it came down to it, he scarcely knew her. In fact, if he asked anyone out . . . but he killed the thought quickly. Patty might fascinate him – she did fascinate him – but she was his enemy as well as being a member of a profession he hated.

It did not occur to him until he was turning into Ashfield Place that Ellen was also a midwife, and that some of the instinctive mistrust which he'd told himself he felt for Patty he should also have felt for Ellen. He was mildly surprised to find that he had no such feelings towards the younger girl, then shrugged the thought away as immaterial. Nurses were nurses, and there were plenty of pretty girls around without even having to consider the nursing profession.

Whistling, he ran up the stairs on to the top landing and headed for his mother's door.

Chapter Ten

Although Ellen had told Patty, after her first week, that she preferred the district to working in hospital, it took her a little longer to realise that the friendliness of the patients, and their open championship for the nurses who looked after them, could never have happened on a hospital ward. Visiting the women in their own homes meant that the nurses really understood their problems and were not merely paying lip service to them.

Ellen revelled in the freedom which she and Patty enjoyed when compared with life on the ward. Mostly they worked together, though as Ellen's experience grew there were some cases which she could deal with alone, and this made the job easier. When in any doubt as to the treatment required, however, Ellen knew she could turn to Patty and always did so. As a last resort, there were doctors, but though some of these were excellent men, as devoted to their patients' welfare as were the nurses, others were not. They did their job well enough but never tried to see things from the patient's point of view. Patty told Ellen that one elderly and cross-grained doctor had actually drawn up a diet sheet for a sick woman which included eggs, fresh milk, poultry and fish. 'Her husband was out of work and she had five children. She could not possibly afford any of the items he suggested, not even as an occasional treat, far less seven days a week,' Patty had said. 'Others recommend that a patient should convalesce in the country or by the sea, when if they only looked around them – used their eyes – they would realise that even a day out would strain the family finances intolerably. We do what we can on the district, though it's little enough in all conscience, but people appreciate that *we* have to make do and mend as they do themselves.'

At first, when Ellen was searching round for a clean sheet or something sustaining for a new mother to eat after her delivery, she thought wistfully of the advantages of having everything to hand on the maternity ward, a cupboard full of clean linen and other nurses to help manoeuvre a heavy or difficult patient. But soon she realised that she had no desire whatsoever to return to the hospital. She and Patty worked well together and never disagreed or argued. They went to Paddy's market to buy piles of rags which they washed and dried to use as nappies for babies whose mothers could not provide for them. They bought cheap sweets which could be given to older brothers and sisters if they woke frightened by their mother's cries, and Ellen soon realised that, as the neighbourhood midwife, she was a person of some importance to patients old and new. Whereas in hospital one met a patient, knew her vaguely for a week and then never saw her again, on the district it was quite different. Patty explained that one of the pleasantest parts of her job was watching the children she had delivered grow up.

'When I was younger, I decided to work in the city until I had enough experience to take on a country practice,' Patty had told Ellen, as they enjoyed a rare day off. 'I still think I'll do so one of these days, but it will be a real wrench to leave these people. I know it sounds like a cliché, Ellen, but they really are the salt of the earth. They'll do anything for each other – think how they rally round when a new baby is born to a family in miserable circumstances – and they'll do anything for us, too. When we have an inspection, they make sure everything in their homes is as it should be, even though perhaps almost all of the equipment has been borrowed from neighbours. Yes, it'll be a wrench to leave my district, though the thought of a little house of my own, and a dog and a nice piece of garden, keeps me going when times are hard.'

The thought of a little house in the country might have appealed to Ellen at one time, but ever since Darky had rescued her and her borrowed bicycle from the tramlines she had known that the best thing about living in Ashfield Place was Darky's nearness. Ever since that first occasion, he had been very friendly towards her. He had actually taken her to the cinema two or three times and always asked her to dance when they both visited the Grafton Ballroom or the Daulby Hall, though Ellen did not kid herself that he was courting her. She knew that Darky had his reasons.

'To tell the truth, Miss Purbright,' he had said when she had tried to thank him for rescuing her, 'I'd ha' done the same for anyone – well, any fellow would – but I had a motive as well. There's a girl in Levers been makin' a dead set at me – Betty Grainger, her name is – so I told her you were my young lady. She won't believe I'm just not interested in marrying again, you see, but once word gets around that I've got me eye on a girl living in my own neighbourhood they'll draw back a bit, I hope.' He had looked at her anxiously, a slight flush staining his cheeks. 'You don't mind, do you? If we could go around together a bit, have a dance or two sometimes, visit the cinema together, then you'd be paying me back double or treble for fishing you out from under that tram.'

Ellen had been grateful to him for his honesty and agreed not to tell a soul because, as Darky had said, once a rumour that he was putting on an act got around, it would be an end to peace at work.

There was no doubt that Ellen enjoyed his company, but she could not help hoping that one day Darky's eyes would be opened and he would stop thinking of her as a friend and start considering her as a future wife. He had never kissed her, never even held her hand, but Ellen told herself proximity often worked wonders. One day, he would realise that she really liked him, was actually giving up the chance of being courted by another feller just to please him, and then . . . and then . . .

Sometimes, Ellen wondered what Patty would say if she knew the true situation. Ellen could not tell her, having promised Darky she would not, but sometimes she thought Patty looked at her rather oddly, no doubt wondering why she, Ellen, did not make a push to go out with Darky more often. However, when her training period finished, Ellen had already made up her mind to apply for a midwife's job on a district and when she was given one adjacent to Patty's the two girls agreed to continue to share the landing house. Darky's presence was an added bonus, Ellen told herself.

By the spring of 1934, the girls were working the two areas between them and managing to do so with such skill that no one had objected. Ellen adored Merrell and told Patty she envied her her little daughter which made Patty grin, though Ellen had no idea why. 'And you're real lucky with Maggie, because the kid's devoted to you and to Merrell,' Ellen told her friend. 'She works ever so well at school – her teacher said so when we met on the Scottie last Tuesday – and she's becoming a real little housewife.'

The only thing which, Ellen felt, caused a slight strain between them was her friendship with Darky Knight. At first she had wondered why Patty disliked him so, for he had the sort of brooding good looks which few girls could resist and he was good-natured too, frequently helping various neighbours by carrying their heavy shopping up the metal stairways and giving Maggie a hand with the pram when it was laden with Merrell, Christopher and the messages. Recently, however, Maggie had decided to enlighten her. She had explained that the very first time Patty had gone dancing with the other nurses, Darky had stopped her on her way home and tried to get a bit too friendly.

'He must have been drunk as a wheelbarrow,' Maggie said wisely, 'because Darky ain't that sort, as you very well know. I expect all he wanted was a kiss, but Patty didn't know that so she struggled and probably hit out. Nothin' makes a feller madder than bein' hit by a woman; I know that because me mam often said so. He must 'ave grabbed her face under the chin, because she had bruises and some on her arm as well. He were real sorry, came round wi' her gaberdine which she'd dropped in the street, said he was sorry . . . but it made things awkward between them. I 'spec' you've noticed they don't speak if they can help it, and if he comes in when we're with Mrs Knight Patty scoots as soon as she can. It's a pity, but as me mam used to say, "There's nowt so queer as folks."'

Ellen was relieved to know that the trouble between Patty and Darky was of a fairly trivial nature. She had long realised that Patty was not at ease with men, treating them all with circumspection and never allowing a feller to walk her home after a dance. Indeed, to Ellen's knowledge, no man had ever entered No. 24 Ashfield Place.

But I do believe she's getting better, Ellen told herself now, as she pedalled along Latimer Street, slowing to a halt as she reached the little shop on the corner of Westmoreland Place. She's been nicer to the fellers she dances with, she isn't afraid to joke with them any more, and though I'm sure she means it when she says she'll never marry, at least the day may come when she isn't actually scared of men.

As Ellen entered the shop and waited for her turn at the counter, it occurred to her that she had never before actually realised her friend was afraid of men. She frowned, thinking it over; being shy was one thing but being actively scared quite another, and she knew Patty well enough by now to realise that it could not possibly have been Darky's attempt to kiss her which had made her fearful of men. Certainly, it had caused a coolness between her and Darky, but an apprehension such as Patty displayed was a great deal stronger and came from farther back than a mere few months. Something awful must have happened to Patty, and Ellen determined to discover what it was. If Patty brought her fear into the open, Ellen was sure that, between them, they could somehow disperse it.

'Can I help you, Nurse?'

Ellen jumped. She had been so immersed in her thoughts that she had failed to realise she had reached the head of the queue and Mr Flowerdew, trim in a brown overall, his moustache neatly waxed and his brown eyes kindly, was waiting to serve her.

'Sorry, Mr Flowerdew, I were dreaming,' Ellen said. 'Could I have two ounces of bull's-eyes and a sherbet dip, please? And half a pound of ginger nuts.'

'Certainly, Nurse,' Mr Flowerdew said, reaching for the big jar of bull's-eyes. He weighed the sweets with practised speed, shooting them into a white, conical bag, then weighed the biscuits. 'Anything else?'

'Yes please; I'd better have an ounce of jelly babies,' Ellen said. Patty did not really approve of sticky sweets for children but Ellen reasoned she could scarcely hand over a sherbet dip to Maggie and share the bull's-eyes with Patty without giving Merrell something nice. The child was bright as a button and beginning to talk and sing nursery rhymes, even chanting the skipping games when she watched Maggie and her pals at play. Ellen would not have hurt Merrell's feelings by leaving her out for anything.

Leaving the shop, Ellen remounted her bicycle and pedalled off in the direction of Ashfield Place. The trouble was, it was difficult for her to have any talk of a private nature with Patty. At home, the children were almost always present, and at work it was impossible to talk confidentially because there was always someone to overhear. At dances, it would have seemed very strange had they huddled in a corner and the same applied to cinema or theatre trips. But if she and Patty took the children to Seaforth Sands on Sunday afternoon, with a nice picnic and a couple of tablespoons and old enamel mugs, then the children could make sand pies and dig out moats and castles whilst she and Patty talked.

Well satisfied with her idea, Ellen swerved into Ashfield Place, parked her bicycle under the first-floor balcony, padlocked the front wheel and began to collect her messages. The bicycle was her very own for she had bought it from an elderly neighbour just as soon as she had saved up enough money and was very fond of it. She always made sure that it was clean and well oiled, with tyres hard and the brakes in good working order.

'Ellen! Where've you been? Ain't it a lovely day though? As soon as I gorrout of school, I picked our Merrell up and played on the swings. I went too high and fell off – see me grazed knee? But I managed to stop Merrell from hitting the ground. She were on me lap and never a squeak did she give when we sailed through the air.' Maggie leaned over the pram and plonked a kiss on Merrell's fair and smiling face. 'There ain't never been a better girl than our Merrell here, has there?'

'I'm sure you're right,' Ellen said.

She picked the baby out of the pram and lodged her on her hip but Merrell squeaked indignantly: 'Merry wanna go down! Merry wanna walk!' so Ellen stood the child on the cobbles, though she retained her hold on Merrell's small hand.

'I've got something nice for us all,' she said as she lifted her shopping bag from the bicycle basket. 'Have you got many messages, Maggie? Can you manage 'em if I take Merrell here up to the house?'

'I've got a great sack of spuds, two cabbages and an orange each an' I can manage 'em easy,' Maggie said briefly. She followed Ellen, lugging the pram behind her with her shopping still inside it, and began to hump it up the noisy metal stairs. Before she had got more than half a dozen steps up, however, Ellen heard her thanking someone and looked round to see Darky Knight taking the main weight of the pram. She smiled at him over her shoulder and he grinned back, saying gruffly, in answer to Maggie's thanks: 'It's all in a day's work, queen. My goodness, but you must ha' done messages for half the landing houses, or else you gals is hungrier'n most Irish navvies! All them perishin' spuds!'

'Some of 'em's for your mam,' Maggie agreed, rather breathlessly, 'and some's for Mrs Clarke. I only shop for our landing, as a rule, 'cos of the weight.' They reached the top landing and Darky went ahead of them, disappearing into his own house whilst Maggie carried the potatoes into Mrs Clarke's kitchen and handed over change. Rather to Ellen's disappointment, when they knocked at Mrs Knight's door it was that lady herself who answered; Darky had vanished.

'Got your spuds, Mrs K.; Mr Knight helped me lug the pram up the stairs though, so I 'spect you already know,' Maggie said cheerfully. She picked up a newspaper-wrapped bundle and handed it to the older woman. 'You wanted an onion and a couple of carrots an' all. They're in the same parcel and there weren't no change.'

'Thanks, queen,' Mrs Knight said. She turned to Ellen. 'I dunno how I'd manage wi'out young Maggie here to do me messages. You off dancin' tonight?'

'Not tonight, but Patty and me might go to the flicks,' Ellen said. '*Dinner at Eight* is showing at the Burlington Cinema in Vauxhall Road. It's got John Barrymore and Jean Harlow and Patty wants to see it as badly as I do.'

'That sounds lovely,' Mrs Knight said, with a trace of wistfulness. 'If you decide to go, come and tell me and I'll give an eye to the girls. Did you say John or Lionel Barrymore?'

'I said John, but Lionel's in it too, and I know you've got a weakness for him,' Ellen said, twinkling at the older woman. 'Why don't you go tomorrow night, Mrs K.? Mrs Rogers on the second landing goes to the flicks most weeks. She's a great fan of Jean Harlow.'

Later that evening, when she and Patty were returning from the cinema, Ellen suggested the trip to Seaforth Sands and was pleased when Patty agreed to go. 'So long as the weather's fine, that is,' Patty added, as the two of them prepared for bed. 'I wouldn't want to traipse all that way and not be able to go on the beach. They're good kids but even a good kid whines and gets difficult when a seaside trip is rained off.'

As soon as they awoke on Sunday, however, it was clear that they were in luck. The sun shone and the air was warm and pleasant, and as the children ate their breakfast Patty and Ellen bustled about preparing sandwiches and bottles of cold tea and getting all the equipment they would need packed into their shopping bags.

'It's a pity we can't take the pram, but it's too big to lug aboard a tram and after cycling about a thousand miles this week I'm not in the mood for a long walk,' Patty said, shoving a wool cardigan each into her bag. 'I've already packed a couple of towels so the kids can paddle but I'm adding the cardies in case we get chilly.'

'We're going to be laden like a couple of camels,' Ellen said apprehensively, eyeing the bulging bags. 'Still, an awful lot of it's food and we shan't be bringing that back.'

They reached the beach in good time to secure an area for themselves. Because of the sunshine, the sands were soon crowded. At first the two girls introduced Merrell to the sea, letting her paddle in and out of the chilly waves and showing her how to dig up the sand and fill the old enamel mug, then turn it out to make a sand pie. Maggie joined in and they had a thoroughly exhausting, happy morning. By noon, they were all extremely hungry and the large carryout which Patty had prepared disappeared in no time. When a 'Stop me and Buy One' appeared, Maggie offered to fetch ices for everyone, but when this treat was over Patty suggested that they might make a little nest for Merrell out of the towels and woolly cardigans. 'She's had a tiring morning so I think she should have a nap,' she said. 'I wouldn't mind one meself, come to that. What do you want to do now, Maggie?'

Maggie beamed at them. 'We-ell, I spotted one of me pals from school further up the beach,' she said. 'Mind if I goes up and has a word, Patty? Only if you'll give an eye to Merrell while she's asleep, then me and Maureen could have a bit of a chat like.'

Rather to Ellen's surprise, Merrell did not object at all when cuddled down on the sands and was soon fast asleep. The two girls exchanged smiles, and with one accord leaned back themselves. 'I wouldn't dream of sleeping because there's no saying when Merrell will wake,' Patty said. 'But a nice rest will be very welcome, don't you agree?'

'I do,' Ellen said. 'That were a good film the other night, weren't it? That John Barrymore, he's every girl's dream.'

Patty chuckled. 'Not if you're me,' she remarked. 'I dream of bricks and mortar – nice little home of me own, in the country . . .'

'. . . with a dog for company and a nice patch to grow vegetables and a few hens,' Ellen finished for her, laughing. 'But wouldn't it be an even nicer dream, Patty, if there were a feller to collect the eggs for you, and share the omelette across your kitchen table? Why, if he were earning good money, you might even have a little car! There's things that are possible on two salaries which you'll never manage on one!'

She had meant to sound comical, but somehow the words came out seriously. Patty heaved a sigh. 'Sometimes I think I must be different from any other girl who ever lived,' she said pensively. 'Ever since I were a kid, I've wanted a home of me own, but I can't ever remember wanting a man of me own. Is that so unusual, Ellen?'

'It certainly isn't unusual when you're a kid,' Ellen acknowledged. 'But I reckon most girls of fifteen or sixteen are beginning to think about love and marriage. Some just want the white dress and the attention, I suppose, but the more practical ones want the companionship and support of a husband.'

'What about you, Ellen?' Patty questioned drowsily. 'What were you like when you were fifteen or sixteen?'

'Oh, I fell in love with everyone who looked at me twice, including spotty youths who delivered bread and some of the older boys in our street,' Ellen admitted airily. 'As for film stars, I loved 'em all. I suppose I always took it for granted I'd get married one day, but once you start nursing . . .' She left the sentence unfinished.

'Once you're in nursing, your opportunities to meet men aren't so good,' Patty agreed. 'Well, you can meet 'em, but getting to know a feller properly is a different matter. Still, you're getting on pretty well with Darky Knight, I'd say.'

'Yes, I do like him,' Ellen said. 'I know you don't agree but he seems a pretty decent sort of feller. However, it was you we were discussin'. Is there a reason why you never think about marryin', queen? I've often wondered, but I haven't liked to ask.'

Patty sat up and stared at her friend with mock amazement. 'You haven't liked to ask?' she said incredulously. 'I can't imagine why, Ellen Purbright, because you're as curious as any cat!'

Ellen laughed. 'If you want to know, I haven't asked because of Merrell,' she explained. 'If I'm going to be frank, you must've liked a man well enough a few of years ago to – to go with him, otherwise Merrell wouldn't be here today!' She was watching Patty as she spoke, expecting to see a blush of mortification on her cheeks or a flash of anger in her blue eyes, but to her astonishment the only look which crossed Patty's face was one of intense amusement. Ellen waited for the outburst, but it did not come. Instead, Patty smiled lazily and put a caressing hand on the baby's fair curls.

'Merrell's father isn't a bad sort of feller,' she said, almost idly. 'But there was never any question of liking or not liking from either of us. He was – he was a widower, lonely without his wife but not looking to replace her.'

Ellen's eyes rounded; so she was getting the truth at last! 'Does – does he know you've got Merrell?' she asked after a moment. 'Didn't he offer to marry you when you told him you were pregnant?'

'I didn't tell him,' Patty said truthfully. 'Why should I? As I've said, marriage had never interested me and Merrell's father wasn't even my type – if I've got a type, that is. It was just – just that I felt sorry for him, I suppose. He had a great many other kids, you see, and soon took on another woman who could help him to bring them up. He knows nothing about Merrell and I mean to keep it that way. The last thing I want is interference; she's my little girl and I know I can give her a much better life than he could. Any more questions?'

'No. And now I understand why you don't like men much. Although you say it isn't so, I think you were taken advantage of and that isn't very nice,' Ellen said triumphantly. 'Only just because Merrell's father was a wrong 'un, that don't mean to say all men are rats.'

Patty smiled affectionately across at her friend. 'Since Merrell's father doesn't know about her, you can scarcely blame him for not asking me to marry him,' she pointed out. 'There was another thing . . .' and then she began to tell Ellen what had happened to Selina. 'Though it was a long time ago, it does tend to colour my feelings, I think,' she finished.

'Yes; that was terrible. But there are good, honest men who deal fairly by the women in their lives, truly there are, Patty,' Ellen said, 'and one day you'll meet the man for you, just see if you don't.'

'Maybe you're right,' Patty conceded. 'There was a feller I liked once . . .' and she told Ellen about her friendship with Toby Rudd and their plan to meet five years later, when they grew up.

284

Chapter Eleven
November 1923

Patty woke early on the morning of 15 November. Five years ago, on this very day, she had said goodbye to Toby Rudd and they had sworn to meet, if it was humanly possible, in five years' time.

On every 15 November since, Patty had always taken a few moments of quiet in which she had thought hard and earnestly of her old friend. They had not known each other for very long, but in the short time that they had been together Patty had learned both to like and to trust him. When they had parted, as the fireworks soared into the dark night sky, Toby had been about to set off for France and Patty supposed that, even then, she had known that his life was not like hers. He was a born traveller, and because he was with the fair he would go where they went and not where he wished. He had said he would come to the rendezvous if he could, and she had known that this was no more than the truth. Toby might be waking up to the warmth of an African sun or to the freezing cold of the Antarctic, for all she knew. He was older than she, so she supposed he might even be married with responsibilities of which she knew nothing, though she did think that at nineteen this was unlikely. Patty sat up on one elbow and glanced towards the window.

She was staying at the YWCA hostel on Hope Street. She had left Durrant House some time previously and was working as a cleaner and general dogsbody at the Royal Infirmary. They would not accept her as a probationer until her seventeenth birthday, but until then she was learning hospital ways, hospital rules and a great deal more beside. The work was hard and the pay poor, but Patty enjoyed it. The patients were wonderful, grateful for every tiny attention, and the junior nurses were nice, too, always appreciative of any help which the domestic staff offered.

The room contained six beds and the other girls still slept soundly. Patty knew that today was special only for her. Laura, had she been at the hostel, would have shared Patty's feelings to some extent, but Laura had returned to her mother's home in the court on her fourteenth birthday. 'As soon as they're useful, able to bring up younger kids, or earn a wage,' Patty had heard a member of staff saying bitterly, as Laura left. 'That Laura's a good little girl, bright enough at her lessons and quick to appreciate anything you do for her. She wanted to be a nurse and she'd have made a good one, but some chance of that now! That mother of hers will have her scrubbing lavvy floors in Waterloo station and she'll take her wages each week. Laura will be lucky to see a penny once her mam gets her greedy claws on it.'

Patty knew that this was true, but there was a still a part of her which envied Laura. Mrs Reilly was slapdash, selfish and unimaginative. She could not understand why her daughter would wish to be a nurse, nor why the authorities at Durrant House had suggested that she should continue her education. Yes, she wanted Laura's wages, yet Patty knew the older woman regarded her daughter with a good deal of affection and would have defended her against any criticism from outsiders. Whenever Patty was free to do so, she went round to the crowded, smelly little house in the court off the Scottie Road. She usually took a bag of buns or a few sweets, but she knew in her heart that the Reillys would have welcomed her had she come empty-handed. They were like that.

But right now, the day for which she had waited so long had arrived and she must make her plans. She had already arranged to take the whole day off, and without telling any of her roommates what she was about to do had borrowed the nicest clothes she could from each of them, so that Toby would not be ashamed to meet her under the clock. The hour of their meeting had been arranged for twelve noon so she had no need to hurry, but having woken, Patty knew she could not remain in bed.

Quickly, but quietly, so as not to disturb her companions, she washed and dressed, then stole down the stairs into the hostel kitchen. Breakfast was never an elaborate meal, just porridge, bread and margarine and a cup of weak tea. And since the porridge was cooked and the kitchen staff already at table, no one objected when Patty helped herself to a bowl of it and sat down.

'You in a hurry, queen?' Mrs Cooper, the cook, raised grey eyebrows. 'You gals work hard enough wi'out startin' an hour early.'

Patty shovelled the last spoonful of porridge into her mouth, then reached for a slice of bread and margarine whilst Cook poured her a cup of tea. 'It's my day off,' she said. 'I'm going round to see me pal, Laura, first, then I've got an appointment I must keep. After that, I might go to the cinema. *The Ten Commandments* is showing at the Gaiety; they say it's the biggest thing ever to hit the screen, with masses of Hollywood stars in it.'

Cook nodded. 'Aye, you're right there. But surely a pretty young gal like you can find some feller willing – nay eager – to buy you a cinema ticket and hold your hand in the frightening bits? When I were your age, I never paid for anything; me young men wouldn't let me.'

Patty laughed, feeling warmth creep into her cheeks. 'Plenty of time for that,' she said airily. 'I'm only sixteen after all.' She finished her food, drained the tea in her mug and stood up. 'I'm off now, Mrs Cooper,' she said, heading for the door. 'I might be in for supper or I might not.'

Once out of the kitchen, she made her way to the downstairs cloakroom to fetch her outdoor things. It was a cold morning, though the sun was shining palely from a sky now blue, now cloudy. Patty hurried along the familiar streets, excitement beginning to mount once more. She had told Mrs Cooper she meant to see Laura but she knew there would be little point in such a visit. Her friend was working in a grocery shop on the Scotland Road, though she still intended to become a nurse one day. Later on, I'll go into her shop and buy some broken biscuits; then, if Toby doesn't turn up, I can take them round to Mrs Reilly. No doubt she'll ask me in for a cuppa, then when Laura comes home we can go to the flicks together, Patty planned, threading her way through the streets which were just beginning to get crowded with Thursday morning shoppers. Friday was usually payday so on a Thursday folk were hunting for bargains.

Patty spent a pleasant morning despite the fact that as noon approached she grew more nervous. Suppose he didn't come? Suppose he did and she did not recognise him? Suppose he did not recognise her and simply walked straight past her and out of the station, ignoring her cries of 'Toby, it's me!' These were all scenarios which Patty had already experienced in dreams. At the time, she had acknowledged that they were dreams, anxiety dreams in fact, but now, it seemed to her, there was a distinct possibility that they might come true. Even worse, suppose he found he did not like the grown-up Patty, nor she him? She knew he must have had an exciting time in the five years since they had last met, knew her own life to be dull by comparison. But, she told herself, this was not a bad thing. No doubt he could tell fascinating stories of his life on the ... the ... gaff, did he call it? And she knew that once she got over her initial shyness, she could tell some amusing stories about life in hospital. Of course it wouldn't compare with the experience of a traveller, who probably knew Britain and the Continent as well as she knew Liverpool, but to Toby it would be something different, something novel. Besides, she remembered him as a kind boy and was sure he would not let her see he found her boring, even if he did.

By half past eleven, Patty was sitting on a bench on one side of Lime Street station, watching the clock like a hawk. It was tempting to remain there, not committing herself, not obviously waiting for anyone, but Patty knew that when the clock struck noon she would be standing beneath it. It would be tragic if he, too, hovered well back, watched the clock, saw no one waiting, and left. Shyness was all very well but it would be downright silly to risk losing her one chance of meeting up with Toby.

Accordingly, at five minutes to twelve, she took up her station beneath the clock, trying to banish ridiculous fears such as the one that he might turn up with a wife and six kids in tow. Suppose he did? They had never been more than friends, never even exchanged letters which would, she supposed, have been possible had he wanted to stay in touch with her. True, he had had no permanent address to which she might write but he could have sent a note to Durrant House. He had not done so, but then she had not tried to contact him either, difficult though it might have been.

She was beginning to wonder why she had not when the clock over her head began to strike twelve and Patty's heart skipped several beats. She glanced around the crowded concourse but could see no one who resembled the young Toby. Despite the five-year gap, she remembered every detail: the soft toffee-coloured hair, the bright eyes and quirky smile. Even at fourteen, he had been a good six inches taller than herself.

But I've grown, Patty reminded herself. Not six inches though . . . and he will have grown as well. Fellers don't just stand still between fourteen and nineteen; their shoulders get broader and they lose that gangly look. We *did* say twelve noon, didn't we? But I mustn't start to worry because I know with all my heart that we agreed on twelve noon. The clock stood at ten minutes past twelve but if Toby were depending on public transport to get here, he might well be a good deal later than ten minutes. Sighing, Patty settled down to wait.

She waited the whole afternoon. People pushed past her; other people came and joined her beneath the clock for longer or shorter periods; young men rushed up to young women, talked animatedly for a few moments and then left, arms entwined. Young women approached young men, apologised for being late, complained about the train services or the buses and trams, linked arms and disappeared. After a couple of hours, Patty told herself she was being an idiot and went and sat on a bench, though her eyes were still fixed on the patch of paving beneath the clock. Every now and again, a tall young man would saunter across the concourse, making Patty's heart beat even faster. But it was always a false alarm; the young man would be greeting a friend or going across to buy a newspaper to read on his journey home, or simply waiting for someone; someone who was not Patty. She told herself fifty times that he must still be in France, that it was impossible for him to reach her, that he would never deliberately let her down.

At half past five, she went to the refreshment room and bought a ham sandwich and a cup of tea, telling herself that her vigil was ended. She would go back to Laura's house and see whether her friend would like to go to the cinema.

Laura was full of sympathy when Patty told her what had happened but bade her friend cheer up and enjoy the film. 'As you say, he's probably in France or somewhere else abroad and couldn't get back,' she said tactfully. 'Didn't you make no other arrangement, queen? You should have said that if 1923 didn't come off you'd be under the clock a year later, and a year after that if you felt so inclined. That way you could still meet up again eventually.'

'Well, we did,' Patty admitted. 'You see, his life is so uncertain, being with the fair and that. So I said I'd come to Lime Street station around noon every fifteenth of November – and I shall,' she added, with a touch of defiance. 'He means a lot to me, does Toby.'

'Oh well, if you've agreed to try again each year,

then it's not too bad,' Laura said cheerfully. 'Tell you what, Patty, real friends always do meet up again because they like the same sort of things. Mind, there's plenty more fish in the sea, so you don't want to be puttin' all your eggs in one basket,' she ended, rather obscurely. 'We're old enough to go to dances and try to get a feller each. What say we do that on your next evening off?'

Patty laughed but shook her head. 'The trouble is, I'm only comfortable with fellers I know well, like Toby,' she confided. 'When I'm with strangers I can't help thinking of Selina.'

'You've got to forget Selina if you're ever going to have a normal life,' Laura said bluntly. 'Selina were a grand girl but she never meant to put you off fellers – decent fellers – for ever. Why, if she knew that what she said to you was turning you into a – a recluse, then it would just about break her heart. You come dancing with me on Saturday night, queen. Promise?'

'Perhaps I will,' Patty said guardedly. 'Now let's go along to the Gaiety and see this perishin' film everyone's talking about.'

'Toby! Are you comin' in for your breakfast or are you goin' to spend all day under that bleedin' traction engine?'

Trixie Flanagan's voice was shrill but the words were by no means unwelcome to Toby, lying beneath the main shaft of the Little Giant, his oil can at the ready. Today was moving day and it was one of his many jobs to make sure that the traction engines which pulled the fairground equipment were in first rate order. However, he had been working on this one since day dawned and thought that it was now roadworthy, so he wriggled out on to the cold wet grass and grinned cheerfully at Trixie. She was a good-natured, blowzy girl who ran the shooting gallery and was the Riding Master's second wife. Following the death of his first wife shortly after Toby had joined the fair, Mr Flanagan had lived with his surviving son, Ted, in the big, comfortable travelling wagon and had been glad enough to let Toby occupy one of the spare bunks. The men had got on pretty well, taking it in turns to cook and clean, but when Mr Flanagan had begun to court Trixie, daughter of Fred Ellington, who owned the shooting gallery, their lives had changed dramatically. Even before they married, Trixie had taken over the catering and fed both families, but once they wed and Trixie moved into the Flanagan van, Ted and Toby had to move out. It had been summer and Mr Flanagan had bought the boys a small tent, which was quite satisfactory while the weather remained clement. The previous winter, however, had not been easy. Both young men had taken to shooting into the Flanagan caravan as soon as they awoke, in order to dress in comparative warmth, and though Mr Flanagan had tolerated this Trixie had made it plain that she considered it an imposition. 'Here's me, tryin' to dress decent and prepare breakfast while there's two fellers in all their dirt sittin' an' starin' at me,' she had exclaimed aggrievedly. 'They ain't a couple o' kids, Mr Flanagan, an' they shouldn't be treated as such. When we're in winter quarters, they should go into lodgings, like the Chaps do.'

Toby knew that the manual labourers who were so essential to the fair, both for the running of it and for the taking down and putting up of the larger rides, were known as 'the Chaps'. He thought himself a cut above the Chaps, but saw Trixie Flanagan's point and agreed to go into lodgings when winter quarters were reached.

Now, however, he strolled over to the living wagon, put his oil can down on the step and rinsed his hands and face in the bucket of water which Trixie always put out for that purpose. Toby knew it had been hot water earlier, but now it was cold and scummy and did very little to get rid of the grease on his hands and face. Most of the dirt, he saw ruefully, had come off on the torn piece of towelling with which he rubbed himself dry, but it could not be helped.

'How many eggs can you eat, Toby?' Trixie asked, breaking some into the big black frying pan balanced precariously on her tiny cooking stove. For most of the year, she cooked outside and the men squatted round the fire, planning the day ahead over breakfast, or discussing how it went at supper time. Today, however, because of the rain which had fallen constantly since dawn, the meal was being prepared in the van, though only family – Toby counted as family – actually ate indoors. Those Chaps who stayed with the fair and were regularly fed by Trixie came to the door and were given bacon and egg sandwiched between great uneven chunks of bread, and a tin mug of steaming hot tea. They would take their food to the nearest shelter – probably the galloper since it had still not been taken apart – and would return the tin mugs later, when they recommenced work.

Toby and Ted finished their meal simultaneously, thanked Trixie, and made for the outdoors once more. The rain still fell steadily from a grey and lowering sky and the pair exchanged rueful looks as they made for the galloper, which the Chaps were already dismantling with all their usual and casual efficiency.

'Goin' to be a bugger of a day to move,' Ted commented as the two of them reached the galloper and began to help the Chaps to heave the segments of the ride on to the huge trailer awaiting them. 'I'd rather pull down in almost any weather other than continual rain – the gaff's like a marsh already.'

'Snow's worse,' Toby pointed out, taking the tail end of one of the dappled, scarlet-caparisoned wooden horses as Ted lifted the head. 'I'm driving the engine pulling this load, aren't I? I want to get a move on because it isn't safe driving after dark in weather like this and we'll be a bit later starting than your dad had planned.'

'Yes, you're drivin' this one,' Ted confirmed. 'I'm takin' the swing boats. We've a good deal of ground to cover, though, if we're to be in by nightfall.' He took his cap off to shake the rain from the brim, then replaced it firmly on his oiled black hair. 'But at least, since we're goin' into winter quarters, we won't have to put up as well as pull down. That's one comfort.'

Toby agreed and the two young men began to work even faster, though both were careful to make sure that neither the horses nor the rounding boards, with the brilliant paintwork which had taken Mr Flanagan weeks to perfect, got chipped or scratched as they loaded. It was noon before Toby was able to climb into the cab of the Little Giant, which he did with some trepidation since, by now, the churned-up ground could have bogged down both the traction engine and its heavy trailer. The Chaps, however, were used to this and were already laying a corduroy road, with planks kept for the purpose. Toby lined up his engine, the Chaps got behind the entire contraption and after a good deal of swearing, pushing and hoarsely yelled advice the Little Giant and its unwieldy trailer lurched across the planks and on to the tarmacked road.

It was a long and exhausting journey and well after dark by the time Toby wearily turned the Little Giant into their winter quarters – a large area outside King's Lynn which had once been meadow, but Mr Flanagan had tarmacked so that the fair might safely overwinter there without fear of becoming bogged down and unable to 'up sticks' when spring arrived. Originally, he had bought the land from a poor farmer, and had tarmacked it bit by bit until now a good half of the meadow was hard standing. Since their own fair did not need so much space, Mr Flanagan rented out to others, and there was always a good mix of people overwintering there. It made life more interesting for all of them, and on dry winter evenings Mr Flanagan would organise the lighting of a really big fire and stand sacks of potatoes and strings of sausages close by, so that everyone prepared to pay a few pence could bake a potato in the embers and impale sausages on a stick and thrust them as near to the flames as they dared. Then the talk would begin, with old and young gradually beginning to tell the tales of past seasons. Men would hand beer bottles around, women would brew tea and the youngsters would drink anything they were given. Very soon, a grand atmosphere of camaraderie would come into being so that, for the entire winter season, each man, woman and child living in this strange, closed-down tober would think of himself as part of an enormous family and act accordingly.

On this first night, however, traction engines, horses and even some motor vehicles were still streaming on to the site, and everyone was soaked to the skin and far too tired to think of anything but a hasty meal and then bed. Toby and Ted ate fish and chips, downed pints of hot, sweet tea and filled up remaining corners with rounds of bread and jam. Then Mr Flanagan handed Toby a dirty piece of paper with an address written on it and told them that their landlady was a Mrs Griffin and that he had paid a month's rent in advance. 'She'll give you breakfast but you'll come back here for your dinner an' supper,' he told them. 'I've paid for a cooked breakfast, so mind you're up in time for it; she says between seven an' eight. You'll mebbe want to sleep in tomorrer so I told her that if she were gone out she were to leave you the makin's in her kitchen and you'd do for yourselves, but other days you'll have to be up betimes.'

'Did you say Roundhey Road?' Ted asked presently, as the two boys made their way through the dark, wet town. 'If so, we go down here; what number was it?'

Toby told him and presently they turned into the tiny front yard of a grey stone terraced house where a light burned behind red curtains. Mrs Griffin answered their knock and ushered them inside, talking amiably as she did so about the terrible weather and the fact that she had not got her washing dried outside for the past week. 'Your dad told me you'd be fed at Spalding's Meadow,' she said cheerfully, 'but I thought a mug of cocoa and a big slice of my rich fruit cake wouldn't come amiss. If you wouldn't mind signing the register while you eat, then I can show you to your room. It's a quiet neighbourhood so you should get a good night's sleep.'

Both Ted and Toby were worn out but the thought

of hot cocoa and cake was a welcome one, so they followed their landlady into the kitchen and sat down to eat and drink. Toby said cheerfully that he would sign them both in and flashed a quick grin at Ted. Not that it would have mattered, he saw, when he opened the page, since the two lodgers who had already signed in that day had both made their mark – a wobbly cross – beside their roughly printed names.

He began to fill in the spaces on the page, then turned to Mrs Griffin. 'What's the date, missus?' he enquired.

'It don't matter about the date,' Mrs Griffin said eagerly, pointing to a couple of lines above that upon which Toby was writing. 'It's there already, see? The fifteenth of November. So all you need is your names and the name of the fair.'

Toby thanked her and began to eat his cake but though he chatted easily enough, he kept getting a nasty sort of feeling that he had done something wrong, or perhaps not done something right would have been a better way of expressing it. As he and Ted made their way up to bed and examined their room – small, but neat and fiercely clean – he was wondering why he should feel that 15 November ought to have some significance for him. His mam's birthday? His dad's? He was pretty sure it wasn't Mr Flanagan's, because Trixie would have commented, and he knew full well it wasn't Ted's or his own.

'I reckon we've fallen on our feet, old feller,' Ted said, as he climbed into the narrow bed, closest to the window. 'I heered some of the chaps talkin' an' they say landladies start as they mean to go on. If they're stingy old bitches what grudges you every mouthful you eat and turn off the lamp before you're halfway up the stairs, to save fuel, and keep a fire no bigger'n a cricket ball burning in the grate, then they'll start by chargin' you extra for a cup of cocoa and hidin' away the coal so you can't make up the fire. But Mrs Griffin didn't need to give us that bit of cake, nor that cocoa, so I reckon me dad's done us proud.'

'Looks like it,' Toby agreed drowsily. 'Ted, is there anything special about today? The fifteenth of November, I mean.'

'Well, it were Victory Day after the war, but I don't see why that should mean anything special five years later,' Ted said, after some moments. 'Night, Toby.'

'G'night, Ted,' Toby said dismally. So that was it! He had promised the little blonde from Durrant House that he would meet her on 15 November 1923, at noon. Now that Ted had reminded him, the whole thing had come back to him. The fireworks, the excitement and Patty's pale little face as they parted . . . yes, Patty, that was her name.

He told himself that he had intended to go, had not meant to let her down, but in his heart he knew that life was so full, so interesting, that he had simply never given the date another thought and had almost forgotten Patty's very existence.

Settling down, he wondered how long she had waited, wondered whether there was any way of getting in touch with her. Over the next few months he would have a certain amount of spare time. Today had been moving day anyway, he told himself; it would have been quite impossible for him to have kept the rendezvous, even had he remembered. Mr Flanagan relied on him both to service the machines and to drive the Little Giant and Toby did not mean to let him down. The secret conviction that, had he explained, Mr Flanagan would have found someone else to drive the traction engine would not be entirely denied, but Toby did his best. Next year, he told himself, I really will go to Liverpool and stand under that clock at Lime Street, just like we planned. She'll probably turn up and then I can explain why I couldn't make it today.

Presently he fell asleep, still trying to justify himself. But though he might satisfy his conscious mind, his sub-conscious was far harder to convince. In his dreams, a small girl with two flaxen plaits and a lost expression on her face waited under the clock and wept for his absence. And in his dreams, Toby wept too.

Chapter Twelve
Summer 1934

'Mammy! Merry don't want porridge, Merry want milk.'

Patty stared down at the small, defiant figure sitting up to the table with the untouched bowl of porridge in front of her. Maggie, so much wiser than she, had warned her that this would happen so she should have been prepared, Patty told herself. Merry's two and a half now and Maggie said she was beginning to feel her feet and exert her will, only she's not tried it on me before. It's good that she wants to drink milk but I'm sure I shouldn't simply give way. Oh, goodness, I wish Maggie were here!

It was a Sunday morning and Maggie had seized the opportunity of Patty's being at home to take her father's money round to Stanton's Court. She meant to spend the day with the Mullins, giving Fanny a hand and playing with the younger children – for Laurie and Gus had been retrieved from the Father Berry Home, and with them had come their older sister, happy to be back with her siblings once more. 'They're me flesh an' blood, an' I love 'em all, even me dad, 'cept when he's drunk,' Maggie had explained, rather bashfully. 'I don't ever want to live there again and I don't suppose I ever shall, but I don't want to lose touch either.'

Maggie made a point of spending time with her family at least once a month, but she never took Merry on such expeditions and usually Patty very much enjoyed being with the little girl, but today was clearly going to be different. Merrell was watching her, the look in her young eyes almost calculating, her soft brows drawn into a frown. Seeing Patty hesitate, she seized her porridge bowl in both hands and pushed it away from her. 'No porridge,' she said decisively. 'Merry want bre'm butty an' milk.'

Patty sighed and sat down opposite the child. It was another beautifully hot, sunny day and perhaps porridge had not been such a good idea, she reasoned. And Merrell was now suggesting bread and butter, which would be just as good for her as the porridge if she had a mug of milk with it. She would, however, doubtless see the bread and butter and milk as a victory and Maggie had impressed upon Patty that it was not a good idea to let a wilful toddler feel she had your measure, so Patty whisked the porridge bowl away and took it over to the sink, saying over her shoulder as she did so: 'Perhaps it is rather a hot day for porridge; you shall have cornflakes instead.' She glanced back. Merrell's mouth was forming into what looked like a large, square hole, her hands were balled into fists and she was screwing up her angelic blue eyes and taking a deep breath. Presently, Patty guessed, her baby's face would begin to go scarlet . . . oh, God, suppose she has a fit out of sheer fury, Patty thought wildly. It isn't unreasonable to ask for bread and butter, after all. Only she usually loves cornflakes . . . why oh why do children have to start to try to prove themselves when they're little more than babies?

Behind her, she was conscious of the small dictator's eyes fixed on her as she went to the cupboard, removed the box of cornflakes and poured some of them into a bowl. She added milk and carried it across to the table and, when Merrell made a spirited attempt to knock it out of her hands, actually gave her small daughter a reproving tap. 'Less of that, young lady, unless you want a spanking,' she said as firmly as she could. 'I agree that today the weather is too hot for porridge, but cornflakes should be just right. Now eat up your nice breakfast and then you and I will call for Mrs Clarke and Christopher and go to the park.'

'Shan't,' Merrell said, though without much conviction. She picked up her spoon and began very, very slowly to scoop up some milk and a couple of cornflakes. 'Don't wanna go to the park, want to play in the road.'

Patty laughed. Playing in the road was a forbidden pastime and well Merrell knew it. Clearly, she had decided this morning that she would be as awkward as she knew how but Patty, having won the first battle, thought she could probably cope with the rest. Accordingly, she picked up her own plate of bread and jam and her cup of tea and sat down at the table, beginning to eat her breakfast as she planned the day ahead.

Ellen had already left the house. She had not said so to Patty, but Patty imagined that her friend was probably having a day out with Darky Knight. At any rate, she had said she would not be back until late and that they were not to wait the evening meal for her. Finishing her breakfast and seeing, with considerable satisfaction, that Merrell was ploughing happily through the cornflakes, Patty reflected, a trifle wistfully, that it would have been lovely to go off for the day. In fact, there was nothing to stop her. She and Merrell could take themselves off to New Brighton and have a day by the sea. It wouldn't cost much and they could have their dinner out, even if it was only a cup of tea and a bag of chips.

She prepared a bag of necessities for a day on the beach and got Merrell into her outdoor things.

'Where's we goin', Mammy?'

Patty smiled and hoisted the child on to her hip, then picked up her canvas bag and slung it over one shoulder. 'We're going to New Brighton, which is by the sea, queen,' she informed her small companion. 'We can't take the pram but you're a big girl now. If you walk for a bit, and then I carry you for a bit, we should get along just fine.'

'But you said the park. I wanna go to the park,' Merrell pointed out. 'Mammy, you said the park, you did, you did!'

'I know, but I thought you'd rather go to the seaside. Do you remember what fun you had on the beach, making sand pies and digging big holes which filled up with water?' Patty asked. 'New Brighton's the seaside, queen, and we'll have our dinners out.'

'Seaside! Seaside!' Merrell squeaked, reaching up and hooking an arm around Patty's neck. 'Merry loves the seaside – Merry loves *you*, Mammy!'

They reached New Brighton and found, to their joy, that the tide was out, leaving great stretches of golden sand baking beneath the June sun on which a child could play for hours. They settled themselves at the top of the beach and Patty produced the old mug and the tablespoon and watched with dreamy pleasure as Merrell fell upon these objects and began to make sand pies, crowing with delight as their number grew. At lunchtime, Patty made her way to a fish and chip shop and bought chips for herself and Merrell and a bottle of fizzy drink, so virulently red that she hesitated at first to let Merrell drink it. However, it tasted all right so she and Merrell shared it, sitting on the sand and revelling in the hot sunshine. Having finished their meal, they were about to begin making more sand pies when Merrell spotted the ice cream van. Patty was reclining on the sand, full of chips and fizzy cherryade, and was not, at first, much inclined to move. But Merrell's ecstatic squeaks made her sit up and take notice and presently she fished some coppers out of the bottom of her bag and invited Merrell to accompany her back to the prom. 'Ess, ess,' Merrell agreed at once, jumping to her feet. 'I see Knighty!'

'That's an odd thing to call ice cream,' Patty said, amused, as the two of them made their way across the sand. When they reached the van, however, she realised her mistake. Just ahead of them in the short queue was Darky Knight!

Patty would have ignored him, would have pretended she had not even seen him, would, in fact, have walked away and gone without her ice cream. But Merrell was not of the same mind. She wrenched her hand out of Patty's and rushed over to Darky, jerking at his jacket and addressing him in a stream of what sounded like complete nonsense, though he clearly understood. 'Well, fancy seeing you, young lady,' he said, his voice friendlier than Patty had ever heard it. 'Just where did you spring from, Merry? I saw Maggie go off early this morning, but you weren't with her, so . . .' He turned and saw Patty and immediately the gentle look left his face, to be replaced by a much more guarded expression. 'Oh, I'm sorry, Nurse Peel, I didn't see you there. Having a day out, are you?'

'That's right,' Patty said, aware that her own voice

had echoed the formality of his. 'Maggie goes back to her own family on a Sunday, if I'm around to look after Merry. Is – is Ellen around somewhere?'

Darky looked genuinely astonished. 'How should I know?' he said. 'Did she mean to join you here, then?'

Patty felt extremely embarrassed. Clearly, she had misread Ellen's intention of having a day out. Wherever her friend had gone, it had not been with Darky Knight. Patty supposed that she had simply assumed the two were still going out together, but now it appeared that, on this occasion at any rate, they had gone their separate ways. Hastily, she racked her brains for a reply which would not give too much away. 'She said she might,' she said cautiously. 'That is, if she got back in time. She's gone to visit friends,' she finished, crossing her fingers behind her back.

The queue was shuffling forward and Darky raised his eyebrows. 'I'll buy your ices,' he said gruffly. 'No need for all of us to queue.'

Patty would have liked to say, frostily, that she would buy her own ices, thank you, but Darky had already turned away and she heard him asking the young man in the van for two large cones and one small one. Besides, she reminded herself, Merrell was clearly fond of Mr Knight and she did not want to offend him. His mother was more than a good friend; she was an essential part of life at No. 24. Patty did not think that Mrs Knight would cease to befriend them even if the situation between Patty and Darky worsened, but she could not afford to take chances. So, when Darky handed her an ice and bent down to give Merrell hers, she accepted as graciously as she could, though she produced her money at once and tried to repay him.

'It's all right,' Darky said shortly. 'I think I can afford to buy a couple of ices now and then.'

Patty began to bristle, then relaxed and gave him a grin. 'Thank you very much, Mr Knight, but why did you only buy three ices? Isn't your mother with you? If she is, you must let me buy a teapot.'

'A teapot?' Darky said, looking confused. 'Why on earth would me mam want a teapot?'

Patty laughed. 'It's clear you don't come to New Brighton often,' she said gaily. 'There's an old woman on the prom who hires you a teapot, full of tea and hot water of course, which you can take down to the sands to make yourself a cuppa. You have to bring your own mugs, but I've got a couple stowed away in my canvas bag which we could have used. Still, if your mother *isn't* with you . . .'

Darky took a deep breath, then turned back to the prom. 'I'm by meself now, though I were with a party of fellers from Levers earlier,' he said. 'But we went to a pub and one or two of 'em had a drop too much. They got quarrelsome and above themselves, so I left. And now you mention it, I wouldn't say no to a cup of tea.'

Patty was astonished, but did her best not to show it, reflecting that perhaps Darky realised the advantages of being friendly, as she did herself. 'Well, we'd best eat our ices first,' she said, trying to talk naturally and easily. 'Let's go and sit by the Perch Rock while we eat them, then Merrell can paddle in the pool.'

Darky agreed, and very soon all three of them were enjoying their ices. When these were finished they got down and Darky rolled up his trouser legs, removed his boots and socks, and proceeded to act, Patty saw with surprise, just like a young boy out on a day trip.

He splashed into the water with Merrell, fished out shells which he put into her sand pie mug, dug channels between the pools in order to drain one and fill up the other, borrowed the tablespoon to show Merrell how one could tunnel under a sand castle, and seemed to be thoroughly enjoying himself. Patty held aloof for a little but Merrell's pleasure was so infectious that very soon she found herself joining in. There was a moment when all Merrell's new-found independence came flooding back and she began to be difficult. It was over the wearing or not wearing of a pink and white frilly sun bonnet, which Patty thought essential in the afternoon glare and Merrell thought a wretched nuisance, but Patty prevailed when Darky joined in the argument, telling Merrell that nothing was more painful than sunburn. Merrell, who had burnt herself only the day before by seizing the toasting fork as it lay on the hearth, grew thoughtful and actually came to Patty to have the sun bonnet tied on more securely when it started to slip.

Patty thought that Darky had forgotten all about the teapot but presently he got to his feet and began to dust the sand off the knees of his trousers. 'I'm parched,' he said, speaking to no one in particular. 'Wharrabout that teapot, then? If you tell me where to go, I'll fetch it while you keep an eye on young Merry here.'

'No, it's all right, I'll fetch it,' Patty said quickly. 'I'm not nearly as wet and sandy as you two.' She hesitated, then added: 'I'll get a bag of buns at the same time, shall I? It seems a long time since Merry and I had our chips and cherryade.'

Darky's eyebrows rose. 'Didn't you have your dinners out, in a café or a tearoom?' he asked incredulously. 'Me and the fellers went to Reece's and had a grand meal, only they aren't licensed and the fellers wanted a pint, so we went along to the pub on the pier, which is where the trouble started and I lit out.' For the first time he looked straight at Patty; she could read mockery in his expression but there was something more, something to which she could not put a name. She was still puzzling over it when he said, in a rallying tone: 'Very well, Nurse, you get the teapot and the buns, but later on I'm takin' all of us back to Reece's for a slap-up supper. I don't mean poor Merrell to go home hungry after her day out.'

Patty could only stare at him speechlessly. Darky's companions, it now appeared, were not the only ones to have had a skinful. To be sure, Darky had behaved as though stone cold sober whilst he played with Merrell, splashing in and out of the water and making sand castles, but now it was clear he must have been inebriated. Why else should he suggest 'a slap-up supper' which would mean he would be spending time in Patty's company when he could easily have excused himself and gone off to find his friends?

'Well, Nurse? Are you going to stand there all day like a bleedin' stuffed dummy? If so, I s'pose I'd better clean myself up and go and find this here teapot—' Darky was beginning but Patty, feeling the heat rush up in her cheeks, cut him short.

'Sorry, sorry, I'm just going,' she gabbled. 'It – it just surprised me that you should even think of taking Merry and me into Reece's. It's – it's awful posh, wi' tablecloths and shiny silver cutlery. If you're still hungry after the buns, we could get more chips.'

Darky laughed, looking down at her with a teasing and somehow provocative glance which set the blood unaccountably racing in Patty's veins. Confused and not wishing to be caught staring, she turned away from him and headed up the beach, calling back over her shoulder in as light a voice as she could manage: 'All right, all right, I can take a hint! I'll be back with tea and buns in two ticks. Now no more sea bathing because the sun's getting lower and I don't want to be nursing a little girl with a cold in the head.'

There was a queue of people waiting to hire teapots but Patty was not sorry. It would give her a chance to assess the situation. Having thought the matter over, she was forced to admit that Darky was no more drunk than she was. It was clear that he was truly fond of Merrell and wanted to give the child a good time, but Patty had enough common sense to realise that he and his mother could have brought Merrell to New Brighton on numerous occasions had they wished to do so. Furthermore, earlier in the afternoon he had played with Merrell, building sand castles and splashing in the sea, without really taking the slightest notice of Patty herself. Looking back, she realised that his attitude had changed subtly during the course of the sunny afternoon. Perhaps, she thought hopefully, he had begun to realise that she was not such a bad sort of woman after all. She had never forgotten how he regarded all members of her profession but knew that this prejudice, at any rate, was definitely beginning to lose its grip upon him. After all, he took Ellen out fairly regularly and he knew as well as Patty did that Ellen and she shared the same occupation. But that did not, of course, mean that his prejudice against herself would automatically lessen. If he had really believed she had encouraged the drunken louts who had attacked her that night on St Anne Street, then she could not blame him for his attitude towards her. Yet today, that hostility seemed to have disappeared and friendliness had taken its place. She thought, as the queue shuffled forward, that it might have something to do with Ellen. If Darky had said unpleasant things about her, Patty, then she was very sure that Ellen would have leaped to her defence. Yes, that must be it; Ellen had told him she was a respectable girl who worked extremely hard and thought the world of her patients. That would change his mind if anything could.

Oddly enough, however, this thought gave Patty no pleasure. In fact she found herself cursing Ellen for interfering. It was not that she wanted Darky's enmity, far from it; it made life difficult. But she did not want his friendship if it was a mere sop to keep Ellen happy. She wanted it, she realised, for herself. Everyone wants to be liked for themselves, and Patty was no exception. If Darky was simulating friendship with her in order to please Ellen – or, for that matter, to please Merrell – then she wanted none of it. At this point in her musing she reached the head of the queue, bought the buns and hired a tray and a heavy teapot and began to walk carefully back across the promenade and down to the beach. Blinking in the bright sunlight, for her thoughts had been far away, she told herself severely to stop lookin' a perishin' gift horse in the mouth. She and Darky might never be truly close – well, she could scarcely expect it considering he was going out with her best friend – but this afternoon must surely herald the start of a happier relationship between them? And if that was indeed so, then she was grateful. Ever since Mrs Knight had taken over the care of Merrell, Patty had had to time her visits to coincide with Darky's absences and this was often awkward. Now, if she was sensible and watched her wretched tongue, things should improve.

Darky and Merrell were sitting expectantly around a large flat sand table and beamed as they saw Patty approaching. Darky got to his feet and took the tray from her, setting it carefully down on his creation. 'See?' he said proudly. 'Me and Merry have got the table all laid and ready, *and* we've washed our hands so we shan't get sand all over the buns. How about that, eh? My, those buns look good enough to eat!'

Patty laughed and handed round the large, sticky-topped buns, then began to pour the tea – already milked and sugared – into the two mugs. 'I didn't bring Merry's little drinking beaker,' she said regretfully, 'but she manages pretty well with the big mug. She'll have to wait till the tea's cool, mind.'

Merrell did not seem at all anxious for yet another drink – she had finished the cherryade some while before – but when the liquid in the mug was cool enough Patty helped her to drink it and was surprised when the child drained the tea down to the last drop. Licking her lips, Merrell said: 'That were nice, Mammy,' and began taking large bites out of her bun whilst Patty poured a cup of tea for herself into the empty mug. Presently, with their impromptu picnic finished, the three of them began to tidy themselves up since Darky had suggested a walk along the prom to the pier.

'If you'll take the tray and teapot, I'll give Miss Merry here a shoulder ride,' Darky said when most of the sand had been removed from their persons. He looked down at Merrell's flushed little face. 'But if we reach the end of the pier before she falls asleep, I'm a Dutchman,' he added. 'Pity we can't snug her down in a pram, but I suppose that great old thing would have been more of a nuisance than a help, what with the ferry crossing an' all.'

It was the nearest he had come to a criticism so Patty only said equably: 'To say nothing of heaving it aboard the tram,' and was glad she had not been cutting when he gave her a friendly smile.

'Never mind,' he said, hoisting the child on to his shoulders. 'Hang on to my head, queen, and I'll hold on to your legs, and if you feel like fallin', fall forward.' The child chuckled delightedly and patted his dark hair, addressing him as 'Horsy' and commanding, in a rather blurred and sleepy voice, that he should go 'clippety clop, clippety clop'.

Darky obviously realised the source of this remark and began to sing.

'Horsy, horsy, don't you stop,
Just let your feet go clippety clop,
Your tail goes swish and your wheels go round,
Giddy up we're homeward bound.'

Patty joined in the chorus and, noticing Merrell's sideways tilt, warned Darky that his passenger was falling asleep in time for him to whisk her off his shoulders and into his arms. Patty would have taken the child from him, but when she tried to do so he shook his head. 'We'll go straight to Reece's and I'll put her gently down on a cushion or an upholstered chair, and she can have her sleep out while we enjoy a meal,' he said. 'I don't want to do her out of her grub, but I honestly think she needs a sleep more. By the time she wakes, we'll probably be back at Ashfield Place and you can put her straight to bed with a glass of warm milk, or whatever it is you women give your kids.'

Patty looked at him doubtfully. 'Wouldn't it be better to go straight home right now?' she suggested.

'After all, it has been a long day and carrying her all the way back to Ashfield Place is no joke. I know she's only a little thing but it's surprising how heavy she gets.'

Darky raised his eyebrows. 'Are you trying to tell me she'll gradually get heavier and heavier while she snoozes in Reece's?' he enquired. 'You should know better, Nurse! She'd be just as heavy if we set off now as she will be in an hour or so.'

Patty giggled. 'Well, yes, but that wasn't what I meant. If we go home now, she'll likely wake when we get aboard the ferry and walk a good deal of the way, but if we take her to Reece's she'll go sound asleep, and then I'm afraid it will mean carrying her all the way home.'

'Well, I happen to be extremely hungry and since *I* shall be the one carrying Merry, I ought to be allowed to stoke up so's I get back me full strength,' Darky said plaintively, making Patty give another snort of laughter. 'Now no more argument, Nurse – I bet you're as hungry as I am.'

Patty realised that this was indeed true; the bun had been nice but not tremendously filling and the day had been a long and delightfully tiring one, so she smiled at Darky and followed him meekly enough back along the promenade, under the canopied walkway and into Reece's luxurious and neat premises.

'I'll order for both of us to save time, and a children's meal for Merrell, too,' Darky said, when the waitress approached, and proceeded to ask for the most expensive thing on the menu. Patty looked at the pile of golden chips and the various meats of which the mixed grill consisted and protested that she would never be able to eat so much. Darky smiled mockingly at her. 'After a day on the beach you'll cope wi' that, no trouble,' he declared, tucking into his own food, and he was rapidly proved right as Patty cleared her plate almost as quickly as he did. Despite her fear that Darky's money had been wasted on the children's meal, Merrell had woken for long enough to eat most of her food before she snoozed off again.

Putting down her knife and fork, Patty leaned back in her chair with a satisfied sigh. 'That was the best meal I've ever had,' she announced. She glanced across at Darky, at his thin, intelligent face and the twinkle of amusement in his dark eyes. He looked more relaxed than she had ever seen him and this prompted her to ask the question which was uppermost in her mind. 'Do tell me, Mr Knight,' she said, 'you've never seemed to like me very much and you certainly haven't approved of me, but you've made today one of the happiest I've ever spent. Why?'

She was watching Darky's face as she spoke and saw his cheekbones redden a little but he did not hesitate before replying. 'It's partly me mam,' he said, rather gruffly. 'She's been on and on at me, saying what a nice girl you are, a marvellous mother to Merry here and a first-rate nurse. She said I were prejudiced against you because – because of what happened when my wife died. Then I took Ellen out a couple of times – she's a nice girl an' all, is Ellen – and I realised it were true what me mam said: "There's good an' bad in all professions, all walks of life." One day, when we were chatting, I actually admitted that if you or Ellen had been on duty when Alison's labour began, I'm sure it would have been a very different story. So, when I saw you in the ice cream queue, I thought – I thought mebbe it were time to try to make amends.' He looked across at her, his expression reminding her very much of a puppy who has chewed up your best shoes and is not sure whether you have yet found the remains. 'Because I knew all along that it were none of your fault you were attacked that night,' he said in a rush. 'I was in the Daulby Hall, you see, and I knew they picked on you because you were alone and very pretty and they were drunk, but I – I told myself that you had brought trouble on yourself by your behaviour, even though I knew it weren't true.'

Patty picked up her spoon and began to trace invisible patterns on the white tablecloth. She admired Darky tremendously for having the courage to speak as he had but realised that she must do likewise, because fair was fair, after all. Accordingly, she took a deep breath and said, 'Well, Mr Knight, you aren't the only one who's not always behaved quite honestly. I was so angry with you after the way you spoke to me when you returned my gaberdine that I wanted revenge, I suppose. So I never told anyone, not even Maggie, that it was you had rescued me from those horrible men. In fact, once or twice, Maggie has said things which make me wonder whether she thinks it was you who had gone a bit too far. Of course, I've never said anything to give her that impression, but then I've never corrected her or tried to tell her what really happened.'

To her considerable relief, Darky did not immediately look away from her or begin to frown. Instead, he grinned broadly and pretended to wipe imaginary perspiration from his forehead. 'Phew!' he said. 'I should say we're well matched, Nurse, because we've each been a trifle hard on the other, wouldn't you say? But I hope that's all behind us and in future we can treat each other as friends. After all, my mam says she thinks of Merry like the grandchild she's never had, so you and I are almost honorary relations!'

At this point, the waitress approached them once more and Darky ordered lemon sponge pudding and custard for them both. Then he paid the bill and the little party set off in the direction of the ferry, with Merrell still slumbering soundly in his arms. They went aboard, Patty noticing with satisfaction that it was nowhere near as crowded as it had been on their outward voyage, and settled themselves in the saloon, since a little breeze had arisen with the coming of twilight and she did not want to risk Merrell's catching a chill. A good many other people had also decided to come below and one of them, a brassy blonde, kept glancing curiously across at them, grinning at Darky and then nudging her companion, a tall tow-headed young man with a loose lip and a knowing eye, who grinned also and gave Darky a mocking salute, which Patty's companion rather grudgingly acknowledged with a curt nod.

'Who's that?' Patty murmured, as the ferry drew away from the quayside.

'One of the fellers from Levers,' Darky said. 'He's with one of the girls from the flakes department; a couple o' trouble makers, I've always thought 'em.'

Patty said no more as the children in the saloon began romping noisily, running backwards and forwards and shouting to one another, jumping over feet and playing various games. Presently, Merrell awoke and began to whine that she wanted to get down.

'Not now, queen,' Darky said, holding her firmly on his lap. 'We're nearly back at the landing stage, then everyone will have to get off the ferry; those noisy brats as well as us respectable folk.'

Unfortunately, as he spoke, there was a moment of silence and Patty saw that several of the parents of the unruly children were giving Darky affronted glares. Before she could warn him that he was offending people, Darky turned his head and spoke directly to her. 'D'you know, I wonder if Merry's got a temperature on her? She's come over all warm – hot, you could say – and I feel . . .'

He gave an exclamation of horror and rose to his feet, holding Merrell away from him as though she were a parcel. Patty followed the direction of his gaze and saw that his light grey trousers were soaking wet and that a puddle had formed on the wooden seat he had just vacated.

'Oh, Mr Knight, I'm so sorry . . .' Patty began, and then the humour of the situation struck her and she gave a breathless little giggle. It was awful and most embarrassing for Darky but she felt she could scarcely blame the child. When Merrell had asked to get down, she must have realised she wanted to wee, but had not had time to explain what was happening to her.

Darky was still holding Merrell out before him, watching with distaste as she dripped on to the deck. Next to him, a large and blowzy woman, parent of some of the noisy children, rose ponderously to her feet. 'Well, look at me decent skirt!' she exclaimed. 'All covered with piddle, an' him so high an' mighty! Well, mister, my brats may be noisy but at least they don't pee on total strangers!'

She had said it half laughingly but Darky clearly

did not see the joke. He tried to thrust Merrell in Patty's direction but the child turned like an eel towards him, throwing both her arms round his neck and clinging like a limpet. 'Daddy! Daddy! I's all wet. Don't be cross with Merry, Daddy.'

It was too much for Patty's sense of humour and she laughed outright, holding out her arms to take the child and saying, penitently: 'I'm terribly sorry, Mr Knight – I'll hold her if you'll go and borrow a mop and bucket from the crew.' She tried to take Merrell, but the child squawked indignantly, clinging to Darky's neck like a burr.

Several of the other passengers had now gathered round, giving advice and plainly delighting in someone else's predicament. A child of about six announced in a high voice: 'There's a man here wet hisself. A growed man! Ooh, there's a great puddle on the seat. His mammy will be cross with him!'

There was more laughter and the couple from Levers came across to them, the fellow saying jeeringly: 'Well, if it ain't our gaffer! I see you've had an accident – them kecks will never be the same again. Good thing you're in a well-paid job and a bachelor wi' no fambly responsibilities.'

The brassy-haired girl, clinging to her escort's arm, put in her own two penn'orth at this point. 'Mr Knight a bachelor?' she said derisively. 'Well, he's got a very nice little daughter for a bachelor, wouldn't you say? I'd say as Mr Knight has pulled the wool over everyone's eyes. Just wait till I tell the girls wharr I've see'd today! Mr Darky Knight, the darkest horse o' them all!'

Darky continued to try to thrust the child into Patty's arms, his face burning, and Patty, who had got the giggles with a vengeance, did her best to take

Merrell from him and presently succeeded. Merrell was giggling too, now, and turned to bury her face in Patty's shoulder. 'I's wet,' she announced, as though making a new discovery. 'Knighty's all wet, too. Is he cross, Mammy?'

Having freed himself, Darky stalked off, saying through gritted teeth that he would fetch the mop, and Patty collapsed on to a dry piece of bench just as the ferry drew alongside the landing stage.

Wiping tears of mirth from her cheeks, Patty began to dig in her canvas holdall and presently withdrew a stout brown paper bag, a small cardigan and a pair of knickers. She stripped Merrell of her wet clothing, which she pushed into the brown paper bag, then dressed her in the dry knickers and cardigan and, after a moment's thought, took off her own light jacket and wrapped the child in that as well. Merrell did not seem particularly perturbed by what had happened so Patty did not waste time in talking about it, but cuddled the child in her arms and prepared to join the queue of people waiting to disembark. She looked round for Darky but he seemed to have disappeared. Presently a crew member came over, armed with a mop and bucket, and cleaned up the puddle, saying as he did so: 'I telled your ole man that we're used to accidents – it's a deal better than puke, if you ask me – so he's gone ahead, like. No doubt he'll be waitin' for you on the landing stage.'

'No doubt,' Patty said grimly. She realised that what had happened to Darky had caused him great humiliation but, even so, she thought he need not have abandoned her without so much as a word. After all, it had not been her fault that Merrell had had an accident; the child had asked to get off his knee but Darky had hung on to her and suffered the consequences. As the queue shuffled forward, she acknowledged that it was dreadfully bad luck that the couple from Levers had seen what had happened, but if Darky had been sensible, made a joke of it, then their barbed comments would never have been passed. What was more, it was his disgust and outrage which had made the other passengers regard the whole incident as hilarious. In fact, though he clearly blamed her, Patty felt that most of his humiliation had been self-inflicted. One cannot laugh at someone who is laughing at himself.

By the time she reached the landing stage Merrell's head was nodding and it was clear that she would very soon be asleep, so Patty walked slowly, wondering how on earth she would get the child home without waking her. To her relief, she saw Darky and gave him a tentative smile which was not returned, though he stooped and took Merrell from her, saying stiffly: 'Give her here. I'll take her to the tram stop.'

'If you hold her fairly low, my jacket will hide the front of your kecks,' Patty said timidly. 'I really am sorry, Mr Knight. What a dreadful thing to have happened.'

Darky shrugged. 'It wouldn't have mattered so much if she hadn't called me Daddy,' he said in a hard voice. 'Thought it very funny though, didn't you? I dare say you've taught her to call any friendly feller Daddy, eh? Makes you seem more respectable.'

Patty could not believe her ears. After giving her such a wonderful day, he was ruining it now – ruining it deliberately, it seemed. She longed to flare up at him, to tell him how she felt, but bade herself, grimly, to count to ten before she did so. After all, being soaked to the skin and humiliated before a great many people might cause the best of men to lose his temper. Darky was hitting out at the only person within reach who could be blamed for his predicament; if she turned away his wrath with a soft answer surely he would come to his senses, realise that what had happened could not possibly have been as a result of anything she had said or done?

Patty fell into step behind him, knowing that this was the most sensible thing to do. If she walked beside him, he would probably make more caustic comments and she might not be able to prevent herself from replying in kind. Then, glancing at his tall, unbending figure, she noticed, for the first time, that sitting in a puddle can be as injurious to the back of the trousers as to the front. There was a very large dark circle right across the seat of his pale grey kecks.

If I walked closer to him, no one would notice, Patty thought, but did not attempt to do so. It also occurred to her that he might tie his jacket round his waist by the arms, which would be equally effective. Indeed, she opened her mouth to tell him so and then shut it again. He would probably only snub me, she told herself defensively, walking along in his wake, and anyway, since he was in sublime ignorance of the state of his nether regions, he might as well remain so.

They reached the tram stop and stood in line and presently climbed aboard a No. 43 which would take them as far as the end of Silvester Street. She would have followed Darky as he got on, but to her great surprise he paused on the step and ushered her ahead of him into the one remaining seat. 'I'll put Merrell in your arms, then we won't have to disturb her again when we get off,' he said ungraciously. 'I'll go to the upper deck; there's bound to be some room up there.'

So Patty sat down and took the child from him. He

turned to mount the stairs and was several steps up when a voice hailed him. 'Hey, mister! Did you know you've sat in suffin'? Your bum's all black.' It was an urchin of eight or nine, standing on the platform having just got on to the tram.

Patty winced as Darky turned and glared at the child before disappearing from view on to the upper deck. Then she settled into the seat with a sigh, conscious that her lovely day had been spoiled and that a budding friendship which she would have valued had been lost through no fault of her own.

Chapter Thirteen

'Where are you off to, son? I hope you're not going to
be long. Supper's all but on the table and I'm doin'
apple pancakes for a puddin' and apple pancakes
isn't something that'll keep hot.'

Darky turned, his hand already on the doorknob.
'Oh, I thought I'd just stroll down to the corner shop
and buy a packet of Woodbines,' he said airily. 'But I
can put if off until after supper if you like.'

'No, no, you go now and you can fetch me back two
ounces of mints. Now that the evenings are drawing
in, it's nice to have a bag of sweeties to suck while I'm
knitting.'

'Righty-ho,' Darky said but he was far from
pleased, since he had had no intention of visiting the
corner shop. Now, however, he would have to do so
and supposed, resignedly, that he might as well buy
the Woodbines as well as the mints. When he came to
think of it, he could do with some cigarettes. He had
been smoking rather more than usual lately.

Darky let himself out of the door and shut it gently
behind him, glancing swiftly sideways as he did so,
towards No. 24. Ever since the dreadful day when he
and Patty had fallen out so dramatically, he had done
his best to avoid the girls next door. To be sure, he had
taken Ellen out a couple more times, but he had
begun to realise that he was being unfair to her by so
doing. He liked Ellen as a friend but knew there
would never be anything more between them. It was

odd, he reflected, that he felt no warmer feeling for her, because she was pretty, light-hearted and good company. When they went dancing, he always danced several times with her and was aware that she found this exciting, that it gave her pleasure and also encouraged her to hope that he was serious. After the time he had spent in New Brighton with Patty and the child, he had known such conflicting feelings that he had become confused, but not too confused to recognise that what he felt for Patty was a stronger and far deeper emotion than that which he felt for Ellen. Therefore, in common decency, he decided he must make it plain to Ellen that they could never be more than friends.

Ellen had not taken it well, had actually wept a little, but he thought that now, eight weeks later, she was becoming resigned. What was more, it was high time he tried to make it up with Patty.

He had known all along, of course, that it had been his fault. The kid couldn't possibly have helped wetting him, half asleep as she was, and in his heart he was pretty sure that fatherless children tended to call any man of whom they were fond Daddy. The truth was, that having made up his mind to mend the rift between himself and his next door neighbour, he had felt doubly humiliated when things had begun to go wrong. After such a lovely day, he should have been able to laugh over the incident on the ferry. He had done so next day, at work, when brassy Bet had tried to make an issue of what had happened. 'Good God, woman, you're pretty keen to make a mountain out of a molehill, aren't you?' he had enquired. 'Me mam baby-sits for our next door neighbour's littl'un, so she's in and out of our house all the time. At that age, they'll call any feller Daddy who looks at them twice. And, though she's pretty good as a rule, every kid has accidents when they're first out o' nappies. We had a good laugh over it that evenin', me mam and me.'

It had taken the wind out of her sails; made her look spiteful and foolish, which meant that he had no more trouble. Why oh why, he had asked himself later, had he not done the same aboard the ferry? Why had he not made light of it to Patty, instead of turning on her as though the whole thing had been her fault?

The fact was, his feelings for Patty were both strong and strange to him. He had loved Alison deeply for she had been a sweet-tempered, biddable little creature, whose only desire was to please him, and he knew instinctively that Patty would never be like that. Sometimes, he thought she was so pretty that he simply wanted her, but the day in New Brighton had forced him to conclude that there was more to it than that. There had seemed to be an affinity between them, a strong bond . . .

Darky reached the corner shop and tried to expel the thoughts of Patty and their relationship from his mind. He was here to buy – what *was* he here to buy? Oh yes, his mam had wanted mints and he was down to his last two Woodies.

'Yes, Mr Knight? How can I help you, my son?' Mr Flowerdew, moustache bristling, looked encouragingly up at Darky who asked for ten Woodbine, two ounces of mints and a half pound box of chocolates – 'Black Magic if you've got 'em.'

Mr Flowerdew raised gingery eyebrows. 'Takin' a young lady to the flickers?' he enquired jovially. 'It's amazin' how much a box of choccies softens up the toughest young lady.'

'No, these are for me mam,' Darky explained, as Mr

Flowerdew reached down a box of chocolates from the shelf behind him and then began to weigh out the mints. 'Now that the evenings are pulling in, she does a lot of knitting and listening to the wireless and she likes to have a sweet to suck, so I thought I'd treat her.'

Mr Flowerdew nodded understandingly. 'She's a grand lady, your mam, and you're a good son to her,' he observed. 'Want a bit o' paper round them chocs?' Darky said that this would not be necessary, shoved the sweets and chocolates into his pocket and left the shop.

He walked slowly as far as the metal stairway, sat down on the lower steps, lit a Woodbine, and began to consider his next course of action. Originally, he had intended to go straight round to Nurse Peel's place and tell her that he was deeply ashamed of his behaviour on the ferry from New Brighton. He had known from the start that the next move was up to him, he just could not bring himself to take it. Patty had every right to snub him, to turn away his apology with withering scorn, but now that he knew her a little better he did not think she would do so. He acknowledged that she was a generous person, not mean-minded in any way, and would probably be as keen for reconciliation as he was himself, though he could not blame her if after eight weeks of coolness she doubted his sincerity.

Reaching their landing, he walked swiftly to the end house and lifted the little brass knocker, letting it fall quite gently; he had no desire to bring his mother out, thinking that someone had come to call on her!

There was a nasty moment while he wondered what he should say if Ellen answered the door, but the worry was short-lived. The door opened. Maggie stood there. She was chewing and there were crumbs on one cheek, but she managed a bright smile. 'Hello, Mr Knight,' she said thickly. 'Does you want a message running? If so, I'll go soon as I've finished me supper.'

Darky swallowed. 'No, it isn't a message, exactly,' he said awkwardly. 'Is Nurse in?'

'Which one?' Maggie said baldly. 'Oh, I suppose it's Ellen you're after. I'll just . . .'

'No, no, don't fetch her,' Darky said desperately. 'I – I wanted a word wi' Nurse Peel but if you're having your tea it don't matter, I'll catch her later.'

'Well you couldn't catch her now, 'cos she's not in,' Maggie said briskly. Was there a hint of disapproval in her tone, Darky wondered. If so, he could scarcely blame her. Maggie was a bright child and must have known full well that there had been trouble between himself and Nurse Peel. 'She's attendin' a confinement on the Scottie; it's the flat above Brannigan's chippie. No tellin' how long she'll be, though it's the woman's fourth baby.' Here, curiosity plainly got the better of her. 'Is there anything I can do? Take a message? Or give you a hand wi' – wi' anything?'

Darky, having recovered his composure, said, a trifle loftily, that he would not trouble her and turned back to his own house. He had intended the chocolates for Patty as a sort of peace offering but now he began to think he might as well give them to his mother after all. The chances of finding Patty alone seemed remote indeed and he had no desire to apologise for his behaviour in front of a kid of thirteen or the young woman he had recently disappointed.

Throughout the excellent supper which his mother had made, Darky pondered his problem, and by the time the meal was over he had made a decision. He would go out, letting his mother believe that he was visiting the pub, but instead he would go along to the chippie on Scotland Road. There, he would buy a bag of chips and ask, with joviality, how the job was going on upstairs. He knew enough about his neighbours to realise that every woman in the street would be well aware of what was happening and would be eager to pass on any news.

'Well, Mrs Brannigan, you've got a fine, healthy boy. He weighs almost eight pounds and he's sleeping soundly. Doctor will be round when he gets back and I'll come and see you again between nine and ten tomorrow morning, but if you have any problems, you know where I live. All right?'

The woman on the bed smiled up at Patty. Her face was drawn with weariness but her eyes were bright, for the baby which lay, respectably cradled, at her side was her first boy, a brother for Betsy, Meg and Sue. 'Thank you, Nurse, you've been wonderful,' she said. 'We're going to call the baby Patrick, after your good self, and I hope as you'll stand godmother to him when the time comes.'

Patty said she was honoured and took her coat from where it hung on the hook behind the bedroom door. Mrs Brannigan was lucky, Patty reflected as she descended the stairs. Her patient could sleep, secure in the knowledge that if the new baby cried the little maid who did her housework, and looked after the children when Mrs Brannigan was working in the shop, would instantly fly to the cradle. Patty had been at the Brannigans' home for almost ten hours, and now would have to cycle home, boil water for a good hot wash, generally clean herself up and find herself a snack to eat before she could climb into her own bed. Furthermore, it had been a difficult birth, a breech presentation, and though Patty had sent for the doctor – Mr Brannigan had gone to his house – he had been unable to attend due to another confinement a couple of miles off.

Patty had not been particularly worried, and all had gone well, but she had had to work extremely quickly in order that the baby should not remain in the birth channel for too long, and by the time the baby was successfully delivered she was shaking from strain and fatigue and longing for her bed. When Mr Brannigan called to her as she descended the stairs, offering a cup of tea and a sandwich, she replied ruefully that she appreciated his kindness but really had to get home. 'I'm afraid I might fall asleep on my bicycle if I stay any longer,' she admitted, making her way to where Mr Brannigan stood by the door of the shop, ready to let her out into the street. 'But thanks for the offer, Mr B.; one of these days I'll take you up on it.'

She emerged into a clear but chilly night – or rather morning, for it was almost two o'clock. Her bicycle leaned where she had left it, down a short alley at the side of the shop. She unlocked the padlock which secured the front wheel, dumped her bag in the wide wicker basket in which Merrell had once travelled, and wheeled the machine on to the road. Stifling a yawn, she was about to mount it and ride off when a voice said, almost in her ear: 'Evenin', Nurse Peel. Can I have a word?'

To say that Patty was shocked was an understatement. She must have jumped six inches, turning as she did so to face the man who had spoken – and saw, with real astonishment, that it was Darky Knight. Immediately, she felt all sorts of barriers rising up around her, and oddly enough a frisson of fear. She could think of no possible reason why he should be walking along the Scotland Road at this hour, but she was too tired to defend herself if he had come to quarrel with her yet again.

'Nurse Peel? I've been meaning to tell you how sorry I was for the way I behaved on the ferry from New Brighton, only it's so hard to get hold of you! We both work long hours and when I'm free and you're at home, so's Ellen and Maggie. So this evening, I thought I'd meet you out of work, tell you I really am sorry.'

Patty stared at him, momentarily speechless. If he had been waiting here for hours just to apologise, she supposed she should be grateful, but she discovered she was too tired even for gratitude. 'It's all right, Mr Knight,' she said in a flat, discouraging tone. 'I dare say I made too much of it, but the fact is, you and I are like fire and water – we just don't mix. Still, at least, in future, we can say "Good morning" or "Good Evening" to one another when we meet on the stairs or in the street.'

She began to mount her bicycle and Darky, with an exclamation of dismay, moved round to block her path, seizing the handlebars as he did so. 'Don't go, Patty,' he said urgently. 'I know you're desperate tired and probably wishing I'd go to perdition, but I really *am* sorry and I want to be friends.'

Patty, now seated on the saddle of her bicycle, felt righteous wrath fill her. How dared he try to hand her an ultimatum, to say that mere neighbourliness would not be sufficient, that he wanted friendship – and after the way he had behaved, too! 'It's rather late for such weighty matters, Mr Knight,' she said, with as much cordiality as she could manage. 'I'm tired out and want my bed because tomorrow is another working day and I've a list of revisits as long as your arm. So, if you'll kindly step out of my path and let go of my handlebars, I'll be on my way.'

Darky, however, did not move so much as a muscle. 'I don't blame you for being angry with me,' he said in a low voice. 'I've never behaved to any woman the way I've behaved to you and I'm downright ashamed of myself. But now I've admitted my fault and mean to mend my ways, surely you'll give me a chance? Could I – could I talk to you tomorrow evening? We could go for a walk . . . sometimes it's easier to talk as you walk . . .'

Patty compressed her lips, but once more felt too tired to argue. 'All right; I'm off early tomorrow evening,' she said. 'I'll meet you outside the corner shop at seven o'clock – just for five minutes' chat, mind.'

She told herself she would have done anything, agreed to anything, to be allowed to go home to bed and was immensely relieved when Darky let go her handlebars and stepped out of her path. 'Thanks, Patty,' he said, almost humbly. 'You won't regret it, I promise.'

Moving off down the road, Patty turned and delivered one parting shot. 'I had better not regret it, Mr Knight,' she said. 'Or I will never speak to you again as long as I live.' And with that, she cycled thankfully away.

It was an hour before Darky crawled into bed, but when he did so he could not, at first, sleep. He had seen Patty emerging from the chippie, looking so white and strained, and a most extraordinary feeling had gripped him; he had wanted to protect her, tell her she must not work so hard, nor become so involved with her patients. Normally, her self-confidence – and her blonde prettiness – was what he noticed and liked. But seeing her worn out by a long day's work had changed everything. He had been aware for the first time that what he wanted from Patty was most definitely not just friendship. He wanted to take care of her with loving tenderness. He wanted her to turn to him, not just as a friend, but as the one true love in her life.

The thought astonished him so much that he sat up in bed, staring wide-eyed into the dark. How could he even think such a thing? He had been telling himself for months and months that he did not even like Patty and only wanted to be friendly with her to ease the situation. To be not on speaking terms with one's next door neighbour made for a good deal of awkwardness, particularly since his mother and Patty were such good friends.

Yet seeing Patty so worn out and defenceless had brought his true feelings rushing to the surface. Lying down again, he thought that he had not felt like this since his marriage. He could remember how he had longed to protect Alison from every wind that blew, and he had never expected to feel the same about any other woman. Indeed, he did not feel the same, for Patty was the absolute opposite of his timid, gentle little wife. Yet she had aroused in him the same fierce, protective emotions – what could this mean?

He lay for a long while, puzzling over it, and was on the very edge of sleep when another thought popped into his head. I love her, he thought, astonished. Whether I like it or not, I, Derek Knight, of Levers, am in love with Patricia Peel, midwife.

A short time before, such a thought would have

outraged him, but now he found himself smiling, glad that he had sorted his feelings out at last. He buried his face in the pillow, reminding himself that he must be up at six, when another thought struck him: Patty most certainly did not return his feelings. In fact, judging from her attitude earlier, she disliked him very much.

The thought should have distressed him, but it did not. I'll *make* her see sense. I'll *make* her fall in love with me, he told himself, just as he fell asleep.

Patty awoke next morning with the uncomfortable feeling that she had committed herself to doing something which would give her no pleasure; quite the opposite, in fact. However, she had slept through the alarm and was already late so she had no time to dwell on the thought. Instead she shot out of bed, washed in cold water, struggled into a clean uniform and set off for the girls' room. Maggie must have heard the alarm through the thin wall which separated the two rooms, as she was already up and dressed and helping Merrell out of her nightgown and into warm clothing, for the morning was chilly.

'Maggie, my dear, I was out until the early hours – it was well past two before I got to bed – and I'm in a tearing hurry since I slept through the alarm,' Patty said breathlessly. 'I'll go through and make the porridge but I'm afraid I simply won't have time to help you to feed Merrell or to do any of the other things I usually do. Ellen will probably give you a hand . . .'

'Ellen's already gone,' Maggie said. 'She had a call just after seven o'clock; Mrs Gruber is in labour. I'm surprised you didn't hear her oldest kid bangin' on the door. As for breakfast, don't you worry yourself.

I cooked the porridge whilst Ellen was getting dressed; it's simmering on the back of the stove, so that's no problem. You get yourself off, Patty, and I'll see to little Merry here and get myself to school before the bell goes. Oh, Mrs Knight says she's goin' to the market and does you want any messages?'

'Oh, Lord, I don't know,' Patty said distractedly, clutching her head. She could feel a tightness behind her eyes which normally presaged a headache; the last thing she wanted on such a busy day. 'Maggie, could you be a real little darling and check the pantry for anything we need? I'm supposed to be off at five this afternoon, but with the sort of luck I've been having lately it'll probably be more like seven.' As she said the words, she remembered; she had actually arranged to meet Darky Knight outside the corner shop on Latimer Street at seven o'clock. Damn, damn, damn! After the way he had treated her, she should have had enough sense to tell him to get lost, to walk away from him. Then she remembered that he had physically barred her way, had not allowed her to even go home as she had wanted. Belated indignation at his cavalier treatment made her cheeks go hot. She thought, vengefully, that it would serve him jolly well right if she stood him up, let him hang around on the corner waiting for her in vain, and decided that she would probably do just that. After all, she could always pretend she had forgotten the appointment in the rush of the day's doings.

Thinking back, she told herself that being horrid to her was not Darky Knight's only sin. He had taken Ellen out, made much of her, danced with her when they both attended the Grafton Ballroom, and had then dropped her for no real reason; certainly he had not taken out any other girl, so far as Patty knew.

Ellen had been heartbroken, had presented a tearful countenance at mealtimes and had shown such a lugubrious face to patients that folk had stopped Patty in the street to ask whatever was the matter with that nice little Nurse Purbright? It had all been Darky's fault, Patty thought crossly now, rushing round the kitchen and eating warm porridge with one hand whilst endeavouring to polish her shoes with the other. Yes, it had definitely been Darky's fault because he had led Ellen on and then dumped her, and Patty, of course, had had to pick up the pieces, apply salve to injured pride and generally put herself out.

The fact that she had never thought Ellen and Darky were right for each other and had been proved correct had not given her the satisfaction she would have expected. But Ellen was now interested in a young army officer, John Bond, stationed at the Seaforth Sands barracks and her heart seemed to be mending nicely. She had met him at the Grafton Ballroom and now he came calling at least once a week and seemed to have cured Ellen of her melancholy, at any rate.

Merrell erupted into the room as Patty was pouring herself a cup of tea. Her fair curls were on end and her blue eyes blazed with excitement. 'Mammy, Mammy, Nanna is takin' me to the market,' she said importantly. 'Me shoes is too small. They're pinchin' me toes.'

Patty gasped. 'Oh, darling, I quite forgot,' she said distractedly. 'Nanna told me you were needing a larger size. If I give Maggie some money, she'll give it to Nanna for the shoes. Is there anything else, queen?'

'Nuffin' else, 'cep' mebbe some sweeties,' Merrell said. 'I love sweeties, Mammy.'

Patty laughed, kissed the top of the child's curly head and fished her purse out of her handbag. She extracted some coins and handed them to the child. 'Take that to Maggie, queen,' she said. 'And now I really must go or I'll never get through my work till midnight.'

Jamming her felt hat on the back of her head and slinging her coat over one shoulder and her black bag over the other, Patty shot across the kitchen and out of the door. She ran down the metal stairs, making a terrific noise, and skidded to a stop beside her bicycle. She was fishing out the key to the padlock, and trying to get it into the tiny keyhole, when someone else came thundering down the stairs. Patty glanced up and saw that it was Darky. The lock parted and Patty shoved it into her coat pocket and began to struggle into the garment. She was so used to being ignored by Darky that she did not even greet him and was pleasantly surprised when he screeched to a halt beside her and began to help her into the coat.

'Can't stop. I'm going to be bleedin' late, but don't forget we're meeting outside Flowerdew's at seven,' he said breathlessly. 'See you later!'

Patty, buttoning her coat, cramming her bag into her bicycle basket and mounting the machine, told herself that there was no chance now of claiming to have forgotten the appointment. She would simply have to go and meet Darky and make it plain to him that she would stand no more nonsense, that this was positively his last chance. She did not think they could ever be friends, but at least in future they could be polite to one another.

Having made up her mind on this point, Patty cycled off, telling herself that life would be a good deal easier if she and Darky stopped ignoring one another completely and occasionally exchanged a greeting.

As she turned into the Scotland Road, Patty saw Darky's familiar figure standing at a tram stop literally jiggling from foot to foot with impatience, and smiled grimly to herself. He was going to be late to work because he hadn't got to bed till the early hours through bullying her into agreeing to meet him – she dismissed his apologies as probably insincere – and it served him jolly well right! She still sometimes remembered the day in New Brighton but it had been pretty well ruined by his behaviour on the ferry. Still, she could not help wishing that poor little Merrell hadn't had her accident on Darky's knee, hadn't called him Daddy . . .

Next year, she decided, she would have to lay the ghost of that dreadful day by returning to the seaside resort and having a wonderful time. I'll take Ellen with me – and both girls, of course – and we'll do all the things we did with Darky and go on the funfair as well, she decided. She and Darky had not visited the funfair because Merrell had been too tired by the time it really got going. But when Ellen and I go, I'll buy one of those little folding pushchairs; Merrell can sleep in that if she gets really tired, and Maggie can keep an eye on her while Ellen and I have a good old go on the waltzers and the merry-go-round and the swing boats, Patty told herself. I've always loved the fair, I suppose partly because it makes me think of Toby.

At the mere thought of Toby's name, Patty gave a reminiscent little smile. She had been so fond of Toby! The one fellow, she thought as she wove her way along the busy road, who had never let her down, never been cruel or nasty, never tried to take advantage. Of course, he had not turned up to meet her under the clock on Lime Street station, though she had gone to the rendezvous six years running. After that, she had been too busy, too involved with her own life to continue the vigil. But the fact that he had not turned up would not be because he had forgotten or grown tired of her. He had probably been abroad, or in the north of Scotland, or down at Land's End with his beloved fair. She just knew he would have come to Liverpool to meet her, had it been possible.

'Watch out, Nurse!' A large brewer's dray swerved to a halt against the pavement in front of her, barrels clattering, and Patty tore her mind away from Toby and returned it firmly to the present. One way of escaping the meeting with Darky would be to get killed, she told herself with mordant humour, but that seemed a bit extreme. Paying more attention to her surroundings, she continued to make her way along Scotland Road.

'Oh, hard luck, madam – hard luck indeed. Why, you're a crack shot. You must ha' been practising for months. A little more to the left and you'd have won the Kewpie doll, but we won't let a bit of bad luck send you away empty-handed, eh? You shall have either a goldfish or a big bag of toffees. Which shall it be?'

The girl thus addressed dimpled up at Toby and pointed to the bag of toffees. 'I'm a bit old for a goldfish,' she said, fluttering her eyelashes at him. 'But no one's ever too old to suck a toffee.'

Toby, agreeing, handed over the toffees, putting a good face on it. Goldfish were tricky little beasts, liable to go belly-up if the weather was too hot or too cold, or if the tank got too crowded or sometimes, he thought, out of sheer spite towards the showman who was trying to make a living. Still, the girl had been pretty and the toffees were home-made. Trixie Flanagan was a dab hand at toffee making and always said that once a customer got a taste of her wares, they would come back again and again as long as the fair remained in their vicinity.

The girl wandered away from the stall and Toby sighed and looked hopefully at the clock which he could see above the roofs of the surrounding stalls. After he and Edie had split up, he had paid Ted to manage the swing boats and had dealt with the shooting gallery himself, but had almost immediately realised that this was not ideal. Takings had fallen startlingly from the very day Edie had left and Toby was quite acute enough to realise that this was because the main customers of the shooting gallery were men and men liked to have a pretty girl to cheer when they hit one of the targets. He had known that if the shooting gallery was to succeed, he ought to look about him for a pretty girl to run it. Edie, he reflected without bitterness, had been extremely pretty and was responsible for the excellent takings from the shooters.

Now, despite the fact that it had been a wet August, the fair had done quite well. The swing boats were bringing in as much as they had ever done; it was only the shooting gallery which was disappointing. This was why Toby had taken over the gallery and let Ted look after the swing boats. But my manly charms, Toby thought ruefully, cannot possibly make up for my not being a pretty girl. I've simply got to get hold of someone like Edie or sell the shooting gallery on, and I don't mean to do that.

He and Edie had never married though they had

lived together amicably for half a dozen years in the large, green-painted caravan which the Flanagans had found for him when he first bought the shooting gallery from Trixie's dad. It still rather annoyed him that Edie had thrown in her lot with Solly Butcher, but Solly was already Riding Master of a large fair of his own and Toby supposed, ruefully, that one could scarcely blame the girl. Besides, though he had been fond enough of Edie, he had never lost his heart to her. She was a hard-boiled young woman who had spent all her life with the travelling fair, and he had not been, by any means, her first partner. So losing Edie, he thought now, had affected his business rather than his heart.

One of the reasons that Toby had been unable to employ a young woman to run his rifle range was that Flanagan's fair was a trifle short on females. The only young, attractive girls were already fully employed, and taking on an outsider was a difficult business because the fair constantly moved on. Besides, he had no accommodation to offer an employee; had he been married, it would have been natural for him and his wife to give the girl a bed in the green caravan – but then if he had been married, his wife would have run the shooting gallery and there would have been no need to employ anyone.

Toby sighed and leaned his elbow on the counter, looking out at the desolate scene. They were due to move on tomorrow and he just hoped that the new gaff would be less soggy underfoot than this one, for nothing put the flatties off more than getting mired to the knees in mud. He tried to remember to which town they were going, then gave up. Once they were on the road, they might well stop half a dozen times in small villages before moving on to a proper town, and such villages were always, he reflected gloomily, muddy.

Despite the fact that, as she had warned Maggie, she had barely finished work by seven o'clock, Patty hurried straight to the rendezvous. She did not intend to put herself in the wrong with Darky by arriving late, though she had a perfect excuse for so doing. One of her patients had developed mastitis and by the time Patty had finished with her, she was already an hour later than she should have been for her subsequent calls. It was a tired and cross Nurse Peel, therefore, who climbed wearily off her bicycle outside Mr Flowerdew's shop. She was still in full uniform and knew herself to be both dirty and untidy, for she had been far too busy to comb her hair or do more than wash her hands and face with carbolic soap at her last call. It would have been nice to have had a good wash with scented soap, to have used a talcum and perhaps to have dabbed a little perfume behind each ear, but instead she would have to face her adversary – for she could scarcely think of him as a friend – with her hair falling out of its bun and the aroma of disinfectant about her.

Glancing around, she thought for one moment that Darky had not yet arrived, but then he emerged from the shop and saw her and a big smile crossed his face. 'Patty!' he said and there was a lift to his voice that Patty had never heard before. 'I were that scared you wouldn't come . . . and last night, I forgot to give you these.' He produced a box of Black Magic chocolates from his jacket pocket and held them out to her, looking so like a bashful small boy that she had to smile as she accepted the gift.

'Thank you, Mr Knight,' she said demurely. She

tucked the chocolates into her own pocket, not wanting them to come into contact with the tools of her trade which had overflowed her black bag and were crammed untidily in her bicycle basket. When she got home, they would be meticulously cleaned and sterilised and put neatly into their proper places, but for the time being all she was concerned about was getting back to the landing house before she fell asleep from sheer exhaustion.

A couple of people walked between them and Patty smiled and began to push her bicycle towards home. Darky fell into step beside her, saying as he did so: 'I can see you've come straight from work; you've had a long day. I'd hoped – expected – that we might take a stroll down to the waterfront so that we could chat.' He peered earnestly into her face across the small distance which separated them. 'Patty, we need to talk – we must talk! I've never been much of a feller for words but now I realise how important they are. Look, if we walk home and you leave your bicycle and take your stuff upstairs, we could be off again in ten minutes. We could catch a tram, or a taxi cab even. It's a bit late for going anywhere exciting, but . . .'

Patty pulled her bicycle to a halt and turned to face him. Above her head, a street lamp spluttered into life in the deepening dusk. 'I need more than ten minutes to get myself decent, Mr Knight,' she said firmly. 'At the end of every day, all my instruments have to be cleaned and sterilised, my uniforms – aprons and so on – have to be bundled up for the laundry or washed at home, and of course I have to wash myself pretty thoroughly as well. If I've been in contact with any sort of bad disease, I have to bath and wash my hair several times. So you see, it isn't a simple matter of going indoors, running a comb through my hair and changing into a clean dress.'

'I didn't know,' Darky said humbly. 'I wasn't thinkin' straight because of course you had a dreadfully late night last night.' He hesitated for a moment, staring down at his feet, then looked up, meeting her gaze squarely. 'I were that desperate to get things sorted out that I suppose I were only thinking of myself.' He grinned ruefully at her. 'When will I ever get things right, eh? And by the same token, why have I descended from Darky to being Mr Knight again? I dare say you'll think I'm just a cheeky blighter, but I don't mean to stop calling you Patty – unless it makes you mad, of course!'

Despite herself, Patty was forced to grin back at him. She supposed that she was being a bit formal, considering he had just given her a very acceptable present – Patty's mouth watered at the thought of a whole box of Black Magic chocolates – so she said: 'I'm sorry, Darky, but it isn't easy to forget how often I've got on the wrong side of you by accident and I suppose it's made me wary.' She hesitated again, glancing up into his dark, intense face as they turned the corner into Ashfield Place. 'Do you think it might be better if we postponed our talk until another evening? Only I'm so tired, and I've so much still to do . . .'

'I'll come in and help you,' Darky said eagerly. 'I can help wi' the kids; I'm quite handy about the house. Why, if you tell me how to sterilise your instruments, I'm sure I could do that for you. Then I could take you out for a bite of supper; do you know the Crocodile Restaurant on Cable Street? They do quite a decent meal, and if we get in before the cinemas and theatre shows finish it won't be crowded.'

Patty laughed. She thought it was time that cards were placed very firmly on the table if Darky was suggesting that he should visit her house and behave like a friend of long standing. 'And what about Ellen?' she asked forthrightly. 'No matter how you may feel, Mr Kni— I mean Darky, I don't think Ellen would be at all happy to have her ex feller running loose around her home. And I believe Maggie has felt a bit unfriendly towards you for some time now.'

'Oh yes,' Darky said, his cheeks reddening. 'I suppose . . . only I never was serious with Nurse Purbright, you know; never pretended to be. It – it were a misunderstanding like, and anyway Mam tells me she's gorra feller now . . . and what business it is of young Maggie's, I've yet to discover!'

Patty laughed again. 'There you go, you see,' she said. 'Taking offence, getting all hot and bothered, making me feel it would be a great deal safer to call you Mr Knight and cross the road when I see you approaching. When three females – four if you count Merrell – share a house, then they get closer – and fonder – than you would believe possible. We're a family, Mr Kni— Darky, I mean – and we behave like one. We take on each other's quarrels, stand up for each other and band together against anybody who seems to be attacking one of our number. I don't think fellers behave the same but you'll find that women, old or young, tend to do just that.'

'I see,' Darky said, a trifle dismally. Patty thought he sounded truly crestfallen and was glad of it. At least he hadn't argued, hadn't tried to prove her wrong or claim that she was making a mountain out of a molehill. If they were to be friends, then he simply had to accept that the situation between himself and Ellen must be put right before he could visit freely at No. 24. 'Patty, I do see what you mean. Suppose I apologise to Ellen for the way I behaved; do you think she'd accept an apology?'

'Ellen is a very generous person,' Patty said primly. 'If you apologise to her I'm certain she'll say that everything's fine and since Maggie was hurt for Ellen rather than for herself she'll be fine as well.' They had reached the foot of the stairs and Patty padlocked her bicycle. 'But I would still recommend that we forget going out this evening; what's wrong with tomorrow evening?'

'There's nothing wrong with it,' Darky was beginning, when someone clattered down the stairs. Patty was too busy transferring the contents of her basket to take much notice, but Darky started forward, standing at the end of the steps with a hand on either banister rail, effectively preventing the descender from setting foot on solid ground. 'Ellen, I've treated you badly,' Darky said. 'Can you bring yourself to forgive me?'

Ellen looked astonished before saying airily, 'Oh, don't give it a thought, Darky. You were right that it were wastin' my time to hang around hoping you'd get serious. Me new feller doesn't need no encouragement; we're already savin' up for a wedding in a couple of years' time.' As Darky stood back, Ellen peered around him and spotted Patty. 'Oh, is *that* why you're suddenly so keen to make a clean breast of it,' she remarked, grinning. 'I might have guessed it weren't just your naggin' conscience which was cutting up rough.' She turned back to Patty. 'I've gorra late call to Mrs Finnigan. She reckons her pains have started so I'll probably be out most of the night since she's a primigravida.'

'Right,' Patty said briskly, heading for the stairs.

'See you tomorrow morning then, queen. Everything all right at the house?'

'Fine,' Ellen said, going over to her own bicycle. She dumped her black bag in the basket and began to unfasten the padlock. 'Merrell and Maggie have both had their supper and I put Merrell to bed almost an hour ago. She was really tired because Mrs Knight had taken the pair of them to Paddy's market to buy shoes, and the little madam has been parading up and down Ashfield Place showing off her new possessions to anyone who was interested and quite a few who weren't. Maggie's sitting by the fire, toasting bread and trying to do an acrostic puzzle which one of the teachers in school gave her. She's done her homework, and by the look of her it won't be long before she's off to bed as well.'

'Thanks ever so much, Ellen,' Patty said gratefully as she and Darky began to mount the stairs. 'If you get into a fix and need help, get one of the neighbours' kids to fetch me. But I expect Dr Evans is standing by, because you said Mrs Finnigan was very slight and . . .'

'And her husband's the size and build of a Herefordshire bull,' Ellen shrieked happily at their retreating backs. 'Thanks, queen, I won't forget.'

'What's a primi thingy when it's at home?' Darky said curiously, as they reached the first landing. 'Here, let me carry some of that stuff or you'll be spilling it all over the place.'

'No I shan't, because I do this just about every night,' Patty said rather breathlessly, though she let him take the black bag from her grasp with considerable relief. 'As for a primigravida, it means a first time mother, that's all. Mrs Finnigan is in labour with her first child, in other words.'

'Oh, I see,' Darky said rather blankly. 'But what difference does it make? That she's a first time mother, I mean?'

'It means she'll probably have a harder time than if she'd given birth before,' Patty informed him, as they emerged on to the top landing. 'The doctor should be standing by, but if he's called to another case and Ellen finds her patient is struggling, then she can either call for me or she can send a message to the hospital for an experienced obstetrician – that's a doctor who specialises in childbirth – to come to her aid.'

'Yes, I understand,' Darky said so quietly that Patty could scarcely hear him. 'That – that was what should have happened with Alison . . . But there's no point thinking of that.'

'No, I'm afraid there isn't,' Patty said frankly. She had no wish to discuss another midwife's incompetence with Darky, particularly since the woman in question had been dismissed from the service as a result of that incompetence. She wondered if Darky knew that, and, since he was still hovering at her side as she began to open her front door, decided to enlighten him. 'Nurse Farthingdale was chucked out of the service as a result of what happened to your wife – but I expect you know that.'

She was looking at Darky's face as she spoke and saw the incredulity and slowly dawning pleasure which crossed it. 'You don't say!' Darky muttered. 'Well, I wonder why no one ever told me, nor me mam either. I hope I'm not a vengeful man but the thought of that awful woman going round doing harm has haunted me for years. If only I'd known, Patty, I'd have been easier in me mind.'

'I think the authorities wanted to keep it quiet, because of course it gives the hospital a bad name when they send out a midwife who behaves as Nurse Farthingdale did,' Patty said quietly. 'But I do think you and your mother – and your wife's mother of course – should have been informed.'

'They might have told me mother-in-law,' Darky said rather grimly. 'But she'd not have said a word to me or me mam. She were a strange, bitter woman and blamed me for her daughter's death. She moved back to Glasgow soon after Alison's death – she only came down for her lying-in – and though we felt obliged to send a card at Christmas she's never followed suit.'

Patty nodded her comprehension, stepping into her living room as she did so. 'I can't understand how she could possibly blame you, but I do understand the deep bitterness she must feel at losing her child,' she said. 'If anything happened to Merrell – oh, I don't know what I'd do. Please come in, Mr Knight,' she added sarcastically, since her neighbour was already in the room. 'Shall I ask Maggie to get you a cup of tea while you wait for me to get ready? That is, if you're sure you wouldn't rather let our chat wait until tomorrow evening, when hopefully I shall be more organised and less weary?'

Patty was genuinely tired and really hoped that Darky would take her point and agree to meet next day, but though he looked a trifle guilty, he shook his head. 'It's got to be right away, because with you and me, anything might happen,' he said frankly. 'I want to get things sorted now while me courage is up.'

Maggie had got to her feet at the mention of tea and now Patty turned to her. 'Hello, queen. As you can see, we've got a visitor. Don't worry – he's apologised to Ellen for what happened, so I dare say you and I can unbend enough to share a cuppa with him.'

Maggie, taking cups down from the dresser, grinned. 'Well, I'm that glad,' she said, rattling the cups into their saucers. 'The thing is though, Patty, I saved you a bit o' blind scouse and a couple o' nice big spuds and if you don't eat it soon it'll dry up and be fit for nothing.' She glanced across at Darky, who was placing Patty's black bag carefully on the draining board. 'And there ain't enough for two,' she finished meaningly.

'It's all right, Maggie, I'm takin' Patty out for a bite to eat,' Darky said, coming towards the table. 'So you can take the food out of the bake oven and tip it into the pig bucket if you've got one.'

Maggie laughed. 'I'm still quite peckish meself,' she observed. 'So if you're sure it ain't wanted, I'll finish it up with me cup of tea.' She picked up the big brown pot and poured the tea into three cups, added a judicious teaspoonful of conny-onny to each and pushed one of the cups towards Darky, then picked up another and followed Patty through into her room. As soon as they were out of earshot, she lowered her voice to a hiss. 'What's up wi' Darky? Come to that, what's up wi' you, Patty? I thought after what happened in New Brighton, you were never going to speak to the feller again.'

'He apologised to me as well as to Ellen,' Patty said briefly. She was pulling her dress over her head as she spoke so her voice was muffled and her face, thankfully, was hidden. 'It's been awfully awkward, being on bad terms with the son of one of my best friends, because we're all fond of Mrs Knight and we rely on her too, don't we?' As Patty's head emerged from the dress, she saw Maggie nodding in confirmation and pressed home her point. 'It's been really difficult, particularly for me, because I had to plan and scheme to go round to the Knights' house only when I knew Darky wouldn't be there. Besides, he's really fond of Merrell, you know. And I think he likes you as well, queen.'

'Oh aye, you're right there. He'll spend hours playing with Merrell, giving her piggy-backs, taking us both up to the playground while his mam cooks our tea so that we can play on the swings and slides,' Maggie agreed. 'I kind of guessed why you and he fell out and I were ever so glad when things seemed to be getting easier. I could've cried when Merrell piddled on 'im in New Brighton and things got bad again.' She looked wistfully at Patty, lathering herself in soap and water as she washed. 'You won't let it get bad again, will you, Patty?'

'Not if I can possibly help it,' Patty assured her, rinsing off the lather and beginning to rub herself dry. 'Hand me my clean dress, would you, Mags?'

Despite Patty's fears, she was ready in a remarkably short time with Maggie's help. When they emerged from the bedroom, Patty was astonished to realise that Darky had done as he had promised: he had taken her bundle of used instruments, washed them in the sink, and then put them in a pan of water which was now boiling merrily on the stove. He had clearly not known what to do with the rest of Patty's equipment but she dealt with it rapidly herself and then bundled her dirty dress, apron, collars and cuffs into the brown sack the hospital provided and put it by the door. Tomorrow morning it would be collected by a van and taken to the laundry, and by evening it would be returned, beautifully cleaned and starched once more.

'Are we ready for the off?' Darky asked hopefully. 'I know you said the instruments had to be sterilised

– they've been boiling for ten minutes, is that long enough? – but I couldn't think of anything else to do. Even Maggie's homework was finished,' he ended, a trifle plaintively.

'I'm astonished at your efficiency,' Patty said politely. 'Who taught you to sterilise instruments, Mr Knight – Darky, I mean? As for being ready, I'll just pop in and make sure Merrell's sleeping soundly and Maggie is all set for the night, and then we can be off.' She glanced up at him, adding wickedly: 'I'm sure you've told your mother that you're taking me out, so she'll be listening for a knock on the wall from Maggie?'

This actually seemed to disconcert Darky. He flushed and said defensively: 'If I say I have, then I'm in the wrong because it would have been before I asked you and before you said yes. But if I say I haven't, I'm in the wrong because that means Mam won't know the girls is alone. Patty Peel, you're enough to drive a feller to drink!'

Patty laughed and opened the door, gesturing him through. 'Just you pop in and tell your mam I'll be out for a couple of hours and will she keep an ear open in case Maggie needs her,' she instructed him. 'Or would you rather I did it? That way, it'll save her knowing you've unbent at last.'

Darky cast his eyes up to heaven but he grinned at the same time. 'You'll make sure I'm in the wrong if it's the last thing you do,' he said resignedly. 'Go on then, you tell her. I'll do my telling later, when I've a day or two to spare.'

After three weeks, during which takings at the gallery never picked up, Toby went round to Mr Flanagan's caravan and found the family sitting round their dining table with a map of Great Britain spread out before them, apparently discussing how they should journey back to winter quarters when the time was ripe. They greeted him jovially, however, and Amanda Ellington, who was fourteen and at the gangly self-conscious stage, moved up to make room for him on the long bench, blushing as she did so. Trixie's sister was a pretty kid, Toby reflected as he took his place beside her, but she was also bright and her parents were determined that she should stay on at school, possibly even take her School Leaving Certificate. It was difficult for fair children to get a good education but Mrs Ellington had been a teacher before her marriage and had managed to see that her daughters kept up with other children of their age even during the spring and autumn, when they were changing schools constantly. If this had not been so, Toby would have asked if he might employ her on the shooting gallery, for she was a lively, intelligent girl who would have brought the flatties streaming to try their luck. But since she was destined for greater things, Amanda, unfortunately, was not an option.

'I think we'll overwinter in Wrexham again,' Mr Flanagan said. 'We can open up for Christmas on the Beast Market, then go on to Chester for the New Year – it's only a dozen miles off – and be back in Wrexham again in time to snug down for the bad weather. I know King's Lynn is by way of being favourite, but there's too many fairs make for the town now for my liking. What d'you say, Trixie?'

'Whatever you think best, Mr Flanagan,' Trixie replied placidly. 'You're right about King's Lynn; they say it's getting mortal crowded and anyway we need the rent.' She turned to Toby. 'But I don't suppose Toby came here to discuss winter quarters! How can we help you, Toby?'

Toby smiled. 'I've come for some advice, Trix. I've got a problem with the shooters.'

'Aye, we wondered how long it 'ud be before you decided you'd have to employ a young woman,' Mr Flanagan said. 'I suppose you're considerin' a flattie, Toby? Only there isn't one gal on the gaff who could be spared, as I'm sure you know.'

'But I can't see a flattie takin' to the life when we're movin' on so constantly,' Toby said. 'What's more, I've no accommodation and winter's comin' on. I couldn't ask a girl who wasn't used to the life to sleep out, and though I know the Chaps find cheap lodgings, I don't think the sorts of places they use would be suitable for a young woman. If I had a wife—'

'If you had a wife, you wouldn't need to employ anyone,' Amanda said quickly, then blushed to the roots of her hair. 'But I see what you mean; if you had a wife, the girl could sleep in your caravan. Is that what you were going to say, Toby?'

'It was,' Toby agreed, grinning at her. 'So what's the answer, Mr Flanagan? I expect you've guessed that I'm losin' money on the shooters, hand over fist. I don't want to sell the gallery, and besides, it's the wrong time of year to get a fair price, but at the moment it scarcely pays for ammo, let alone anything else.'

He meant that the gallery was not even earning its own ground rent, but did not mean to say so. Others, however, were not so tactful.

'You won't be making the rent Mr Flanagan charges you,' Amanda said, nodding. She turned to her brother-in-law. 'I wish I could help out – I s'pose I could work in the evenings, couldn't I?'

Mr Flanagan shook his head. 'No, that wouldn't

answer,' he said gruffly. 'Your family would kill me if I even suggested it.' He cast his wife a quick glance and Trixie, though she smiled, shook her head. 'Tell you what, Toby. I don't want to lose you, but this dilemma had got to be solved an' I can only see one way of doing it. What you want, lad, is a permanent fair, one that don't move on, like. Then you can get a local girl to work for you over the winter – just until you've got things sorted. There's a number o' funfairs what are permanent now, pertickly at the seaside, and as it happens I know of one Ridin' Master who's on the lookout for a shooting gallery. Your best bet, Toby, is to visit the place as soon as we reach winter quarters; it ain't far from there, so you won't be gone for more'n a day and the train fare won't break the bank. Write a letter first – Trix here will help you with that – an' then go up as soon as we're settled in at Wrexham. What d'you think?'

'Capital, Mr Flanagan,' Toby said gratefully. 'I'll do exactly as you say an' I'd be real grateful if Trix would help me with the letter. But don't you think I'm leavin' Flanagan's, because I ain't. I'll be back just as soon as I've got a respectable young woman to run the shooters for me – I suppose that's what you mean by getting things sorted. But I don't mean to settle down permanent, not me.'

'If she's a reliable sort o' young woman, the trustable kind, I see no reason why either Trix or one of the other women shouldn't give her a bed,' Mr Flanagan said. 'You won't get no one having a young fly-by-night in their van – too risky – but a gal who's worked wi' you for three or four months an' likes the life . . . well, that's a different matter.'

'And if you choose right, mebbe you'll end up making an honest woman of her this time,' Trixie said, giving Toby a reproving glance. Toby knew she had disapproved of his relationship with Edie. She had told him frankly that the girl would never have left him had he done the decent thing by her. But Edie had never suggested or seemed to want marriage and now Toby was glad of it. He was heart whole and fancy free with none of the responsibilities and shackles – albeit broken – of an unsuccessful marriage hanging round his neck.

However, it would not do to say so to Trixie, so he gave her his most winning smile as he left the caravan. Whistling happily to himself, he fetched his writing materials and retraced his steps. Trixie would not write the letter for him since he was perfectly capable of doing so himself, but she would advise him on the best way to approach the man who might become his temporary boss. Amanda was coming down the caravan steps as he approached and grinned cheerfully at him as their paths crossed. In another half-dozen years she's going to be a real little smasher, Toby told himself, smiling back at her. I wouldn't mind marrying the boss's sister-in-law at that – and how she'd bring the flatties lining up at the shooting gallery!

Chapter Fourteen

It was a Sunday morning in mid-December, and although it had rained in the night the sky was now blue and a faint wintry sunshine lit the scene. Patty had glanced through the window earlier and was relieved to see the sun; at least it meant that the children would be able to play when they reached the recreation ground. Mrs Knight had taken them off to St Martin's for a quick go on the swings and then on to her friend's in Hornby Street, who had two little girls of her own and would entertain Mrs Knight with a large pot of tea and a plate of home-made biscuits, whilst the children played in the garden.

Ever since she and Darky had buried the hatchet – and not in each other's skulls either – the two families had begun to share their weekends so that these now fell into a regular pattern. Mrs Knight looked after the children on a Saturday if Patty was called into work, but otherwise Patty, Maggie and Merrell, strapped into her pushchair, did their messages up and down the Scottie, sometimes having their dinner at a canny house. Quite frequently, Maggie deserted them as soon as the cinema opened and went to the tuppeny rush with several hundred other children and Patty and Merrell returned to Ashfield Place where, more often than not, Mrs Knight had prepared a light meal for herself and Darky which she invited them to share.

Sundays followed a similar pattern. Patty would

take the children to early service at St Martin-in-the-Field's church, close by the recreation ground; a service which Mrs Knight and Darky also attended. After it, Patty and Darky would walk home together, chatting amicably, whilst Mrs Knight, Maggie and Merrell made themselves scarce until it was time for dinner, which Patty herself always cooked since it was the only day in the week when she had time to make a proper roast meal with a hot pudding for dessert.

When Ellen was not on duty she spent her weekends either in Formby with her own parents, or in Ellesmere Port with John Bond's people. Mrs Knight and Darky often came to No. 24 for their Sunday dinner while Patty and the girls went to No. 23 for tea.

Right now, however, Patty knew she should be checking on the dinner, though judging from the delicious smell it was doing pretty well by itself. She swung open the oven door, seized a large metal spoon, and basted the joint of beef and the large dish of roasting potatoes before closing the door with a sigh of satisfaction and glancing up at the clock. In half an hour the Knights and the children would be coming in, so it behoved Patty to keep her mind on her work and get a move on. She liked to have the meat cooked, the gravy made and the pudding – it was treacle tart today – ready by the time they arrived.

She began to lay the table and found her thoughts wandering back to the moment when she and Darky had faced one another across the table at the Crocodile Restaurant on Cable Street.

'Patty, you know how sorry I am for the way—' Darky had begun, but Patty had cut him short.

'You've done enough apologising for a whole

lifetime,' she had said bluntly. 'I've said it's all right, I've forgotten all about it and we're going to start anew, but I tell you, if you're going to apologise every time we meet, then we won't be meeting often!'

Darky had laughed and leaned across the table to take her hand. Patty had snatched it away. 'Don't jump the gun; there are several steps between starting again and holding hands, Darky Knight! If we're going to be true friends, then it's step by step, not rush, rush. Just remember, it were only a few weeks ago that you were taking young Ellen dancing and out to the flicks – and no doubt holding her hand – and now you're trying to do the same with me. I'm not like Ellen, you know; I'm not looking for a feller or a fancy wedding or anything of that nature. Me and Merrell and young Maggie are already a family. We need friends, I'll grant you that – your mam's one of the best – but the girls don't need a father and I don't need a husband. Can you understand?'

Darky had looked taken aback, almost stunned, but then his face had cleared and he had laughed. 'So you don't believe that two wages are better than one, eh?' he said. 'You don't want a strong arm to carry your coal in for you, or a feller to share the worries when someone's ill or out of sorts? I can see I'm going to have me work cut out to persuade you to let me pay for two tickets for the cinema.' He cocked his head enquiringly, his eyes twinkling. 'Wharrabout the meal we've just ordered? Fish and chips twice and a roly-poly to follow? I suppose it's all this women's emancipation and you'll insist on buying my dinner. Well, I don't mind if it means you'll take me in your strong arms when we get home and give me a goodnight kiss.'

Patty had tried to be cross but all she could do was

laugh at the picture he presented. That evening had set the pattern for the many other occasions on which he had taken her out. He behaved like a perfect gentleman, but always, at some stage, he made some attempt to get closer to her and when she repulsed him, as she unfailingly did, he never became annoyed or offended but turned it off as a well-worn joke, always managing to make her smile.

Patty knew that she was learning a lot about men in general, as well as about Darky himself. From conversations with Ellen, she gathered that no matter what they might pretend, all men had one object in mind. They expected a girl who had accepted their company on an evening out to give at least some small return, and this meant that one should accept both kisses and cuddles, provided the kisser and cuddler did not try to go too far. Patty, however, did not mean to give Darky the impression that either kisses or cuddles were to be a part of their friendship. She had set her face against matrimony, and in her view it would have been unfair to allow him any liberties since she was not in the marriage market.

On their third date – a trip to the cinema – she had told him on the walk home that if he was looking for a wife he was wasting his time on her and should look elsewhere. Darky had grinned and then asked her, perfectly seriously, why she imagined that he had marriage in mind. 'Maybe I'm like you and just looking for someone to go about with,' he said blandly. 'I don't know what gives you girls the idea that men are so keen on settling down; most fellers would run a mile sooner than walk up the aisle.'

Patty had laughed and changed the subject, but she was still very sure in her own mind, after several weeks of going about with Darky, that he would want to marry again, some day. She had several times surprised a look in his eyes which almost embarrassed her with its intensity, and made her more determined than ever to keep him at a reasonable distance.

The bubbling of the water in the big black saucepan brought her back to the present and she carried the colander of finely chopped cabbage across the kitchen, tipped it into the boiling water and put the lid on the saucepan. Then she glanced around the room with some satisfaction. Apart from making the gravy, everything was ready for dinner, so as soon as she could pull the cabbage a little off the fire she would go into her bedroom and tidy herself up. She liked to present a neat and pleasant appearance when Darky and his mother came in for their dinner, and never allowed herself to wonder why this should be if she was as uninterested in Darky as she insisted. After all, it was Sunday and their only real day of rest.

Later in the week, Patty came home from work tired out and cross to find no food on the table, the fire almost out and no sign of either Maggie or Merrell. She went at once to Mrs Knight's house and that lady came to the door, very pink and flustered.

'Oh, Patty, such a to-do we've had,' she said as soon as she saw who her visitor was. 'Maggie left Merrell with me and went round to see her dad after school – it were something to do with Christmas, I believe – and the doctor was there. The three youngest kids have got the perishin' measles so Maggie came flying back, explained what had happened and said she'd have to stop with her family for a few days. She was sure you'd understand, but of course it's thrown my plans out somewhat. Still an' all, we'll have a chat presently, see what we can work out.'

Patty's hand flew to her mouth. 'Your visit to your sister!' she said. 'Oh, Mrs Knight, you've simply got to go!'

'I don't see how I can,' Mrs Knight said worriedly. 'Glasgow's a long way off; it's not as if I could just pop up to see her for a couple of hours. It's a shame, because she does need me, especially towards Christmas time. But it's just one of those things; I don't mean to let you and Merrell down, and I simply don't see how you could possibly manage without me *or* Maggie.'

'If only I could take a few days off! But for some reason Ellen and I are rushed off our feet and likely to be so until well after the New Year,' Patty admitted. 'Babies always seem to get born in batches, and we've both got half a dozen confinements, at least, due before Christmas. I wonder whether Ada Clarke might be able to arrange something for Merrell? She's obviously done so for Christopher.'

Mrs Knight looked a little self-conscious. 'Young Christopher is going to Mr Clarke's sister, the one what lives in Coronation Court, with all them kids,' she said. 'If I were you, I'd not let Merrell go to that little lot. I suppose there's no chance of Maggie taking her to her home? I mean, I know there's measles, but she'll be bound to get 'em one day, anyhow.'

'No, I'm afraid not,' Patty said. 'It – it's as unsuitable as Mr Clarke's sister, if you see what I mean. But don't worry, Mrs Knight. I'll think of something. Can you keep Merry for another half-hour or so, while I clean up next door and get her tea? Only poor Maggie left things in a bit of a state.'

Mrs Knight agreed and Patty went home and began wearily to persuade the fire to burn briskly and to pull the kettle over the flames so that she might have a hot wash.

Thirty minutes later, clad in a clean skirt and blouse and wrapped in a calico apron, Patty was setting the table for tea when the door opened and Mrs Knight, with the child in her arms, appeared.

'I've had a grand idea,' Mrs Knight said triumphantly, standing Merrell down on the floor. The child rushed to Patty, squeaking 'Mammy, mammy, mammy', and was immediately picked up and kissed warmly before being sat down in a corner amongst her toys.

Patty turned to her friend. 'Well, I'm glad you've thought of something because I've racked my brains and haven't come up with one single plan,' she admitted. 'Go on then, what's this grand idea?'

'How about if I take Merry to Scotland with me? She's not three yet, so she'll go free on the train, and she's no trouble, the little darlin'. Me sister's often said as how she wished she could see Merry – she's rare fond of kids is my sister – and you know she'd be well looked after.'

'Oh, Mrs Knight! But wouldn't it make things awkward for your sister?' Patty asked anxiously. 'I mean, you're going up to Glasgow to help her with her Christmas shopping; won't Merry get terribly in the way?'

'No, in fact she'll be a help,' Mrs Knight said. 'Me sister can walk with a pushchair quite well; she won't need to use her sticks at all. Honest to God, Patty, if you're prepared to let her come with me, then I'll be tickled to bits to have her, an' so will me sister. What d'you say?'

'I say it's just like you to put yourself out for me and not to think of yourself,' Patty said gratefully. 'Tell you what, Mrs Knight, when Ellen comes home, we'll have a talk and see whether we can come up with some sort of solution, because I still think it's unfair on you, but I imagine we'll be jolly grateful to accept your offer. Now, I'm only going to make baked beans on toast for supper, but if you'd like to join us you'd be very welcome.'

Mrs Knight smiled but shook her head. 'No, because I've done the tea for Darky and meself, though thanks for the offer,' she said. 'I'll come round later and we'll discuss the details – unless you think of something else, that is.'

On the following day, Patty saw Merrell and Mrs Knight off, waving energetically at the train until it had steamed out of sight. Then she began her day's work aware that despite Mrs Knight's kindness, she was in for a difficult week. Because Mrs Knight had taken Merrell, she had felt obliged to tell Darky that he could come round for a meal any time, and though he had said he would not bother her but could manage perfectly well alone, she still knew that she owed the Knight family a good deal.

Maggie was up to her eyes in looking after her own family now and though she had come round to No. 24 earlier that day, looking white and tired, she had not entered the house. 'I don't want to give you measles, Patty,' she had explained. 'I thought I'd had 'em when I was a little 'un but me dad says it weren't so, which means I could go down with them any day – or I could pass 'em on to someone else.'

'I wonder if I would get them? I never did when all the other kids had 'em at the Durrant,' Patty said positively, but even if she did have some mysterious immunity Maggie decided it was safer to keep clear, and, in view of her job, Patty agreed that this would be best.

The house seemed strangely quiet without the two youngsters, but after a few days Patty found herself quite enjoying her new-found freedom. She missed Merrell and Maggie – and her kind neighbour – very much indeed, but it was pleasant not to be constantly examining her watch when a delivery went on longer than it should have done, and she and Ellen sat round the fire and gossiped about their patients in a way which would have been impossible had Maggie been present. It was easier to scratch together a meal for two than for four, or to fetch in fish and chips, but Patty knew that this freedom was not really freedom at all. The house was beginning to look neglected and meals got scrappier and scrappier until she told Ellen severely that they would have to pull themselves together and get into a proper routine.

'If we weren't so busy, it might be fun to go to the flicks or to a dance without having to make arrangements for the children,' she said to Darky one evening when he had popped round to see how they were getting on. 'But the truth is, Maggie has become a real little housewife and she's even beginning to cook pretty well. I don't mean dinners – she's always been able to do that – but baking and such. So did you say you were off this Saturday?'

Darky nodded. 'That's right. So I thought we might go Christmas shopping, just the two of us. It may be our last opportunity, because Mam will be bringing Merry home next Monday and I dare say young Maggie will be back around then, so we might as well make the most of it.'

Patty agreed and the two of them had an excellent day investigating the big stores on Bold Street and

Ranelagh Street, coming home laden with parcels which were stowed away in various hiding places.

'And now let's round off the day with a visit to the Grafton Ballroom – after you've made me a good high tea as a thank you for me pains,' Darky said as Patty pulled the kettle over the fire and went into the food cupboard for the loaf of bread. 'Tea and toast is all very well, young Patty, but I'm a fellow with a big frame and I need plenty of fuel to stoke up me fire.'

Patty giggled. 'You mean you've got hollow legs,' she told him, briskly cutting two thick slices off the loaf and impaling one on a toasting fork. 'Here, hold this while I warm the butter and find up a jar of honey.'

'Oh well, if it's all that's on offer.' Darky sighed. 'I s'pose there's not much time to make a proper meal or we'll miss the dancing.'

'I don't mind missing the dancing,' Patty said, emerging flushed and tousled from the food cupboard. She plonked the jar of honey down on the table and pushed back her thick blonde curls, which had somehow managed to escape from their bun as they shopped. 'Why do you want to go dancing all of a sudden?'

'Because it's the only way to legally get me arms round you,' Darky said, his tone light. 'Tell you what, Patty, if you aren't in the mood for dancing, why don't we go over to the fair at New Brighton? I remember you telling me once that you and Ellen were going over there when summer comes so's you could remember what a nice day we'd had before I spoilt it all. If you and I were to go together and have a good time on the fair, d'you reckon that would convince you that I'm not such a bad feller after all?'

He spoke lightly but Patty thought she'd heard an underlying seriousness in his tone and suddenly felt sorry for him. He had been so good to her, so kind to Maggie and Merrell, such a gentle and undemanding escort. She might at least give him the satisfaction of scotching the feeling that he had ruined her life by his behaviour that day in New Brighton! 'All right,' she said therefore. 'I'm not saying you're a saint, Darky, but you've been really good to us, same as your mum has. I guess I'll enjoy the fair with you a good deal more than I'd enjoy it with anyone else.'

Darky's face lit up but he said nothing, only holding out the toasting fork to the fire, and presently, their hunger and thirst satisfied, the two of them set off. It was strange, Patty reflected as they boarded the ferry, that she felt so excited and light-hearted. Perhaps it was because the outing was such a spur of the moment affair, an unexpected treat after a long day of slogging round the shops. It was a nice evening, what was more, despite the fact that it was 22 December. The air was cool but crisp against Patty's face, and overhead the stars blazed down from a sky of velvety blackness. Patty stood by the rail with Darky beside her, and when the ferry docked at New Brighton and Darky slid an arm round her waist she did not object. In fact, she put her own arm round him, telling herself severely that they must not get separated as the crowd jostled and pushed its way down the gangplank. Darky made no comment, but as they reached the shore and walked along the pier towards the promenade, he released her waist and slid his hand down her arm until he was clasping her fingers. 'Is this permitted, Nurse Peel?' he said laughingly, gently swinging their clasped hands. 'Only if not, I do suggest you tuck your hand in me elbow, because the crowds at the fair are going to be something awful. Can you hear it?'

Patty could. In her present mood, however, she was quite content to hold Darky's hand, and indeed, when they reached the fair, it became a necessity to cling to one another, or they would most certainly have got separated. The fair was brilliantly lit with smoking naphtha flares and electric lights around all the larger attractions. Everyone was in holiday mood, and when Darky bought two ridiculous 'kiss me quick' hats and a large bag of chips, with so much salt and vinegar on them that Patty's eyes watered, she felt that she was becoming a different person, the person she ought to have been – light-hearted, fun loving and eager for all the enjoyment the fair had to offer.

'Swing boats first,' Darky shouted in her ear. 'We can swing slow while we eat these chips and then go on the other things once our hands are free. How do you like the cake-walk and the bumper cars?'

'I like everything tonight,' Patty screamed above the din, as he helped her into a swing boat. 'But don't forget, Darky, this is my first ever time on the fair. I don't know what a cake-walk *is*, nor yet a bumper car – only I'm sure I'll enjoy both of them, because it's that sort of evening.'

Patty was soon proved right. She loved the soft, swooping motion of the swing boat and shouted to Darky that she was sure that if she opened her mouth she would presently swallow the stars, which made him laugh. She wasn't so keen on the cake-walk, which jiggled about and lifted her skirt above her knees, causing her to give squeaks of dismay. In order to hold her skirt down, she had to let Darky put both arms about her to stop her from being jiggled over, and it was a laughing, crimson-faced girl who came off the cake-walk and headed eagerly for the bumper cars, and then for the merry-go-round and the waltzers.

After the waltzers, when she had clung very close to Darky and hidden her face against his shoulder, they bought pink candyfloss and shared a bottle of ginger beer between them. Then Darky steered her away from the more rumbustious entertainments towards the part of the fair where the sideshows were – hoop-la, penny-falls, darts, test your strength and similar attractions. 'I'll prove I'm the strongest man in the world,' Darky told her, handing over his money, seizing the huge mallet and raising it above his head. 'I'm so happy this evening that I swear I could pick up the whole fair and hold it above me head if I'd a mind.' With that, he thwacked the mallet down on to the platform, making the indicator shoot up to the very top of the tower, so that bells jangled madly.

'Well, if that don't beat the Dutch,' the man on the nearby shooting gallery called out, emerging from behind his stall. 'Don't do that again, mister, or likely you'll bust the spring and then where will we be?'

He was laughing, coming towards them, and Patty turned at the sound of his voice and stared. Then she jumped forward and grasped the man's arm. 'Why, I do declare, it's Toby Rudd, isn't it?' she said, her tone incredulous. 'It *is* you, isn't it, Toby? I don't suppose you remember me, but . . .'

The young man turned and stared at her, then lifted the 'kiss me quick' hat off her blonde head and whistled, a slow smile spreading across his face as he replaced the hat. 'Not remember you?' he echoed. 'Why, as if I could forget! You're Patty Peel, me very first girlfriend!'

*

It had been a joyful reunion, Patty reflected as, very much later that evening, she and Darky made their way back towards the ferry. Toby had been absolutely charming to both herself and Darky, even going to the length of getting a young lad to take over the shooting gallery so that he could entertain them both in his large green caravan. Patty was fascinated as he bustled about, getting out tin mugs, making tea in a big brown pot and producing, from a small cupboard, a very large and delicious-looking fruitcake.

'What a wonderful cake! Did your wife make it?' Patty asked disingenuously, and was rewarded by a quick, laughing glance from Toby's dark eyes.

'Me wife? Now wharrever made you say that?' he said, grinning. 'Does your husband like fruitcake, Patty?'

'Since, as yet, I have no husband, I couldn't say, I'm sure,' Patty had said demurely, smiling at Darky. 'I did introduce you, Toby; I said that this was my friend Darky Knight. Don't you remember?'

'Oh aye, but then if you look round this caravan you'll see there isn't any sign anywhere of a woman's presence,' Toby assured her. 'As for the fruitcake, there's a baker's shop in Rowson Street. Mrs Howe delivers a fresh-baked loaf every other day, a fruitcake once a week an' apple pies, crumbles and puddings every two or three days.' He cut three large slices of cake and handed them round, then sat down and picked up his mug of steaming tea. 'Well? What d'you think of me little home, then? Ever been in a travelling caravan before?'

He was looking at Patty as he spoke but it was Darky who answered him. 'I don't reckon either of us have, since this is Patty's first visit to the fair,' he observed. 'It's a deal bigger than I'd imagined and plenty of room for more than one. Why, you could bring up a family in here!'

'That's right; I bought a decent-sized van because I like a bit o' space about me and because I've always meant to settle down one day, get me a wife and then some kids,' Toby said easily. 'But when you're travelling on all the while, never staying more than a day or two in one place, you never get the opportunities, like.'

'What about the fair girls? There's lots of them,' Patty asked. She felt the warm blood rush to her cheeks and hoped it wasn't too obvious to the men. 'I thought fair people intermarried . . . at least, I don't suppose I've thought about it at all really, but now you mention it it seems the obvious thing.'

'Aye, fair folk do intermarry,' Toby agreed. 'But I've always fancied quite a different sort of girl meself, someone with a more practical outlook. D'you remember when you were a kid, Patty, you always said you were going to be a nurse? I really admired your single-mindedness. At an age when most kids dream of goin' on the stage or becomin' a fillum star, you were just dead set on nursing, helping folk. I always admired you for that.' He grinned across at Darky. 'An' now I suppose you're goin' to tell me that she's the manageress of a smart dress shop or a secretary in a big insurance firm,' he ended ruefully.

'He will tell you nothing of the kind,' Patty said indignantly. 'I *am* a nurse – a midwife, actually – and I love my work. I'd be bored to death in a shop or an office because every day would be just the same and you'd meet the same people. In my job every day is different and all the patients are different too.'

Toby nodded. 'I always thought you'd stick to what you said,' he assured her. 'It's the same with me. Remember how I always swore I'd work the fairs and one day be Riding Master on my own gaff? Well, maybe I've a way to go before achieving that, but I own the shooting gallery and at the end of this season I reckon I'll mebbe buy me a hoop-la stall. Though if I'm to branch out I shall have to start thinking seriously about marriage. So you can put the word about that I'm in the market for a nice, steady little wife – a blue-eyed blonde preferred,' he ended, grinning at them both.

Patty giggled, but Darky answered Toby at once. 'If that's a serious suggestion, I don't think Patty here would do for you at all,' he said bluntly. 'She loves her work and I don't think she'd take to a travelling life at all. Come to that, I've never heard of a travelling midwife, have you?'

'Ah, but haven't you guessed? I'm thinking of settling down,' Toby said at once. 'That's why I've come to New Brighton, which is a permanent fair and stays here all the year round. So you see, I might not be movin' on when spring comes, not if I've found meself a nice little wife by then.'

'Oh, well, in that case, we'll ask around for you,' Patty said blithely. 'Because I'm not thinking of marriage, why should I? I've got my own nice little home and my own nice little family and we all rub along just fine, without any man to interfere.'

'An' wharr've you gorra say to that, Darky?' Toby said equally lightly, but Patty fancied that his question was more serious than it sounded. 'Aren't you plannin' to wed this lovely lady one o' these days?'

Patty looked across at Darky and saw a shutter

come down behind his eyes, though he spoke perfectly pleasantly. 'Patty and me's good friends, real good friends, and I want to keep it that way,' he said firmly. 'Now, queen, if we're to catch the last ferry, it's time we were movin' on.' He turned back to Toby. 'Many thanks for your kind hospitality. Any time you're in Liverpool, there'll be a welcome for you at the Knight house.'

'I'll come with you, just down to the pier,' Toby said eagerly, getting to his feet as they did. 'I'd come all the way but it would mean swimmin' home if you're catchin' the last ferry.' As they left the caravan, he tucked Patty's hand into the crook of his elbow, patting it and saying confidentially: 'I don't mean to risk losin' touch with you again, Nurse Peel. Let me see, tomorrow's Sunday, so I'm off all day. How about meeting? I could come round to your place and then we could go out somewhere. Or you could come over to the fair and let me introduce you to all me pals. It were impossible tonight because the stallholders were all busy, but tomorrow everybody will be off, the same as me.' He turned to Darky. 'We're such old friends, d'you see? I've thought about her for years, hoping to get back to Liverpool so's we could meet up again, tell each other what's been happenin'. And wi' Christmas so close, I guess I've got to seize me opportunity like.'

Darky muttered something which Patty could not catch but she was too excited at the thought of seeing Toby again to wonder how Darky felt. 'You must come to my place,' she said at once. 'I usually cook a big Sunday dinner around one o'clock. Can you be there by then? I live at Twenty-four Ashfield Place – Darky and his mam live next door – so all you've got to do is catch a ferry and transfer to a number forty-three or forty-four tram. Well, I suppose any tram heading for Scotland Road would do, come to that; it'll say on the destination board. Then you want to get off at the Silvester Street stop and walk along Silvester Street until you reach Latimer on your right. You go down there until you get to Ashfield Street and we're just off that; it's a landing house and we're on the top floor, right at the end of the balcony. Think you can find us?'

By now, they had reached the pier and could see the ferry waiting. Patty disengaged her arm from Toby's as he replied that he would find her with ease, would be with her by noon, if that was all right. 'We'll have a good old talk, and since you're treatin' me to dinner I'll take you somewhere for a high tea,' he said gallantly. 'See you tomorrow then, queen. Tara, Darky, nice to have met you.'

'Well, wasn't that the strangest thing?' Patty said as the two of them climbed aboard the ferry and took their places in the bows. 'To tell you the truth, Darky, I never expected to see Toby again, not once he'd escaped from the children's home and joined the fair. In fact, the last time we met, we made one of those silly kids' arrangements to meet again in five years' time. I – I went to the meeting place, but of course Toby must have been miles away and couldn't manage it. He was a good friend to me when I was in the Durrant, so it'll be grand to hear what he's been up to since then, and to tell him how I've fared, of course.'

'Aye, I'm sure it'll be grand,' Darky echoed rather dismally. He hesitated, glancing awkwardly at Patty. 'These fair folk, they're real fly-by-nights, you know, queen. I'm not sayin' there's anything wrong with Toby, but from what you say it's been years since you last met. Fellers change – I dare say girls do, too – so the kid you knew when you were at Durrant House . . .'

'I know what you mean, but Toby's different,' Patty assured him. 'Perhaps it's because he spent a lot of time away from the fair, but he is reliable, truly he is.'

'Patty, you can't know that,' Darky said obstinately. 'I told you, folk change as the years pass, and it sounds as if most of his adult life has been spent with the fair. I'm not trying to interfere, I'm just trying to warn you . . .'

Patty turned on him, feeling the hot blood rush to her face. Didn't want to interfere indeed! Why, she had felt from the first that he did not like Toby, considered him no fit companion for a girl like herself. But he was wrong, totally wrong! 'I don't need advice from you or anyone else, Darky Knight,' she shouted into the windy darkness. 'He's my pal and he's never been nasty or unfair to me once. He didn't ask questions which made me feel uncomfortable and he certainly never suggested that I couldn't run my own life. Just you save your warnings for those who need them.'

Even in the dim light aboard the ferry, Patty could see the colour rise in Darky's lean cheeks and she waited, half fearfully, for the explosion which would surely follow. Instead, however, he just said quietly: 'I'm sorry, queen I didn't mean to offend you. I expect he's a grand chap really, but the truth is . . . well, the truth is, I felt a bit jealous. It's taken me weeks and weeks to get you to so much as hold my hand, but this evening you'd no sooner set eyes on Toby than you were in his arms.'

'I was nothing of the sort,' Patty blazed. 'I – I may have taken his hands . . . I know he took my hat off . . .

375

oh, for goodness' sake, I refuse to quarrel with you, Darky, no matter how annoying you may be. You've been a grand friend to me; none better, just like your mam, and I wouldn't want to fall out with either of you. Only don't say nasty things about Toby, understand?'

The ferry was drawing alongside the Pier Head and Darky nodded resignedly, then took her arm. 'All right; we'll play by your rules. I just don't want to see you get hurt,' he muttered, as they made their way on to the landing stage.

Patty considered the remark carefully and decided that it was harmless; in fact, it was the sort of thing his mother might have said to her, had she been present. And she had been speaking no more than the truth when she said she did not wish to quarrel with Darky. When they had been bad friends, life had been so difficult, so complicated. So she said, in a small voice: 'I know you're only trying to do what's best. And now let's talk about something else, like Christmas. After all, it's only three days away.'

After he had seen Patty safely into her own house, Darky returned to No. 23. The fire had burned very low so he stirred it up with a poker and put fresh fuel on, then pulled the kettle over the burgeoning flames. It was very late, but he knew that if he went straight to bed he would simply lie in the dark thinking bitter thoughts and that would never do. A nice hot cup of tea and one of his mother's currant biscuits would help to relax him, and he would try to work out what his strategy should be with regard to Toby Rudd. For there was no doubt in Darky's mind that Toby posed a very real threat to his, Darky's, relationship with Patty. She had long insisted that she was not interested in marriage and had no wish for the complication of a man in her life. But both he and his mother had lately noticed signs of softening in her. This very evening, when he had slid an arm round her waist, she had actually responded and put her arm round him, and both in the bumper car and on the waltzers she had snuggled up to him, pushing her face into his chest so that the scent of her soft hair had caressed his nostrils intoxicatingly. When he had held her hand, she had not objected in the slightest, and he had been planning how gently and lovingly he would kiss her goodnight on their arrival home, when Toby had burst into their lives.

It was all very well telling himself that Toby knew very little of the grown-up Patty. After a few meetings – and clearly Patty intended to continue to meet Toby – that argument would no longer hold water. What was more, Patty and Toby seemed to have shared a warm and loving friendship as children which meant they could look back on a happy past together. Darky knew that his own past, so far as it involved Patty, was a pretty black one. He had done his best to discredit her with anyone willing to listen to his criticisms, and this could scarcely have endeared him to her. Further, he had pulled no punches so far as Patty herself was concerned. He had snubbed her, criticised her conduct to her face, or ignored her completely. He had taken her best friend out and then dropped her, leaving Patty to deal with Ellen's unhappiness as best she could. It would have been simple for Patty to tell Ellen what an unpleasant sort of man Darky was. To comfort her by explaining how Darky had treated Patty himself, but he knew she had done no such thing. And what had he done? He had met Patty at New Brighton the previous summer and spent a gloriously happy day with her and Merrell and then, just because the kid had widdled on his lap, he had spoiled it all, losing his temper and bawling Patty out for something which was most certainly not her fault.

So what should he do? He neither liked Toby nor trusted him, though the feeling had no foundation so far as he could see. He could not, however, deny Toby's undoubted attraction. He was handsome in an exciting, rakish sort of way, and working the fairs was a good deal more interesting than working in a soap factory, no matter how good your employers nor how stimulating your fellow workers. Whoever married Toby would also marry the fair; Darky realised that, even if Patty did not, but this was not not necessarily a disadvantage to a girl whose life had been as circumscribed as Patty's had. Even if it was true that Toby meant to remain in New Brighton – and Darky doubted this – Toby's wife would be involved with the fair. So if they married and Toby moved away, Patty would be bound to follow.

At this point in his musings the kettle boiled and Darky heaved it off the stove and made the tea. Then he slumped back in the fireside chair once more, sipping the hot liquid. Another worry, now that he came to think of it, was that Toby had a home to offer Patty whereas he, Darky, did not. The caravan was delightful, what was more. Every inch of space was put to good use and every modern convenience which could be installed in a mobile van was ready to hand. He had seen Patty's admiring gaze sweep around Toby's home and had bitten back the desire to point out how tiny it was, how cramped and confining it would be for Maggie and Merrell. He knew now that such criticism would only alienate

Patty and turn Toby from a possible rival into a probable enemy.

Darky finished his drink, got to his feet and made for his bedroom. It was pointless driving himself mad by anticipating the worst. He would simply have to wait and see what happened and how Patty reacted to the adult Toby when she knew him a little better.

He was actually in bed and settling down when another thought struck him. So far as he was aware, Toby knew nothing about either Merrell or Maggie. When he found out that he was expected to take on a girl of fourteen and a baby of three, perhaps his enthusiasm for Patty would wane. Come to that, Darky told himself drowsily, it was quite possible that he was not even considering marriage, and Patty was far too conventional to simply move in with a fellow. Darky thought Patty was brave and hard-working as well as deliciously pretty, but that didn't mean to say Toby would feel the same. Toby was an adventurer, a go-getter; his attitude to women would be coloured by the ones he knew best, and they would be fairground girls who understood his way of life and were probably a good deal more suited to it than dear little Patty Peel. Furthermore, Darky's mother would return the day after tomorrow. Once she was back, he would be able to consult her on the best way to deal with the menace of Toby Rudd.

Much comforted by this thought, Darky fell asleep at last.

Chapter Fifteen

Patty woke on Sunday morning and was immediately aware of a feeling of great happiness and contentment. With her brain still fogged by sleep, she thought at first that it was because Mrs Knight and Merrell were returning today, but then she remembered that this was Sunday, not Monday, and that the feeling of well-being was because she and Toby Rudd had met up once more and he would be having dinner with her this very day.

Patty jumped out of bed, heaved her nightgown over her head and began to wash. She had bought a small joint from the butcher on Limekiln Lane, and an assortment of vegetables. Fortunately, the joint would be plenty big enough for two, since she had meant to ask Darky to share her meal with her. It seemed a bit mean to exclude him but she had already decided that the old saying 'two's company, three ain't,' was particularly true so far as Darky and Toby were concerned. Throughout the lovely evening they had spent together, she had been uneasily aware that Toby had not taken to Darky and that the feeling was mutual. She and Toby needed to be alone, she decided, dressing hastily, for her bedroom was very cold. She wanted to know exactly what had happened to him after they had parted company all those years ago, and though she did not mean to ask where he had been in November 1923, she rather hoped that he might tell her of his own accord.

Then she had so much to tell him! Oh, it would not be exciting and adventurous as his life had undoubtedly been, but it had its high spots. Finding out that her mother may have been a nurse would surely interest Toby? And then – and then there were all the examinations she had had to take; her first job as a general skivvy at the hospital, her gradual ascent of the ladder until at last she had become a State Registered Nurse, and the final accolade, when she had passed her midwifery examinations with flying colours and had taken up her first post in the community. Patty finished dressing and hurried through into the kitchen. She went straight to the pantry and found a packet of rice, smiling with satisfaction as she took it down from the shelf. She would do a savoury rice dish to go with the mutton, potatoes, swede and cabbage, and make a lemon sponge pudding for dessert. This would mean a hasty rush down to the corner shop for a lemon and some icing sugar – how she longed for Maggie at that moment – but it would be worth it to show Toby what a good cook she was.

Humming a tune beneath her breath, Patty decided to make a Victoria sponge, fill it with butter icing and jam, and cover the top with white frosting. Then she would write 'Welcome Toby' in pink letters and he would know himself truly wanted.

She glanced at the clock on the mantelpiece and saw that it still lacked ten minutes to nine. Good, she had plenty of time. For the first time since Mrs Knight had carried Merrell off to Scotland, she found herself grateful for the child's absence. She loved Merrell dearly but knew that, had she been present, it would have been impossible to work with the necessary speed, impossible to concentrate quite so totally upon her expected guest.

Whenever she remembered that Merrell would return the following day, however, she was suffused with a warm glow of love. Into her mind there flashed a picture of the little girl as she was now; she could see the child's clear skin and bright eyes, the soft blonde curls which clustered over her small, round head, and the way she smiled, showing her tiny, pearly teeth. I am so lucky, Patty told herself, slipping into her coat and making her way to the corner shop. I've got the prettiest, sweetest little girl in the world, a nice home of my own and a great many good friends. I love Merrell so much that if I had to give up work in order to take care of her I'd do it, though I love my work too. But I'm lucky enough to have Maggie, who is worth her weight in gold, and Mrs Knight, the best neighbour in the world. And then there's Ellen . . . not everyone would have been as patient and forbearing as Ellen had been, taking her turn with the all the housework, baby-sitting when I was working late at night . . . yes, they don't come much better than Ellen.

At this point in her musings, she reached the shop and made her purchases and presently, back in the kitchen once more, her thoughts returned to the day ahead and what she should say to Toby. She did not want to bore him with a blow-by-blow account of the last – heavens! – decade or so, yet she wanted him to be as familiar with her life as she hoped to become with his. She wondered what would interest him most: how she had come to take on Merrell, or the relationship between the two girls, or how she had struggled up from hospital skivvy to the position of trusted and respected midwife.

Sighing to herself, Patty began to get the ingredients for her cake out of the cupboard and arrange them across the kitchen table.

Toby arrived punctually at twelve o'clock and took a good look around while he was at it. Because it was so near Christmas and a cold day, there were no more than half a dozen children playing out in Ashfield Place and Toby was agreeably surprised at their clean and almost prosperous look. Patty's found herself a good neighbourhood, he thought, slowly ascending the metal stairs and peering inquisitively along each landing as he reached it. The houses were all smartly painted, with shining windows, decently curtained. Toby's opinion of Patty's home rose. The house was conveniently situated for her work, she had told him, and he supposed he had half expected to find her living in a crowded court or a rundown little back to back, but here she was, in what seemed to him a very superior dwelling indeed. Without really thinking much about it, he had assumed that his proposal of marriage – should he make one – would be happily accepted since it would be taking Patty up in the world. She would live in his grand caravan and her only real work would be that of keeping the van clean, doing all the usual domestic tasks, and appearing, like an actress on a stage, behind the shooting gallery every evening. Afternoons, being nowhere near so busy as evenings, could be managed either by himself or one of the youngsters on the gaff.

Toby told himself he was not conceited, but he knew he was very popular with the fair sex and had little doubt that he could win Patty round. He had seen her with Darky, but they were clearly just friends. So there should be nothing to prevent his beginning to court Patty, for he had speedily decided that she was the girl for him. She was pretty, intelligent, fun-loving . . . but it was not, if he were honest, any of those things which mainly attracted him. It was that glorious mass of gold, curling hair. Oh, she tied it back, scraped it off her face, pushed it out of sight beneath her hat at work no doubt, but he was sure she would see the sense of wearing it loose when working the shooting gallery. He told himself jubilantly that Patty's glorious tresses would have everyone gaping, open-mouthed, and not just the flatties either. Other fair folk would see its attraction at once and would marvel at his perspicacity and good fortune.

Having made up his mind, he would most definitely make it clear to Patty that he was serious. A man came down towards him as he ascended the steps to the top landing and murmured 'Good morning' but did not stop. It was Darky Knight and Toby remembered Patty had said he was her next-door neighbour. Thank goodness, he thought, Patty's invitation had not included the other man. He hurried along, checking the numbers as he went, and presently knocked on the door of No. 24. As he waited for Patty to answer his knock, he smoothed down his hair, which had been rumpled by the stiff wind coming off the Mersey, and prepared to charm.

Toby put down his spoon and heaved a satisfied sigh, then grinned across the table at Patty. 'That was one of the best meals I've ever had,' he said truthfully. 'You're a grand cook, girl! So come on, tell me why someone hasn't snapped you up and carried you off to his mansion to cook meals like that for him three times a day!' He blew out his cheeks expressively. 'You're a bleedin' marvel, Patty Peel, because I know your mam didn't teach you to cook like that. You must be a natural.'

'It's not quite so simple as that,' Patty said, returning his smile. She looked even prettier, he decided, when flushed both from cooking and from his praise. She really was a darling, and he was going to be the luckiest of fellers. 'When I decided to do my midder – that's my midwifery course to you – I lived with an older woman, Mrs Ruskin, and she taught me all about the job. Only, since we were sharing a house, she also taught me to cook and I must admit I took to it like a duck to water. I suppose it's because I enjoy my food,' she added, glancing down at her empty plate. 'Anyway, though in theory Ellen, Maggie and myself share the cooking, it's usually me who does the slightly more complicated things. Oh, and bread and cakes and fancy puddings and so on,' she ended.

'Well, I'm not a bad cook meself,' Toby told her. He leaned across the table and patted her pink cheek. 'Now you just sit yourself down by the fire and I'll make us both a nice cuppa and begin the washing up. We fellers who live in caravans have to be pretty handy . . . I'll show you what I can do, and whilst I do that you can tell me all about your life since we last met. I've done most of the talking so far, so now it's your turn.'

He pulled the kettle over the flame and made the tea when it boiled. Then he poured the rest of the water into the sink, topped it with cold and began to wash up the plates. Patty had obediently begun to talk, growing more eager and enthusiastic as she warmed to her task, but Toby only listened with half an ear. He was planning his strategy. He thought he would take her back to New Brighton presently and introduce her to all the fair folk, show her round, let her have a go on the shooting gallery, take her up in a swing boat. The fair was always closed on a Sunday so they would be able to muck about without having to worry over flatties. And then they would have a grand high tea in New Brighton and return to his van for a nice cup of cocoa and a piece of fruit cake before catching the ferry back to the 'Pool. This time it would not be the last ferry, so he could bring her home and whisper sweet nothings into her ear – perhaps even have a bit of a kiss and a cuddle – before he had to return to the fair.

By the time he had finished the washing up and had dried all the dishes, pans and cutlery, Patty seemed to have reached the time when she had finally become a midwife and moved into the landing house. To be honest, Toby had hardly listened at all once he realised that her story was going to be mainly about passing examinations and learning to deliver babies. I'm not a squeamish feller, he told himself right-eously, scrubbing industriously at the inside of the baking tin, but I really don't want to hear about this poor woman with a dozen kids . . . oh, God, I can tell the poor woman's going to die . . . I do think Patty might remember that fellers don't want to hear all the disgusting details about childbirth, no matter how much they may enjoy the part before that!

Diligently, therefore, Toby simply stopped listen-ing and turned his thoughts to some work he meant to do on the caravan to bring it even more up to date. He heard Patty's voice rising and falling as he finished the clearing away and wiped his hands. Then, since she seemed to have paused for a moment, he turned to her, smiling.

'Well, you've certainly been busy whilst I was earning my place at the fair! So when am I going to see this paragon child of yours? This Maggie?'

'I don't know; didn't you hear me say that her

father sent a message round this morning to say she's gone and caught the measles?' Patty said, sounding rather puzzled. 'Oh, I suppose it's the names that confuse you – Merry and Maggie do sound rather alike.' She had been sitting by the fire, sipping her tea, but now she stood up and crossed the kitchen, getting her coat down off the hook behind the door. 'I really ought to tell Darky – that's Mr Knight; you met him yesterday – since it may mean a lot of extra work for—'

'He's gone out. I met him as I climbed up your stairs,' Toby said quickly. For all he knew, the chap might have returned already, but he did not want Patty distracted today, especially not by another feller. 'Shall we go now? I want to introduce you to me pals on the gaff, and since it's a Sunday and the place is closed we can have a go on just about anything. '

Patty, beaming, agreed at once, and without more ado the two of them set out. Patty chattered on, largely about folk who were strangers to Toby. She talked of a Nurse Purbright and a baby – Toby was not sure whose baby – and various other people whose lives interwove with Patty's. Toby, who very much disliked listening to stories about people he had never met, simply ceased once again to pay attention. On the walk down to the ferry he looked into shop windows or gazed at other girls – none as pretty as Patty – and once aboard he enjoyed the ship's movements, the tingling freshness of the air and the cries of the seagulls. He reminded himself that, when summer came, he would be back with the Flanagans once more, moving on every few days, living the roving, adventurous life he loved.

He was sure that Patty would very soon realise

they were made for each other. Oh, she might cling to her job and her friends for a bit, but once she had grown used to the fair, grown used to the free and exciting life – grown used, in fact, to his company – he had no doubt that he would be able to persuade her to try the road.

Smiling to himself, he put an arm round Patty's supple waist and gave her a squeeze, and, when she pulled back, laughed at her and reminded her that they had been pals for a long, long time. 'I wouldn't ever do anything to upset me pal,' he told her caressingly. 'When we were kids you were the only girl I'd ever really cared about, and now . . . well, now I'm wondering how I ever managed without you all those years.'

And Patty, smiling shyly up at him, told him that she was beginning to wonder the same thing.

'Are you nearly ready, Patty? Oh, how I hate a wet Monday morning, but a snowy one is worst of all!'

Ellen, cramming toast into her mouth, spoke thickly and Patty, gulping tea, nodded. 'I don't know that I particularly hate Mondays, but this one's bound to be perfectly frightful. Christmas Day tomorrow, so we've got a pile of visits to get through before the holiday, then Mrs Knight and Merry coming home later in the day, only the snow will complicate things so you can bet their train will be late. And Darky's on an early at the factory . . . Still, no use meeting trouble halfway. Did you have a good weekend?'

Ellen sighed blissfully and picked up her mug of tea. 'It was one of the best! John gets on so well with me mam and dad, and Gran came for the day and she liked him too . . . then we went and picked the Christmas greenery – he'd never done that before and thought it grand – and put the ivy round the picture rails, the holly behind the pictures themselves and the mistletoe in bunches over doorways.' She grinned wickedly at her friend. 'You should have come over and brought Darky; I bet he'd have made good use of the mistletoe!'

'Actually, I went out with someone else yesterday,' Patty said demurely. She and Ellen were meeting for the first time since Friday. 'Someone I knew from way back . . . Ellen, you won't believe it, but you know that feller I've talked about, the one who ran away from the orphan asylum when I did?'

'I know. The feller who promised to meet you and then never turned up,' Ellen said, making more toast. 'Don't say he did – turn up, I mean!'

'That's right, he did. It was quite a coincidence, because I had no idea he was anywhere in the vicinity. Darky suggested that we should visit the funfair at New Brighton . . .'

The tale was soon told and then Patty admitted that she had invited Toby to Sunday dinner. 'And after that, he took me back to the fair and I met everyone,' she said enthusiastically. 'They were so friendly, Ellen, they let me go on their rides for nothing and the women took me round their caravans and said I was welcome there any time. Everyone likes Toby – the men respect him, but the girls all vied for his attention. Honest, he made me feel like a queen, squiring me round the whole of the gaff – that's the fairground – and explaining everything to me. He's turned out really well. He's self-confident, charming . . . well, you must meet him some day and then you'll see for yourself.'

Ellen said that she would look forward to meeting this paragon – the only man, it appeared, who had ever had a chance with her friend.

Patty sniffed. 'He's just a pal,' she insisted, scurrying about to collect all that she would need on her rounds that morning. 'Still, I dare say you will meet him. In different circumstances I would have asked him back here to share our Christmas dinner, but since Mrs Knight has already asked the girls and myself to go next door, that's out of the question. Besides, there's a grand spirit amongst fair folk and I gather he's been invited to spend the holiday with a family who are in winter quarters not far away, so that's all right.'

'What about Boxing Day?' Ellen asked, beginning to pack her own black bag, though she was still crunching toast. 'Mind, I'll not be back until the twenty-eighth, so I won't see him even if he does come round then.'

'If I can arrange it, I'm seeing him tonight,' Patty explained. 'The fair's opening for a special Christmas Eve event tonight so he'll be busy, but I promised I'd go over to New Brighton if I could get away and help him on his shooting gallery. But of course that depends on whether Mrs Knight can keep an eye on Merry, since I don't think our Maggie will be back for a week or so yet.'

Ellen groaned. 'And I'm off home as soon as I finish work, so I can't come wi' you and spy on him,' she said cheerfully. 'Never mind, we're sure to meet up eventually. Oh, by the way, what has Darky had to say about this Lothario?'

'He hasn't said anything,' Patty said, looking mildly surprised. 'Why should he? If I've said it once I've said it a hundred times: Darky and myself are just good pals. Why, I say it to him and he never contradicts.'

Ellen, now struggling into her mackintosh, shook a

reproving head at her. 'If you're trying to convince me that Darky isn't interested in you, then you're fair and far off, queen. The feller's crazy about you; I've known it for months and months. Why, in me heart I knew it when he were taking me about, which is why I didn't make more of a push to keep him. Not much point in hoping when you see that look in a feller's eyes every time they rest on your best friend!'

'Well, I don't see it,' Patty said obstinately, struggling into her own coat and checking with her eye that the fire was damped down and the place in reasonable order. 'He's proved to be a good pal, better than I'd ever hoped, but that's all there is to it. And anyway, I remember Mrs Knight telling me all about his dead wife. Meek and sweet and compliant were the words she used. And you can't pretend, Ellie, that I'm any of those things.'

'Perhaps that's what he likes about you,' Ellen said. 'So he was charming to your Toby, was he? Stepped into the background like? That's a loud 'un, I'll be bound! Pull the other one, queen, it's got bells on!'

'I'm telling you, Ellie . . .' Patty was beginning crossly when there was a loud knock on the door. The girls looked at each other, then Patty went across and pulled it open. 'Yes? Can I . . .' she began, then recognised her caller and held the door wide. 'Darky! Whatever's happened? You should be at work!'

Darky came into the room carrying a carpetbag. He was so wet that he could have just emerged, dripping, from a suicide attempt in the River Mersey and Ellen, the irrepressible, immediately told him so. 'Well, when I heard the news it was what I felt like,' he admitted, still grinning. Then he turned to Patty, the grin disappearing. 'You're right, I should be at work, queen, but there was a phone call at Levers from me mam and the boss gave me special permission to come back here and tell you meself. Mam rang as soon—'

'What's happened?' Patty demanded, feeling the blood drain from her face. 'Oh, don't say your mam's been ill . . . don't say Merry's been hurt!'

'Measles,' Darky said succinctly. 'I'm awful sorry to be the bearer of bad tidings, queen, but Mam called the doctor in yesterday, even though it were a Sunday, because the littl'un were so poorly. Mam were real worried, but this morning, first thing, the rash had come out and the doctor called again and confirmed it were the measles. Mam says she's got Merry tucked up in bed wi' plenty of fruit juice to drink, some lozenges to suck because her throat's sore, and me aunt's little wireless set beside the bed and the curtains down because they don't want Merry trying to use her eyes too much. The doctor's some sort of specialist in children's complaints, it seems, and he's anxious that there should be no eye strain, Mam says.'

'Oh, the poor little darling . . . and your poor mam, stuck up there nursing Merry, when it's my job really,' Patty said, much distressed. 'I ought to go to her. . . but how can I? I'm busy every minute of today and I'm on call tomorrow for emergencies . . . oh, Darky, I'm so sorry! But I'll go up there just as soon as the authorities can find someone to replace me.'

'Mam said as how you'd want to be up there, but she also said you shouldn't do anything so mad,' Darky said comfortably. 'She says what can you do that she and her sister can't, just for a start? Then she says you've never had the measles, and what good would it do for you to catch them?'

Patty was forced to agree with this eminently

sensible point of view, though her heart yearned to be with Merry, to see for herself that everything that should be done was being done. However, as Mrs Knight had said, it was pointless for her to expose herself to infection. Grown-ups were apt to get children's diseases really badly, so Mrs Knight and her sister could end up nursing a thoroughly sick patient and cursing Patty's foolishness in coming to Scotland.

'You're quite right of course – or rather your mam is. I'd be more of a hindrance than a help if I went up to Glasgow,' Patty agreed. 'But oh, poor little Merry! And poor Mrs Knight! And how selfish I'm being because this is going to ruin your Christmas, isn't it? Though, naturally, you'll come here for the day, instead of us coming to you as we'd originally planned. I know Mrs Knight was having her turkey cooked at Kelly's bakery, so I'll collect it for her tomorrow morning and bring it back here, if that's all right. I'll do the potatoes and the veggies and steam the pudding, of course. So you'll get your Christmas dinner, Darky.'

Ellen had been listening to every word and now she said impulsively: 'Why don't the two of you come over to me mam's for your dinners? I don't like to think of you all by yourselves on such a day.'

Darky looked embarrassed, though he smiled his thanks at Ellen. 'Well, I don't think as I'll be around tomorrow,' he said slowly. 'I talked to the boss and he's agreed I can take a week off wi'out pay so I looked up the trains and I'm going up to Glasgow meself, if that's all right by you, Patty. You see, I've had the measles and I'm a pretty handy sort of feller about the house, so I can be really useful to Mam and me aunt, getting the messages and so on. So if you've got any Christmas gifts already parcelled up, I'll stick them in the top of me carpetbag and pretend I'm Father Christmas. The truth is, I'm really fond of Merry and she's fond of me, so when the ladies want a bit of a rest, like, I can amuse Merry.' He glanced anxiously from Ellen to Patty. 'If you agree, that is,' he ended.

Ellen, making her way to the door with her bag slung over one shoulder, slapped him on the back as she passed. 'You're a grand feller, Darky,' she said appreciatively. 'There ain't many as would give up their Christmas to look after a sick kiddie, especially if it means travelling on Christmas Eve; I reckon the trains will be packed today.'

'Oh, I don't mind the journey, or missing Christmas in Liverpool,' Darky said easily. 'I'll miss you, though, Patty. Still, I dare say your pal Toby Rudd will keep you occupied.'

'I don't know about that,' Patty said doubtfully, moving towards the door and following Ellen out on to the landing. 'He's got his own plans for Christmas Day, though if he knows I'm at a loose end I suppose he might come round and share the turkey. Anyway, I'm so grateful, Darky, that I scarcely know what to say. If you're up in Glasgow, then I know everything will be just fine and Merry will soon be home and fit again.' Abruptly, she clapped a hand to her mouth, then spun round and headed back to No. 24. Unlocking the door, she shouted over her shoulder to Darky: 'The presents! Hang on a mo', they're in my room. Shan't be a tick.'

With the gaily wrapped parcels reposing in Darky's carpetbag, the two of them began to descend the stairs. When they reached the bottom, Patty unchained her bicycle and prepared to mount. Ellen had gone, and just for a moment Patty's gratitude to Darky was so great that she felt tears come to her eyes. He was a good man and no one could have a better friend, but to tell him so would only embarrass them both, so she said lightly: 'What time does your train leave, Darky? You mustn't miss it.' By now, she was cycling slowly across Ashfield Place with Darky keeping pace beside her. He hitched his watch out of his waistcoat pocket and consulted it.

'I leave in forty minutes,' he said briefly. 'I'll get a tram on the Scottie and be there in no time.' As they reached the main road, Darky slowed and Patty dismounted from her bicycle. For a moment they simply stood there, Patty staring into the dark face above her own, whilst a mixture of extraordinary emotions swirled into her mind. She suddenly realised that she would miss Darky, miss him badly; that the week of his absence stretched cold and empty before her. But this was ridiculous! He was only a friend, only a friend, and she had lots and lots of those. Besides, Toby would be here, taking her out, making much of her, introducing her to life on the gaff. Resolutely, she banished the feeling that she was being abandoned and held out her hand, smiling up into Darky's face.

'We'd best say goodbye now. I can see my tram bearing down on us,' Darky said, grasping her hand. 'Take care of yourself, Patty, and you can be sure Mam and I will be taking good care of Merry.'

Almost as he spoke, the tram drew up alongside in a flurry of water and descending passengers. Darky swung himself on to the platform, lifted his hand in a half-salute, and then he was gone and the tram was rocketing away towards Lime Street station.

Patty sighed and remounted her bicycle. The day

felt oddly flat, as though all possibility of pleasure had been leached out of it by Darky's departure, but of course there was still her work. And Toby Rudd.

Patty began to pedal towards her first patient.

Darky caught the train in good time and actually managed to acquire a corner seat, so it was with some expectation of an interesting journey that he settled into it as the train drew out of Lime Street station. The snow, which had fallen desultorily earlier in the day, had stopped and now a light rain drizzled against the panes, obscuring his view of the fleeting countryside passing by. The carriage was full and most people had brought books and magazines with them, including Darky, who spread out his copy of a national daily and began to read. After a few sentences, however, his mind insisted on returning to its present preoccupation, which was whether he had done a very wise or a very foolish thing in catching the train for the north and leaving the field to Toby Rudd.

For some time after his mother's telephone call, he had fretted over what was best to be done. He told himself that he did not dislike Toby Rudd, but knew that he did not trust him. The other man wanted Patty all right but Darky thought he wanted her for the wrong reasons; in fact, Toby needed her. He was an unmarried man, living alone in a pretty sumptuous caravan, and he badly needed help on his shooting gallery. What was more, Toby had big ideas. He wanted to be a Riding Master with his own fair and this would only be possible if he had a wife to help him as he built up his various fairground attractions.

Darky had not gained his information about Toby by mere guesswork, however. For some years, he had been friendly with one of the young men who helped on the New Brighton funfair when he was not working at Levers, and on Sunday morning he had visited Jack Evans and been given the low-down on Toby Rudd.

'He's a grand feller, but of course his whole living is made by getting people to trust him, same as all fair folk,' Jack had said. 'Mebbe the sights of his rifles are all straight, mebbe the guns throw a bit to left or right, but you can be sure of one thing: every show is designed to part the flatties from their money. And to give them a good time on the way, of course. It ain't cheatin', it's life, and Toby Rudd didn't always have an easy time of it. There were a woman who ran off with another feller, takin' half Toby's profit with her, and now he's desperate to find himself a decent, steady girl who'll marry him and help him with the shooting gallery. What's more,' he went on chattily, 'I heard him tellin' someone yesterday that he's found himself a girl who would suit.'

Darky had guessed that Jack was speaking of Patty and had gone home thoughtfully to Ashfield Place. It had been terribly tempting to go round and spill the beans to Patty, tell her everything he had learned, but some instinct, older and wiser than he, advised against it. Let her have her head for a bit longer, a small inner voice told him. You don't want a woman who's half in love with someone else, you want someone who loves you for yourself – loves you only. Give Toby Rudd enough rope and he'll hang himself, and give Patty enough rope and she'll find out the truth about him and learn where her heart really lies.

But suppose her heart doesn't lie with you, Darky Knight, another voice asked cruelly. Suppose she really is in love with Toby? If so, was it sensible to

397

leave them alone for a whole week while you go gadding off to Scotland?

Darky took a deep breath and pushed the little voice out of his conscious mind. Whatever anyone says, he told himself, I know I'm doing the right thing. If she really loves Toby Rudd, then it's best that she marry him even if he doesn't love her, because once they're living together he won't be able to stop himself falling for her. Look at me, I've never even kissed her, but I'm as deep in love as I could possibly be. So I've done the only sensible, logical thing; I've cleared out so that she can really get to know Toby and decide for herself just what she wants without having to consider me at all. But I'll rely on Patty's good sense. She'll see through Toby, and once she's done that she'll be able to make the decision that is right for her. After all, if she wants an adventurous life, the fair and Toby can satisfy that want, but if she wants real love and the comfort of someone who adores her, then she'll settle for me and whatever I can offer.

Satisfied at last that he was doing the right thing, no matter how many objections the small voices might make, Darky wiped the steam off the inside of the window and fixed his eyes on the passing scenery. After all, a week was only seven days, even if it was going to feel more like seven months; surely he could bear to be parted from Patty for that long?

When she finished work on Christmas Eve, Patty bustled about banking up the fire, getting herself and Ellen a quick snack, and then tidying herself up so that she would present a neat appearance behind the shooting gallery. She and Ellen exchanged Christmas presents and Patty looked rather ruefully at the small gift she had bought for Darky. Why on earth had she not handed it over when she had given him the presents for his mother and Merry? But in her secret heart she knew; she meant to give the present – twenty Woodbines and a pair of grey woollen gloves she had knitted herself – to Toby. She could always buy Darky something before his return in a week's time.

Then, when she and Ellen were ready, they had set off, the one to New Brighton and the other to Formby. They had walked to the tram stop together and then wished one another a grand holiday and gone their separate ways.

When she reached New Brighton, Patty made straight for the big green caravan where Toby welcomed her warmly. 'You don't think I'm taking advantage, do you, queen? Only you said you'd like to help, so I thought . . . I thought . . .'

Patty laughed. 'I'm really looking forward to it,' she said gaily. 'It'll be an adventure, Toby, and one that doesn't often come my way. Is there anything I should know? Anything I need to do? Suppose someone asks to be allowed to have three shots instead of six, do I charge them half?'

Toby laughed too but shook his head. 'It's a fixed price for six shots,' he said positively. 'There's a black and gold japanned box with different compartments which is tucked away under the counter, and that's where you put the money when you've got time.' He reached across and handed her a leather apron with a pouch in front. 'Wear this; you'll find you won't have time to use the box when there's a queue of flatties waiting, so you just pop the takings into the pouch and only go to the box when you need change or have time to empty the apron. You've got a float, of course, but . . .'

'What's a float?' Patty asked curiously. 'Money doesn't float, unless it's notes, of course, and I dare say they'd just go soggy.'

Toby laughed again. 'Your float is a quid in small change,' he told her. 'And the only thing you need to do is to take off that smart nurse's coat and hat, put on the apron, brush out your hair and be yourself. They'll love you, I know it.'

It was a mild night, so Patty felt she could not object to the removal of her hat and coat; she had noticed that the fair folk seldom wore such garments, but she felt self-conscious over freeing her long, wheat-coloured hair from its trim bun. However, she complied with Toby's request, though she told him that it seemed rather silly since her long hair would fall across her face.

'Yes, but the bun is so severe,' Toby told her, putting out a strong, brown hand and touching the little fronds of curl which surrounded her face. 'Just for this evening, I want you to look as unlike a midwife as possible, if you don't mind. Tell you what, I'll get Jessie Tate to lend you a couple of tortoiseshell combs. They'll keep the hair out of your face, but the flatties will still be able to admire it. Is that OK?'

Patty agreed, somewhat self-consciously, and when the combs arrived, and Toby arranged them in her hair, she had to admit that she was pleased with the result. Certainly nobody would think she was a nurse, she told herself rather ruefully, gazing at her reflection in a large mirror by the caravan door. She wished that the combs had been less elaborate – they had tortoise-shell butterflies decorated with paste diamonds above the actual teeth – but they certainly added a touch of glamour to an appearance she had always thought, privately, was far too plain and sensible.

And whether or not it was the combs, Patty certainly enjoyed a great success as the mistress of the shooting gallery. For the entire evening, men were queuing up to take their turn with the rifles, chaffing her and telling her she was the prettiest thing on the fair, though since most of them were showing off their skills to their girlfriends Patty took these compliments with a pinch of salt. A good many of her customers returned again and again and far too many, Patty thought apprehensively, were winning prizes, though Toby told her that this was no bad thing, was in fact a good thing since it encouraged others to try their luck. 'We don't have no sharp cheats on our gaff because the flatties wouldn't return week after week, year after year, if we did that,' he said virtuously. 'It ain't only me as runs an honest show, everyone's the same. We wouldn't have it otherwise.'

So when Patty returned to the caravan to have a bite of supper when the fair closed at eleven, she was all aglow with the excitement of the evening. She put down the box, heavy with money, on the caravan table and basked in Toby's admiration as he carefully counted it and told her she was worth her weight in gold.

'I dunno how you do it, but you've even got all the money in the right compartments,' he said admiringly. 'It makes counting up the take a good deal easier, I can tell you. And how hard you worked, dearest Patty! But the main thing is, did you enjoy it?'

Patty thought, then beamed at him. 'Yes I did,' she said truthfully. 'It was a bit embarrassing because some of the men said things . . . but it was all in good fun, I'm sure, and I was too busy for anyone to pester me. Oh, but I'm so thirsty. Is that ginger beer for me?'

'It is, and presently someone will be delivering bags of chips; I've ordered one each.' Almost at the same moment there was a bang on the door, which flew open to reveal a short, stout man with a basket piled high with newspaper-wrapped parcels.

'I'm playing Santy Claus tonight,' the small man squeaked, tipping two parcels of chips on to the table. 'You've got yourself a real little smasher there, Toby,' he added, eyeing Patty appreciatively.

'Don't I know it,' Toby said fervently, unwrapping the chips. 'And she took five times more money than Edie ever took.'

'It's the hair,' the little man said, turning back towards the door. 'The flatties always go for blondes, they tell me. Well, good night both.'

Rather baffled by this unexpected remark, Patty wondered why on earth people should be more willing to part with their money because of her hair, then forgot it as the recollection of what she meant to say to Toby came rushing back. She wondered how she could say, tactfully, that she would be on her own next day, but as it happened Toby's next remark led her straight into the subject.

'I'll see you home, of course,' he said. 'Unless Mr Knight means to meet you, that is?'

Patty took a deep breath. 'Mr Knight has gone to Scotland to be with his mother and the baby,' she said. 'They were supposed to come home today but the baby's caught the measles, so they won't be home for two to three weeks.'

Toby stared at her and Patty could see comprehension dawning in his dark eyes. 'The Knight family are in Scotland?' he said incredulously. 'But – but you were going there Christmas Day! I remember you told me that it were all arranged and that they were coming to your place Boxing Day. So what'll you do now? You can't be planning to spend Christmas Day alone!'

'Well I am,' Patty said baldly. 'Ellen's gone home to her people and everyone else has already made their plans. But don't worry. I enjoy my own company and a quiet day will probably do me good.'

Toby leaned across the table and clasped her hands in his. 'As if I'd let you be alone, come Christmas,' he said reprovingly. 'You come to the Flanagan's with me. I've borrowed Sid's motorbike and it'll take two.'

'I'm on call on Christmas Day for emergencies,' Patty said regretfully, 'so I'm afraid that's out of the question.'

'But how about if I came to your place? I guess you've already got food in, but I'll share the cost willingly. What do you say, Patty?'

In a daze of happy anticipation, Patty said, 'Yes,' but as she got into bed that night and snuggled down she found that there was a faint niggle of unease at the very back of her mind. She lay there for some time, racking her brains as to what it could be. It was not until she was almost asleep that the reason came to her: Toby had not once said how he meant to get in touch with the Flanagan's, who were supposed to be his hosts on the following day. Surely he would not simply let them down, leave them worrying over his whereabouts, perhaps even delaying Christmas dinner for him?

How ridiculous you are being, Patty Peel, she scolded herself. What on earth makes you think that Toby would behave in such an unprincipled way? The answer, of course, was simple and one which she wished she did not have to face. In her heart, she knew that Toby had let her down not once, but many times. She could tell herself that he had been far away, unable to keep their rendezvous at Lime Street station, but thinking it over now she realised that there are always ways to get in touch. He could have sent a message to the station master, explaining his inability to meet her, and it could have been read over the loudspeaker system. She had heard several such messages while she waited for Toby – indeed, it was one of the reasons she had hung about for so long. Also, Toby had not attempted to explain why he had never come to Lime Street station on the appointed day. In fact, when she had timidly raised the subject of past years, he had brushed it aside, given her a hug, told her that they must forget the past and concentrate on their happy future.

I wouldn't have done that, Patty felt herself thinking. I wouldn't let the Flanagans down, either; I'd make jolly sure that they knew I had other plans. But then she thought of the telegraph office – was it open on Christmas Day? – and decided that Toby would undoubtedly send a telegram as soon as the office opened on Christmas morning. She knew he was an adventurer, that his charm and gaiety probably made it unnecessary for him to apologise for past mistakes, but she told herself stoutly that he was not irresponsible, not selfish. As soon as he arrived at the house next morning, she would ask him how the Flanagans had reacted to the news that their party would be one short, and he would tell her how he had telegraphed, or telephoned, or got in touch with them somehow.

Almost satisfied with her own explanation, Patty slept.

Chapter Sixteen

In Glasgow, winter dusk falls early, so Darky found himself trudging through the streets towards his destination under the glow of the lamplights, with people intent on last-minute Christmas shopping all around him, though thankfully, since the Scots celebrate the New Year more enthusiastically than do the English, the streets were not as crowded as they would have been – probably were – in Liverpool.

He had telegraphed his mother to say that he would be arriving as soon as possible, that he would stay for a week and that she was not to worry, for he had guessed immediately, from the sound of her voice alone, that she was worried to death by her situation. His aunt was not an easy woman at the best of times, and so his mam would be dealing not only with a sick child far from home and her mother, but with an increasingly fractious woman in her seventies, who could do very little for herself since she was crippled with rheumatism.

'I know poor Patty won't be able to come and give me a hand because for a start she's not had the measles,' his mother had said, her voice thin with worry. 'I were wondering whether Ellen might be free, only I know she were going home with her young man for the holiday . . . and your poor Aunt Beryl can't remember whether she took the measles when she were a child . . . you can't blame her, it were a mortal long time ago . . . and although she can manage to get her messages in the ordinary way, at Christmas, what wi' the crowds in the streets and the prices . . . well, I feel that guilty, landing her with a sick kid and meself . . .'

'Don't tell me she isn't glad to have you over the holiday,' her son had protested. 'She's spent weeks trying to persuade you to go up there for Christmas, or else for Hog . . . Hoggy . . . oh, well, for the New Year!'

'Aye, she's pleased in a way, and it's Hogmanay,' Mrs Knight had said. 'Darky, love, I don't suppose . . . it's a lot to ask but I know how fond you are of Merry and as it is I can't leave the kid for a moment . . .'

'I'll come just as soon as I've sorted things out wi' Levers, and Patty,' Darky had promised at once. 'I may not be able to get away today, but by this evening I'll have got things sorted. So don't worry, Mam, help is on its way!'

He had heard her laugh, heard her voice take on a lighter note, with considerable relief. He knew, none better, what a good woman his mother was and he knew, too, that Patty would have caught the first train north had it not been for the fact that she would be less of a help than a hindrance, seeing that she was liable to catch the infection herself. So it had been good to be able to relieve his mam's mind of at least some of its worries, and as he trudged through the dark streets he reflected that though he was a long way from Patty, at least he would be able to discuss what he had done with his mother, the wisest woman he knew. She was one of the most unselfish people he knew as well, which meant that if she thought he had done wrong to leave Patty to the mercy of Toby Rudd she would say so, even if it meant losing her son's help a little earlier than they had planned.

He reached the narrow little street, where the tops of the houses overhung it so closely that they almost touched, and knocked on the door of No. 121. It was a narrow, granite-built dwelling with a street lamp right outside, and as he knocked he heard a small voice that he knew well. 'Nanna, Nanna, vere's a knock, vere's a knock! Is it me mammy come to give me a hug an' a kiss, or is it Santy Claus wiv me presents? I know you said he might be late, Nanna, 'cos of me not being in me own lickle bed, only – only Santy's a magic man, like Jesus, so I thought – I thought he *might* come!'

Darky looked up and saw that the window above his head was slightly open, for though it was dark it was still remarkably mild for the time of year. He grinned to himself, then shouted up at the little, greenish glass panes of the window. 'It ain't your mammy, little Miss Merry, 'cos she's turble busy around Christmas, but it's your old pal Darky Knight. What's more, I met Santy as I was catching the train at Lime Street station and he gave me a grosh o' presents for a poor little kid what's gone and got the squeezles just in time for Christmas!'

There was a shriek from above and a small, pale face appeared, distorted by the thickness and colour of the glass but immediately recognisable to Darky, who felt his heart contract. Poor little girl! Far from home, stuck in bed, no doubt feeling both ill and miserable, but she was beaming down at him, jumping up and down on something invisible so that she could see him more clearly.

'Darky! Oh, Darky, come up an' see me, please, please, please!' she entreated just as the door opened.

Mrs Knight stood there, her arms held out. 'Oh, my dearest lad!' she said. 'I can't tell you how welcome you are! Your aunt has been very good and patient but she can't gerrup the stairs without a deal o' help and I dare not bring Merry down, not until her temperature drops to normal, and . . . and I've been trying to do everything and worrying that Merry may get worse . . . I can't tell you what a relief it is to know I'll have your help, if only for a few days.'

'I told Patty I'd be here a week, but in fact the boss said to stay until I could bring you and the littl'un home wi' me,' Darky told her as the two of them entered the tiny front room. He went over and hugged his aunt, who was squeaking with excitement and telling him how much he had grown and what a fine fellow he was, then turned back to his mother. 'I'd better get up them stairs, though, Mam, because Merry came to the window and shouted down to me and I imagine that if I don't go up she'll come down!'

'You're right there,' his mother said, smiling. 'She feels a little better today and that means she's forever trying to come downstairs, so she can see more of what's going on. I *thought* I heard voices when I came to the door to answer your knock . . . I might have guessed the young madam would be consumed with curiosity as soon as she heard someone at our front door. You run up, then, whilst I make a pot of tea and cut some sandwiches. I dare say you're hungry?'

'Starving,' Darky said promptly – and truthfully, for he had not had a chance to get himself a bite as the train roared northwards. 'I'll come down as soon as I can, since I dare say you could do with some messages running, now that you've got one extra for Christmas dinner!'

He headed for the stairs as he spoke and heard his aunt, behind him, chuckle. 'Your mam's scarce had a breath of fresh air since the bairn took ill,' she said.

'You stay wi' the wee one. I'll mek something for your supper, and Nellie here can nip down to the market, for it'll be in full swing until ten or eleven this night.'

'Right,' Darky said, mounting the narrow little stairs which led, ladder-like, to the upper floor. He knew his aunt never came up here and guessed that his mother and Merry had been sharing the big bed where his aunt had slept in happier days, but he was still surprised to find that the stairs led straight into the bedroom, which was clearly the only one. He looked around him, at the low, beamed ceiling and the small room totally dominated by the huge bed and containing no furniture other than the bed itself and a deep window seat set into the small bow of the window.

'Knighty! Oh, oh, Knighty, have you come to take us home?' Merry enquired hopefully, hugging him as he sat down beside her and sank into the feather mattress. 'Mammy didn't have the spotties when she were little, so she can't come, Nanna says. Oh, I's so bored!'

Darky returned her hug but said prosaically: 'I can't take you home, queen, until there's no fear of you passing on your squeezles to someone else. But I'm here to keep you company and help Nanna Knight and Auntie Beryl until you're well enough to go home. Does that suit your majesty?'

'Yes, that's all right,' Merry conceded, leaning back on her pillows. 'And it's measles, not squeezles, you silly Knighty.'

'You called it spotties,' Darky pointed out. 'Look, I'm going to carry you downstairs so that you can sit and watch me eat my supper and then I'll carry you up again. But you must be very, very good and do exactly as I tell you; understand?'

Merry, who had begun to look very tired, perked up at once and presently Darky was sitting down to a meal of ham sandwiches with hard boiled eggs on the side and chatting to his aunt, whilst Merry sat curled up in an ancient fireside chair, sucking her thumb contentedly and gazing at the flickering flames behind the doors of the old-fashioned range.

Christmas Day dawned bright, though cool, and Merry was once more carried downstairs to open her presents. She was feeling a little better with each day that passed but needed to be in company since, left to herself, she scratched her spots until they bled. She ate very little of the roast fowl, potatoes and other vegetables which Nellie Knight had bought the previous evening, but she played with her toys and helped Darky with a large jigsaw. His aunt often bought jigsaws to keep her brain active, she said, and this one taxed Darky's ingenuity to the utmost, but at least it kept his fingers occupied whilst his mind flew back to Liverpool, and Patty.

I wonder what she's doing now, he asked himself, several times an hour. I wonder if she's opened her presents yet. I bet she and that Toby feller are sharing a cosy dinner in the kitchen at No. 24. Oh, what a fool I was to leave them alone together at such a time of year!

But when he saw how much happier his mother and aunt were, and how Merry clung to him, he did not regret his long journey north – was glad of it, in fact. He was needed here, but he still did not know whether he was needed – or, indeed, wanted – in Liverpool.

I did right, he told himself continually, but

410

knowing it did not stop him wondering how Patty and Toby were getting on.

The first thing Patty had asked Toby when he reached her house on Christmas morning was how the Flanagans had taken the news of his defection. Toby, hanging his overcoat and cap on the back door, had looked faintly surprised. 'Defection? How could I tell you that, queen? I won't be seeing them now until the day after tomorrow, or mebbe later. What makes you ask?'

'Well, I didn't know whether the telegraph office would be open, or whether someone at the fair is on the telephone,' Patty explained. The look of amusement on his face made her feel, obscurely, that she was interfering in some way, being nosy in fact. But she told herself it was a perfectly normal question and continued to wait for his answer.

Toby walked over to the table and sniffed appreciatively at the good smells coming from the oven, for Patty had fetched the turkey from the bakers and roasted some potatoes and onions and now the rich aroma of the food filled the room. 'Isn't that a grand smell now?' Toby said. 'An' it's a grand cook you are, Patty Peel. Me mouth's watering already.'

Patty, however, decided not to be deflected. 'Yes, it's going to be a good dinner, but what did the Flanagans say?' she persisted. 'Or did you telegraph?'

'No, I didn't telegraph and I didn't telephone either,' Toby said easily. 'They're good friends, the Flanagans, and they understand how things are. They'll guess something came up to prevent me being with them and they'll just continue as though I'd never said I'd spend Christmas in Wrexham.' He glanced curiously at her, dark brows rising. 'What's wrong with that, Patty Peel? Good friends – real friends – understand.'

Patty stared at him but before she could make any other comment he had produced a small parcel from his pocket. He moved towards her, pressed the packet into her hand and, before she could prevent him, kissed her lightly on the nose. 'Happy Christmas, Patty,' he said softly. 'And a prosperous New Year.' He grinned at her. 'Which is as good as wishing meself a prosperous New Year since I'm hopeful that we're going to be travelling into 1935 together. Go on, open me present. I'm longing to see what you think of it.'

Hastily, Patty pulled open the drawer in the big kitchen table and produced the gift which she had intended for Darky. She had not rewrapped it but had changed the label on the front so that it now read, 'To Toby, best wishes for Christmas 1934, from Patty.' She handed it to Toby, feeling vaguely ashamed of herself, and then opened the fascinating little packet he had given her. It contained a very pretty brooch in the shape of a four-leafed clover which was almost certainly gold. For a moment, Patty could only stare, then she lifted her eyes to his and saw that he was watching her intently. 'Do you like it?' he asked softly. 'It isn't new, it belonged to me mam, but she gave it to me just before she died and told me it were real Irish gold and I were only to give it to the woman I wanted to marry.' Patty began to protest, but he shushed her with a finger across her lips. 'Don't worry, I'm not trying to force your hand. I just want you to know what you mean to me.'

Patty looked wistfully at the pretty little brooch in its nest of cotton wool but shook her head firmly and put the box down on the kitchen table. 'I can't take it,

Toby. I know we were pals when we were kids, but we scarcely know one another as adults. Maybe one day we'll both feel differently and it would be too bad to take such a gift until I was certain sure.'

Toby sighed but pushed the box towards her once more. 'Look, Patty, it isn't like an engagement ring. It's just a really pretty brooch, and you know four-leafed clovers are supposed to bring good luck. If you decide that I'm not the feller for you, you can give me the brooch back. But in the meantime, wear it and enjoy it. After all, it's a Christmas present and you can't just hand them back.'

'Well, all right,' Patty said, half grudgingly, pinning the brooch to the lapel of her navy wool frock. 'But it makes my gift to you . . . oh, well, open it!'

Toby opened the parcel and professed himself delighted both with the Woodbines and with the grey, woollen gloves. 'I'll be rare glad of the gloves when the fair opens up again,' he said enthusiastically. 'Me hands get freezing handling all the change; these will suit me a treat.' He pulled one on. 'Yes, nice and roomy.'

Patty was about to say *Darky's got bigger hands than you*, but she caught herself in time and giggled weakly. 'I'm not a very good knitter,' she confessed. 'As for size, I just had to guess. Most of the men I know smoke Woodbines, so I took a chance with them as well.'

Toby sank down on to one of the fireside chairs and began to open the packet of cigarettes. 'All the fellers I know smoke Woodbines,' he said contentedly, putting a cigarette into his mouth and leaning forward to get a light with one of the tapers which stood beside the fire. 'Want a drag, queen?'

Patty had never begun to smoke and didn't meant to start now, so she said she would have a cup of tea and a biscuit instead and the two of them began to discuss other things. Vaguely, in the back of her mind, Patty was aware that Toby's answers to her questions about the Flanagans had not been very satisfactory. But she did not really know fair folk; perhaps their friendships were indeed so casual – or so deep – that they would not mind if a guest simply failed to turn up. Perhaps the arrangement had never been a particularly definite one; perhaps the Flanagans had merely indicated that Toby would be welcome if he arrived.

At this point in her musings, the meal announced itself ready. Presently Patty found herself simply enjoying Toby's company and his obvious admiration, and ceasing to worry about his easy-going attitude to life. After all, she supposed, like herself he had been forced to make his own rules to a certain extent, since those which applied in the children's home did not help much in the outside world.

Satisfied on this score, she settled down to enjoy her meal.

Rather to his surprise, Darky found himself thoroughly enjoying Christmas and Merry's cheerful, if demanding, company. She was an affectionate child, neither shy nor diffident, and though he could not promise her treats until the infection had run its natural course, she seemed quite content to play with her Christmas presents, do the jigsaws which Aunt Beryl provided and listen to the tales in the story-books she had brought up with her from Liverpool. Darky, reading the story of the Three Little Pigs, or the tale of Simple Susan, marvelled at the child's memory, for should he skip a sentence, or even a word, she was on him like a little tiger, stabbing a forefinger at the book – quite often hitting the right word – and telling him that he had missed a bit.

'She'll be reading before she starts school,' Darky told his mother. 'She's bright as a button, she can count up to twenty and if you give her simple sums with pennies to represent numbers, she'll get 'em right nine times out of ten.'

'Oh aye, she's a bright kid right enough,' Mrs Knight said. She glanced sideways at Darky, a smile lurking in her eyes. 'I'm real proud when she calls me Nanna, to tell you the truth. I wish I really were her gran but I reckon I'm the nearest thing she's got to one, so that'll have to content me.' She cast another sly glance at Darky. 'For now,' she finished.

'I know what you mean; I'm mortal proud of her meself,' Darky admitted. 'I were proud of her in Liverpool because she was so pretty and nice to people. She always had a smile for me mates when they came round to the house, and she's been chattering away to anyone who'd spare a moment for the best part of a year now. But this is the first opportunity I've had to spend twenty-four hours in her company and I tell you, Mam, it's made me certain sure of one thing. I'm not going to be a widower for the rest of me life if I can possibly help it. I want a family of me own.'

The two of them were sitting in Beryl's living room whilst Beryl taught the child to make gingerbread men; a task which was apparently full of humour since frequent bursts of laughter came to the Knights' ears. Once more, Nellie Knight gave her son a shrewd look. 'All kids ain't like Merry,' she told him. 'D'you know what you're really saying, son? You're saying you'd like Merry to be your own little girl, which means you wish Patty—'

'Yes, well, wishing butters no turnips,' Darky said quickly. He realised he was actually afraid that if his mother voiced what was in his mind, it might mean that his dream would come to naught. You're a superstitious fool, Darky Knight, he told himself robustly. Mam and I both know that I want Patty for me wife, but neither of us knows whether I've got a chance.

Mrs Knight raised her eyebrows. 'Oh, so now you're putting words into me mouth, is that it?' she asked genially. 'I were just thinkin' that Patty must be mortal fond of you to let you take her place with the little one over Christmas. So it follows that you're mortal fond of her to take on such a task, see?'

Darky decided that the time had come to tell his mother how things stood and ask her advice. Because Merry had been so poorly upon his arrival, he and his mother had had few opportunities to talk, but now Darky stood up and went over to the kitchen doorway. 'Auntie Beryl, is it all right if Mam and meself get some fresh air for half an hour? Only you and Merry seem pretty occupied and it would be grand to see a bit of the city in daylight.'

The gingerbread makers, scarcely looking up from their task, agreed absently that the Knights might go out and welcome. 'Only I'm serving tea and scones at four o'clock sharp, so don't you be late,' Aunt Beryl said. 'And if you're both very good, the bairn and meself might even let you have a gingerbread man apiece; what do you say, Merry?'

'I'm having the one with the walking stick,' Merry said at once. 'But Knighty and Nanna can have the man with only one leg and the one whose head has run a bit.'

Darky peered at the gingerbread men set out on the table. 'That's not a walking stick. You've give the poor feller three legs,' he said accusingly. 'You only want that one because it's got the most gingerbread and I'm a lot bigger'n you, so that one should be for me really.'

Merry, flushed and excited, promptly disputed his claim, so Darky gave in gracefully and then he and his mother left the house. For a while they walked in silence, enjoying the fresh, cool air and the sights and sounds of the city, for it was New Year's Eve and the streets were crowded with shoppers, but presently they came to a quiet little square and Mrs Knight turned to her son. 'Well? I know you want to talk; I can always tell. I s'pose it's got something to do with the doctor saying that Merry would be infectious for another ten days and that he prefers her not to leave for another fortnight. It's disappointing for Patty, I know, but she's got her work and her pal Ellen, and I dare say Maggie will be back in Ashfield Place by now, so I'm sure she'll understand that it's for the best. Is that what's worrying you, son?' Mrs Knight's voice was indulgent. It was clear she thought her son was worrying about nothing. So Darky took a deep breath and began to explain.

'Well, Mam, it all came about because of me taking Patty to the New Brighton funfair on the Saturday before Christmas . . .'

When the story was told, Mrs Knight gazed at her son with considerable concern in her pale blue eyes. 'That is a facer,' she admitted after a long moment. 'But to my way of thinking, son, you've done absolutely the right thing by coming away. It was a brave thing to do and a kind thing as well, and Patty's no fool; she won't mistake either braveness or kindness for indifference, she'll see it for what it really is. As for this Toby Rudd of yours . . .'

'He ain't none of mine,' Darky protested, grinning for the first time since he had begun his tale. 'I don't like the chap, nor I don't trust him, though it queers me to say why.'

'It's a figure of speech,' Mrs Knight said reproachfully. 'And well you know it, young feller-me-lad! No, I've said it once and I'll say it again, you've done just as you ought and I don't think you should go home one day before you have to. I admit there'd be folk as would advise you different, but I ain't one of them. Patty's as sweet and level-headed a girl as I've ever met, and when push comes to shove she'll see where true worth lies and make her decision accordingly.'

'I know what you mean, but . . . but he's a good-lookin' bloke, Mam, and he's got a beautiful caravan and his own business. What's more, there's a sort of glamour attached to the fair which don't apply to Levers.' He saw his mother begin to smile and added hastily: 'You know what I mean! He's been places and done things that I've never even dreamed of. He can offer Patty foreign travel and excitement, but all I can offer is a regular wage packet. In other words, he's the prince and I'm the peasant.'

Mrs Knight was not a demonstrative woman, but now she stood on tiptoe, pulled Darky's head down to hers and kissed him resoundingly on the cheek. 'And I suppose you ain't good-looking?' she said derisively. 'I suppose you don't have half the girls in Levers swooning over you? As for the glamour of travel, or whatever it was you said, I reckon Patty's a real home bird. I'm telling you, son, you've done the right thing, and when we get home all you'll have to is pop the question.'

Darky snorted. 'And risk her saying no and spoiling what I have got? We're good friends, Mam, and I can see Patty and Merry whenever we aren't working, but if I propose and she refuses, she might feel too embarrassed to so much as come to a flick with me ever again.'

It was Mrs Knight's turn to snort. 'Faint heart never won fair lady,' she quoted. 'Am I to call you a coward, son? Afraid to chance your arm in case she turns you down? Now I want you to promise me that when we get back to Liverpool you'll ask young Patty if she'll marry you; and if she says she won't, I'll eat my Sunday hat.'

Darky took a deep breath, intending to say he would do no such thing, and found himself meekly promising to do just as his mother had asked. Strangely enough, having made the decision, he felt happier than he had done for days, and even began to share his mother's optimism over Patty's reply to his proposal.

When the telegraph boy came to the door, Patty's heart sank into her sensible wellington boots. She had just come in from a gruelling round of calls and wanted nothing more than a hot cup of tea and a nice sit down before the fire. However, she ripped the little yellow envelope open with a dry mouth whilst the boy stood patiently, saying over and over beneath his breath: 'Any reply, miss? It's a penny a word.'

The telegram, however, did not bring bad news of Merry's health. It merely said: MERRY STILL INFECTIOUS STOP COMING HOME 14TH STOP LETTER FOLLOWS STOP KNIGHTS.

Patty was so relieved that, for a moment, the room swam around her. Then it steadied and she told the telegraph boy that there was no reply, shut the door and tottered to the nearest fireside chair, where she collapsed, reading the telegram again and feeling a stab of dismay that she would see neither the Knights nor Merry for another nine days.

However, she must look on the bright side. Bringing Merry home too soon could easily result in nasty complications and, as a nurse, Patty was well aware how damaging these could be. Measles was dismissed by some as a childish ailment which everyone had to go through, but she knew how often a child sick with the measles could run such a high fever that hallucinations and worse could follow. Patty had known cases where otitis media had had children screaming with earache; she had nursed a child whose untreated measles had caused encephalitis and another whose eyesight had been so severely affected by corneal ulcerations that she had lost most of her sight. So she must count herself lucky that Merry was merely staying in Scotland for an extra nine days and not suffering from any of the various ills which could have come as a result of the infection.

Maggie, however, was now back at No. 24 for a couple of days each week, since the children were all pretty well over their illness. She said, confidently, that she was sure she would be back at Ashfield Place full time in another week or so. When she came in presently and heard that Merry was remaining in Scotland for another nine days, her face fell, but she said bracingly: 'It'll be for the best, Patty. I know you said that the younger the child, the less chance of real damage, but even so we wouldn't want our girl takin' that long journey in such horrid weather before she's properly fit, would we? And anyway, it means we'll be able to give Toby a bit more time on a Saturday, because he does need help with the shooting gallery, even though Christmas and New Year are over.'

'Business slows almost to a stop from now on,' Patty reminded her. 'It's in January that all the repair work gets done. They repaint the gallopers – that's the merry-go-rounds, Maggie – and the swing boats, renew the ropes, oil the rifles and go to the wholesalers to buy new prizes for when spring comes again. So even when they're not open for business, they're still extremely busy.'

Maggie nodded. 'Yes, I'm sure you're right. As you know, Patty, I don't like Toby as much as you do, but think how we would have missed Darky and Mrs Knight if it hadn't been for him!'

Patty smiled. 'I don't know what I would have done over Christmas and the New Year without Toby and the fair,' she admitted. 'He is so full of fun and so good-tempered, even when things go wrong. And the fair folk are the same. They've made it clear that they consider me one of themselves because I'm Toby's pal. When I was truly worried about Merry, Toby was really sensible, telling me that worry never did anyone any good and pointing out that if I made myself ill my work would suffer. And then, of course, he can always make me laugh. I know you have your doubts about him, queen, but you've not known him as long as I have.'

'It isn't that I have my doubts exactly,' Maggie was beginning when the door flew open and Ellen tumbled into the room. She sank into the fireside chair opposite Patty's and turned to beam at Maggie. 'Oh, it's grand to have you back, Mags,' she said, 'even if you're only here for a few hours.' She began to pull out the contents of her bag and tip those instruments that needed sterilising into a cake tin. 'Are your instruments in the oven already, Patty? If not, we'd better sort them now, then they can sterilise together.' She turned back to Maggie. 'What's for supper, queen?'

Patty fetched her own black bag and tipped her used instruments into the sterilising tin, then turned towards her bedroom. 'I've worked my hands raw today,' she said in a tired voice. 'I'll just get into a clean dress and then I'll give Maggie a hand with the supper. When I've changed, I'll throw the laundry bag out so you can add your stuff, Ellie, and then we can begin to relax.'

'I can't. I'm going to the flicks with me John as soon as I've eaten,' Ellen said cheerfully. 'Wharrabout you, Patty? Are you seeing Toby?'

'Not tonight,' Patty said, poking her head back into the room. 'To tell the truth, I feel a bit low. Darky sent a telegram saying they won't be coming home until the fourteenth – it seems an age away. Still, I know it's for the best; the journey would be too much for Merry in her present state.'

Ellen agreed and presently, alone in her room, Patty began to consider the past couple of weeks. She had worried about Merry, of course she had, but she trusted Mrs Knight and knew that Darky would do anything he could for her small daughter. He had been awfully good, writing to Patty every single day and giving a progress report which was so detailed that she had almost imagined herself to be present in the narrow little house in Glasgow.

Then Toby's constant, loving companionship and his deep interest in everything she said and did was a great comfort. The amusements and entertainments to which he took her often kept her mind from Merry for several hours together, and working on the fair was something so new and exciting that it was like a different life. She had grown accustomed to the chaff and chatter with which her customers on the shooting gallery greeted her and was able to chaff and chatter back, giving as good as she got and thoroughly enjoying the light-hearted repartee. Toby had told her afterwards that she might have been born to it.

'I'm beginning to believe you love it as much as I do,' he said, his eyes twinkling. 'I've spent me life looking for someone who'd fit in and enjoy the fair and now I've found her! I tell you, Patty Peel, you and me make a grand team.'

Patty had laughed, pushing back the strands of golden hair from her flushed face, but she had enjoyed the compliment and, when she was with him, she often thought that she really could become a member of the fair family. They were so friendly and warm, so good-naturedly anxious to help one another. Even Maggie, who was still a little doubtful of Toby, adored life on the gaff. And Merry's so young that she would take to it as a matter of course, Patty told herself. Oh, but I do miss her! And to think that Toby's never even met her! Well, he's in for a pleasant surprise, because a sweeter, prettier child was never born.

Thinking it over now as she gradually relaxed, she reminded herself that Toby truly needed help from someone on his shooting gallery. She was useful to him, but she was sure this was not the only reason he was beginning to court her. She believed he was genuinely attracted by her. She imagined that the fact that she had run the shooting gallery so well over Christmas was a sort of delightful extra. Going over what he had said, how he had behaved, she decided that he probably did mean to propose marriage when they had spent rather more time together. The only fly in the ointment was his genuine liking for women – all women. Several times, when he had been making her pretty speeches, she had noticed his attention wandering, his eyes roving speculatively over a couple of pretty girls as they walked, arms linked, past the caravan. She guessed that he had not yet seriously considered the chief responsibility of marriage, which was to remain faithful to one's marital partner. He had volunteered to move in with a pal so that she might stay in his caravan for a couple of days, get to know both life on the gaff and himself a little better, but so far she had not taken him up on the offer. It was going too far and too fast for Patty, who liked to think out every move before she made it. I'm staid and dull, except when I'm with Toby, she told herself sadly. But that's the way I am and I can't change it. If I move into the big green caravan it will be as Toby's wife, not as an experiment!

One thing Toby had done for her, however, was to dissipate her fear of physical closeness. He had never taken advantage of her but had constantly cuddled, kissed and squeezed, telling her that this was natural and normal between two such old friends who hoped to become, in time, more than friends. Patty had actually begun to enjoy this mild form of love-making and to think that maybe – just maybe – marriage might be quite a pleasant thing after all. As for Toby's roving eye, that, she imagined, could be easily dealt with once the knot was tied.

Then Ellen had told her, only the previous day, that she was becoming quite human. 'I can't say I like Toby the way I like Darky,' Ellen had said frankly. 'But then I've never been out with Toby, so I don't know him the way I know Darky. Toby never takes much notice of me, come to think. That's natural, of course, since it's plain as the nose on your face that the feller's going to ask you to marry him any day now. What'll you say when he does, queen?'

'I think Toby should be the first person to know that,' Patty had said primly, but with a smirk. In fact, she had no idea what she was going to say when – or rather if – Toby asked her to be his wife. She, an orphan without a relative to her name, was immensely attracted by the idea of belonging to the extended family of the fair, for she was quite acute enough to realise that this was probably why Toby himself had taken to the life. What was more, Toby had a definite effect on her. He was light-hearted, easy-going, permanently pleased with life and happy go lucky. When she was with him she felt the same; her worries receded and she simply lived for the moment.

Of course, there was the other side of the coin. She knew herself to be a dedicated member of her profession; ever since Selina had first talked to her about her nursing career she had longed to follow in her friend's footsteps. It isn't that I'm a do-gooder, Patty told herself, brushing her teeth hard and spitting into the remains of her washing water, then emptying the bowl into the slop bucket. No, I'm not a do-gooder, but I've worked like a galley slave to get the job I have, and I really enjoy helping my patients, delivering their babies, teaching them how to look after their little ones. Toby has said I need not give up my work, could continue with it either in New Brighton or even in my present district, if I could manage the journey to and from work each day. But if I married I would want children of my own and that would put a pretty decided stop to my career. To my hopes of a small country cottage, animals of my own, a proper garden ... well, I suppose I might have them in time if I married Toby, since he has said he would stay in New Brighton if that was what I wanted.

Clad in her clean dress, Patty went back into the kitchen to join her companions.

It had been a long train journey for all of them, but perhaps especially trying for young Merry, Darky thought, as they reached Lime Street station. The carriage was full but he managed to get out on to the platform first, then turned and held up his arms as his mother lifted the sleeping child and handed her down to him. Poor little kid, Darky thought, looking down into her flushed face. She had been good as gold, playing games, listening to stories and trying not to scratch, for though the rash had disappeared it had left dry and flaky patches of skin on the insides of her elbows and the backs of her knees, and Mrs Knight had been most anxious that she should not rub and make the dry skin worse.

Darky tucked the child into the crook of his arm and grabbed the suitcase which his mother was shoving towards him. He stood it on the platform and gave Mrs Knight a hand down, then thanked a fellow passenger who passed him his own carpetbag. Mrs Knight had dozed a little as daylight faded and now she knuckled her eyes, pulled her hat further down on her brow and picked up the suitcase.

'Put that down, Mam,' Darky said. 'I'll let you take the carpetbag because that's not too heavy but I can manage Merry and the suitcase. It's not for long, because we're getting a taxi.'

'A taxi?' Mrs Knight said, sounding scandalised.

'What's wrong wi' a tram, son? You've lost three weeks' pay as it is; you don't want to go throwing your money about on taxis.'

Darky laughed. It was typical of his mother to try to save a bob or two of his hard-earned money, but he had no intention of hanging about in the cold with a child who had only just recovered from a nasty attack of the measles. He said as much as they made their way towards the taxi rank on Lime Street and Mrs Knight grudgingly agreed that she supposed he was right.

'She's been such a good little girl, she don't deserve to have to hang about in the cold, you're right there,' she agreed. 'My goodness, I'll feel like a queen driving up to Ashfield Place in a cab! I wonder what Patty will say when she sees us getting out of a taxi?'

'She won't say anything because she won't be at home,' Darky pointed out. 'It's only four o'clock and I never said in my telegram which train we were catching because I didn't want her to feel that she ought to meet us. She works terrible hard, Mam, and needs time to get through her rounds each day. But think what a nice surprise it will be when she gets back from work and finds we're all settled in again, with a meal on the table and the fire blazing in the stove.'

Mrs Knight groaned. 'I hadn't thought – I suppose the fire will be out and there'll be hardly any food in the cupboard . . . oh, and what about milk? Conny-onny's grand watered down, but Merry's been used to having a mug of real milk before she goes to sleep at night.' She turned anxious eyes on her son. 'I know Patty must have been hard pressed, only having Maggie at weekends, but do you think she'll have had time to do the messages? If not, perhaps we'd better get the taxi driver to drop us off at the corner of Latimer Street so that we can pop in and get some groceries from Mr Flowerdew.'

'Patty will have got food in,' Darky said comfortably, helping his mother into the back of the waiting cab. 'And she'll have damped down the fire, so all we'll have to do is stir it with the poker. I don't know whether she'll have seen to things in number twenty-three or twenty-four, but I'm sure we shan't go into a cold house. Patty's reliable as well as kind, you know, Mam. He hefted the suitcases into the cab and followed his mother into the back. He had already told the driver their destination and now he sank back on the worn leather seat with a contented sigh. 'This sure is the best way to travel,' he remarked. 'My, but I'm gasping for a cuppa. Oh, Mam, I'm that glad to be home!'

'Work tomorrow,' his mother said prosaically. 'Back to Levers and soapflakes and girls giving you a mouthful. Wharrabout that, eh?'

'Oh, Levers ain't so bad,' Darky said drowsily. 'But being up in Glasgow and having time to meself has made me think. I'm a good electrician and I've had a deal of experience these past ten years or so. I'm thinking about having a go at working for meself.'

His mother stared at him, but before she could speak, Merry, who had been sleeping soundly, woke up with a cry. 'Where is we? What's happening?' she demanded fretfully. She turned in Mrs Knight's arms and patted her. 'Oh, you're still here, Nanna. I dreamed a big, big monkey had stolen you away and was swinging through the trees with me tucked under one arm. Only then he dropped me and I was falling . . . falling . . . Oh, Nanna, I were frightened, so I were.'

Mrs Knight gave her small charge a loving hug. 'It's all right, queen, we're nearly home,' she said consolingly. 'And as soon as we get indoors, Nanna will put the kettle on and we'll all have a nice cup of tea!'

When they reached Ashfield Place, Darky's optimism was confirmed. As they stepped into the warm, firelit kitchen of No. 23, there was a note leaning against a pot of chrysanthemums in the middle of the kitchen table. Darky read it aloud to his mother and Merrell. 'Welcome home! Meat and potato pie on shelf in pantry, only needs warming through. I'll be back sevenish. Lots of kisses for Merry, Patty.'

'There, I told you so,' Darky said, walking over to the fire and pulling the kettle over the flame. Whilst his mother unwrapped Merry from her layers of garments, he checked the pie in the pantry and came back into the room smiling broadly. 'It's a huge pie,' he said gleefully, 'big enough to feed an army, and there's a jam roly-poly for afters. There's a jug of milk standing in a bowl of water on the cold slab and a Victoria sponge under the gauze cover, so we shan't starve.' He rubbed his hands together and walked over to set out teapot and cups on the kitchen table. 'And in two hours or so, Patty will be home.'

As he spoke, there was a rattle as though someone had thrown a handful of gravel up to the balcony. Mrs Knight went over to the window and glanced out. 'Weather's taken a turn for the worse,' she observed. 'The wind's got up and that rattling sound were hail. Poor Patty! It looks as though she'll need a good, hot fire and a decent meal when she gets home.'

Chapter Seventeen

By the time Monday morning arrived, Patty was so excited that she had to speak severely to herself; they can't get home before early evening and if they miss a connection they won't be home then, so it's no use getting into a lather. It would have been lovely to meet them at the station but she had a hectic day ahead of her, with a great many revisits to patients who had given birth over the past couple of weeks and to three expectant mums who were already overdue.

As they got ready for work, she and Ellen discussed the day ahead and Patty said that she was longing to take half an hour off that afternoon and see if she could meet the train which the Knights and Merrell were most likely to be on. Ellen smiled sympathetically but said sadly that her own duties made it impossible to stand in for Patty, even for half an hour. 'Mrs Reynolds has three children under five and the twins, who aren't yet a week old,' she explained. 'If I don't turn up there at around quarter to five, no one will get a meal and Mrs Reynolds will be in tears by the time her old man gets home. Then he'll be angry and we can't have that, not with all those little kids around.'

The girls were not supposed to have favourites among their patients, but Mrs Reynolds was a sweet, generous person who did her best for everyone and was usually both cheerful and efficient.

Unfortunately, the birth of the twins had been difficult and had left Mrs Reynolds completely washed out, liable to burst into tears if the least thing went wrong and incapable, for the moment, of running her own life. Mr Reynolds was a pleasant little man who worked in a large grocery shop on Heyworth Street. In normal circumstances, tea would have been on the table and the children washed and ready for bed by the time he arrived home, and he could not understand why things should be different simply because two babies had arrived instead of the one which had been expected. Patty and Ellen both knew that Mr Reynolds would never use violence towards his wife, but they also knew that when he came home tired and hungry and found nothing on the table, and a weeping wife sitting helplessly before the fire, he would shout, perhaps even call names, and this would only worsen Mrs Reynolds's condition. So, in a way, it was in Ellen's own interest to see that Mr Reynolds got his supper on time. Experience showed that a mother recovered from the depression which sometimes followed childbirth within a relatively short period, provided she was treated with sympathy and understanding.

'Yes, of course. I never really thought you'd be able to stand in for me today,' Patty said, shovelling her instruments into her black bag. 'And it isn't as if I know what train they'll be catching, because Darky never said. I spent all last evening cooking so there's plenty of food in the house and I made up the fire in number twenty-three and damped it down before I put my uniform on, so that's all right. I'll write them a bit of a note, telling them I'll be home sevenish. I'll do that right now and then get off; you never know, I might get through my visits early for once.

*

After Patty had left her, Ellen bustled about doing all the little jobs that the two girls and Maggie normally shared between them. The previous evening, Patty had told her that she must go round to the Knights' at supper time, since there would be plenty of food for all of them, so at least she did not have to make any preparations for the evening meal, but she damped down the fire and carried the big black kettle over to the sink, filling it with water and standing it on the hob so that it could be easily pulled over the fire when needed.

She was packing her bag and preparing to leave the house when there was a knock at the door. Ellen heaved a deep sigh and picked up her bag. She opened the door expecting to find a child or the husband of one of her patients preparing to ruin her carefully planned day, but instead Toby Rudd stood there. He was wearing a ragged cap and an equally ragged jacket and did not look at all like the dapper young man whom Ellen had met only twice when he had come to call for her friend.

Ellen opened her mouth to tell him that Patty was not at home, but Toby spoke before she could do so. 'Where's Patty? I've got to talk to her,' he said urgently. 'I've had a message from the Flanagan's; young Ted Flanagan's been took bad – they think it's appendicitis – when he were halfway through dismantling the engine which turns the big galloper. It could be a couple a'weeks before he's out of hospital and fit again and there's no one, apart from meself, as knows how to put the engine together again.'

'Oh dear,' Ellen said politely, wondering what on earth this had to do with Patty. So far as she could remember, the Flanagan's were the family who owned the travelling fair Toby had belonged to before he came to New Brighton. Why should young Ted's afflictions affect him now? But Toby was pushing past her, clearly both impatient and worried – and determined to speak to Patty. Ellen grabbed his arm. 'It's no good, Toby. Patty left for work ten or fifteen minutes ago,' she said briskly. 'But I'll be seeing her this evening – can I give her a message? I take it you want to let her know that you're going off to – to wherever the Flanagan's are, to put this here engine back together?'

'Not here?' Toby looked aghast, as though it had never occurred to him that Patty's work took her constantly from home, Ellen thought crossly. 'Not here? But it ain't even half past eight yet; I made sure she'd still be at home.'

'Well, she isn't,' Ellen said firmly. She stepped out on to the balcony and held the door so that Toby could go past her. 'What's more, she won't be back until around seven this evening, but if you've a message for her I might manage to see her at some time during the day.'

'No, no, that's not good enough; I need to know what her answer is,' Toby said wildly. 'I'm relying on her to run the shooting gallery this evening because otherwise I'll be letting the New Brighton Riding Master down. Tell me, where am I likely to find her if I set off right now?'

Ellen thought briefly. She knew roughly in which direction her friend had gone. If only she could concentrate . . . but it was difficult for she herself was running late. 'Look, walk down with me to my bike while I think,' she commanded. 'She had a delivery the night before last – she'll probably go there first.

Yes, and it's probably the nearest. You'd best try Mrs Ratner at Number Five, Ellesmere Court. It'll be a fairly long visit, but if she does happen to have moved on – Patty, I mean – she'll likely have told Mrs Ratner who she'll be visiting next.' She eyed Toby rather uncertainly for a moment, then added: 'But just you remember she's a working midwife, Mr Rudd, and don't try and hassle her. Patty's an excellent nurse and her patients come first. She won't thank you for butting in on her round unless it's an emergency, and what is an emergency to you may seem pretty trivial to her.'

By this time they had reached her bicycle and Ellen was unlocking the padlock and slipping it into her pocket, aware that her voice had sounded a trifle cold, but not caring very much. She thought that Toby was trying to make use of her friend, and did not like it.

Toby stared at her, his eyes very bright. 'Mrs Ratner, Number Five, Ellesmere Court,' he repeated. 'Nurse, you know I want to marry Patty, don't you? I wouldn't ask her to put herself out unless I was serious, would I? I ain't the sort of feller to take advantage of me pals.'

'I should hope not,' Ellen said, still rather coldly. She was beginning to wonder whether she had done right to tell Toby where he would find Patty; after all, this evening the Knights and Merrell were returning from Scotland.

She said as much to Toby, who flashed her his most charming smile. 'Yes, but the fair closes at ten tonight, so she won't be late,' he said. Ellen opened her mouth to tell him that her friend would have had an exceedingly long day by seven o'clock and would be in no fit state to work another three hours, but she did not get the chance. Toby raised a hand, gave her another charming smile and strode off, calling over his shoulder: 'Tara then, and thanks for the address.'

Ellen mounted her bicycle and set off towards the home of her first patient. Was he right, she wondered? Would Patty really consider the shooting gallery so important that she would set off for New Brighton before even seeing Merry and the Knights? Of course, she might be able to make arrangements for Maggie to return home, just for the evening, and Patty had already worked very hard to make the homecoming a success. She had prepared all the food, warmed the house through, and had, in fact, left the Knights little to do but pop Merry into bed when their supper was eaten. Besides, Ellen thought, I'll probably be home before seven, so I'll give an eye to Merry if Patty's gone to the fair.

She turned into the little street which housed her first patient and thought, suddenly, of Darky. She knew he was keen on Patty and now she wondered how he would take it if Patty simply swanned off to the fair on his first night home. Darky had a temper and a sharp tongue; she found herself hoping devoutly that Patty would tell Toby where to get off. Life had been so comfortable since Patty and Darky had become friends; a resurrection of their former enmity would be horrible indeed.

'Thanks very much, Nurse Peel. This baby's a rare good 'un, norra sound out of 'im last night. He drinks his supper and falls straight to sleep like me milk were drugged. See ya tomorrer, then!'

Mrs Evans stood on her doorstep, surrounded by her children, all waving vigorously. Patty, smiling, mounted her bicycle, thinking that it was always a joy to visit the Evanses. The children were fat and healthy, though seldom clean, and Mrs Evans was the wife of Joe Evans, who owned a small bakery shop nearby. The family took life lightly and, far from resenting her yearly pregnancies, Mrs Evans was apt to say, blithely, that kids were gifts from God and you couldn't have too many of them.

'Goodbye, Mrs Evans, and thanks for the cuppa. I've only got two more visits and then I'll be off home,' she called cheerily. 'Good thing, too, because I wouldn't be surprised if we had a storm later; the wind's blowing up a hooligan.'

And presently, as she pedalled along towards her next visit, Patty's words were proved right. It began to hail, the stones bouncing off the road and lashing against her unprotected face so hard that she was forced to dismount and push her bicycle. When the hail eased off, Patty remounted and set off as fast as she could, intent upon reaching her next patient before the wind grew worse or the hail started again. She was cycling with considerable care, aware of the treacherous road surface, when she thought she saw a familiar figure on the farther pavement. 'Darky!' she gasped, her heart leaping with unexpected delight. Then the man turned towards her and she realised he was a total stranger. Momentarily distracted, she forgot the slippery surface and felt the bicycle shudder, then slide away from her, felt herself falling . . . falling . . . She struggled to save herself, clutching the bicycle wildly, and saw the road rushing up to meet her. There was a screech of brakes, several voices exclaimed and a woman screamed, then Patty felt a violent blow on her head and blackness enveloped her . . .

'Derek Knight, if you go to that window once more I

shall go mad,' Mrs Knight declared, wagging a finger at her son. 'I know it's a wild night and I know young Patty said sevenish in her note, but you know how conscientious she is. Why, if she were called to a lying-in, she'd have no choice but to go, you know that as well as I do.'

Darky turned away from the window. It was ten past seven and it had begun to thunder; the storm was clearly some way off but, he thought, heading in their direction. 'I reckon if she were at a lying-in, she'd have sent us a message,' he said worriedly. 'There's always kids around who'll take a message for a penny or so and Patty isn't the sort of girl to let anyone down. Oh, Mam, suppose she's in some sort of trouble?'

'There you go again, leapin' to conclusions,' his mother said wryly, but Darky could see she was worried. 'Ah, I hear a step!'

Darky flew across to the door. 'At last! We thought you was . . .' His voice faltered to a halt as Ellen came into the kitchen and began to take off her soaking coat and hat, beaming round at them as she did so.

'Sorry. I suppose you thought I were Patty,' she said cheerfully, shaking a small river of rain from the brim of her hat. 'She's gorra full day, I'm tellin' you, or she'd have been back by now unless—' She put a hand to her mouth, then looked wildly round the room. 'Where's Merry? How did she manage the journey? I dare say she's worn out, poor kid. Oh, listen to that weather!'

'Merry's in bed in me mam's room because she were too tired to stay up any longer,' Darky said evenly, 'and just what were you going to say, Ellen Purbright? What do you really think has happened to Patty?'

437

Ellen, hanging her garments on the hooks on the back of the door, turned and smiled at him. 'I think mebbe a patient is taking longer to deliver than Patty hoped, or mebbe she's found all her calls have taken a bit more time than expected,' she said, with a glibness which did not deceive Darky for one moment. She knows Patty better than most people and she really is worried, he thought. Well, anyone would worry if someone they loved was out on a perishin' bicycle in a storm like this. Still, there's no point in getting in a state yet; as everyone keeps saying, she's probably been kept late with a patient.

When eight o'clock came and there was still no sign of Patty, however, all three of them sat around the kitchen table and looked at one another with considerable anxiety. At his mother's insistence, Darky had agreed that they should have their meal, but as the minutes ticked by he had found it increasingly difficult to swallow and in the end had pushed his plate away with a good half of his slice of the pie still untouched. 'You can say what you like, Mam,' he said miserably, getting restlessly to his feet and going over to peer out of the window for the umpteenth time, 'Patty would have sent a message. She knew we were coming home today and she knew how we'd worry. Why, even Ellen can't tell us where she is.'

He looked accusingly at Ellen as he spoke, certain that she knew more than she was telling. For a moment, Ellen stared back at him, then she heaved a deep sigh and spoke. 'Well, I suppose it must be . . . oh, Darky, you've got to try to understand. Toby Rudd called this morning . . .'

Darky crashed both fists down on the table, the

blood draining from his face. 'I *knew* I were being a bloody fool to take meself off to Scotland for a week, lerralone three,' he shouted explosively. 'I s'pose you're tryin' to tell me that she's run off wi' the bugger. Well, I'm not having it; whether she knows it or not, it's *me* she cares for, *me* she's going to marry.' He turned on his mother, his eyes flashing angrily. 'And it weren't only me, it were you! You said I were doin' the right thing, you said give him enough rope and he'd hang himself, and now look where we are.'

'Eh, you've a nasty side to your nature, Darky,' his mother said placidly, wagging her head sorrowfully. 'You don't even know what's happened to the girl and you're turning round and tryin' to blame someone else rather than facing up to facts and listening to explanations. No, don't flare up at me,' she added as Darky opened his mouth to speak, 'let's hear what young Ellen has got to tell us.'

Ellen smiled at Mrs Knight then started to speak. 'The fact is that Toby Rudd came round this morning to ask for Patty's help. A pal of his has been whipped into hospital leaving some work half done, from what I could gather, and Toby was asked to go and finish it off.'

Darky gave a sort of growl beneath his breath. 'So what's that got to do with Patty?' he asked truculently. 'I don't see—'

Mrs Knight leaned across the table and shook a warning finger just under Darky's nose. 'If you don't shut your gob I'll give you a clack, big as you are,' she said wrathfully. She turned to Ellen. 'Carry on, queen. If there's owt we don't understand, we'll ask you to make it clear after the story's told.'

'Thanks, Mrs Knight,' Ellen said gratefully. 'I'm not telling it very well because Toby was in a rush and seemed to think I knew more than I really did. But the gist of it was that he had to go away pronto and he wanted our Patty to man his shooting gallery this evening. He said it were a real emergency and if she couldn't make it, he'd be letting all the fair folk down.'

'And she agreed to go, knowing that Merry and me mam and me were coming home this evening?' Darky asked incredulously. 'Why, she left a note saying she'd be home sevenish.'

His mother opened her mouth but Ellen shushed her with a quick movement. 'It's all right, Mrs Knight. I'm afraid I got it all a bit haywire. I should have explained that Patty had already left for work when Toby arrived, so he asked me to give her a message if I should meet her, but then he decided that he needed to know her answer before he left so he got me to give him the name and address of the patient she was likeliest to visit first and went off at a gallop, heading for Number Five, Ellesmere Court.'

'I . . . see,' Darky said slowly. A frown creased his brow; he was obviously thinking hard. 'But what good would Patty be on a shooting gallery? She can't shoot, can she?'

Ellen giggled. 'It isn't like that. Patty's been helping out at the shooting gallery ever since Christmas – he's an old friend, after all – so she knows what to charge and how to load the rifles and so on. I think it would be fair to say that she can manage the gallery as well as Toby can himself, and it isn't difficult. Why, a couple of times young Maggie's given him a hand and she's only a kid.'

She looked expectantly at Darky, who nodded slowly. 'Yes, I can see she'd help out a pal at a difficult time,' he admitted grudgingly. 'But surely she'd have left us some message?' He turned to his mother. 'Can you credit it, Mam? That Patty would just go off to the fair, knowing we was coming home, without so much as a word? From what young Ellen tells us, she might well not have even known Toby had been to number twenty-four first, especially if he met her in a house full of squalling kids. I mean he'd just be intent on getting her full agreement.' He put both hands over his face and rubbed vigorously, then got up. 'I'm going over to New Brighton,' he announced. 'I can't imagine that the fair will be going strong in weather like this, but at least if Patty's there I'll be able to find out just what has been happening and what lies Rudd's been telling her, because there's something strange going on and I mean to get to the bottom of it,' he finished grimly.

He got up from the table as he spoke and went over to the door where he began to struggle into coat, cap and boots. 'I think you're doin' the right thing, son,' Mrs Knight said approvingly, as Darky seized his scarf and wrapped it around his throat so violently that he looked as if he were trying to strangle himself. 'But don't go bawling the poor girl out the minute you see her, because you're quite right on one thing: there's no way Patty would have gone off without leaving a message for us. She might have pinned a note to the door and it might have got torn off by the wind, or she might have given a young lad a message and he got the wrong address. Oh, there's a million things that might have happened and one thing that might not; no way would Patty have left us to stew.'

Darky was snatching the door open but he turned to grin at his mother as she spoke. 'Haven't I been saying that all along?' he asked. 'I knew Patty wouldn't let you and Merrell down, even if she fancied a bit of worry would do me good! As for bawling her out, what do you think I am?'

'I think that you're a hot-headed young fool who's been cutting off his nose to spite his face ever since Patty moved into Ashfield Place,' Mrs Knight said, raising her voice to a shout as Darky opened the door and the rain and wind swirled in. 'But take care, son – and good luck!'

Darky ran down the stairs and across Ashfield Place. The weather was as bad as he had feared, making him more certain than ever that the fair would have been forced to close by now, even if it had opened earlier in the evening. As he sloshed his way through the puddles towards the tram stop, he told himself with mordant humour that he had often thought that he would go through fire and water for Patty, but had not expected to do it literally – the water part, anyway. He hoped that the ferries would be running, but suddenly began to doubt it; it was perfectly possible that they would not set sail in such conditions. In that case his trip would be abortive – unless, of course, he decided to swim it. But keen though he was to know what had happened to Patty, he did not really anticipate diving into the surging waters of the Mersey to find out.

When he reached the main road, however, he discovered he was in luck. A tram was bearing down upon him, its destination the Pier Head. He climbed aboard, handed over his fare and asked the conductor in tones which he strove in vain to keep casual whether the ferries were still running.

'I guess they is,' the conductor said easily. 'It's a wild night, sure enough, but the tide's on the ebb and there are shift workers wantin' to get across to Levers and the docks and such. The ferries don't usually stop going across except when the sea's terrible rough.'

Darky thanked him, chiding himself for having had to ask. After all, he himself caught the ferry in both directions every working day, and though the boat might be late, he could not remember a time when he had been left on the wrong side of the water. Sure enough, when he reached the quayside, the ferry was just about to depart. Darky shouted and gesticulated and just managed to get aboard by the skin of his teeth, settling down to make the best of an extremely uncomfortable journey.

Two hours later, he threw open the door of No. 23 once more and trudged heavily into the kitchen. 'Any sign of her? Any news?' he asked in a weary voice.

Mrs Knight shook her head. 'There's been no word and it's clear from the look on your face that she weren't at the fair. So where is she, Darky? Were the fair folk able to tell you?'

'No, no one knew. All they could say was that she hadn't been to the fair at all, to their knowledge. But since the really bad weather started at around five o'clock, they were mostly tucked up in their caravans and wouldn't have seen Patty if she had turned up. To tell the truth,' he added, collapsing into one of the fireside chairs, 'they seemed right surprised that Toby should have asked her to give an eye to the shooting gallery. The old woman I spoke to said that though Friday and Saturday nights are quite lively, the rest of the week is so poor at this time of year that only the really big attractions bother to open, and not all of them, either. Which means that Rudd could have gone off and left the shooting gallery unattended without letting anyone down, or being in any way worse off.'

'Then why on earth did he ask her give up her evening and go over to New Brighton?' Mrs Knight asked, her voice bewildered. 'There ain't no sense in it, son.'

'Oh yes there is,' Darky said grimly, holding out his hands to the blazing fire. 'I'll take a bet it were done to show me whose girl Patty really is. In other words, he were proving that Patty thought so much of him that she'd miss our homecoming, just for his convenience. Well, it didn't work, because Patty never turned up at the fair, I'm sure of it.'

'Then what's happened to her?' Mrs Knight wailed. 'You don't think she went off with him?'

'If she did, he bleedin' well abducted her, because there's absolutely no way that Patty would have left Liverpool on the very day that Merry came back from Scotland,' Darky said positively. 'And if he's abducted her, and I know my Patty, he'll suffer for it.'

'If there's been any hanky-panky, you ought to go to the scuffers,' his mother said decidedly. 'Abducting young females is illegal, and even if he's only tricked her into going away with him, the scuffers ought to know about it. Besides, you don't know she's with him. Why, she might be lying in a hospital bed somewhere, not knowing who she is or where. Have you thought of that, son?'

'I've thought of nothing else ever since finding she wasn't at the fair,' Darky admitted. He glanced around the kitchen. 'Where's Ellen, by the way?'

'Gone home to bed. She's on call tonight,' Mrs Knight said briefly. 'Are you going to the scuffers or aren't you, lad, because if you're froze I'll make you a quick cup of tea and then I'll nip along to the station meself.'

Darky heaved a sigh and got to his feet. 'I've

already been to the scuffers; a fat old sergeant wrote all the details down and said he'd put the word about that a young woman was missing, but he didn't seem particularly worried. He knows Patty, you see, and thinks her far too capable to be taken in by a rogue like Rudd.' He did not add, as he might have done, that the sergeant had reminded him of the white slave trade and of Patty's long blonde hair, because he knew that such a remark would terrify his mother and with cause. He had been terrified himself when the sergeant had advanced his theory. Then he had remembered that Patty would have been in uniform and his fears receded slightly. A district nurse was far too obvious to be carried, unconscious, down to the docks. Someone there would certainly be suspicious and would doubtless alert the authorities.

'Then if you've been to the scuffers, where are you going now?' his mother asked, rather plaintively, as her son settled his cap firmly on his head and turned towards the door. 'There's no point in wandering the streets.'

'I'm going to the hospitals,' Darky told her. 'It'll be easy enough to find out whether she's been admitted. Young women in district nurse's uniform aren't exactly ten a penny.'

'I wish I could come along o' you, so's we could split the hospitals between us,' Mrs Knight said ruefully, 'but I'll have to stay to keep an eye on Merrell. I couldn't let Ellen take her in case she's called out, so Merry's still in the truckle bed in my room.'

'It's all right,' Darky said, glancing at the clock as he began to open the door. It was getting on for half past ten and he was already weary to the bone, but he knew he would not stop hunting until he had found

Patty. 'Don't wait up for me, Mam. I may be gone a while.'

Toby had actually got the galloper back into working order before darkness fell and could have set off at once to get back to New Brighton before the fair opened for the evening. However, in such vile weather, he knew very well that no one would bother to open up the attractions. He had not managed to get hold of Patty, but of course Ellen might easily have done so, in which case he had no doubt that Patty would be at the fair right now. He hoped that she would take shelter in the green caravan or, at any rate, with one of the other fair folk, because he really did not want her dancing attendance on the Knight family, the way she had done before he came on the scene. Toby would have said that he did not have a jealous bone in his body, but he did acknowledge that it worried him a little that Patty was so thick with her next-door neighbours. Suppose the charms of Mrs Knight and the little granddaughter she had taken to Scotland with her proved greater than those of Toby and the funfair? Although Toby continually stressed the fact that he was her oldest friend, he acknowledged secretly that she must know the Knights a good deal better than she knew him.

So, 'all's fair in love and war', Toby had told himself when he had formulated the plan to keep Patty by his side on this most crucial of days – the day that the Knights came back from Scotland. Of course he had not been able to be present himself because of the desperate SOS from the Flanagans, but he had done the next best thing; he had commandeered Patty to run his sideshow and was sure she would not let him down – not if she got the message, that was. If only he could have spoken to her himself, he just knew she would have promised immediately, but it seemed that Ellen had been mistaken in her assumption that Patty would go first to Ellesmere Court. When he had got there, the child who answered the door had said that Nurse would not be along before noon. 'Me mam's gone to see Auntie Ivy what's gorra poorly chest,' the child had told him, taking a swipe at his nose with the ragged sleeve of his jumper and leaving a sticky path across one cheek. 'Is there a message?'

Naturally, Toby had left a message, couched in terms calculated to send Patty flying off to New Brighton as soon as her rounds were over, but though he made the child repeat what he had said twice, he still hoped that Ellen and Patty had met up. He was sure the kid would do its best, but three hours inside such a tangled head could well result in some much-scrambled gobbledegook when Patty finally arrived in Ellesmere Court.

'Toby! Supper's ready!'

Toby smiled and got to his feet at the sound of Trixie Flanagan's voice. He had agreed to spend the night with the Flanagans and had been offered the use of their couch. He had told them about Patty, how well she did with the rifles, how the flatties were attracted by her mass of gold hair and had noticed, with amusement, the jealous look in Amanda's eyes. If only she were a couple of years older, I wouldn't worry myself over catching Patty, he found himself thinking. Patty's good, or as good as a flattie can be, but Amanda was born to it. The thought made him remember how Amanda Ellington had teased him when he'd mentioned Patty's name. 'Patty the flattie, Patty the flattie,' she had chanted. 'Or shall we just call her Flattie Patty?'

He had been quite hurt at the time, but fortunately her gleefully smiling face had made him see the funny side, so he had forgiven her though he had said loftily: 'She won't be a flattie. Once she's married to me and working on the shooting gallery, she'll be a fully fledged member of the community in no time.'

'Tobeee! Me sister's shouted you for supper twice and she won't let the rest of us start our meal until you're sat down at the table, so get a move on.'

'I'm coming, I'm coming, don't be so impatient,' Toby pretended to grumble, making his way past her and grinning apologetically at the rest of the family, already seated around the long table. 'Sorry, Trix. I were getting cleaned up and grease ain't all that easy to shift.' He slid on to the bench and sniffed appreciatively at the good smell coming from the big black pot in the middle of the table. He picked up his spoon and fork and smiled seraphically at his hostess. 'Judging from the smell, that's an Irish stew, my favourite food. I bet you've all been cursing me making you wait, but I'm here now. Let's go!'

Darky was in luck. He drew a blank at the David Lewis Northern Hospital on Great Howard Street, but when he tried the reception desk at the Stanley Hospital the trimly uniformed woman behind the desk said at once that they had had a district nurse admitted earlier. She consulted a large ledger, then smiled up into Darky's worried face. 'It's all right, chuck, don't gerrin a state,' she said comfortably. 'It says here she come off her bicycle in a hailstorm, or some such, banged her head on the pavement edge or the tramlines – something hard at any rate – and broke her arm. The doctor said she realised she was falling and tried to save herself, but fell with one arm at an awkward angle. It was a nasty break and she had to go to theatre to get it put right. We didn't manage to get her name because the knock on the head had concussed her.'

'Well, if she's blonde and pretty as a picture, she'll be Patty Peel, a young district midwife who lives next door to me in Ashfield Place,' Darky said at once and found himself praying that it was his Patty lying in a hospital bed, somewhere quite near him now. Concussion and a broken arm were no joke, but compared to the alternatives – lying dead in a mortuary, being the victim of white slave traders or an abducting Toby Rudd – a broken arm and a bump on the head seemed almost trivial.

'I haven't set eyes on the girl myself, but the nurses were talking about it when I came on duty,' the receptionist admitted. 'You'd best go along to the ward, Mr er . . .'

'I'm Derek Knight,' Darky supplied at once. 'Can you tell me the way to the ward, Nurse?'

The receptionist immediately abandoned her desk, though only to call a night porter across. 'Can you take Mr Knight along to Ward Ten? He's a relative of the young nurse who was brought in earlier.'

Darky did not correct her but followed the porter along a great many gloomy, ill lit corridors, until they reached a pair of swing doors with the legend *Ward 10* written above them. The porter pushed the doors apart and a nurse sitting behind a small desk, further down the long room, rose to her feet and came swiftly towards them, a finger on her lips.

'Relative of one of the patients,' the porter whispered hoarsely, indicating Darky. 'The one we don't have a name for; Mr Knight'll identify her if he can.'

449

The nurse, who had looked rather forbidding, smiled at Darky and indicated that he should follow her. They walked almost the full length of the long ward and then the nurse came to a halt beside a bed in which lay a figure Darky recognised. It was Patty, white-faced, with an enormous blue bruise on her forehead. She lay neatly on her back with her head turned to one side and someone had plaited her long tresses so that she looked very young, no more than a schoolgirl. Her right arm was outside the covers and encased in gleaming white plaster, and a tube led from a bag of some sort of liquid, suspended above the bed, into her wrist.

Darky's heart smote him. He had thought such awful things at first, suspecting her of going off with Toby and simply forgetting her responsibilities to Merrell and his mam. But now that he saw her looking so pale and vulnerable, pity welled up in his heart and he felt that he could never do enough for her. He told himself that if she truly preferred Toby to him . . . but at this point his thoughts broke down in confusion, and anyway the nurse was tugging at his arm.

'I can tell by your expression that you've recognised her,' she hissed. 'Can you come back to my desk, please, and give me the details?'

Darky complied, and when the nurse had finished filling in the form he glanced wistfully back up the ward towards the pale little figure in the bed. 'She looks awful frail, Nurse,' he said uneasily. 'And that's a whacking great bump on her forehead, as big as a hen's egg. Is she going to be all right? When will she wake up, do you reckon?'

The nurse smiled at him. 'Are you her husband?' she enquired. 'Yes, she'll be just fine. She came round after the anaesthetic but she was still very confused, so when she fell asleep we decided to put off asking any more questions until morning. Besides, concussion is quite commonly followed by a degree of memory loss so there's little point in asking questions of someone who cannot, as yet, tell you the answers.'

'I see,' Darky said rather doubtfully. 'When do you think it will be possible for me to come and see her, then? I could stay all night, of course, but my mother is dreadfully worried because we had no idea what happened to her – Patty, I mean – so I really should go home and relieve her mind. Besides, I suppose there's no point in my sitting beside her bed if she doesn't know I'm there.'

'No, no point at all,' the nurse said firmly. 'Having someone on the ward is disturbing for other patients, and because you would not be able to help looking at your wife's face your gaze might well wake her before she was ready. No, you are quite right, you should go home. Get a good night's sleep and come back after eleven o'clock tomorrow morning, if you are able to do so. Doctor's rounds usually take place between ten and eleven, so there may be more news of your wife by then.'

Darky smiled and nodded, but decided he had better come clean since, sooner or later, someone would realise that a married couple with different surnames was unusual, to say the least. 'I'm not Nurse Peel's husband,' he admitted. 'Not yet, at any rate. She's my young lady.'

'Oh I see,' the nurse said, but vaguely, as though she had not been really listening. 'In that case, could you get in touch with her parents for us? Only, until she's fully conscious and can give us their address—'

'She's an orphan. So far as she knows, she has no

living relatives,' Darky said quickly. 'But my mam's been as good as a mother to her and I know she'd like to visit – if you'll be keeping Nurse Peel in hospital for long, that is.'

'That's for the doctor to decide,' the nurse said primly. 'And now, Mr Peel, if you don't mind . . .'

'It's Mr Knight, actually,' Darky said rather wearily, deciding that the nurse was either tuppence short of a shilling or simply worn out after a too-long shift. 'I did tell you I wasn't Nurse Peel's husband, remember?'

'I'm awful sorry,' the girl said, and for the first time Darky looked properly at her and saw how white she was and how shadowed her eyes. 'The nurse who normally does the night shift has been taken ill so I've been on duty since six o'clock this morning and look like having to remain on duty until tomorrow. I'll be relieved before eleven o'clock, though, so I'll leave a note for the ward sister explaining that you would like a word with the doctor and to see the patient; I'm sure there will be no difficulty.'

Darky cast one last, longing look towards Patty's still figure in the bed and then set off on the walk home. Despite Patty's plight, he found that he was feeling rather light-hearted as he strode along the glistening wet pavements. He had found her and, though clearly far from well, she was in good hands. She would get better and as soon as she was fit again he would stop shilly-shallying and beg her to be his wife.

Back at No. 23, he stole in his stockinged feet to his mother's room and peeped round the door. She was not asleep and sat up in bed at once, though cautiously, making as little noise as possible. She was just a dark shadow amongst other shadows, but

Darky did not have to see her face to read the painful enquiry which he knew it would wear.

'I've found her!' he whispered. 'She's in the Stanley Hospital with a broken arm and a bit of concussion, but the nurse says she'll be fine and I'm to go back tomorrow at eleven to have a word with the doctor. Oh, Mam, I'm that relieved! I was imagining the most dreadful things, so a broken arm and a great bump on the head doesn't seem nearly as bad as it might have.'

'You weren't the only one,' his mother whispered back. 'I've been lying here imagining the most dreadful things. White slave traders, murder and mayhem . . . you name it, I've thought of it.' Mrs Knight sighed deeply. 'Well, now that we know the worst – and you say it isn't too bad really – I'm going to get my head down and try for a few hours' kip, and you'd best do the same. Good night, son, I'll see you in the morning.'

Chapter Eighteen

Da

Patty awoke. At first she could not think where she was, for the light above her bed seemed both strong and intrusive, not in the least like the soft light that filtered through the curtains of No. 24 Ashfield Place. Then she remembered that it was wintertime and was more puzzled than ever. She was pretty sure the alarm had not gone off, yet someone had switched the light on right above her head and she could hear a good deal of muted noise, far more than that caused by herself, Ellen and Maggie getting up late on a Sunday, for instance.

She was still puzzling over it when her mind gave a sort of click and everything fell into place. Of course. She was in hospital and had been here for several days. She had broken her arm and cracked her head against the tramlines and she had consequently suffered from concussion and a degree of memory loss. The nurses assured her that she would be soon be back to normal, but Patty, a patient for the first time in her adult life, found herself longing for Ashfield Place, for the girls and for her familiar routine as ardently as she had ever longed for anything.

She sat up, wincing as the change of position made her injured arm ache, and looked about her. Jenny Sales, in the bed on her right, grinned at her. 'Tea trolley's on the next ward so it won't be long before we get our cuppa,' she said cheerfully. 'How do you feel today, queen? I feel just grand meself 'cos I'm goin' home after me dinner. It wouldn't surprise me if they let you out today an' all. How long have you been in, any road?'

'Five perishin' days,' Patty groaned. 'Oh, what wouldn't I give for a delicious home-made meal. I don't know how they can call the stuff they give us food. Do you?'

Jenny looked doubtful. 'What's wrong wi' it? I admit the breakfast porridge is a bit thin but that stew we had last night were pretty good and there were plenty of it.'

Patty immediately felt guilty. She knew from her own experience that a great many people in the city ate poor quality food, and that was clearly why Jenny had enjoyed a meal of watery stew so bulked out with vegetables and gravy that it was impossible to say what meat had been used. Hastily, she said: 'Yes, it was the breakfasts I meant; the other meals have been prime.'

The two girls continued to chat idly as they drank their tea, made their way to the washroom for their daily ablutions and ate their breakfast. Once that was done, however, the patients were free to amuse themselves until doctors' rounds started. Patty lay back on her pillows and allowed her mind to wander over the past few days.

Although children were not allowed to visit, Darky had brought Merrell to the hospital and Ellen had pushed Patty in a wheelchair into the reception area. The wheelchair had not been necessary, since there was nothing wrong with Patty's legs, but the sister on the ward disapproved of patients wandering about the premises and had insisted on the chair. The reunion had been glorious, with lots of hugs, kisses and tears on both sides, particularly when Patty had had to tear herself away since Sister had warned her severely not to be absent from the ward for longer than ten minutes. She had doubled that and had still left her dear little daughter – for Patty would always consider Merry her daughter now – with the utmost reluctance and had cried all the way back to the ward.

She had had a good many adult visitors though; Darky had come on every available occasion, Mrs Knight had popped in, and most of the other neighbours on her landing had either come in person or had sent messages and small gifts. Even her patients had either visited or sent good wishes by Ellen, though poor Ellen had had her work cut out doing Patty's rounds as well as her own and had not been as frequent a visitor as she would have liked.

Toby, however, had come even more frequently than Darky once he found out where she was. Of course, it was easier for him since the fair was closed now except at weekends, but it was a long journey from New Brighton to the hospital and Patty appreciated that it was not every young man who would have paid a girl to whom he was not even engaged such close and loving attention.

The other women on the ward openly admired both Toby and Darky, though Toby was considerably the more popular of the two. He chatted and laughed with the girls in the beds nearest Patty's, complimenting them on their pretty nightgowns or elaborate bedjackets, teasing them about their young men and behaving as if he had known them all his life. He often mentioned the fair and invited them to come across to New Brighton when they had left the hospital, promising free goes on the rides and generally cheering everyone up. Once, Patty had asked him if he was embarrassed by being the only man in a room full of nightgowned women and he had clearly been astonished by the question. 'Embarrassed? Why on earth should I be embarrassed?' he had asked. 'The only one who embarrasses me is that sister with a face like a hatchet, and she makes me feel I ought to be ashamed just to be a feller!'

Darky, on the other hand, though he smiled and exchanged greetings with the rest of the patients, came to see Patty and no one else and his eyes seldom left her face, though he and Patty chatted and laughed with an ease which Patty had once thought they would never attain.

'Hey, Patty, are you asleep?' The husky voice of Sadie, the patient in the bed on Patty's other side, broke into her thoughts. 'Ain't you the lucky one though, just to break your perishin' arm? I'll bet you'll be signed off today or tomorrow and able to go home, but the doc said yesterday I'd be here for a full three months. Why, you can walk about the ward, go down to reception, all sorts, but all I can do is lie here on me back with me perishin' leg up at a most unladylike angle and worry about what's goin' on at home.'

Patty smiled sympathetically. Sadie had descended from a tram into the very same hailstorm that had caused Patty's accident and had slipped on the pavement edge, crashing down with her leg bent at an awkward angle. She had broken both tibia and fibula, and although she was by nature a cheerful and outgoing woman, she was worried that her family would be unable to cope.

Patty was about to comfort her, to say that she herself would go round to Sadie's house and let her know how things were progressing, when the doors at the end of the ward opened and Sister ushered in Mr Watkin and his team. Immediately, all conversation stopped. Patients who had been knitting or reading hastily hid work and books under the blankets and the nurses whizzed backwards and forwards, whisking covers straight and kicking any slippers or knitting bags on the floor out of sight under the high beds.

Patty had worked in hospitals for so long that the routine was familiar to her and she did her best to help the nurses by keeping the area around her own bed and those of her neighbours clean and neat. She had got Jenny to tie back her long hair since she could not do it herself whilst her arm remained in plaster, and now she settled primly back against the pillows and waited hopefully; surely Mr Watkin would see the sense of letting her go home where she was needed, would agree to her being signed off.

Toby slicked down his hair with water and pressed it back, though he knew that within ten minutes of going out into the brisk wind his soft, toffee-coloured hair would flop over his forehead once more. He considered the violet-scented hair oil which the Flanagans had given him for Christmas but decided against it, for though this evening was important he did not fool himself that Patty's decision would be affected by tidy or untidy hair.

There was a decent-sized mirror beside the door in the green caravan and Toby stood before it and checked his appearance. He was wearing navy-blue trousers and a thick, matching sweater with a white silk scarf knotted around his neck. Over these garments he wore his heavy black winter coat and he carried a trilby hat, though he had no intention of wearing it. Liverpool was always a windy city and he had no desire to see a three and sixpenny hat sailing off his head to land on the bosom of the Mersey. He wondered whether he should change the navy-blue jumper for a scarlet one, or even the green, which Edie had knitted him the winter before she left. It would look more cheerful, certainly, but he rather thought that seriousness and sobriety should be his watchword this evening. He intended to propose marriage to Patty, and knowing her adult self as he now did he thought it best to play down the more flamboyant side of his character and to show Patty what a faithful and hard-working husband he would be, as well as a loving one.

Having decided on his appearance, Toby buttoned the overcoat so that only the white silk scarf showed at the neck and picked up the bunch of violets from the jug of water close by the door. They were hot-house violets, of course, and he had paid what he felt was an extortionate sum for them only that morning. Then he picked up the single red rose which he had purchased at the same time and threaded it into his buttonhole. Satisfied, at last, he opened the caravan door and was met by a blast of wind so strong that he had to tuck the violets inside his coat for fear they would be blown out of his grasp and scattered across the fairground. Then, tucking his head into his collar, he set off for the hospital, comfortably sure that he had done everything he could to make his suit acceptable to Patty. Not that he had much doubt of her answer. If he had seriously worried, the small jeweller's box nestling in his inside pocket would not have been there. But, of late, Patty had been so sweet and carefree when in his company that he could not believe her indifferent.

He had had a word with the sister last time he visited and she had been pretty sure that today would be Patty's last day on the ward. 'They'll send her back home tomorrow; Mr Watkin as good as told us that she was able to manage at home now,' she informed him, with a twinkling smile. 'Then you'll be able to have her all to yourself, Mr Rudd, and I know that will please you.'

Toby had agreed, of course, though in fact this was anything but the case. Once she was home with the girl Maggie and Nurse Purbright constantly in attendance and Mrs Knight and her son right next door, he knew that his opportunities for seeing Patty alone would be severely limited. What was more, the difficulties she would encounter with her broken arm in plaster for a number of weeks might make her short-tempered and less willing to consider changing her status. No, he must propose whilst she was still in hospital, strike while the iron was hot in fact, or else risk a rebuttal.

He was aware that Darky Knight was in love with Patty, of course he was, but could not fathom how Patty felt about the other man. They were friends, it was true, but he did not think that Darky meant to ask Patty to marry him. Why, otherwise, would Darky have come slogging all the way to New Brighton on the day following Patty's accident just to tell him in which hospital she lay? If Darky had had intentions there himself, surely he would not have let the opposition know where she might be found. Toby knew that in similar circumstances he would have said nothing to Darky, would have done his utmost, in fact, to keep the other man in the dark. And I'm not a bad sort of feller, Toby told himself as he battled his way aboard the ferry. I'm as generous as the next man, but only an idiot – or someone not really interested in the girl – would let a rival know how the land lay.

He got off the ferry at the Pier Head and was lucky enough to catch a tram immediately. He had come early deliberately, partly because he knew that Patty always had plenty of visitors between seven and eight and partly to give himself more time since he wanted to discuss with her just where and how they should get married and where she would like to go for a brief, three-day honeymoon. He knew most women wanted white dresses, and bridesmaids, but hoped that practical Patty would be different. He wanted a nice register office ceremony to be performed as soon as possible, followed by a few days away, perhaps in Southport, a town he had always liked, and then a return to New Brighton and the green caravan until around April, when he would want to move back to the Flanagan's fair.

Thinking it over as he swung off the tram and faced into the wind once more, dodging the great shining rain-dappled puddles which almost hid the paving stones, he decided that probably Patty's broken arm was a blessing in disguise. The ward sister had told him it was a nasty fracture and might take as long as three months to heal properly. If they got married almost immediately he would make sure that Patty had a thoroughly enjoyable three months, living in the green caravan, helping out occasionally on the shooting gallery and savouring a freedom from work which, he guessed, she had never known. Oh aye, he told himself, splashing onwards, at the end of three months he was sure she would willingly give up this so-called career of hers in favour of himself and the fair he loved so well.

'Well? Not that I need to ask, Patty Peel, your face tells it all.' Sadie's own face wore a delighted beam. 'So they're letting you out tomorrer, eh? Now don't you forget what you promised. You'll nip round to Hetherington Court just as soon as you're able, to check on me old feller and me kids.'

Patty was coming down the ward from an interview in Sister's office and beamed back at her friend. 'Yes, I'm to go home tomorrow,' she said blithely. 'I had to promise that Mrs Knight would pop round to help out until I settle in and have learned to do things one-handed. The nurses have been wonderful, letting me help them in the kitchen and the sluice, so that I've got used to not using my right hand. There are all sorts of tricks which help. I can't carry a tray, but if I put things into a bag I can manage several objects at a time, and simple things like making a cup of tea and chopping vegetables can be done with one hand if you put the vegetables into a smallish container and then wedge the container in a corner. But of course peeling potatoes just isn't possible, so Sister said to cook them with their skins on; they're better for you like that, anyway.'

'And you'll have Maggie pretty soon,' Sadie reminded her. 'But you're going to be a lady of leisure for some time to come. Well, if you're bored, you can always hop on the tram and come to visit me. I wish you would, because I'm certainly going to miss you. Perhaps you'll get lonely when Maggie's in school,' she finished hopefully.

'I'll have Merry, don't forget,' Patty reminded her friend. 'She's grand company even if she is only three. I've often wished I could spend more time with her and Maggie.'

Sadie was beginning to reply when the doors at the end of the ward shot open and a large, red-faced woman in a scruffy white apron appeared, pushing an enormous trolley. 'I've brung your suppers, lassies,' she shouted. 'It's mince and mashed spuds wi' a nice spoonful of swede on the side and a good old chunk of jam roly for afters. Is anyone bedbound or can you all come and get your plates filled up here?'

'I think mince and mash is the meal they do best,' Patty said presently, scraping her plate clean. 'It's a pity the jam roly-poly is always cold by the time we finish our first course, but I suppose they can't perform miracles. What's more, I'd dearly like a cup of tea to follow straight away instead of having to wait twenty minutes for it.'

'Yes, and I could drink a gallon of tea instead of just a cup,' Sadie agreed as the two girls waded their way through the rather solid jam roly-poly. It was not easy for Sadie to eat anything, lying on her back as she was, but she had perfected the technique of leaning up on one elbow, just as Patty had grown accustomed to eating everything with either a spoon or a fork and no other implement. 'Never mind, me old feller's visiting this evening, and my sister Maisie, because my Auntie Flo's baby-sitting.'

When both roly-poly and tea were finished, the two girls settled down, Sadie to continue doggedly knitting a jumper for her youngest son whilst Patty performed the gentle exercises which the staff had taught her, moving her fingers as though playing an invisible piano and then balling her hand into a fist and stretching her fingers out as far as she could. She was engaged in this exercise when the ward doors swung open once more and a familiar figure came through them. It was Toby Rudd, drenched to the skin and looking, for a change, thoroughly bad-tempered. 'I fell gettin' off the bleedin' tram,' he announced crossly. He looked down at himself with distaste. 'I put on me best clothes an' that, to make a good impression, 'cos Sister told me you were goin' home tomorrow, and now look at me.' At this point, his sense of humour got the better of him and he began to laugh. 'Here was me, wantin' to show you what a respectable feller I am an' I end up lookin' like one of the Chaps in ragged old kecks.'

Patty laughed too and took his hand, giving it a reassuring squeeze. 'I don't care what you look like,' she said bracingly, 'it's what you *are* that counts and you're my oldest friend, whether you're dry as dust or wet as water. But fancy you coming out on such a night! Even in here we can hear the rain lashing against the window panes and the wind screaming down the sides of the building. I bet it was a sickly sort of voyage on the ferry, wasn't it?'

'Oh, it weren't so bad,' Toby said airily. He was clearly recovering his aplomb, Patty thought. He began to struggle out of his overcoat, saying as he did so: 'D'you mind if I hang this over the end of the bed? Only it's so wet . . . oh, damn and blast it!' A bunch of what looked like violets had fallen to the floor and scattered in the pool of water that had formed around Toby's feet.

Patty could not help herself; she began to laugh as Toby threw his coat on to the floor and started to gather up the violets, muttering curses as he did so. 'Are they for me?' she asked gaily. She picked up the coat and his discarded trilby whilst he was still collecting the flowers, and headed for the ward kitchen. 'I'll hang this up for you and then fetch a vase for them. Poor Toby, what a catalogue of disasters!'

When she came back, order had been restored. Toby was sitting in the visitor's chair, holding the now neatly bunched violets and teasing Sadie for having grown too lazy even to swing out of bed and help him to pick up a few flowers, but as soon as Patty returned his attention switched back to her. He pushed the violets, now more than a little crushed, into the vase she offered him, and stood them on her bedside locker. Then he got to his feet and took her good hand in his. 'Come into the kitchen with me for a minute,' he cajoled. 'I told Sister I wanted to be private with you and she said it would be all right, just for a few minutes. After all, today's your last day on the ward so I've got to make the most of it.'

Patty hung back, suddenly all too horribly aware of what he was about to ask her. She felt it was too soon – much too soon. He still hadn't met Merry, scarcely knew Maggie, had only known Patty herself out of her natural environment. Oh, he had spent Christmas Day with her and they had both enjoyed themselves very much, but that was not an ordinary day. He could not possibly realise how all-consuming her work was, nor how having Merry complicated things. Slowly, she followed him obediently into the kitchen and sat down on a table.

She had half expected Toby to stammer and stutter, but she had underestimated him. He came straight out with the question which, she supposed, was uppermost in both their minds.

'Patty, I guess you know how I feel about you. We were old friends from way back but now we've met up again and got to know one another properly, I hope we'll be more than friends. I want to be with you always and I don't want to waste any more time. I want to start our new life together at once. If you want a smart white wedding, I dare say it'll take a bit longer, but if you're content with a register office and a special licence, we can tie the knot in a week to ten days. I know you've a nice home and you're fond of it, but it's only rented, ain't it? The green caravan's my own property and there's plenty of room for three.'

'Three?' Patty said. 'Why three?'

Toby looked puzzled. 'Well, seeing as how Maggie's your daughter, I thought . . . I thought you'd want her to come along,' he said rather lamely. 'Does she have other plans? She seems rather young to go off on her own, don't you think?'

Patty laughed. 'Maggie isn't my daughter,' she said. 'She's a dear good girl and a great help, but in fact I pay her a small wage and her keep so that when I'm working she can look after Merry for me.'

'Merry?' Toby said blankly. 'But I thought she were Mrs Knight's granddaughter? I thought she were Darky's get? I remember you telling me Darky's wife died in childbirth, and then Mrs Knight took the kid to Scotland . . .' He hesitated, the bewildered look deepening. 'What else were I to think?'

Patty was about to reply when she was struck by a sudden recollection. As clearly as though it were happening now, she could hear her own voice on that Christmas morning, carefully explaining to Toby things which she had told no one else in the world. She had explained how she had attended Mrs Mullins's lying-in and how the poor woman had given birth to twins, one dead, one alive, before dying tragically herself. She had gone into details then, explaining how she had taken the baby in, pretending that it was hers, because she could not bear to see the tiny scrap put in an orphan asylum to suffer as she herself had suffered all those years ago. She had told him about Selina, to explain why she had become a nurse; in fact she had bared her soul to him, confiding things that she had kept locked inside her heart all her life.

And now, looking searchingly at him, she really saw him for the very first time. Toby was handsome, charming and excellent company, but he skimmed the shallow waters of life, she concluded, and never descended to the depths. When she had been pouring her heart out in the kitchen of No. 24, he had not even bothered to listen, because she had been talking about herself and her worries and responsibilities, and not about Toby Rudd. She had no doubt that if she told him about Merry this minute, repeating everything she had said in the kitchen almost a month ago, he would listen with attention because now, he believed, it concerned him. With another flash of intuition, she realised that Maggie was an asset, a growing girl who would be useful on the fair, might take to it and look forward to a career amongst the fair folk. She did him the credit to believe that he would accept Merry, maybe even enjoy the baby's company, for he was not ungenerous, merely self-centred in a way she had never come across before.

'Patty?' His voice was anxious now. 'What does it matter, anyhow? It's you an' me that matter. Damn it, queen, I'm askin' you to be me wife. I'm not askin' Maggie, nor this Merry, I'm askin' you, Patty Peel.'

Patty took a deep breath, meaning to be kind and gentle and explain that she needed more time to get to know Toby better, and suddenly realised that she knew him very well indeed, that she did not need more time, that her mind was made up. 'No,' she said baldly. 'No, I won't marry you.'

It did not end there, of course. Returning to the ward after one of the most miserable and exhausting half-hours she had ever lived through, Patty told herself that she had earned all the disappointed, angry and ultimately spiteful comments which Toby had delivered. She had not intentionally led him to believe that she would become his wife but she had certainly never attempted to push him back and had always fallen in eagerly with his plans. The trouble was, she told herself now, going over to her bed and loosening her hair from its bun, that she was more than half in love with the fair and the life which Toby led, and this had blinded her to faults in his character which she would otherwise have spotted at once.

Perhaps it was best to know a man's bad side first, to be thoroughly disillusioned in fact, and then gradually to begin to see the good things about him, she decided as she brushed out the long blonde curls. She remembered how she and Darky had disliked one another, how he had snarled and shouted at her, or completely ignored her. At the time, she had almost hated him, but even her strong dislike had not blinded her to his many good qualities. Perhaps if she had not seen Toby through the rose-coloured spectacles she had worn as a child, she might have been less eager for his company, less willing to accept the faults which she now saw so clearly. After all, he had started letting her down years ago, when he had failed to turn up at their first rendezvous. It was not until he met her by chance in New Brighton that he had attempted to resuscitate their old friendship. Patty now acknowledged, sadly, that it had been need of someone to help him with the shooting gallery, rather than a deep affection for an old friend, which had prompted Toby to begin courting her. And because of her own attitude he had been far too sure of her, so sure that he had actually purchased a small sapphire and diamond ring to celebrate their engagement.

Patty sighed and began to roll her hair up once more, ready for when the visitors arrived. She had felt most dreadfully guilty over the engagement ring, but one of Toby's less pleasant remarks led her to wonder now whether he had purchased it for sixpence from Woolworths. When she had offered to give him back the gold clover-leaf brooch, he had told her that she might as well keep it. 'I gorra job lot as prizes for the shooting gallery, an' I've given 'em away to any girl who's been willing, from Land's End to John o' Groats,' he had said nastily. 'So you can have it as a keepsake or chuck it into the bleedin' Mersey; please yourself.'

The remark had been meant to wound but, unfortunately, Patty had laughed and this had led Toby to make other, even less pleasant comments. He told her she was a tease, had deliberately led him on, had lied about her child, kidding him that Maggie was hers and not mentioning the other brat. 'I suppose you an' that black-browed bugger what lives next door made the kid between you,' he had flung at her. 'Well Toby Rudd don't need to accept another man's leavings, even though that hair of yours would have been worth a deal o' money to me shooting gallery, so I ought to be grateful that you've let me down.'

Patty had bitten her lip and had tried to tell herself that the things Toby was saying came from disappointment and not from the heart, but in the end her temper had got the better of her. 'Let *you* down?' she had screamed at him, completely forgetting to keep her voice down. 'You're saying *I* let *you* down? Why, Toby Rudd, you let me down once a year because *I* turned up on Lime Street station for six bleedin' years, hoping – and expecting – that you would come. I told myself you were probably miles away, couldn't make it, didn't understand that you could have left a message with the station master, but now I know better. And talking of messages, I never told you that I got yours on the day I had my accident . . . some tomfoolery about running your shooting gallery. As if I'd do any such thing on the day the Knights and Merry came home! It just shows that you never knew me at all. In fact, we never really knew one another and the only reason you want to marry me is to get free housekeeping and someone to help with the shooting gallery, so let's stop kidding ourselves. Love doesn't enter into it. What you were proposing was a business arrangement and that's what I'm rejecting, so why all the hysterics?'

For a moment, she had thought he was going to laugh and, somehow, that would have made every-thing all right. But instead, he had snatched his coat and hat from the hook on the back of the door, crammed his trilby down over his ears and marched out of the kitchen. She had followed him, reluctant to part on such very bad terms, but he had been unable to resist a parting shot. 'Well, this is goodbye, Nurse Peel,' he had shouted over his shoulder, setting off along the corridor. 'At least when you're an old maid tottering on the brink of the grave, you'll be able to tell folk that you had one proposal from a decent, hard-working chap – and turned it down like the silly bitch you are.'

Patty was so angry that she actually pursued him some way down the corridor. 'If I die an old maid, it'll be from choice,' she shouted. 'And the way you've behaved this evening has certainly taught me a thing or two. You turn up again in my life like a bad penny and expect me to fall into your arms, when all you really want is a bleedin' slave. Why, marriage to you would be hell on earth. I hope to God I never set eyes on you again, Toby Rudd.'

'You won't,' Toby had shouted back. 'Because I'm off back to the Flanagans just as soon as I've worked out a month's notice. I never meant to stay in one place and I never mean to come back to New Brighton again.'

Patty had taken a deep breath to scream that she had known all along he was lying to her when a hand fell on her arm. Staff Nurse O'Hara was pink-cheeked and round-eyed, though obviously smothering giggles. 'Patty, do hush,' she had said urgently. 'Sister sent me out of the ward to find out who was screamin' like a fishwife; you go along to the lavvies now and I'll say it were one of the cleaners. If you come back to the ward in ten minutes and ask who were making all the row, it'll probably save everyone trouble.'

Patty had been glad to comply but the silence from Sadie and the other women made her suspect that, even if Sister was in ignorance, the other patients could have made a pretty good guess at who had been shrieking down the corridor. In fact, Sadie, gazing dreamily at the ceiling above her head, remarked in a soft voice: 'Well, well, well! Fallen out wi' lover boy, then?'

'Yes,' Patty said through clenched teeth. 'And I shan't be falling in again, either. I never used to trust

471

men, never wanted to have anything to do with them, and now I think I was right. The things he said! Sadie, you wouldn't believe . . .'

'I take it he axed you to wed and you turned him down; that always makes 'em mad and then they say things they don't really mean,' Sadie said comfortably. 'Never mind, chuck, he'll come round.'

Patty was opening her mouth to scream 'I don't *want* him to come round' when the doors at the end of the ward swung open and the visitors arrived. Sighing resignedly, knowing she was still pink-cheeked and tear-stained, Patty slipped quickly on to her bed and tried to smile welcomingly as the new arrivals surged up the ward. She saw Darky at the back of the crowd and her heart missed a beat. However was she going to bear a whole hour in the company of a member of the opposite sex? She felt she could not be natural, yet she had no wish to tell Darky what had just transpired. She wished ardently that he had been accompanied by his mother, or by one of her other friends, but it was not to be. Darky, beaming at her, came across and settled himself in the visitor's chair. 'You're looking remarkably fit and well,' he said amiably. 'There's a lovely flush on your cheeks, and you're eyes are as bright as stars. Don't tell me, you're coming home tomorrow!'

Settling down after all the visitors had left, Patty concluded that she really need not have worried. Visiting hour had passed swiftly and delightfully. She and Darky had discussed the means by which she would return to Ashfield Place, how she would manage with only one useful hand, and what Darky and his mother could do to ease matters.

'I've took tomorrow off,' Darky had said, 'because

472

they told me yesterday that they thought you'd be going home. But to tell you the truth, I've talked to my boss about leaving, setting up in business for myself, and he's been very understanding. I promised I'd stay on for three or four months to train someone else, so when I explained you was coming out of hospital and needed a bit of a hand on your first day home, Mr Clitheroe said that would be fine.'

'Goodness, going into business for yourself,' Patty marvelled. 'I suppose you'll have a little shop? Your mother has mentioned you were thinking about it but I hadn't realised you were so serious.'

Darky shrugged. 'It's still only an idea,' he reminded her. 'It may yet come to nothing, but I'm definitely considering it and one of me pals from work, Tom Fraser, is thinking about joining me. We're both electricians so we might go into partnership. But anyway, that's for the future. Right now, I'm more concerned about settling you back into Ashfield Place.'

Amongst other good news that Darky had brought was the fact that the Mullins felt they could manage without Maggie at last. 'Maggie says she'll stay with you full time when she leaves school at the end of the summer, but of course she's keen to get a proper job, say in a factory,' he had explained. 'Then Mam asked her whether she'd consider pupil teaching because that would lead to her being a teacher herself one day and it would be awfully convenient for you, once Merry's in school. So now that Maggie isn't nursing the measles, she's going to enquire about pupil teaching. What do you think of *that*?'

Patty had been delighted at the idea. It would make an enormous difference to have Maggie working only whilst Merrell was at school, so there would always be someone at home during the holidays to keep an eye on the little girl. Of course, Patty had known that Mrs Knight would step into the breach, as she always had, but Darky's mam was not getting any younger and there would undoubtedly come a day when she would find the care of a lively young girl rather too much.

Patty was also delighted by Darky's attitude towards her, which was just as brisk and businesslike as it could be. He laughed with her, told her funny stories about Merry and her antics, teased her about hospital dinners and how happy she would be to leave them behind; but there was never anything in his attitude to embarrass her or remind her of her recent experience with Toby. In fact, it was only as he was leaving that he gave her a penetrating glance and asked: 'You all right now, queen? I've done most of the talking, I'm afraid. There's nothing you need to tell me?'

If there was a trace of anxiety in his voice, Patty decided to ignore it. She gave him her widest smile, saying airily: 'I'm fine, Darky, and I'll see you at ten o'clock tomorrow morning and not a moment later. Oh, I can't wait to get back home – and what a hug I'll give Merry!'

Perhaps because she was exhausted by the quarrel with Toby, Patty slept deeply and soundly until she was woken next morning. In the bustle which preceded breakfast she found she had very little time for quiet thought, but one thing she did know, she told herself firmly. She would not even think about marrying anyone until the awful scene with Toby was forgotten. Eating her breakfast porridge, she scolded herself for even letting the thought cross her mind that Darky might suggest marriage. Why should he, after all? He had behaved like her good friend for months and months now and, the previous evening, had not indicated by a word or a look that he expected to be anything other than a good friend in the future. And that is how I want it, she told herself firmly, refusing to acknowledge the little flicker of disappointment which accompanied the thought. They had teased her on the ward about her two admirers; in the space of half an hour she had sunk from having two admirers to having none, it seemed.

'Miss Peel! If you've finished your breakfast, Sister said you'd best get dressed, so I've come to help you.'

Patty thanked the young nurse and went over to her bed, and the nurse drew the curtains around it. As she began to struggle into her clothing, Patty became aware of mounting excitement; she was going home!

Promptly at ten o'clock, Darky came into the hospital, though he was not allowed on to the ward since the doctor's rounds were in progress. Patty saw him peering hopefully through the glass doors, however, and said a hasty goodbye to the friends she had made before setting off, joyfully, in the direction of freedom. As soon as she emerged through the double doors, Darky took her suitcase and ushered her along the corridor, saying: 'Well, thank heaven for that! One of the nurses said you wouldn't be able to escape whilst a medical round was in progress, but she was obviously wrong. I've got a taxi waiting, so you'll be home before you know it.'

Patty gulped and realised, suddenly, that she was nervous. The cold air of the outside world was not as welcome as she had expected. She clutched Darky with her good hand, saying in a desperate undertone: 'Don't go so fast, Darky. My legs are still shaky and I don't want to risk falling again.'

475

'I'm not surprised,' Darky said, steering her towards a seat. 'Stay there while I put your suitcase in the car, then I'll come back and give you a hand.'

The waiting taxi driver, however, left his cab and came towards them, taking the suitcase from Darky's grasp, and presently Patty found herself sitting comfortably on the back seat with Darky beside her. He tapped on the glass and said something to the driver, then leaned back and looked smilingly across at Patty. 'Well? How does it feel to be back in the big, wide world? I guess it must be pretty strange after six days in hospital. Are you looking forward to learning how to housekeep with one arm in plaster? Mam is all set to come in whenever you want her, and of course Maggie is thrilled to be back in what she considers to be her own home. You were really lucky with Maggie; you couldn't have found a better girl to help you in the house and to look after Merry.'

'Has Merry moved back into number twenty-four yet, or is she still with your mam?'

'She slept at number twenty-four last night, since Maggie had moved back in, and I understand she had breakfast there,' Darky assured her. 'But of course Maggie's in school now so Mam's taken over again. She and Merry have gone shopping to buy something special for your dinner, so you can be sure of a good meal when you do get home.'

'Oh, I thought they'd all be lined up waiting for me,' Patty said, only half jokingly. 'Still, I suppose they might be back from shopping now.'

Darky, however, shook his head. 'No. I've told them you won't be home until noon at the earliest,' he informed her calmly. 'I've hired this taxi to drive us out into the country so we can have a bit of a talk. The truth is, Patty, I never seem to see you alone. I know

Toby Rudd usually came to the ward out of visiting hours, and I thought it wasn't fair on the staff to try to follow suit.' He smiled across at her, his dark eyes gentle. 'I know he came to see you last night, before the visitors arrived, because one of the nurses told me. But never mind that. Just tell me, queen, are you thinking of marrying Rudd?'

Patty stared at him, her eyes rounding. 'You kidnapped me!' she said indignantly. 'Darky Knight, take me right home this minute!'

'I'll take you home just as soon as we've had our talk,' Darky said quietly. 'I've tried to play fair by you, Patty, and by Rudd, though I don't honestly think he deserves it, but now the time has come for plain speaking. I left you pretty much to your own devices, going off to Scotland the way I did, but I thought Merry was more important right then than anything else. I hope you agree with that?'

'Yes, of course I do,' Patty mumbled, feeling the heat rise to her cheeks. 'But what do you mean, you played fair by me? I don't understand.'

Darky heaved a sigh. 'First of all, I went off to Scotland for three weeks, hoping that, whilst I was gone, you and Toby might get to know one another well enough to be able to decide whether you were truly in love. Then when I got back and found you in hospital, I went straight across to New Brighton and told Toby where to find you – but I take it you knew that?'

'No; how could I?' Patty said. 'You never told me you'd done that and of course Toby never said a word. Come to that, I never even asked him, so perhaps in my heart I did know.'

'Perhaps you did,' Darky agreed, 'because, whatever my faults, I'm not mean-natured, and it would have been a mean thing to cut you off from one of your oldest friends. I know he came to the hospital regularly, I know he gave you a very pretty gold brooch . . .'

Patty laughed. 'Oh, very pretty,' she agreed. 'He bought them by the gross and handed them out to any girl who, as he put it, was willing. He told me that last night after I'd turned down his proposal of marriage.'

'He's already asked you?' Darky said, the colour draining from his cheeks. 'My God, he's a quicker worker than I thought; I'd made up my mind he'd wait until your arm was out of plaster, or at least until . . . until you were more yourself.' He suddenly seemed to realise what she had said and reached across the cab, turning her so that she faced him. 'Oh, Patty darling, can you look me in the eye and tell me you truly aren't going to marry Toby Rudd? I knew you were mortal fond of him, or had been when you were both kids, but I never thought you were right for each other. Only . . . only I was afraid you'd been blinded by all that charm and . . . and he's a handsome feller an' I was so horrible to you when we first met . . .'

Patty gave a shaky laugh. 'He was worse than either of us knew,' she observed. 'It's true, I was taken in for a while, but I was beginning to ask myself just what his game was even before I came off my bicycle and broke my arm. In fact, I reckon I've had a lucky escape, one way and another. I truly don't think I'm the marrying kind. I love my work and I love my little family and that will just have to be enough. Believe it or not, I don't need a man in my life.'

Darky gave a muffled groan and then Patty found herself in his arms. She gave a squeak of fright but his mouth found hers and suddenly it no longer seemed to matter that they were sitting in the back of a black cab and driving through crowded streets. All that mattered was Darky's mouth, and his arms around her. Patty, who had just announced that she did not need a man in her life, felt her bones melt and cuddled against him, kissing him as hard as he was kissing her and only pulling herself away when the pressure on her broken arm became unbearable.

Darky sank back in his seat and whistled expressively. 'For a girl who doesn't need a man in her life, you kiss awfully well,' he said breathlessly. 'Oh, Patty, have you any idea how much I love you? I believe I've loved you since the first moment I met you, though heaven knows I fought hard enough against it. I felt that loving any other woman was letting Alison down, but loving a midwife seemed – oh, it seemed like spitting in her face. I hated myself for loving you so I was just as nasty as could be and kept snubbing you and trying to believe the worst about you. Then I was mad with jealousy over Merrell's father because I was sure you must have loved him deeply, or you would never have had a baby by him. But the love was there all right and when I saw you with Rudd and thought I'd lost you, I wanted to top myself. Only – only you've turned him down, and now I've got to ask you if you'll take me instead? You don't have to answer right away,' he added hastily. 'I don't mind how long you take, so long as you say yes.'

His voice was so humble, so pleading, that Patty found her eyes filling with tears. He was so different from Toby, such a good and loving man – what was the point in keeping him waiting? In her secret heart, she had known for ages that Darky meant more to her

479

than almost anyone else, and when their lips had met she had realised that her feelings for him were real love, the sort that went on and on, growing deeper with every passing year. 'Yes please, Darky, I'd love to marry you,' she said in a small and slightly shaky voice. 'But there's one thing you must know first. It's – it's about Merrell's father.'

'It doesn't matter; I don't think I want to know,' Darky said. 'The only thing that matters is that we love one another and we're going to marry. I love Merry, you know, and I'm mortal fond of Maggie, so it won't be any hardship to take them into our family.' He had recaptured her hand and now he squeezed it gently, leaning across to brush her cheek with his lips. 'What I'm trying to say is that Merry's beginnings are really none of my business because I wasn't around at the time. She'll be our little girl just as though I were her father. Can you understand that?'

Patty moved across the seat and cuddled against him. 'You must be the kindest man in the world, Darky Knight,' she said dreamily. 'Accepting another man's child is never easy – God knows, I see enough examples of how such children suffer in my work – but you are willing to take it all on board, aren't you? Even when you think I've been in love with some feller and have let him . . . well, let him father Merry . . . you don't reproach me or hold it against the child.' She turned in his arm to look up into his face, her eyes suddenly mischievous. 'But how will you feel, my love, when I tell you that Merry isn't mine any more than she's yours? You see, her mother died giving birth and the father couldn't cope with the tiny baby and wanted me to put her in an orphan asylum. Only – only she was so small and sweet that I couldn't bear to let her go, so I kept her and now she's as much my own as though she had truly grown inside me for nine months.'

Darky stared down at her, his eyes rounding in astonishment. 'She ain't yours?' he asked incredulously. 'But – but . . .'

'No, she isn't mine, though I couldn't love her more if she was. In fact, Darky, she's Maggie Mullins's baby sister. You see . . .'

By the time the story was told, the cab was cruising through open country, though the occupants only had eyes for each other and scarcely noticed the passing scene. Patty had also seized the opportunity to tell Darky all about Selina and her own childhood in the Durrant House Orphan Asylum and this brought out all Darky's protective instincts and made him hug her so tightly and kiss her so passionately that she actually saw the driver tilt his rear view mirror in order to keep an eye on the proceedings. As they drew apart, she nudged Darky. 'This isn't really the time or the place,' she whispered, indicating the driver's stolid back with a significant glance. 'And shouldn't we be heading for home? I'm sure your mam and Merry will have returned from their shopping trip by now and they're bound to wonder what has become of us.'

Darky nodded reluctant agreement and leaned forward to tap on the glass panel which separated them from the driver. 'Thanks, mate. Now will you take us back to Ashfield Place, please?' he said loudly, as the little panel shot back. 'Only don't hurry yourself. We shan't be missed for another half-hour at least.'

The driver, grinning, turned his cab when the next opportunity occurred and headed back to Liverpool once more whilst Patty, bathed in a glow of happiness, decided that she must ask one vital question. 'Darky, can I ask you something?' she said rather timidly. 'It seems very brassy of me but I feel I need to know.'

'You can ask me anything you like,' Darky said contentedly. 'Fire ahead, my darling.'

'It's – it's about Alison,' Patty said shyly. 'I know how much you loved her and I know how terribly you've missed her and mourned for her, but you've never said what she looked like, or what sort of a person she was. Your mam scarcely ever speaks of her either. I – I'd feel happier if I knew a bit more.'

For a moment, she thought that Darky was not going to reply, for he sat staring straight ahead, his eyes fixed almost blankly on the back of the driver's head. When he spoke, it was gently and without a hint of resentment. 'She was small and very pretty, with reddish-gold hair and a great many freckles,' he said reflectively. 'I know her eyes were greenish-hazel and I know she had a soft, Scottish accent, but the truth is, Patty, that we weren't married for very long, barely nine months, and she's been gone almost six years now. It's difficult for me to remember much detail, to tell you the truth. She was a very quiet girl and meek, never arguing or putting forward an opinion of her own. I – I've sometimes wondered how we would have gone on if she'd lived, because since her death I've realised that pretty, biddable girls ain't really for me. I like a woman with spirit, who's got opinions and convictions of her own, someone who doesn't agree with everything I say but who will answer back and fight for what she believes is right.' He turned to smile at her. 'In fact, I want a fiery blonde, who can shout as loudly as I can and who'll stick to her guns and force me to back down every time I'm wrong.'

Patty sighed deeply. 'So long as you aren't marrying me as – as a sort of Alison substitute,' she said dreamily. A thought suddenly occurred to her. 'You know when we tell folk we're getting married, they'll immediately assume that their worst suspicions were right and that you really are Merrell's father.'

'Then we'll let them believe it,' Darky said, grinning. 'Not that we'll be in Ashfield Place for very much longer, my love. As soon as I have worked out my notice at Levers and got my own business established, I'm going to rent a cottage in a smallish village. I know you want to continue with your job, but once the babies come that won't be possible. But if you're set on staying in Ashfield Place for a few years, I can always tell me boss I've changed me mind.'

Patty drew in a deep, ecstatic breath. 'A cottage in the country,' she breathed. 'We could have a dog and a cat and I could keep hens – I've always wanted to do that. Oh, and Darky, could we have a garden? A proper one with currant bushes and apple trees . . . perhaps even an orchard!' She glanced shyly up at him. 'The country's a proper place to bring up children, wouldn't you say?'

At this point, the cab drew up in Ashfield Place. The driver put Patty's case down on the pavement and Darky helped her tenderly from the cab. He paid off the driver and then put a proprietorial arm round Patty's waist and led her towards the iron stairs. 'Provided it's a home with love in it, children can be happy almost anywhere,' he said gently. 'But if you want a country cottage with a big garden, then that's just what we will have, even if we have to wait a while to get it.' He began to lead her up the stairs, still with his arm firmly about her. 'My, what a surprise for me mam when I tell her our news,' he said contentedly. 'You've made me the happiest feller on earth, Patty.'

To find out more about Katie Flynn why not join the Katie Flynn Readers' Club and receive a twice yearly newsletter.

To join our mailing list to receive the newsletter and other information* write with your name and address to:

Katie Flynn Readers' Club
The Marketing Department
Arrow Book
20 Vauxhall Bridge Road
London
SW1V 2SA

Please state whether or not you would like to receive information about other Arrow saga authors.

*Your details will be held on a database so we can send you the newsletter(s) and information on other Arrow authors that you have indicated you wish to receive. Your details will not be passed to any third party. If you would like to receive information on other Random House authors please do let us know. If at any stage you wish to be deleted from our Katie Flynn Readers' Club mailing list please let us know.

A Kiss and a Promise

Katie Flynn

Michael Gallagher is an Irish seaman, fighting with the British Navy. He comes ashore in Liverpool when his ship needs repairs and meets lovely young Stella Bennett on the quayside, searching for her lost kitten.

The young couple fall in love and want to marry but the Bennett's have other plans for Stella and when she gives birth to a baby, Ginny, Michael is dismayed by the child's ginger hair and convinced she is not his.

He returns to Ireland, leaving the sluttish Granny Bennett to rear Ginny. The child accepts her lot, expecting little from life but knows that, in order to escape from the slums, she must attend school. Granny Bennett prefers Ginny to skivvy for her, but when a sympathetic teacher, Mabel Derbyshire, comes into her life, Ginny decides she must better herself and the obvious way to do so is to find her father . . .

arrow books

Down Daisy Street

Katie Flynn

It's 1934 and Kathy Kelling is eleven years old. She has always lived in Daisy Street in Liverpool, the only child of elderly parents. Her best friend is Jane, who has half a dozen brothers and sisters, and her worst enemy is Jimmy McCabe, who lives nearby, the eldest of a large and penniless family. He calls Kathy spoilt and posh because she goes to a private school.

The girls are forced to grow up fast when war breaks out in 1939. But it has its advantages: Kathy is enchanted to meet Ned Latimer, a handsome RAF pilot from Norfolk. He is delighted with Kathy's wit and personaliity, but it is Jane who uses her good looks to steal him away.

Broken-hearted, Kathy joins the WAAF, determined to do her bit. But fate has not finished with her as she is thrown together with Ned again, at Britain's most deperate hour . . .

arrow books